SISTERS
IN
ARMS

SHIDA
BAZYAR

TRANSLATED BY
RUTH MARTIN

SCRIBE

Melbourne • London

Scribe Publications
18–20 Edward St, Brunswick, Victoria 3056, Australia
2 John St, Clerkenwell, London, WC1N 2ES, United Kingdom
3754 Pleasant Ave, Suite 100, Minneapolis, Minnesota 55409, USA

First published in German as *Drei Kameradinnen* by Kiepenheuer & Witsch in 2021
Published in English by Scribe 2023

Typeset in Adobe Garamond Pro by the publishers

Printed and bound in the UK by CPI Group (UK) Ltd, Croydon CR0

Scribe is committed to the sustainable use of natural resources and the use of paper
products made responsibly from those resources.

978 1 761380 10 5 (Australian edition)
978 1 915590 20 6 (UK edition)
978 1 957363 52 3 (US edition)
978 1 761385 19 3 (ebook)

Catalogue records for this book are available from the National Library of Australia and
the British Library.

The translation of this book was supported
by a grant from the Goethe-Institut

GOETHE
INSTITUT

scribepublications.com.au
scribepublications.co.uk
scribepublications.com

Inferno on Bornemannstraße

Aggressive and blinkered: Saya M. from R. was radicalised in plain sight.

'At school, Saya was always looking for an argument, she was constantly provoking people,' a former acquaintance says. 'She just had this anger inside her, it's, like, part of her DNA.'

Was it this anger that cost so many people their lives last night? The authorities may still be saying they don't want to comment on an ongoing investigation, but witness statements paint a clear picture.

Former neighbours report that in the early nineties, Saya M.'s family started taking in suspected Islamists who came to Germany on tourist visas. It is unclear which groups these people belonged to — but it may be assumed that Saya M. grew up in an atmosphere of radicalism.

It seems that M. was attempting to recruit others until the very end: for several years, this young woman had been running workshops in schools, under the guise of careers advice. Even on the morning before the crime, she was preaching to the students of the Wilhelm Gymnasium: 'Learn Arabic, it's the only language with a future!'

Shortly afterwards, she assaulted a man outside a cafe on Bornemannstraße while shouting 'Allahu Akbar'.

Volker S. is currently receiving medical treatment. He has released a statement via his lawyer: 'We have been tolerant for long enough. People like Saya M. are threatening our country's security with their ideologies. How many more attacks do there have to be?'

The assault on Volker S. took place just hours before the deadly fire on Bornemannstraße, which Saya M. is suspected of starting. It is already being described as one of the most devastating since World War II. The authorities are still refusing to call it an Islamist terror attack. This arsonist seems to be shielded by the left-wing leanings she liked to flaunt.

Reports that the building destroyed in the fire was home to a member of a patriotic group are so far unconfirmed, though they do point to a possible motive for Saya M.

I want to be fair, to clear up all the misunderstandings, and make no secret of what this text is and what it isn't, right from the start.

No, that isn't what I want.

I want to be fair, to clear up all the misunderstandings, and explain who I am and who I am not, right from the start. I am not: the spawn of our integrated society. I am not: the girl you can gawk at, so you can look all sympathetic and say you've really paid attention to the migrants and, well, it's all very dramatic, but so admirable, too. I am not: the girl from the ghetto.

I am: the girl from the ghetto. But that's a question of perspective. There are real girls from real ghettoes who'll laugh at me for using that word, when they find out I grew up in a grubby corner of some provincial town — and there are girls who wouldn't have lasted a day there.

I am not: a girl. I'm too old to be called a girl; if certain things in my life had been different, if a few things had gone wrong, I could already be a mother to girls who'd be calling themselves teenagers

1

now, not girls. But I'm not. I do, however, wear a ponytail and a skirt, and both, combined with the absence of children, make me a girl in the world's eyes. Until I start spitting and shouting and making a noise. Then I'm a hysterical woman.

Writing this is my way of trying to pull myself together for just one night. To refrain from throwing anyone out of a window or becoming an internet troll, for just one night; to wait. To wait for them to release my friend Saya, who's been put inside.

I say inside because I'm trying to sound casual about it. Because even as a child, I liked the words that sounded more casual. I'm not saying inside because it's a relic of where I come from. You can grow up in a ghetto that isn't a ghetto, where criminality and fighting are part of day-to-day life, and still know as little about being inside as the horsey girls a few streets over know about real horses.

But when I say inside and look the way I do and speak the way I do, the horsey girls nod knowingly to me. Sure, they think, inside. Where you went to visit your father as a child; where your first boyfriend spent a few months, and when he came out he'd suddenly changed; the place you think of nostalgically, sometimes.

But I've never been inside and I don't know anyone who has, either — at least not in Germany. Until now. But the last thing I want is to end up behind bars as well, and so I am sitting myself down here, at this desk, once the island of my degree dissertation, now the island of my — no kidding — eighty-three job applications, the island of my unemployment-benefit decisions, and writing.

So, back to what I actually wanted to say, to this attempt to spend the night waiting for my friend to be released. She'll come to my place as soon as she can, because she's staying here for a few days before she flies back to her city and her own life. She was supposed to be having a holiday here with me, and going to Shaghayegh's wedding.

It's Friday night, 2.28 am, and I'm trying to start from the beginning. That won't work, because the beginning would be a time before we were born. So I'll go back a little way, but start kind of more in the middle. With last Monday. Because every week begins with a Monday; that way it can pretend to be a new thing. And then we don't notice everything's just carrying on miserably, miserably carrying on, and nothing's happening. But Monday was before Saya arrived. Saya got on a plane in her city on Tuesday afternoon and landed in Hani's and my city on Tuesday evening. So let's start with Tuesday.

∧ ∧ ∧

'I smiled at him, and it was just a nice smile, clearly not flirtatious, and he smiled back, and it clearly was flirtatious, and he spoke to me,' Saya said, handing us the beer bottles, 'in English.'

'In English,' I laughed, taking the two bottles and passing one to Hani, 'how considerate!'

Hani laughed as well, albeit a little uncertainly, gave the bottle back to me, and held out her lighter. The only smoker out of the three of us, she had the necessary equipment, but no idea how to take the lid off a bottle with it.

I gave her the opened bottle back, clinked mine against it and said: 'I bet he had a thick German accent, as well.' I imitated a thick German accent by saying something in English. I did it twice in a row, so we could clink bottles and giggle twice — initial, awkward giggles, the kind you do when you've laughed together plenty of times before but haven't seen each other for ages.

'Not only did his English have a thick German accent, it was also full of mistakes, of course,' Saya went on, resting her chin on her bent knees and looking out over the city. 'That's the most embarrassing thing about these people who think they have to speak English to us: they can't even do it.'

'It's okay to speak bad English, though, right?' said Hani, whose English wasn't so good either, of course — and to be honest, nor was mine. Hani's wasn't good because she'd been to a bad school, and in my case it was because I'd never needed it before I moved to this city, where it was good manners to start speaking English as soon as a foreigner came to hang out with you. Saya's English was world-class. She'd only found a use for it after school, too, but then she'd travelled round the world with it, lived in this metropolis and that, had relationships, done a degree.

'You shouldn't *have* to be able to speak English, I know that,' she said, 'but that's the really weird thing about these people. If you're not that good at something, then you wait and see if you actually need to do it or not, don't you? You don't just start yakking away at poor defenceless people. Guys like him think our German must be so non-existent that their abysmal English is a better way to communicate with us.'

'And what did he say?' I asked. 'Did you answer in German?'

'No way,' said Saya. 'The flight was an hour and a half and he was sitting right next to me. If I'd answered in German, I'd have ended up having a whole conversation with him. I said in English that my English wasn't very good. And then he just looked really sympathetic and smiled.'

'And what if he was simply a nice person who was trying to accommodate you?' Hani asked, looking out at the city, too, or rather across it, as if somewhere beyond its rooftops and church towers lay the proof that people only ever mean well. 'You were on a plane, after all, you never know who comes from where. He might have spoken to you in German if he'd met you on the street. He probably just wanted to chat.'

'Yeah, whatever, but this story isn't over yet,' said Saya.

She'd been with us for half an hour, had put her hiking rucksack in my room, checked whether she still knew my current flatmates in the kitchen, waited patiently for Hani to come back from the corner shop with the beer, and was then adamant that we had to go up to the roof, because she felt too constricted inside flats right now. It was only when she got up here that she would tell us how her flight had been. 'Catastrophic,' she announced; she'd sat next to this infuriating man. She always ended up sitting next to infuriating men, on every flight she took. So then she told us the story, and the look on her face wasn't at all catastrophic. In any case, she looked like someone who would ride out any catastrophe, and know just how to get comfortable again afterwards. Saya sounded completely normal. Like she was glad to be telling an everyday kind of story, to warm us up to one another again. The way she told it was offhand, incidental. So we really had no inkling of everything that was about to happen.

'Then a woman got on the plane wearing a hijab,' Saya went on.

'Uh-oh,' I said.

'Uh-oh, indeed,' said Saya. 'The people around me started to shift nervously in their seats, glancing around. I mean, the woman might have had a bearded man in tow, that's always a risk — and he'd probably start harassing all the other women and then set off a bomb.'

'No, he'd oppress his wife first,' I said.

'Right,' said Saya. 'First, he'd quickly oppress his wife, and *then* he'd set off a bomb.'

I wanted to say more, to go one better. But we hadn't warmed up yet.

'Are you two making fun of terrorists now? Or of those passengers?' Hani asked, glancing at us. We were still looking at the surrounding roofs, the way other people stare into a camp fire. We could hear car horns and the low sound of people talking on the street below. I didn't want to respond — I thought Hani could have let us go on a bit longer. But since Saya had started telling us about her flight, Hani had been wondering if this was a story to be indignant about. That was what she feared, whenever Saya started telling stories: that the whole point would be getting indignant at the end. But so far in this story, everything was still fine.

In fact, when Saya got on the plane, the whole world was still fine. Saya could almost have forgotten that the world was a place that filled her with indignation. She had a window seat and got to board in the first group, without having to pay for the privilege. That evening she was going to see us and drink her inhibitions away. The most beautiful city in the world was waiting for her, and Saya didn't even have to think about its rental prices. When the guy with the bad English sat down beside her, she found it more amusing than annoying.

Then the woman got on. And Saya would have taken no further notice of her, if the woman hadn't looked at her ticket, then the seat numbers, then her ticket and back at the seat numbers, with a slightly lost expression on her face. Something was wrong; her seat appeared to be occupied. She said so several times, said it to the people sitting in front of Saya, enough times for them to listen, eventually, and tell her no, her seat was the aisle, not the window, and that seat was still free. There was a brief moment in which the woman said something like, 'But it's A, B, C!' as she pointed to each seat in turn, and the woman sitting in front of Saya replied, 'No, it's A, B, C,' starting at the opposite side.

'Could you sit down, please, there are other passengers waiting behind you!' the flight attendant said at her back. She was surly but also correct: a queue of people had formed, squashed together and scowling as they waited on the small plane. Saya knew that in this endless A-B-C game, the woman in the hijab was correct, but she also knew that in a minute, the woman would probably just sit in the wrong seat rather than get into an argument with the flight attendant as well. After all, having a window seat wasn't that important. And in any case, the flight attendant was annoyed; she sounded like an old-fashioned governess and looked like she was starving herself to keep her figure. It's no good arguing with hungry people.

But the woman — let's call her Yağmur for the sake of simplicity, because she looked like Yağmur from the TV series *Turkish for Beginners* — made a move that was completely new and interesting to Saya. 'Here's a suggestion,' Yağmur said to the woman who was sitting in her seat, 'let's just swap — then you don't have to get up, and I'll sit in your aisle seat.' It sounded like the most generous offer ever, and Saya really wanted to see the face of the woman in front of her. Next, Yağmur turned to the flight attendant and said, 'I'm glad you're here. Could you help me with my case? I'm not allowed to lift anything heavy.' She stroked her belly with both hands to emphasise how pregnant she was. In fact, there wasn't an obvious pregnancy bump, but that isn't something you can really point out.

The flight attendant had no desire to help, of course, and Saya had no idea if that was actually part of a flight attendant's job or not. But with a roll of her eyes, she eventually lifted the case into the overhead compartment, just to get things moving. 'Hand luggage has to be under twelve kilos,' she hissed at Yağmur, groaning under the case. No one gave her a hand. Probably because they were all afraid of her. Or because they all wanted to watch her being useful to make up for her unkindness: a pregnant woman, a carry-on suitcase, a good deed. 'Twelve kilos,' the flight attendant repeated sternly, as soon as the case was stowed. She sounded like she was going to get her whip out at any minute and spur the standing passengers into performing strictly timed production-line work.

Yağmur's voice shook as she said: 'Your colleagues told me that already — they weighed the case before I got on. Thank you for your help, it's very kind of you.' The 'very kind' was uttered so shakily that Saya realised she was shaking with anger rather than anything else. Saya, sitting in the row behind, was overcome with the two emotions she knew best. Anger and solidarity.

Solidarity isn't an emotion, Hani would have put in, if Saya had told us all this as I've described it here. But Hani also wouldn't have objected if I then closed the subject with a simple, 'Yes, it is.'

Because when you know a person like we know Saya, you know that solidarity is an emotion and unkindness is a reason for raging anger. And that's why it's also silly to call Yağmur Yağmur, because the Yağmur in the TV show never displayed such dignified anger as the woman on Saya's plane, and if you can think of another woman on German TV who wears a hijab, just give me a call and I'll change the name.

So, when Yağmur's case was finally stowed, she sat down in her wrong seat and took off her hijab. 'Ugh, this weather,' she said, running her hands through her curls. It had been raining while they were boarding, but thanks to the headscarf the rain hadn't ruined her hair.

The people finally started moving, albeit haltingly, down the plane, and when the woman who had the aisle seat in Saya's row approached, the man sitting next to her immediately leapt up to take her case. Saya leaned forward to see if this woman was pregnant as well, but couldn't say for sure. The only thing she *could* say for sure was that he was going to drone on at this woman in German for the next hour and a half.

'And did she like that?' Hani asked, because now, at last, the moment had arrived when she judged the story to be interesting.

I stopped listening for a second; a warm breeze enveloped us and, down below, someone was yelling something I couldn't quite hear. The haze of flowering trees hung in the air, the spunky aroma that floats over the city at this time of year, along with the smell of exhaust fumes and Hani's cigarette. It smelled so good. Everything was so good. The voices below grew louder as passers-by responded to the person yelling, and it was lovely to be sitting up here and have no part in it. No need to fear for your life, be a good citizen, pay attention, intervene. All the alert mechanisms that become second nature when you live in a big city are no use on the roof. We can't see or hear nearly enough up here to be relevant in any way. It's great. To have Saya's voice, Saya's body beside me, is great, and to know that Hani will put the dampers on anything that might sour the mood is great, too. Everyone is doing what they're best at, and my beer is tepid but it's still the best drink in the world.

Saya told us how the man next to her tried and failed to flirt with the new woman beside him, and then she finally got to the point. I'd been looking forward to this part all along, because I already knew what was going to happen; I'd been thinking it from the start, knowing that Saya had done exactly what I would have done myself in her situation.

'Then the flight attendant came round with drinks. Everyone said things like "tomato juice" or "Diet Coke" all expectantly, and then looked disappointed, because they'd been given a half-full, flimsy paper cup that makes you more sad than happy. The guy next to me, quite the gentleman, alerted me to the fact that drinks were being offered, but that he was happy to wait, and said "Ladies first" in English.'

Hani and I booed him, but not for long, because we wanted to find out what had happened next.

'Then I craned my neck forward and said to the flight attendant, in German, "A coffee with milk and sugar, please," loud and clear and without any accent.'

Hani and I roared with laughter and applauded and said, 'Well? How did he look? Did he say anything?'

'Of course not. He acted like nothing had happened. Later, when we were disembarking, I did it again, and said, "Bye, have a nice evening," as I passed him.'

'And did he reply?'

'No, he was too busy chatting up the woman who wasn't in the headscarf.'

Saya wrapped herself in her shawl, which was like a huge blanket, and I thought that I, too, should have realised that these shawls are a good look. It's just that, as always, I'd been too lazy to try them on. When I see clothes in shop windows, the risk is always too great that I'll try them on and realise I'm wasting my time, so I stick with what I know. Saya doesn't shy away from risks. Saya tries on, lays aside, tries on, buys, throws away, exchanges, and in the end she looks good.

Even the dilapidated old bench in the middle of the roof looked better for Saya's visit. Because she'd spotted the potential and the problems at a glance, and then brought all the cushions in the flat up here. And now we were sitting here like pensioners on the North Sea coast with their own wicker Strandkorb, on this roof, in the city that belongs to us.

We never used to have any doubt about that, Saya and me. When we thought about one day leaving the estate, the only place we considered making our new home was this city, with all the promises it held. The promise of adventure and freedom, but above all the promise that here, at last, we wouldn't stick out.

'Here's to a higher weight limit for pregnant women's hand luggage,' said Saya, raising her bottle and taking several gulps from it.

Hani reached for her beer, confused, not knowing whether we were really supposed to drink to that, whether Saya was serious and we were going to become the lobby for pregnant women now, until there was someone else to be saved from oppression.

∧ ∧ ∧

When Saya's mother was pregnant with her, she was in prison. I'm saying 'in prison' this time because, when someone gets shut away for political reasons, wanting to sound casual doesn't really seem right. And anyone who found themselves there in times when the photos were not only analogue but black and white has even more right to have people say they were 'in prison' rather than 'inside'. We were about fourteen when we looked at the photos, sitting on the rug in Saya's living room.

It was pretty rare for our entire families and their endless guests to all be out at the same time, so we had an agreement that when this happened, the three of us would meet at the flat of whoever had the place to themselves. In a matter of minutes, we became very grown-up, going to the fridge, making snacks, and putting our plates in the dishwasher afterwards. It was a thrill to sit on the finally vacant sofas and watch an episode of *Beverly Hills 90210* in peace, with no fathers and mothers to frown at us. We drank juice from the champagne glasses that our parents never used.

And Hani always had a weird need to get up in the ad breaks and stand out on the little balcony, which looked exactly the same in all our flats, because the flats our families lived in were all exactly the same. But Hani was the only one of us who lived in a flat that smelled of cold cigarette smoke, accidentally let in from outside, and the difference between her balcony and ours was what it was used for, and what it wasn't.

Sometimes, when people say things like 'have a good weekend' or 'a nice evening', this is the precise image that comes to my mind. Me, sprawled on a sofa that would usually be occupied, champagne glass in hand, spellbound by the ecstatic adverts on RTL, while Hani stands pointlessly on the balcony, looking out over the roofs of the town. The perpetual smell of those flats, the smell of feet, old wallpaper and dried herbs, different herbs depending on whose flat we were in. Just as our mothers' languages and the taste of their cooking were different.

So, when we were at Saya's place one day and her parents were out, she showed us the photo album, and the reason Hani and I were so reverent wasn't that we were such good friends, but because we knew this was a private object, in a space where the adults had no private life. Where the children had no private life, either. Where no one had a private life, because there was just no room for it in these flats, and no understanding of it when life and habits were communal. Most objects in these flats were either useful or decorative.

Saya had only seen the photo album for the first time herself a few days previously, when a friend of her uncle's had come to visit and brought it with him. The album must have taken a convoluted path to get here, being passed from one trusted pair of hands to the next over the years. Saya's parents had left their apartment and their country without saying goodbye, and ever since, it had been waiting to be restored to them along with the rest of their former possessions.

Saya was fourteen when she saw pictures of her parents as young people for the first time. Hani and I had no idea this was a formative experience for her; we just found it fascinating to see what these boring old people had looked like in their younger days. Saya showed us a photo of her mother with a bob, wearing a military shirt, one foot on a rock and one hand on her hip. In my eyes and Hani's, she might have looked young, but she also looked pretty uncool — and then Saya pointed proudly at it and said, 'That was just before she went to prison.' Then she added with even greater pride, 'So, just before she got pregnant. She might even have been pregnant with me in this photo, and just didn't know it yet.'

From then on, I was quite envious of Saya. Because of her mother, who had been to prison, and because that meant Saya herself had been to prison, in a way. Who would have thought that one day I'd be sitting here, wishing Saya had never been in prison, not then and certainly not tonight. Why does she have to take after her mother in this, of all things?

Anyway: when we were sitting on the roof and Saya had got to the part of her story where she was feeling solidarity with the pregnant woman on the plane, she made it sound like pregnancy was a blessed time, a happy time that mustn't be clouded under any circumstances. And that's ridiculous, if only because her own mother was pregnant just once, and during her pregnancy she was cooped up with ten other women and being taken off for interrogation every day, not knowing if her husband was still alive. My mother was pregnant five times, and every time, all she could do was hope the child in her belly would survive her night shifts in the laundry.

As a rule, our families were the only people we heard these kinds of horror stories from, and so, even when we were little, we chose to focus on other people's reality, as if our own didn't exist. Which was also important if we wanted the other kids to understand what we were telling them. So in summer we talked about 'going on holiday', although in our case that never meant going to the beach and renting a beach house. All we would do was go to visit our parents' friends for a few days, and spend the whole time watching TV in their small flats.

We still do it sometimes, even now; we take the things that have been sold to us as reality and paste them over our own biographies. And in this reality, pregnant women are happy women, spending a wonderful, intense time inhabiting their bodies, and you should support them in this and help to eliminate all nuisance factors from their lives. If someone doesn't show them respect, then, according to Saya, you have to step in and fight for their rights.

'Is Shaghayegh pregnant?' Saya asked, and for the first time it occurred to me that such a thing might be possible.

'Why do you ask? Because she's getting married?'

'Yes. Why's she getting married?'

'I don't know.'

I didn't know why we were sitting on the roof and talking about that instead of nice things, or why Saya then suddenly threw her bottle cap down into the street, like she didn't know it might hit someone and hurt them. All at once, I no longer had a good feeling about being up here.

'Weren't you surprised she was getting married?' Saya said. She made the idea of marriage sound preposterous, as if you needed a really good reason for it.

'No,' I said. 'I was surprised she invited us. But I think there are worse things than wanting to get married.'

'It isn't a crime,' said Hani. 'I'm happy for Shaghayegh.'

'I just don't know what there is to be happy about,' Saya said. And then she let rip, and I hoped the lecture she was embarking on wouldn't be a long one, because the subject bored me. But it did go on a bit; I'll just give you her main points. 'People get married because films have taught them that's the happy ending, but in reality, marriage only exists so that men can bind women to them, control them, and make them dependent. The fact that the concept has survived this long is only down to the two million tax benefits that married couples get, and that amounts to financial, conservative blackmail, which is disgusting, and by the way, for the past few centuries it's also been a means of excluding everyone who doesn't fit the heterosexual mould. All this time, those people who don't go mad with joy at the idea of being a classic husband and a classic wife have had to literally pay for it and be shamed by it day after day. That's the whole point of marriage. I mean, of course I'm glad Shaghayegh invited us, but I just want to know what's gone wrong with her before we get there.'

'Gone wrong? That's overstating it a bit, isn't it?' Hani asked.

Saya shook her head. 'Not in times like these. Doing something as trivial as getting married in times like these is a luxury you have to be able to afford. Something *must* have gone wrong with Shaghayegh for that to be her priority.'

So that was going to be Saya's mission in the days before the wedding: to find out why exactly Shaghayegh was getting married before she could celebrate with her. Because it was the celebration that had made her take the long trip here from the city where she'd chosen to live.

Two hours later, we had as much booze inside us as I wish I had right now, and our dirty laughter echoed in the streets below us.

The city was pretending to be peaceful. From the roof, it looked like a sheltered, silent place.

It was six years since we'd last got drunk together on a roof in this city. On another roof, on New Year's Eve — and even then, everything had been strangely reverent and peaceful. So peaceful that we had no objection to the barrage of fireworks in the distance, nor did we feel sorry for the refugees from war, the ageing veterans and neurotic dogs sitting in their flats, scared to death while everyone around them was producing a wartime level of noise because this was their one chance to let loose. Maybe our lack of sympathy was also something to do with the fact that there weren't any refugees or ageing veterans left in the part of town where we were celebrating, and our sympathy for the hipsters' dogs had its limits.

It was six years since we'd been together for New Year — not with new groups of friends, new partners, or new partners' friends, but quite naturally together, on the roof of the block where I used to live. And we were sitting together quite naturally again now, as if not a single day had passed since then.

Hani's laugh still made her sound like a giant, as if it came from some vast soundbox, as if it could make the earth quake. She threw her head back and slapped her thighs as we talked about something that had happened at some point, about which Hani had made some comment at the time. Saya's laugh was throaty, as if she was enjoying every note of it, and I laughed, too — but I couldn't stop watching the other two laughing as well. When they were laughing, they didn't notice me staring at them, trying to imprint every detail of them on my memory.

There aren't many people you know so well that you have to keep bringing yourself up to date on how they currently look. So that later, when you think back on this moment, you'll see them exactly as they were. How do you do that, I wonder, when you're properly old and thinking about an indistinct past? Do you see the fashions in your mind's eye, the haircuts, as they were? Or do you just do your best to imagine all that because you want to make the picture as true to life as possible? I do it when I write, and when I think: I don't want some weird, spectral silhouette of the people I'm thinking about; I want to see them the way they looked at that point in time, and it's lucky that I can, or I wouldn't be able to describe everything that's happened to us.

Hani, by contrast, is not usually very good at describing what's happened to her, but we listen all the same. At some point she began telling us about some flight she had been on where the flight attendant did absolutely everything wrong. It took quite a while. And we didn't completely understand, which meant it took even longer, because Hani was going to great lengths to ensure that in the end, we did in fact understand the point she was trying to make. It was about a man who was sitting in the wrong seat, and some people who complained, and a flight attendant who tried to help, but who didn't listen properly and then made the wrong man get up, and Hani drew a little picture in the air of who was sitting where and who was in the wrong seat and where she was sitting herself. It went on forever, this story, and Hani didn't realise how much space she was taking up, and eventually Saya said she needed to go to bed soon, and Hani said, 'Hang on, just one more cigarette,' and in the end she smoked another three cigarettes, so that we would understand *something*, and we only went to bed after reassuring Hani that she had definitely been in the right on that plane.

Hani stayed over, and I enjoyed the fact that Saya *had* to stay at my place, because she was a guest in this city, but Hani *wanted* to stay at my place, just to be close to us. And so I was what I was brought up to be: a good hostess.

ᴧ ᴧ ᴧ

I'm going to stop writing now. There's no point: I keep trying to imagine who you all are, while you're trying to imagine who we are.

We're not so different from you. You just think we are because you don't know us. Because you didn't have a childhood that smelled like ours, and because you don't have friends to share that stinking childhood with.

In any case, you're currently thinking various different things. You're already thinking Hani is an unsympathetic character, and you're now imagining Saya is pretty. You're waiting for the moment when I tell you which of us comes from which country. And that's something you need to know before you can put yourselves in our shoes. For you, that information is about as important as knowing which small German town we grew up on the outskirts of, and how old we are, and which of us is hottest.

I'm not telling you that. You'll have to manage without it. I mean, I don't know anything about you, either. Maybe you'll read this, and maybe you won't, depending on how the press deals with the case. If they try to contact me — and they will — then I won't give any interviews, because I know how interviews work; I've read the paper often enough and seen the public broadcasters' political talk shows. I'm going to print out this manuscript. I'm going to cut my finger and drip my blood onto it. I'll give it to the tabloids, to *Bild*, and then you can let rip, writing about us.

I'm describing Saya the way she is, and you can make of her what you will. If I finish telling this story before the night is over, I'm just going to write it again. Maybe from your point of view. How the story would go if one of you had written it. Oh, wait: if I want to know that, all I have to do is spend a few hours reading the papers or looking online.

So, I'm not going to stop writing after all. I'll carry on, though all I have to drink is tap water and tea, and the neighbours' cold cigarette smoke is coming in through the half-open window, and I'd prefer to be drinking beer, and today I'd even prefer to be smoking. But both of those would require me to leave the building. And that's something I never really want to do, and certainly not today.

The people outside are totally unpredictable, and I don't want to have to dodge past them just so I can buy something to drink.

In any case, the guy in the corner shop over the road always tells me — and he phrases it like a question — that I'm getting prettier: 'You get prettier every day, don't you?' Then I do a fake giggle, because I don't know what you're supposed to say to that. Probably because there's nothing you *can* say, because the point is not for you to say anything. The point is for him to say something. I'm afraid he'll feel like an idiot for saying something so uncalled-for, and so I laugh and pretend it doesn't make me uncomfortable.

And then sometimes I feel a phantom hand touching my backside, although the guy is standing behind the counter, keeping his hands to himself. I get that sometimes: my body recalling unwanted contact on buses and trains and dancefloors, when someone is annoying me in a way that isn't physical. Perhaps it's my body trying to motivate me into a belated reaction and make me punch someone. I don't do that, of course, because the corner-shop guy doesn't deserve it. So I usually just do nothing.

Which reminds me of a story I should tell about Saya, because Saya always does something; she doesn't let things be. She puts her foot down even if that means trampling on something, though that doesn't automatically make her more violent than other people.

I mentioned New Year just now. The one six years ago, our last together. It was a special New Year's Eve: everything was still lovely and exciting. Though I would say that about everything that happened more than three years ago, because three years is the cut-off point, after which things in the past become lovely and exciting, as long as they weren't actively bad or boring.

There were people I knew at this party, and people my flatmates knew, who I didn't know so well. And there were two people I knew inside out: Saya and Hani. The three of us weren't together in the hours leading up to midnight; we were with various other people, laughing and drinking and flirting, oh yes, I was definitely flirting with this cute flatmate I had at the time, and because he'd only just moved in, we hadn't yet reached the point where you either have to sleep together or stop flirting.

I didn't yet know that at some point he would start always making his coffee when he heard I was in the kitchen, and that I would therefore stop laughing at his jokes and cocking my head to one side when he was telling me something. But at New Year we still found each other fascinating. That's the way it always is with crushes and flatmates. They're important as long as they're current, and as soon as you move out, they disappear from your eyeline and your life. I even had to think for a while just now before I remembered his name: it was Felix, the kind of name that people have when they were born in the eighties and everything is going great for them.

Felix had a mate who was completely irrelevant — who was irrelevant even at the time — and who knew nobody at this party except Felix, and somehow also me, because I'd made him a coffee once when he came to see Felix. And because he didn't know anyone, he came and stood with us and disrupted our flirting, because the minute someone is watching you flirt, you start feeling ashamed of what you're doing. It's only exciting when you can kid yourself you aren't flirting. The friend, then — let's call him Gabriel because of his angelic curls — was standing with us, making our flirting visible, but not involving himself in the conversation. In short: he was being a pain in the arse.

At some point, when Hani just happened to be standing beside us, I seized my chance and introduced the two of them to one another. From then on, I observed their conversation from the corner of my eye. He asked where Hani was from, and Hani answered truthfully. He asked what she did, and Hani told him she worked in office management. He asked if that was what you might just as well call being a secretary, and embarked on a dubious historical survey of job titles, to which Hani eventually said something like, 'I do bookkeeping and administration; there's some maths involved as well.'

Hani stood there, carrying on the conversation because I'd introduced her to Gabriel and of course she couldn't know he was an insignificant person. She didn't exactly look amused, but she stayed and chatted. Gabriel acted like he couldn't quite hear what she was saying, which might actually have been true — in any case, he leaned further and further in, inclining his beautiful head towards Hani's mouth. You can't maintain that posture while keeping all your other body parts to yourself, so he placed one hand gently on Hani's upper back as he asked her what kind of company it was she worked for. Hani likes hands on her back and she likes curly-haired men, so now she had one more reason to stay and talk to Gabriel a while longer, besides the politeness she thought she owed to me.

She told him about the company she'd just started working for, using words that the company itself used for this purpose: it was about animal protection, but a kind of animal protection that takes into account the rules of capitalism; uniting the two was the only way for animals to really thrive in the world we live in; there was no sense in trying to do it any other way. Gabriel had plenty to say on the subject, as if he'd spent days and weeks thinking about whether that made sense. Hani actually had spent days and weeks thinking about it and had already decided it didn't (though it did now provide her with an income and dominate her day-to-day life), and she didn't find his arguments interesting, relevant, or good. And at that point she stopped caring about the hand and the curls, and quickly asked: 'So, what do you do?'

I could see from her face that the future of the conversation depended on his response. When he replied, the positions they were standing in didn't change at first, though his reply did go on a bit, and because of the conversation I was having myself, I didn't understand what he did for work. But the expression on Hani's face told me that she didn't have a clue about his job either, or think it sounded nice, and her posture gradually began to change. Her ear moved away from his inclined head and constantly talking mouth — though that didn't do much good, because he followed it. When Hani started taking small steps away from him, his body followed hers, quite effectively, because his hand had a good purchase on Hani's back and it told him where she was going.

'Just popping out for a cigarette,' Hani said — an escape route I'd often envied her for. Smokers can always get away when a situation becomes uncomfortable, always make other people wait for them, always find new people to talk to with an instant topic of conversation — smoking — if need be. But then, inconveniently and much to Hani's surprise, Gabriel said, 'I was about to go for one as well.' He didn't look like a smoker, and she hadn't yet seen him out on the balcony. Later, on the roof, everyone would eventually start smoking, but this early in the evening the only people feeling the call of the outside were those who needed to go.

So they headed for the balcony, and as she turned around, his hand tried to move down and graze her lower back for a moment — but Hani seemed to have sensed this, and managed to prevent it by moving swiftly away towards the balcony door.

I stayed behind with Felix (who at that point, as I said, I found thoroughly witty and interesting), feeling a bit guilty that I'd used Hani to get rid of Gabriel. But I also told myself that Hani was a grown-up and could walk away if he was annoying her, and that he wasn't actually that annoying. He'd asked the usual, not very original questions — well so what, there were worse people to talk to, and he did also seem genuinely interested in Hani's life. And so I chose to carry on talking to Felix, about growing up in the countryside, and village parties, instead of worrying about two adults who could easily communicate to one another that they no longer wanted to communicate with one another. When I saw that Saya was heading for the balcony to fetch a cold beer, I thought no more about it.

It was three, maybe four minutes before Hani and Saya came back to us, laughing and looking a bit shell-shocked, and I heard Saya saying, 'I couldn't stand that for another minute.' We didn't see Gabriel again for the rest of the evening; after he took off, we opened the schnapps. It was a home-distilled one, from the countryside, where Felix grew up, made from his parents' quinces, and my conversation with him went on until midnight, until everyone, as I said, was out on the roof, looking out at the seemingly peaceful city. That evening, that New Year's Eve, Saya had said or done something I didn't dare ask about, but if for example she'd given Gabriel a smack in the face, I would definitely have heard about it sooner or later. On the other hand, I hadn't seen Gabriel come back in from the balcony. I just never saw him again, not that evening or any time afterwards, and when I mentioned his name several days later, everyone just looked embarrassed and changed the subject.

I've imagined what happened so often that I'm now sure my version is true. My version goes like this: Saya stepped onto the balcony, bent down to the beer crate, and overheard enough of Hani and Gabriel's conversation to assess what was going on. She opened her bottle on the railing and stuck around so she could keep listening. She listened and the other two smoked and talked, which is to say, Hani was mostly smoking and Gabriel mostly talking, until he looked at Saya and asked if he could help her. At that, Saya put her beer down, gave him a friendly smile, grabbed him by the shoulders and threw him over the railing. Gabriel spread his wings like an angel, activated his halo, and flew off, not turning back to look at the uninterested, smoking Hani and the strong, not-smoking Saya. That's what will have happened, because Saya always finds a way to protect her friends.

Hani might be less solution-oriented than Saya, but she's always fine. If Saya hadn't stepped in, Hani would just have spent the whole evening with Gabriel, and kept drinking until he was smart, prudent, discreet, and ego-free. Then she would have solved the problem by not finding it a problem. This strategy has always helped her have a better time than Saya and me.

In the last few years, for instance, when we've been patted down outside clubs or festivals, Saya and I have regularly gone berserk with rage, while Hani just giggled. She honestly giggled because she liked the friendly female bouncers patting her down — it tickled, and so she was always on good terms with those people, who never heard a word of greeting, let alone thanks, from Saya and me. Hani walked into clubs feeling great, while we first had to let off steam.

When Hani moved to the estate, we were just hitting puberty. We read the copies of *Bravo* magazine that the other kids on the estate borrowed from their older brothers and sisters, and we read them outside so our parents wouldn't catch us. Saya, two years older than me, always read the Dr Sommer pages, and I noticed her reading them, but without any real interest. At that time, it meant that Saya had a brightly coloured magazine open on her lap at pictures of naked teenagers — alright, let's say young adults. An editorial decision that eventually made *Bravo* scandalous, and which they later reconsidered.

When we were entering puberty, the Dr Sommer column was already much less scandalous, but it still hadn't been cut from the magazine, and it made a valuable contribution to our sex education, which of course no one else thought to give us. Sometimes we showed the pages to each other to make ourselves crack up laughing. I remember one picture that showed a young man who'd sprayed dabs of whipped cream onto his girlfriend's naked body so he could kiss them off. We couldn't stop laughing. I can still hear Saya to this day, gasping, 'Look at this, he's put cream all over the place!' — and I can see our immature bodies doubled over with laughter. Hani stood beside us and giggled along, though always in a slightly more reserved way. At some point that changed, probably when she understood more German and could stop pretending she was one of us, because she actually was one of us.

Various languages wafted around in the back of Hani's mind, languages she would never need in Germany, and would never be recognised as a skill or an in-built advantage here. Her curiosity and interest in learning from us what you had to learn so you wouldn't stand out was written on her face. Not because she was all that hungry for knowledge, but because anything else would have caused problems. And problems were what she'd left behind. Hani's parents, her brother, and she had escaped the war — a bloody, unrelenting, merciless war — and no one here praised or pitied them for it. People were just vaguely aware of them and hoped, because Hani's family hadn't come too far, that they'd go back as soon as the war was over. I don't know if Hani and her parents, a white-haired, moustachioed man and a cheerful young woman with curly blonde hair, hoped that, too. They always gave the impression that the most important thing to them was to be here and to be safe. To smoke on the balcony in peace, to be able to enjoy the sun and welcome their children's friends into their home.

Hani watching us read *Bravo* was somehow important. We felt more grown-up when she was there. Partly, I think, because in the beginning, when she kept quiet, it made us think she knew a lot more than we did and had no need of *Bravo*.

Hani's arrival put an end to that phase when Saya's imagination would run away with her and we'd believe everything she said. By 'we' I mean a few other girls from the estate and me. It was always clear who was boss, because Saya just had a talent for it, and life would have been dull as hell if anyone had usurped her. Saya told us stuff about the world and we believed her, because it made the world better.

The wrecked cars without any number plates, rusting away in the parking spaces outside our building, were a good example of that. We didn't care about them; we had no interest in cars and we never thought to interrogate the crappiness of our neighbourhood. Until Saya told us a heart-breaking story. An old man, Herr Zimmermann, had parked those cars there, she said, and then he got very sick and had been in hospital for years. Poor old Grandpa Zimmermann was going to be out soon, and he'd be really sad to come back and see the state his cars were in now. We needed to help him, Saya said; we had to clean the cars up for him. That was the kind of thing only Saya could pull off: getting five people together to start washing some rusty old bangers. If someone had seen us and asked, we might have realised Saya had made it all up. But because no one did and because her story sounded totally plausible, we did everything we could to spare Herr Zimmermann this sight.

When Hani came and we were just old enough not to fall for any old crap we heard, Saya knew she couldn't get away with those stories anymore. Hani, the observer, would have exposed her without even saying a word. But I think by that age, Saya had lost interest in telling her stories, as well — otherwise we wouldn't have been sitting outside the building with the magazines.

But now I've got the order of things mixed up. I was writing about Tuesday, the Tuesday Saya got here, when everything was still fine.

Though that night, already, things weren't fine. That's something you can say later, in court. Or to Saya's psychotherapist — that might be important, if you want to find out whether she's mad or not.

We went to bed, Saya and me in my bed and Hani on a mattress on the floor. We'd all used the same toothbrush, which we thought was a less disgusting option than none of us brushing our teeth. There has actually never been a point in our lives when we thought one toothbrush between three people was acceptable, but what are you supposed to do when two out of three of you have forgotten your toothbrushes and you've already got that stale aftertaste of beer? We got into bed, murmured our goodnights, and soon I could hear Hani's soft snoring, which, in contrast to her loud laughter, made her sound like a little girl.

You never hear Saya at night. You can't hear if she's awake, and you can't hear if she's asleep. With other people, you can hear when their breathing gets deeper or more regular, but you can't hear Saya breathing at all — and then eventually she just wakes up.

I closed my eyes and opened them again at once, because my head was spinning. But I was so tired that my eyes kept on wanting to close. There was a huge drunken dilemma going on in my weak body, which had been getting too much coffee recently and not enough love. I closed my eyes very slowly and opened them again, closed and opened them. Again and again, so that my body would start to understand it was just imagining the spinning and I was lying there quite safely, quite undeniably in my bed.

I tried to calm myself down, and quite honestly the easiest way to do that was to think about Lukas. That's awkward for me — after all, I was the one who left him, even if I'm not quite sure the rest of the world sees it like that. But it's also awkward because you're either single or you're not; there's no in-between state in which your mind is allowed to be dependent on someone else. It's annoying to still be a little bit dependent all the same, at least dependent to the extent that you find it easier to fall asleep at night when you think about the other person. But what the hell, I decided. The important thing was to fall asleep as soon as possible, and anyway I hadn't mentioned his name once that evening. That was not just a win; that was proof. Even if I didn't know exactly what it proved.

Unfortunately, I'd now kept my eyes shut for longer than my body could cope with, and to compensate I had to not only open them again, but get myself a bit more vertical to prevent everything coming back up. Propped on my forearms, I was now lying there and feeling ashamed that my two friends, who'd drunk exactly the same amount as I had, seemed to be handling it better, and then suddenly there was a loud crash, which clearly came from Saya, a horrible impact noise that went right through me and could only be made by someone with a lot of strength — and I didn't know Saya was that strong — hurling their whole body against the wall, as if trying to break it down with their own weight.

I cried out, looked at her, and couldn't believe that her eyes were still closed and she was lying there on her back as if nothing had happened. But then she reared up again. My heart was racing, and hers seemed to be filled with panic or anger, as she leaned back ready to hurl herself full force against the wall once more. I was frightened for her, and the next second I heard myself saying, 'Saya, Saya,' at a normal conversation volume.

It was Hani, not Saya, who replied, 'Yes?'

'Go back to sleep,' I said. That was meant for both her and Saya, and they both complied. But my heart wouldn't stop pounding, and I spent a good half an hour looking at Saya in the half-light. It was only then that my eyes closed. At least the shock had sobered me up.

Saya doesn't carry any trauma around with her. None of us do. That is, we probably all do — the kind of trauma that people like us always have. Crying parents, shouting parents, figuring out for yourself what is different about you when you're still young. Teachers who treat you like dirt and treat your parents like even worse dirt, no money, no garbage collection, too many ambulances, and too few books.

We have a whole lot of little traumas, but we don't function in the way you imagine when you've watched news reports and you're filled with empathy, and you've speculated — though only with your oldest friends — about how those poor refugees came across the Mediterranean and so must have nothing to do but dream incessantly of the Mediterranean.

No, sure, you're not like that, and that isn't how you think at all: for a while you helped to sort clothes and give out cuddly toys, and you don't have those prejudices anymore. And you were nice to everyone on your relief program, even the people you were a little bit afraid of; you were very brave and you were nice. Even when you wondered if there were any terrorists among the people in your care, you went on being nice — but also racist. You were nice racists. And doing all that aid work, you saw that these refugees are always good for a surprise; you can't pigeonhole anyone, it takes all sorts, and now every time you have dinner with friends you can tell them all the things you've learned. So you've set aside your prejudices, but — and this also nicely rounds off the story about Felix the flirty flatmate — when it comes down to it, people like you, which is to say, all people, suddenly know exactly what psychological state those refugees, which is to say, all refugees, are in.

When one of the rooms in the flat we lived in back then came free, because Giulia left the city suddenly but went on paying rent for another three months, none of my flatmates, including flirty Felix, wanted to let 'a refugee' move in, because refugees are traumatised and we wouldn't be able to deal with that. None of us would. Traumatised refugees are the nightmare of untraumatised non-refugees. And so the latter can deny them their help while claiming to be empathetic people. Because they're grown-up enough to turn down a responsibility they can't handle in advance, instead of finding they're not up to it later and having made the suffering of the poor refugees even worse.

But what I really want to say is that Saya wasn't carrying around any trauma that she hadn't worked through, anything that could have driven her to her scary nocturnal wall-attacks. On the contrary, she's more like an untraumatised non-refugee, if there is such a thing.

One evening when we were maybe seven, by which I mean I was about six and she was about eight, I went on an outing with her family. People who lived on the estate didn't go on outings unless a relative from another country was visiting. Before and after that, nothing ever happened beyond the stone steps up to the blocks, beyond the field behind Saya's building, and beyond what I call the ghetto, because that's what it was intended to be. Its sole purpose was to banish people like us to an obscure corner of the town. And it worked pretty well, because we settled in nicely there, even if the garbage collectors didn't come round for weeks at a time and the fishy bin bags sat rotting in the sun.

Saya's family had visitors. Some relatives or other had come to stay, bringing their three children, all a few years older than us, and a mother-in-law. And Saya's parents had transformed themselves from the boring, serious, quiet folk who were only of interest to me when they allowed Saya to do something, into people who were full of love and laughter.

We drove out down country lanes and through the woods. Saya's father went back and forth several times in his rusty Polo until we were all there: at a locked log cabin with a fire pit outside, in the middle of a huge field at the edge of the woods. The fire pit was the real destination. Saya's father lit a fire, and the other people kneaded meat onto metal skewers that they held expertly over the flames. The fat dripped, the flames crackled, and Saya and I ran endlessly round and round the fire.

Today, of course, I know you're supposed to hire the barbecue cabin, if you're a Hans-Werner celebrating your fifty-eighth birthday with the boys; I know there's a fridge, plates, and cutlery inside, proper benches and tables; and that even when we were kids, no one drove out there just to use the half a square metre of earth where you were allowed to light a fire. No one but those people who were pining for a world where picnicking was a national sport that all families played; people who had ended up in a world called Germany, where open fires were confined to a small patch of ground you had to hire.

We children didn't wonder at the locked hut. We rattled the door for a minute, but then we were more interested in the balustrade around the verandah, which was perfect for climbing and balancing on. Saya's mother had brought liquid soap that smelled of raspberries, and her father tilted a canister of ice-cold water so that we could wash our hands in the irregular stream before sitting down on the woollen blanket and filling our bellies with the fat-dripping meat.

In the evening, the adults kept the fire going as they sat around it and sang songs that, in my memory, all sounded like 'Bella Ciao', except that 'Bella Ciao' wasn't among them, and I didn't even know 'Bella Ciao' at that point.

Saya and I took our blankets and lay down on the barbecue hut's covered verandah. Her uncle drummed on the now-empty water canisters, and the songs that followed were so sad they made me want to cry. But they were also so beautiful they made me want to cry. Apart from the singing and drumming, all you could hear were the crickets and the trees swaying in the wind, and then out of nowhere, as if the mood was now exactly right for sharing secrets, Saya said, 'I think that's the uncle who was there when we rode over the mountains.' She said it as if this was new information to be added to a story she'd told me previously. But she hadn't told me any story, so I didn't know what to do with the mountains and the riding, at least not officially. In reality, I knew what she meant at once. No idea how. 'He sang that song on the horse, as well,' she said. The uncle, who had children older than Saya, had taken people across the mountains to safety. Mountains where there was no paved road, snow-covered mountains that seemed to go on forever. With children no older than four.

Saya hummed along with the song. Her voice, which had never passed for a light child's voice, even when she was a child, was so soft and beautiful against the distant men's voices that I wished the rest of my life would consist of nothing but this one evening.

Afterwards, I was allowed to stay over at Saya's for the first time because, when we finally got back to the estate, our parents couldn't separate us. There was never really room for a guest in their small flat, and certainly not that night. But Saya, the three other children, and I all squeezed into the little room that Saya usually shared with just a few cuddly toys.

Saya slept as Saya sleeps. Normally. She fell asleep without a sound, and woke up without a sound. At night there was never any restless shouting or angry raging. When she told stories, it was like she was still humming along to revolutionary songs in that hoarse voice she had as a child. Earnestly, but without any urgency.

After that, years later, we often went to barbecue cabins together. There was a phase when everyone was having big parties for their eighteenth birthdays. By everyone, I mean everyone at school, at the selective Gymnasium that Saya and I went to. Though she and I never even considered throwing a big birthday party. Maybe because there were too many hurdles. Parents who wanted to be there. Money for beer and sausages that we didn't have, and couldn't ask our parents for, either. And all kinds of reservations about explaining to our parents why we were so full of ourselves, wanting everyone to make a fuss about our birthdays. As utterly different as Saya's parents and mine were, sometimes they were utterly united, without even realising it. Of course, we were still invited to other people's eighteenths, and the parties made that school year much more exciting than the ones before; they were where the majority of our social lives played out. That's how it is in places where you can't go out normally, unless you get organised, know people with cars, and can get to better towns nearby. The parties were held at various cabins, but never at the one where Saya's family had used the fire pit illegally. Maybe it no longer even existed by that point. Anyway, I'm very glad that the memory of that one evening wasn't overlaid with all the times we got wasted together.

We took Hani with us to one of these parties, probably one of the early eighteenths, maybe thrown by one of the boys in our year who we hung around with. It was late summer and still so hot during the day that the nights weren't chilly, and we stood around the fire pit getting drunker and drunker and it wouldn't ever have crossed anyone's mind to drink anything but beer or smoke anything but tobacco and cannabis.

I was in love with a boy called Alex, and it was so lovely to be in love with him, because there was finally a point to it; we'd reached the age when you weren't just in love and then nothing happened — no, we had proper conversations about films and teachers, and it was lovely to talk like this and feel your heart fluttering and to wonder if he might be interested in you, too. Alex was older than me and he was smart and sweet. And that was why the party was so important to me: because I was bursting to find out whether something might happen between Alex and me. I'd brought my favourite hoodie and was wearing the trousers with the big rips in them. I would have liked to put the hoodie on, because I thought I looked nice in it, but it was so warm that it wouldn't have made sense.

Alex was a bit shy, and we spent an entire half-hour talking to one another. Then he had to go to the toilet and he didn't come back, and I waited where we'd been standing. I thought he'd come back — I mean, he'd only gone to the toilet. But Alex didn't come back, because then, as you do, he got talking to other people about films and teachers, and stayed standing with those other people. But I went on waiting, in that spot by the fire pit, because I hoped he'd remember that he'd been standing here with me and that we'd been having a really good chat, and of course then I was too afraid to move away, because if I did then he wouldn't be able to find me when he came back.

Meanwhile, Saya as always hadn't declared any interest in anyone. Saya was never in love, at least not officially. That might have been a reaction to no one ever officially being in love with Saya. Probably because at parties like this one she never did what you're supposed to do: chat, take the piss, say witty things that people will remember you for, show an interest, be interesting. For some reason, Saya was always having a serious discussion with someone. It was the same that night. She was sitting in a corner on one of the few benches outside, in the middle of three boys, three nerds from the year above, talking about the Iraq War. A topic that no one has ever been desperate to talk about, and no one now wants to talk about at all. But Saya *was* desperate; she still wanted to talk about 9/11, and George W. Bush, and the USA. She's let the topic slide now, thankfully, but when we were all eighteen and Saya was twenty, the USA was her favourite subject, and that might have been partly because the USA offered the most controversial fuel for discussions.

The nerds around her, all drunk and dressed in various heavy-metal T-shirts, were telling her what they'd read on the internet: that the Americans had instigated the 9/11 attacks themselves, to give them an excuse to invade Iraq. At the time, Saya herself might have put forward outlandish theories like this to provoke someone, but that evening she argued against them, purely for the sake of arguing, and in the end someone held up an American dollar bill, on which some symbol or other was supposed to reveal something.

That's so old hat, Saya said bluntly, surely no one still believes that — and this, too, she only said because it was a killer argument. If something wasn't current, it no longer had any meaning, somehow. I have no idea whether anyone had held a dollar bill up in front of her before and decrypted some symbol or other, or whether she just said the old hat thing to sound like she was smarter than the others.

Why did someone have an American dollar bill with them in the first place? What becomes of people who take foreign currency to parties at the age of eighteen, as props to help them explain conspiracy theories? Maybe they're the same ten people who are now responsible for the 30,000 hate-speech comments online.

Anyway, Saya was sitting there, well dressed as usual, surrounded by men as usual, and with this completely asexual aura that at the time I found kind of unsettling, because I hadn't yet realised that we didn't all need to go around being so massively oversexualised. That's something you need to learn: first you're confronted with a world in which all films, adverts, jokes, and representations of women are oversexualised, and then you have to not be at all oversexualised yourself, under any circumstances. And all the confusions and uncertainties that arise from this are only laid to rest once you're actually having lovely, regular sex, which is an unexpected chain of causality: oversexuality being healed by lovely sex. That was something I wanted at the time, but it would be a long while before I had any.

Hani, however, did have lovely sex that night. Not for the first time — I know that for a fact, because I know all about her first time — but it was the first time everyone got to hear about it. And now, years later, I am suddenly overcome with sympathy for Hani as I think about this story, although, as I said, it was a really nice thing to have happened to her. But at the time I didn't feel any sympathy; I didn't have any proper feelings at all, because I didn't yet properly understand what had happened and how you were supposed to judge it out in the big, wide world. After that, Hani didn't come to our parties so often, though we did keep inviting her. But we invited her because not inviting her wasn't an option, and somehow Hani understood that.

So, while I was standing there by the fire, waiting for Alex and not even daring to turn round to see where he was, some people were standing nearby laughing loudly and making dirty jokes about a slut. It was a word you used back then. There were people, and there were sluts. Said slut had just had wild sex with someone in the little room where the foosball table was. Slut and someone — it didn't interest me all that much, but I kept listening. They were slagging off her clothes and how she'd been behaving all evening, and saying that she'd been begging for it from the word go. I was inclined to see it as kind of uncool that there was a girl at the party who was so desperate for sex.

Only then did someone ask who they were talking about, and someone else said, 'Oh, the one with the Russian accent and the prostitute stick,' which was mean. Hani smoked her cigarettes with a cigarette holder because that's what her grandmother had done, and her accent isn't even slightly Russian and was already so good that you could only hear it if you were really listening out for it.

But to be completely honest, that wasn't my immediate reaction. My first thought was: shit, they're talking about Hani, and shit, I brought Hani to the party and now she's misbehaving.

When we saw one another again, later that evening, her mascara had run unflatteringly down her face. Of course, she realised that everyone had heard, and that the older girls wouldn't forgive her for it. Nor did it escape her that the guy she'd just been getting to know was having a pretty good evening; afterwards, he won every round of beer pong. But at least I know that Hani had fun, because when she and I swiped the last four bottles of beer and went to sit at the edge of the woods to watch the sun rise, drunk and sad, she told me that it had been really lovely sex and she'd had a really lovely orgasm. I was still too inexperienced and ashamed to just be pleased for her, and hoped instead that she would immediately forget what she'd just said and stay at home when the next party was on.

Maybe we would all have had more fun at these parties if we hadn't distributed ourselves around various men, but stayed together, the three of us. But honestly, then we might just as well have stayed at home, because the whole point of these parties was to meet men, who we still called boys, and we were always taken aback when someone said something like, 'All men are pigs,' because 'men' were the actors our mums idolised, or they were dads, or teachers, not the guys from school we ran around after.

Saya, who by the time the sun came up had long since gone to bed, was somehow dissatisfied with how this party had gone, and only later admitted that she'd made out with someone that evening.

Not with one of the nerds, of course; they might have hung on her every word, but they were never going to make anything that might have passed for a pass at her. No, it was Leo, the class hottie, who everyone secretly wanted to kiss. Leo, who then became Saya's first boyfriend and who now only serves as the subject of a single anecdote, which I could perform right now if I wasn't still on the barbecue cabin and their first kiss. I'm going to store that anecdote away for later. Anyway, I could have sworn I'd had sight of Saya all evening and there hadn't been a moment when she could have been making out with Leo. But in all likelihood it did happen, and somehow she managed to avoid the gossip.

And I could leave that memory at this point, because the outing my mind has just been on to the barbecue cabins of our youth has actually been pretty nice. I could just leave what happened to Saya that evening, at that party, there — but that wouldn't be right. Because I still have a very clear memory of one part of the discussion that Saya and the nerds were having that evening, at that cabin, and so I know this was the summer that Saya began to roll the grubby word 'racism' around her tongue when she was talking about her own experiences, and I know that this summer, because of this conversation, she stopped saying it again for a while.

You see, this was the summer when Saya's aunts came to visit them in Germany. That in itself should be explanation enough. But because once again, you people don't understand and always need to have things explained to you in great detail before you object, I'll take a bit more of a run-up at it. I will explain in more detail than Saya did to the nerds, so that afterwards you can't say you just didn't quite grasp the situation.

So, it was the summer that Saya's aunts came to visit. At this point, Saya and her parents were no longer driving to locked barbecue cabins, because by now they knew what was allowed and what was categorised as illegal, and so Saya and her aunts did normal estate things, with long walks, decadent food shopping, marathon cooking sessions, and endless communal meals. The aunts were there to see Saya and her mother and father, not to have exciting times in an exciting foreign country. In any case, they were much too old for all that. They were actually too old for this trip, full stop, as you could tell when they arrived at the airport and wanted to sit quietly in McDonald's for a bit rather than get straight in the car. The aunts were so old that everyone realised: they'd travelled to Germany this time, yes, but they probably wouldn't be able to make this same journey again.

Saya wasn't worked up or emotional when she and her father met the aunts at the airport with a rose for each of them. She was proud. Who else could say she'd spent her early years with three strong women who had now travelled specially to celebrate her twentieth birthday with her? The twentieth birthday thing was admittedly just what they'd put in the visa application as a suitably innocuous reason for the trip, but Saya's birthday really was coming up, so she'd decided this was the truth, and in return she was going to make it her duty to look after the aunts and pay them the respect they deserved.

When they got to McDonald's, the aunts sat down and Saya and her father went to place their order. Soon she was walking back towards the table in a sunny corner of the restaurant with a tray filled with fries, Coke, and a lot of ketchup. While Saya was carrying the tray, she still felt quite normal. But as she approached the table where the three ladies were sitting, she suddenly felt like she was stepping onto a stage. The aunts were being stared at, both by people at nearby tables and by those sitting further away. Saya distributed the cartons of fries, had kisses bestowed on her in thanks, and suddenly wanted to be somewhere else, ideally alone with her family, so that she could be pleased her aunts had come to visit without having to think about the people all around them.

Over the two weeks that followed, she couldn't shake this feeling. They walked the footpaths through the fields around the estate and strolled through silent woods, and everything would seem alright. Until a walker, a young man with a dog, or an older couple with walking poles approached. Apparently, when you encountered three women wearing hijabs, it was compulsory to stare at them, and Saya could still feel the eyes on them long after the walkers had disappeared round the next bend. And then when Saya was out on her own, walking to school, meeting up with us in the afternoon at the deserted woodland play area — wherever she went, eyes were still looking at her. No one could see her, and yet she felt so visible. The aunts didn't seem to notice. In any case, they were too busy constantly singing Saya's praises.

One evening, Saya, her parents, and her aunts were all sitting round the table, eating. When Saya mentioned some homework she had to do, the aunts praised her for being so conscientious, such a hard-working student, such a clever girl, and at first Saya was flattered, but then she went into her room and felt how angry she was.

Initially, she thought it was because she wasn't hardworking at all, just clever, but then it occurred to her that this wasn't true. She'd always worked hard. Done what was expected of her, never distracted the other children or the teacher, did her homework, put her hand up when she knew the answer. She'd done everything good girls were told to do. 'She got into the Gymnasium, what an achievement!' her favourite aunt had said admiringly, back then, on the phone, and today the youngest aunt had repeated it, because Saya's final exams were coming up.

Saya recalled that her parents had sent her to the Gymnasium because that's what they wanted, but it was also what Saya wanted, and she had a report card full of good 2s and not too many 3s. Plus her parents thought that the extra year in kindergarten and voluntarily repeating the first year of school had been enough to catch up on the language deficit. They'd been right about that: Saya's essays and dictations were no different to those of her classmates.

All the same, the official recommendation had been that she should go to the local high school.

As Saya was sitting over her maths homework, she wondered whether she just hadn't realised what was really going on this whole time. Had people been looking at her the way they now looked at her aunts? Judging her by standards that seemed to differ from the general standards? They'd made her repeat the first year of school. Who the hell has to repeat Year One?

Was it really so horribly straightforward? Couldn't it actually have been for her own good?

The next day, Saya and her aunts took the bus to a local shopping centre; the aunts wanted to buy presents to take back with them, and were particularly interested in electrical items *Made in Germany*, and because Saya's parents had to go to work, Saya and her aunts went shopping by themselves.

As they got on the bus, the driver growled at her favourite aunt: did she have a ticket? The favourite aunt turned to Saya in confusion, and Saya, equally confused, said, 'No, none of us have tickets, I haven't bought them yet. Four, please.' The bus driver printed the tickets without saying a word or looking at her, and nor did he respond when she said 'Thank you' and 'Goodbye'.

Saya and the aunts got on the bus and were offered seats by other passengers. Saya made an effort not to keep thinking about the bus driver, but she couldn't help it. She couldn't seem to convince herself that he was just a bad-tempered man who was dissatisfied with his life and his job, and was taking his mood out on everyone else. Because that led her to consider whether he was taking his mood out on everyone indiscriminately, or only on some people.

Saya talked to her aunts on the bus, but she kept her voice low, because she felt uncomfortable speaking too loudly in their shared language. The aunts spoke quietly as well, because they were trying to fit in and thought that this was what you did on German buses.

The next thing that happened to Saya that day was similarly troubling and ambiguous, and maybe it really was just an unfortunate coincidence that she had two of these experiences on the same day.

They were ambling around the electronics store, their trolley piled with hairdryers, electric can openers, shavers, and a rice cooker. Saya was by the CDs, looking for something for herself; the aunts wanted to buy her a present she couldn't have afforded on her own as a thank-you for giving good advice and translating for them. She was still wavering between an album by a young female pop singer who she liked, but was slightly ashamed of liking, and a new record by an indie band who she also liked, though she'd be buying it mainly because it was a better fit for the image of herself she wanted to project.

But then the store detective came over and asked Saya and the aunts to follow him. He was friendly and had a prancing gait, and Saya noticed that he treated the aunts with the respect that, in her opinion, should be shown to older people. All the same, he asked them to come with him, it really wouldn't take long, it was really just routine, and when they left the little room again, because their coats and handbags obviously weren't full of stolen goods, he said apologetically to Saya that these were random checks they sometimes had to carry out.

Saya then of course had to explain this to the aunts; their faces had taken on a quizzical expression, and they were waiting for her to tell them that this was all perfectly normal, and nothing to worry about. Saya translated the words of the kindly store detective, but not without doubting both them and herself, and then changed the subject and hoped fervently that she wouldn't have to say any more about it.

On the way home, Saya felt eyes on her again, though she and the aunts were the only people on the bus and this time there was a friendly man at the wheel. But the eyes weren't just there; they were inspecting her, making Saya sit up straight and check her reflection in the window, check whether she'd got rid of all her facial hairs that morning and given herself a straight parting. The aunts had closed their eyes by this point, weary from the day's excitement.

At first, Saya kept all this to herself, until she'd gone over it in her mind again and again, and come to the conclusion that it was something you could talk about — though she was still uncertain of how other people would take it. The summer holidays were drawing to an end, and the aunts said their goodbyes and shed some tears and went back to their real lives. That September was so hot that the first parties of the new school year were held outdoors and still smelled of summer, and at one of these parties Saya told people about what had happened with her aunts for the first time.

That evening, like I said, Saya spent a really long time with this handful of nerds, who idolised her, but were also scared of her, and she was feeling the need to talk and had drunk enough to turn what had happened with the aunts into the subject of a discussion, which she was keen to have, because she always loved a good discussion. With the self-confidence of a woman who can express herself well enough that other people find it intimidating, she told the nerds that Germany quite clearly had a big problem with racism, that it was really noticeable — you could see echoes of the original Nazis in their grandchildren and great-grandchildren — and that all you had to do to come to this realisation was get on a bus. But the nerds — though out of respect let's call them something else, let's call them 'the lads' — were suddenly much less keen for a discussion, and Saya also suddenly seemed less attractive to them.

That was a weird thing to say, one of them put in; at just thirteen he'd made a name for himself in his history class by having memorised all the dates and figures of World War II. You really couldn't accuse Germany of that now, he said, after all the things that first the Allies and then the people from the 1968 student movement had brought in. 'There's the German Restitution Laws, Control Council Law No. 10, and have you ever heard of reparations payments?' He went on listing names and numbers, while the other lads waited for the point at which they could start talking about something more interesting.

Saya felt uneasy, as if she'd introduced a topic she could actually know nothing about. It was a feeling that's familiar to her even now: when you've thought something through and you talk to people about it, but you still believe everyone else's opinion counts for more because, as in this case, you don't appear to have the necessary expertise, which is something you only have when you can cite facts and figures off the top of your head. Though there were no facts and figures for what Saya had experienced.

She said again that Germany was a racist country.

If it was racist, the history junkie retorted, that would likely mean people believing in race ideology, and he didn't think anyone in Germany who was in their right mind still did that.

With that, the discussion was over, and it was only years later, really quite a lot of years later, let's say this year, that Saya realised she'd never stood a chance in these discussions, because everyone, herself included, saw her role as merely to throw provocative statements into the ring and argue fiercely with everyone. Her role was not to be right about things. And that might have been why this was the last time for a while that Saya attempted to discuss whether people in Germany were racist. Instead, she sought out another challenge, so she could chalk up a win that evening, and in some mysterious way she ended up kissing the class hottie.

But I'd heard Saya's conversation from my spot by the fire, and I understood her. This wasn't one of those made-up stories she used to tell us when we were kids, the stories that had induced us to do the most ridiculous things. She wasn't seeing how far she could go and how much people would believe of what she told them. Saya didn't have to say anything more; I understood what I'd been ignoring up until then. The moment she said 'Germany is a racist country,' I connected what had happened to her over the summer with all the other, earlier transgressions against us. Things that had happened with other kids; constant questions about how often we washed, who ate what root vegetables, whose father looked like he was in some criminal gang, whose money must come from dodgy businesses — all of that. Saya had now drawn a line between all these pinpricks, and it created a picture like those ones you used to get in the little puzzle books from the pharmacy. I saw that picture with absolute clarity.

And maybe that was why I didn't make a good partner for a discussion on the topic: I knew Saya was right. I imagined the aunts on the bus and felt ashamed that I wouldn't have wanted to sit with them. Even minus the encounter with the bus driver, I would have found the aunts embarrassing. You absolutely could not be seen out like that, with those aunts.

Hani wouldn't have made a good partner for that discussion, either, by the way, as Saya had very quickly figured out. Hani didn't want to hear any of this, because it hurt to have to admit it. Because the world into which she had fitted very nicely since she came to Germany and learned to speak the language would suddenly be shown in a different, sad light. Because maybe she secretly knew that this light didn't shine the same on her as it did on us, when people perceived us differently at first sight. And because she just couldn't be bothered with it anymore. Hani had been classed as belonging to one group or another much too often in this life already, and she'd had enough of labels, alliances, consequences, of the supposed differences between supposedly hostile groups. She'd left all that behind. Hani's strategy was simple and, though I would never have admitted this to her outright, incredibly powerful: problems didn't exist as long as you could ignore them.

So Hani and I were no help to Saya. It was a while before Saya found the people she could have fruitful conversations with. She found them abroad, in London, Bogotá, New York, and Tel Aviv. She found people who had their own facts and figures about racism, who used the word more times in one evening than she'd heard it in her whole life, who gave her reading material and helped her to make sense of everything she'd seen in the world. Once she began to regard the things that happened to her as phenomena that were part of a larger structure, she could soon find the right term for them, and the literature to back it up. She discovered a whole lot of new tools, and realised she was anything but alone. All these phenomena, in various guises and degrees of complexity, were also to be found in other places.

Saya felt as if, in her twenties, she'd suddenly improved her eyesight, and could perceive colours she didn't use to see. Now they were everywhere and she couldn't believe they'd escaped her notice before. She sought ways to describe all these colours to the people who consistently overlooked them. She was almost obsessed by it; she wanted to explain things to everyone who made some ignorant remark or asked her a question that overstepped a boundary, and she wanted to keep explaining until they understood.

She armed herself by going online and reading comments under articles and posts. That isn't a joke, though it just made me laugh for a second myself. She spent night after night confirming what she already knew: the world was full of bastards who never tired of propagating their misanthropic world view. Saya couldn't stop reading, viewing it as research for the ongoing struggle. She would go through the odd phase of arguing back, using a fake white profile she'd set up for the purpose. But because, as expected, there was no sign that her efforts were appreciated, she'd eventually stop using her fake white profile and go back to just spending hours watching the naked hatred in silence. Afterwards, of course, she wouldn't be able to sleep, and would just wait in despair for the next morning to break. She passed the intervening period by reading more comments.

At that time, the three of saw one another at irregular intervals, but we did still see one another. And the first thing Saya and I did was admit that the two of us had now come to the same realisations, and knew the same concepts and definitions, though I hadn't needed to read a single online comment in order to know them.

Hani couldn't ignore the fact that Saya and I were so united on everything, and she was only able to make peace with our concepts when we stopped being angry and arguing over these phenomena and started making fun of them instead. 'Will you two stop whining?' she sometimes said as we laughed. 'Where would our parents and their parents be now if they'd all kept whining about injustices?'

And just once, she also said something like: 'Bad enough being a minority. Don't be a whiny minority.' As she said it, she suddenly sounded exactly like Saya usually does, and Saya had to take it, because neither she nor I could think of a good answer to that.

Hani, couldn't you have said something like that to Saya this morning? Or on Tuesday? Or the days after that? Why ages ago and then never again?

I'm carrying on in no particular order, by the way, all you German teachers and children of German teachers. From an intellectual perspective, it's perfectly reasonable for me not to start with A and stop when I get to tonight, and not to introduce the people you need to know in order to understand my report on the past few days by giving you every little detail of their biographies. I mean, it isn't like the world provided *us* with an order that would make sense. So why should I stick to one? A fixed order is just a tool to help German teachers rein in our stories. What stories would you end up with, pray tell, if you always had to stick to beginning-middle-end? Sedate, well-behaved stories from sedate, well-behaved children.

When German teachers impose an order on things, they're just trying to make sure we keep our stories to ourselves. One time, I received a handwritten note in red pen at the end of an eight-page story: 'You've neglected the structure.'

'That doesn't matter,' I should have written underneath, ideally also in red pen. 'That really doesn't matter, because the stuff I'm writing is awesome.'

So, children of the world: write those words underneath your teachers' comments.

After that note, I always put things in the right order, but I would have written better stories if I hadn't. And the German teachers would have realised that, too, if they'd ever thought about it. If they'd thought about how odd it was that under the essays in which I'd stuck to the structure, they wrote, 'What a great story!' and then only gave me a 2 for it. That must have seemed odd even to them, surely? Great stories deserve a 1, or they aren't actually great stories and thus deserve suggestions for improvement. That really made the hypocrisy obvious, because there was nothing I could have done better. And yet 2 was the best mark available to me. I was supposed to be satisfied with that and pleased that I was allowed to go to the Gymnasium and get on the path that would take me to university. Other people hadn't got in, but I had, so what was I doing demanding top marks as well?

Though on the other hand, these essays were the best preparation for real life, which is now grinning back at me from my desk in the form of rejected applications. Real life also tells me that I've done great at everything, but sorry, bad luck, that doesn't mean things are going to be great for me.

On Wednesday, after a short, confusing night, I had an appointment at the job centre. Since then, the folders of applications have been sitting here on my desk; I got a new burst of motivation and fished them out of the drawer. The burst of motivation didn't happen in the job centre, mind you, but following the meltdown I had afterwards. I hate the job centre. Maybe I hate it even more because in the beginning, I thought it was there to help me.

When I graduated, I spent a whole weekend dancing. Because I wanted to shake off the stress, because I was proud of myself, because I enjoyed university but was still glad to have finished, and because I'd graduated with a first-class degree. I'd worked hard for it, but most importantly I loved what I was learning. I loved working on my dissertation, the weeks of reading and writing in the university library, discussing things in the evening, doubting everything at night, coming up with good ideas the next morning, the topic, the connections that were always emerging between the world around me and the essay I was writing. That's why I studied sociology, and that's why I was so frustrated by the people who asked me what I was planning to do with it. Because that wasn't the point. Or so I thought. If you were going to learn something just so you could get a job, you wouldn't be so naive as to go to university; you'd do an apprenticeship. The sole reason I wanted to do a degree was the degree itself.

I spent weeks explaining this to my parents, and I suspect they still don't understand it, because the question of when I'm going to start earning money is still more important to them than the question of what my brain wants. I kept telling them that degrees like sociology most likely wouldn't exist if the jobs that required them weren't there at the end, but that was rich-people logic. My parents' eyes told me that this logic doesn't usually work for poor people. 'If you're going to study, then why not teacher training?' my mother asked, as if wanting, just for the record, to give me a vivid example of her poor-people logic.

So, while my parents thought I was wasting valuable time, I was learning and feeling relieved, because the reality of university was just as I'd imagined it. And the best thing about it? People there left me in peace. No one put their hand up in lectures and told unsolicited stories from their boring private lives, and the lecturers were so absorbed by their own work that they didn't interfere too much in mine. I spent nights reading and researching, and I passed my exams with flying colours, and I was sure I'd made all the right decisions in life.

Then came my first appointment at the job centre, which — absurdly — I was actually looking forward to. It was an introductory appointment; they'd given me two forms to fill in, and as yet I didn't know that I would have no clue what the questions on these sheets of paper signified. So much for what my degree had done for me in relation to real life: I didn't understand what I was being asked. But I would only realise that once I got home.

At the job centre, I smiled at people to show that I would be a good patient. They called me a client, which I thought was kind of nice. I'm friendly and I smile as both a patient and a client. I learned that from watching my mother, who in reality often has absolutely no reason to smile. But somehow, even early in life, that made me feel less sorry for her, because her smile showed that she wasn't going to let anyone get her down. So, I thought: if I go in there, into the job centre, young, smartly dressed, with my first-class degree and a burning desire for someone to suggest challenging jobs to me, I'll make the adviser's day.

Of course, the world had already taught me that the job centre and unemployment benefits were just scroungers' excuses for laziness, frowned on by the rest of society. I was also familiar with the job centre's usual clientele: I'd grown up with them. They lived next door and upstairs and downstairs. I'd heard and understood every word they yelled at each other; I'd played with their children, taught them swearwords — hello, by the way, yes, that was me — but I wasn't one of them. I was someone who would only be taking up this offer from the welfare state for a brief period, and would then start paying into the social-security coffers at the first opportunity, and give it all back. That, I thought, was something the professionals at the job centre would spot at once.

Then came the first appointment. Frau Duncker sat diagonally opposite me. I didn't know enough about women like Frau Duncker at this point. I didn't yet know that they had been patients once themselves, and then, because there were no jobs for them, had become part of the job-centre family, where you accrued points for getting rid of people like me again asap. And for their purposes, 'people like me' meant everyone. Everyone who came in should be out of there again straightaway. In that respect, patient is actually a better word than client. Though the job centre isn't about treating the illness, just the symptoms.

'So, you studied sociology?' Frau Duncker asked me, and I nodded proudly, the gleaming First emblazoned on my forehead, hoping Frau Duncker wouldn't feel inferior because she hadn't been to university. That's okay, Frau Duncker, I thought, we're all in the same boat.

'And now you think your degree gives you career prospects?' she asked then. I didn't entirely understand the perspective that would make her ask a question like that, but it couldn't be the perspective of a woman who felt inferior to me because she hadn't been to university — that much was clear.

She flicked through my CV and the applications I'd given her to show I was already making an effort, no need to worry about that. She skimmed the lines on the pages without taking the trouble to lower her head; she kept her head up and only lowered her eyes, so it almost looked like she was asleep. I knew what was on those pages, of course, and thought surely she must see how great everything is. A semester abroad in Spain, foreign-language skills, a bit of voluntary work, top of my year, that was all in there. But Frau Duncker's expression, which lay somewhere between incomprehension and disdain, didn't change. Eventually she put the folder to one side, which looked like new energy for new action and briefly gave me new courage.

'Frau R.,' she said, and henceforth mumbled my surname, so as not to show any weakness or make any effort, 'I don't see all that many current vacancies for jobs that might fit your profile. And that's not to do with your qualifications, it's because this city is full of people like you.'

I looked at her and thought that wasn't true. What this city was full of was people like Frau Duncker. People who never had to struggle, who never wanted to achieve anything and never did. This city was certainly not full of people who'd fought their way through my forests and still arrived here full of hope.

'Where I do see real opportunities for you,' said Frau Duncker, with a sudden sparkle in her green eyes, 'is at the call centre.'

I didn't say anything, although the words *Dude, seriously, a call centre?* were booming in my head.

Frau Duncker practically grew wings at this idea. 'It would give you a permanent job, where you'd be challenged, and a good chance of quick promotion.'

And I, who already knew places like the call centre from the inside because that was where you worked in the holidays — but not where you ended up after university — was still trying in all seriousness to keep the look of scorn off my face, trying not to give her the impression that I had no respect for people who work in a call centre or a job centre or in any other kind of centre. Because I do respect them. I just didn't know what the point was of having put myself through the last few years of hard work, against financial and familial resistance, if at the end of it all I was supposed to think of the call centre as the workplace of my dreams. But I didn't say that. I took the job ad from her, and from then on was scared of my appointments at the job centre.

At least I never saw Frau Duncker again, and got a moderately friendly adviser, who never seemed disdainful, though she was never especially helpful, either. Every few weeks I have to go and see her, and every few weeks I panic at the thought of being sent away again, relieved of any self-confidence I might have had and without having taken a single step forward.

After my first interview there, I met up with Lukas and cried. And after that, I knew I wouldn't have to deal with this job-centre business alone. So on Wednesday, before my appointment, I found myself thinking about Lukas again, and about how nice it would be if he was still coming to all these appointments with me and I didn't have to go on my own. Of course, I was thinking this precisely because I wasn't on my own this time. Saya had come with me, primarily out of curiosity, I think. She'd never seen the inside of a job centre, because when her father was unemployed and she had to go to various official appointments with him to translate, the modern job centre didn't yet exist. And she'd steered her own life into a permanent job and a promotion after her degree without having to take a detour through the benefits system. But above all, Saya wanted to come to the job centre with me because she knew I was scared of my appointment.

We'd had breakfast together, the three of us, Hani missing half of it because she had to smoke on the balcony with her coffee, while Saya and I nibbled our rolls, which aren't good in this city because there are no proper bakeries. Neither of us admitted how hungover we were, and I didn't know whether or how to ask Saya about the nocturnal act of violence she'd committed against herself and the wall. Was it my duty to talk to her about it, because a good friend has to care? Or was it better to pretend I hadn't witnessed it? So instead of asking, I kept looking at the clock, because my greatest fear was being late to the job centre; it would show me and my attitude to work in a bad light and confirm everything they suspected about me as soon as I walked into the building: doesn't want to work, doesn't stick to arrangements, isn't worth the effort, will never amount to anything, you can see that right away.

'I can come with you, if you like,' said Saya between two sips of espresso, and I said, 'I don't think you're allowed into the actual interview.'

'Of course I am,' said Saya. 'I mean, I always used to go in to translate.'

'You can come with me and translate what all the depressing stuff they say really means.' We both let out a short, mischievous laugh.

Hani came in, poured herself the rest of the espresso from the pot, and sat down with us.

'So quiet, out the back here,' she said. 'This neighbourhood always feels like it's Sunday. You always think you have to go to school tomorrow and you haven't done your homework yet.'

'Is that what you think on Sundays?' asked Saya. 'I always think one of those states in the old East is having an election again.'

We understood at once. Because actually, you're constantly waiting for the next election in one of Germany's eastern states, even if you don't have the exact date in your head. Weeks go by, and you think: surely it must be over by now? And when it actually happens, you think: at least we've almost got through it. The result, by the way, is never good. It's never surprising, either, even if the rest of Germany is always surprised. The right-wing Flügel party gains votes or holds on to a lot of votes. It's a shitty situation — not just in the east of the country, of course, though that might have been a nice illusion at one time or another. Anyway, the only thing that would surprise the three of us was if the right-wingers were to disappear into thin air again.

'Not cool, talking about the east like that, by the way,' said Hani. 'Don't you go into eastern schools sometimes? Do you talk to those kids like that? You tell them stuff about prejudices, and there you are, thinking of them as Ossies?'

For years, Saya had gone to cities in the former GDR to stop demos by right-wing groups by sitting her backside down on the bare tarmac. And afterwards she'd come weeping back to the west, moved by the left-wingers who lived in the eastern states and didn't get the hell out. They had her heartfelt appreciation. According to Saya's logic, her knowledge of the anti-fascist structures there allowed her to take a massively prejudiced attitude towards everyone else in the east. To Hani, she said drily: 'Well, you're the one who just used the words "eastern schools".' Then she giggled.

'I really don't find that funny,' said Hani. 'There's a lot of people over there campaigning for their voices to be heard, and that's exactly what you're always calling for as well. You just need to listen to them for a minute. The differences between them and you aren't actually that huge. Honestly, I watched this documentary, and they were kind of colonised by West Germany!'

Now Saya burst into loud laughter. 'Right! Colonised! And they're still being enslaved and shipped across the world and put in zoos wearing grass skirts, and their skulls end up in museums.'

'No, come on, you know what I mean. Overnight, their system became worthless, and they had to change their whole lives without being allowed any say in it. And that wasn't necessarily any different for your parents, or mine, or …' She faltered and glanced at me, because my parents didn't fit into her story, which was more about freedom and survival than work and making money.

The last time we had one of these conversations about the east, there was actually an election happening there, and we disagreed just as much then, too. We were watching one of those political talk shows that we usually avoid for good reasons. It was an evening a hundred years ago. We listened to what the so-called experts on the east of the country had to say about the election results for the right-wing camp.

When we watched TV, we usually spent the whole time laughing. But we didn't laugh once that evening, of course, because the only thing to laugh at was the dialect of the people from the east. And if we hadn't laughed at that dialect on stand-up comedy shows on the commercial stations, we weren't going to laugh now, when Nazis were getting elected over there. There was nothing funny about that.

'They're at 23 per cent,' said a man on the politics show, full of himself because he was a man and a journalist and knew exactly what to say on a panel like this to get a large share of the airtime, which everyone thinks is right and proper, in the belief that he genuinely has something to say. He continued: 'It's a catastrophe, no question about that. But we mustn't get hysterical about it. It's still only 23 per cent. And that means 77 per cent of people didn't vote for this party.' The other members of the panel nodded.

And if this was just about mathematics, there would have been nothing further to add. But it was quite clear that the journalist and the people nodding had no idea what they were talking about. They were white Germans, white East Germans for all I know. And they liked that calculation. It gave them the sense that there was still time, because not everyone had started voting for Nazis yet. As if we all now had the opportunity to observe the catastrophe calmly for a little while before having to freak out. It was like finding a disgusting, stinking animal that wasn't quite dead but had stopped being a danger to anyone. You could poke it with a stick and nothing bad would happen. In fact, you could have a really nice chat about it later.

Meanwhile, Saya, Hani, and I, who had just happened to meet up on this scary election night, one of these many scary election nights, felt like we were the animal lying on the floor, dying. Or like children listening secretly at the door while people are talking about their future. What's being discussed isn't meant for their ears, but it affects them all the same.

The presenter finally began talking to a woman from one of the conservative parties about the debate over her party's leadership that had been going on in recent weeks and months, and whether the decision they'd ultimately reached might not have been the wrong one — might even have been the reason the election had gone so badly for them. There was evidence that a lot of their former voters had gone straight over to the Nazis.

Hani lit a cigarette, though there was usually no smoking in her flat. Saya lit one of Hani's cigarettes, though she didn't actually smoke. I lit a cigarette because I didn't know what else to do. I wondered if I should say something. It would have been something like, 'As if Nazis start voting for Nazis because they're so invested in the leadership of some other party.' I wanted to say, 'Let's send out some thank-you cards to the 77 per cent who didn't vote for Nazis.' I wanted to say, 'As if it hurts less when only 23 per cent of people want to put your existence up for discussion, rather than everybody.' But I stayed silent; those were thoughts that Hani and Saya had already had themselves.

After the cigarettes, Hani got up to go to the toilet, and when she came back, she sat on the remote control, which switched the TV off. A brief, surprised silence descended on the lilac-painted, smoky room, and Saya said, 'Thank you.'

'Shall I switch it back on?' Hani asked, and Saya and I said, 'No,' in perfect unison.

The last words that the TV had broadcast were 'a swing to the right'. What a strange term. As if it was an unstoppable, mechanical movement, happening all of a sudden to a nation that was totally taken aback by it. It would have been a much stronger foundation for the panel discussion if they'd said 'a swing into the shit' rather than 'to the right'. Everyone would instantly want to stop a swing into the shit, instead of acting like, sadly, this was just part of life. And that's what I ended up saying — because finally, this was something that the other two might not already have thought — but I could see from their faces that they didn't find it as revolutionary as I did.

I remember later that evening, Saya read out posts by people who'd been shoved, hit, and chased down the street by roaring election winners. These things happened all over Germany that evening, though that didn't stop Saya from focusing on the eastern states, and Hani objecting again.

I opened the window to exchange smoke for bitter cold, and looked out. It was dark and quiet outside, the swoosh of the cars so regular that you could mistake it for silence. Elsewhere, people had gathered to rejoice in their election victory, the German word for 'victory' being a purely positive one for them, with no historical associations.

'Why are you defending them?' I heard Saya asking, and Hani said something that only reached me as an indistinct murmur, though with real urgency behind it. They continued their discussion for a long time, and I was relieved that they did. I always felt kind of like the two of them were their best selves when they had each other to discuss things with. Things that I cared as little as possible about. It was better than relinquishing ourselves to the silence and the sadness that we carried inside us, which no one wanted to let out. And it was less stressful than thinking through the nuances of the situation, which of course were also unspoken.

Because these weird easterners were people like us. I don't mean in the sense of all people are equal. I mean the non-white people in the east; they're like us. Why were we acting like it was only white scumbags who lived over there? But nuance just makes you sad; you need strength to deal with it. So I preferred listening to the two of them discussing things they had no clue about; I preferred listening to two women who had grown up in the west of the country and had never lived or spent much time in the states that made up the old GDR and yet had become experts on the east, which you were allowed to make huge generalisations about, to trivialise or demonise as you saw fit. In a strange way, that played to my sense of justice. We ignored the earlier elections that had been held in the western states, the results of which were different but no less scary, and carried on waiting for a miracle.

That Wednesday morning, there was no time for further discussion. Hani had to get to work and I had to get to the job centre. No: Saya and I had to get to the job centre. I didn't have to get my things together, take a last despairing look in the mirror, and set off for that dismal building alone. We went together. I went in silence; Saya was in an unusually good mood.

∧ ∧ ∧

As we sat down in my adviser Frau Suter's office, she wondered at the fact there were two of us. She probably thought Saya was my partner, and so didn't want to seem overly curious. Totally fine with her, lesbians, totally fine, totally normal. But maybe she was also surprised that I seemed to have a life outside her office and applying for jobs. Well, you forget these things sometimes. I'd have been equally surprised if Frau Suter had come to the office with her date. Robots don't normally go on dates.

Frau Suter and I talked about my current applications and the rejections that went with them. I'd brought the folder where I kept the rejections, my Folder of Shame. I was anxious about forgetting to bring it, because then I'd have no proof that I'd really tried. But most firms didn't even send a rejection, and that annoyed me, because I was collecting credibility points in that Folder of Shame and I couldn't do that if they didn't contribute.

'I've found a few vacancies for you,' Frau Suter said, looking at her computer. She was already familiar with the folder, which actually never interested her. I left the photocopied rejections on her desk, and she probably put them straight in the recycling after the appointment. 'There's a job in northern Bavaria that might be a good fit,' said Frau Suter.

I pricked up my ears. She'd never said that before. Something that might be a good fit for me! Something that Frau Suter thought might be a good fit: so after all this time, Frau Suter had understood who I was and what I was qualified to do. Maybe it was because I was always nice to her and always so well prepared, and maybe also because I was never furious or annoyed or made snide remarks to Frau Suter, because I knew she was just doing her job. Maybe after all this time Frau Suter was actually going to help me.

Saya was staring at Frau Suter as if she hadn't heard what she'd just said. She was searching her face for signs of human emotion, for any kind of feeling or expression she could work with. I should have pre-warned her that these things didn't exist here, but it was okay and they didn't necessarily have to.

'It's a full-time position, forty hours a week, on a permanent contract,' Frau Suter was reading from her screen, unable to see my euphoric nodding — not because of the forty hours, but because of the permanent, obviously. 'Regular CPD,' Frau Suter muttered, before finally spotting what she was looking for. 'Focusing on the empirical analysis of migration movements and ways to promote integration,' she said triumphantly, beaming at me, 'with the Migrant Services office.'

If Saya really had been looking for emotions in Frau Suter's face, they were now on full display for a second and a half. But the next moment she was already turning back to the printer, and handing me a list of addresses. 'Here's the contact details. We looked at these other vacancies last time, but it might be worth giving them another call, the deadline for applications has been extended for this one, so you can try again. I wouldn't get your hopes up. But you do have to show some interest if you want people to notice you.'

If Saya had been allowed to translate, at this point she would have looked at me and said, 'Frau Suter says: Blah blah blah.' But of course Saya didn't do that. She stared at Frau Suter's finger, which was still on the address that was such a good fit for me.

'Migration?' Saya asked, and Frau Suter ignored her and took a highlighter to the address. 'But migration isn't your area at all,' Saya said to me. She was right — and had no idea that this didn't matter. That you didn't send off applications according your area of expertise. That I can make anything my area of expertise in return for a desk, social security, and a monthly salary. 'So why is this job supposed to be such a good fit for her?' Saya asked, with a hefty dose of the emotions that the adviser herself had withheld so professionally.

Frau Suter heaved a deep sigh, sorted the papers, turned slowly and deliberately back to her screen, and checked when my next appointment was. She never normally told me that. I usually had a few weeks of peace before the dreaded letter arrived inviting me to the next humiliation session. Now she told me the time and date so that she wouldn't have to give Saya an answer.

'Thank you,' I said, getting up hastily. But Saya had no intention of getting up, and went on staring at Frau Suter.

'Is this job such a great fit because having an immigrant background is a marvellous qualification for immigration jobs?' Saya asked, and I hoped fervently that Frau Suter wouldn't answer that. Nor did she. Because by this point in her career, she'd learned to deal with escalation and provocation.

She held out her hand to me and tried to smile. 'See you next time. Good luck.'

Outside, Saya went off on one. 'See you next time,' she laughed; her cheeks were red, and she was suddenly striding along at an unusually fast pace. 'Why did she say see you next time? I thought you were supposed to be finding a job! And if she was any good at hers, there wouldn't *be* a next time!'

In the cafe, where we had planned beforehand that were going to treat ourselves to something nice, she said the same thing again; she said all the things I already knew, and she said them very loudly. The people at neighbouring tables looked away with an air of embarrassment, which is always a bad sign in people at neighbouring tables.

'So what was the point of going to see her? She could have sent you that information by email. Even the algorithm could have sent it.'

I started to cry. Because Saya was right and I didn't want her to say these things. Because actually I should have said these things myself and Saya should now be making me feel better. I was also crying because I believed there was genuinely nothing Frau Suter could do about any of this, and to cap it all off I was still ashamed of myself when sitting in front of Frau Suter. It hadn't been a good idea for the two of us to go to that appointment together.

I was also crying because Lukas had come with me to those first sessions, though he didn't come in to see Frau Suter with me; he waited outside the door. That was the best possible consolation: sitting inside, feeling shabbier and shabbier with every unsuitable suggestion, but knowing that, outside, love and justice were waiting for me.

I cried as the waitress brought the coffee, and I cried as Saya put an awkward hand on my forearm and said, 'Don't cry. That means they've already won,' which I didn't even understand. But then I realised that crying was a good thing, because Saya found it disconcerting, and a disconcerted Saya wasn't going to go on any kind of angry rampage. I kept crying, and she stopped ranting, and I imagined Lukas being there. To be honest, that was what made me start crying in earnest, because he wasn't. And because I realised the appointment had been quite a bit shorter than usual, which meant I should really be grateful to Saya. But she'd shown me up; she'd put a dent in the one thing I had going for me — my impeccable behaviour in Frau Suter's office. I blew my nose loudly, and it felt good to let it all out.

'Okay, now you're sobbing,' said Saya. Maybe that's what they teach you when you're training to work in education: state loud and clear what people are currently doing, so they feel somehow seen. 'You're sobbing and you're quite right to, it's the only rational response. There's a lot to cry about in this country right now. And the other thing I was going to tell you is that I was lying yesterday, obviously.'

'What?'

'The story about the plane, I obviously made it up to avoid upsetting Hani.'

'What did you make up?'

'The woman saying all that stuff so nonchalantly and then it turning out that she wasn't even wearing a real hijab — and everyone going ooh, she's not actually wearing a hijab. That wasn't true.'

'So what really happened?'

'Come on, you know this already,' said Saya, and of course I had known from the start that the story was bullshit. In reality, the woman had sat in the wrong seat despite knowing it was wrong, and kept her mouth shut, and everyone — the flight attendant, the other women in her row of seats, and the people in the queue — had made it clear with their looks and their snorts that the fault must lie with her, must lie in her very existence. No one had helped her with her luggage, and no one had felt ashamed. Saya's flight hadn't been a lesson in how to be a total badass; actually, what had happened was what always happened.

'So you had a really cruddy flight, and you didn't want to tell Hani? Do you think she's that weak and vulnerable?'

'I thought I'd do Hani a favour and create some peace and harmony myself, for a change. And it wasn't really that dramatic, the plane thing. It was just like it always is. I spent the rest of the flight reading. I read and read and read, I couldn't stop. But I didn't want to talk about that.'

'Why not?' I asked. 'Were you reading something obscene?'

'Yeah, the transcripts of those group chats.'

'Oh.'

'I downloaded them all.'

'Can you do that?'

'If you use the right websites, yes.'

I didn't probe any further. I'd stopped crying, and that was enough. It had become public knowledge two days ago: the far-right terrorist group that had been living in the underground for years and had killed Muslims in particular, Muslim women in particular, had a group chat going with other Nazis. Jeez, Nazis chatting. Bastards chatting to other bastards. Murderers chatting to their accessories. The murderers had been young when they went underground, so the photos of them that were doing the rounds made them look young, too, though in reality they were forty-year-old losers with no qualifications, who hadn't managed to kill themselves before getting caught. And they must really have had a lot of secret helpers, if they'd kept living and killing for all those years without a permanent job or any benefits.

But what am I doing here? Why am I telling you about the background of the murdering Nazis? You know all this already. You've heard it before; the papers were full of it a few years ago. And if you didn't hear about it, then I know more about you than you could imagine.

I know how white and how sheltered your lives are, how free of violence, how free of fear. I know you're definitely white people with no history of migration or religious affiliation worth mentioning, because otherwise there's no way you could have been oblivious to this story. It's the most horrific story since your Federal Republic of Germany was founded, and it tells us so much about this country. If you didn't hear about the group 'unmasking themselves'; if you didn't see the pictures of the people who were killed; if you didn't hear that the police and the Office for the Protection of the Constitution had opportunities to do something about the group and didn't take them, preferring to 'maintain surveillance' on the Nazis, meaning they just accepted that more totally normal people were going to get murdered — then for fuck's sake do me a favour and use the internet, do a little bit of research, and find out what bloody country you're living in. Take a quick look at the simplistic excuses that one informant who was proved to be present at a murder used to talk his way out of it, and think about whether you're convinced by 'He was on the phone at the time, so he didn't hear anything'. Take a second to look up what the victim's relatives went through when the authorities thought the relatives themselves had done it; they knew from the beginning that it must have been racists who killed their loved one, but the rest of the world thought that that motive was somehow too far-fetched.

When these losers unmasked themselves, it was a caesura, a revelation that must surely make every last one of you realise that it's not fucking *sensitivities* we're talking about when we talk about racism. Shame you didn't hear about it, but hey, there were probably other things that were more important to you at the time. People do have a life outside the news, you know. But then you probably also didn't hear that the trial started on Thursday, in the most fucked-up way it could possibly have started, and then you definitely won't have heard about all the stuff the Nazis said in their group chats. I didn't hear about that either, mind you. I'm not going to read what Nazis have written; I'm not perverse. I don't want to read it, I don't want to see it, I don't want anything to do with it.

'I just couldn't stop reading,' said Saya, 'it's so ridiculous, it's so unbelievable, the way they describe their lives, the things they say about who they're going to kill when, and that they'll kill themselves if it all gets out. I can't stop reading it.'

Saya showed me her phone, onto which she had evidently downloaded all these horrific messages. It looked like a regular group chat, like it was just a conversation between Saya and friends of hers and not a copy of what the murderers had discussed when they weren't off murdering someone. I didn't want to know. I wanted never to have heard of this group, the murders, or the transcripts. The most I could bear was imagining there were elections going on in the east again. I pulled the printout of the job ad out of my bag and looked at it.

'You're not going to apply for that, are you?' Saya asked, adding in a soft hiss: 'In northern Bavaria …'

'Well of course I'm going to apply, I don't have a choice,' I said, sticking my chin out.

'Is that why you were crying? Or was it because the woman was crap?'

'The woman wasn't crap. She's okay, compared with the others.'

'Was it something else, then?'

'Yes. Lukas,' I said, and of course Saya had been angry the whole time, but this clearly dialled her anger up a notch.

'Lukas? Why the hell are you thinking about *him* now?'

'I miss him.'

'Why? Because he was a shit in such a beautiful way?'

I nodded.

'You should be crying because you have to apply for bullshit jobs!' said Saya, and we waited a while for me to carry on crying, but nothing happened.

'And did you make up the bit about the guy on the plane as well?' I asked, thinking at least this was a topic we could still have a bit of a laugh about. Unsolicited flirting complete with English chat-up line, followed by a witty comeback: that was an obvious way to lift the mood. I had a very precise mental image of this man Saya had mentioned, although she hadn't described him in any detail. But in some mysterious way, what I saw in my mind's eye was the same image you're going to find in the papers in a few hours' time — though more of that later. I could just imagine this figure of fun. But unfortunately, Saya didn't look like the figure of fun was going to take her mind off everything else; her face hardened, as if she was wondering whether she should really voice what was going through her head, or whether there might be some danger in it. She'd been planning to keep her mouth shut, but now I had asked. She leaned forward slightly and blinked.

'Kasih,' she said, 'I didn't make that guy up. He was real. But it was nothing like I told you.'

'No flirting, then?'

Saya shook her head gravely for a long time. 'Of course there was no flirting. There was hatred. Disgust. Arrogance. He sat down beside me and looked at me as if my very existence disgusted him. He sat down and because there was no avoiding talking to me, he did it in English. It wasn't ignorance, it was calculated, naked hatred. He didn't want to share his fucking German with me.'

'How do you know all that?' I asked, and was instantly annoyed at myself for doubting her words.

Saya was still looking me straight in the eye, not shifting her gaze a millimetre in either direction, and she said: 'Man, I could just feel it. I could see it, in his whole manner. He was arrogant and certain of victory, and not because he felt the airline was taking such good care of him; in a really disgusting way, he'd internalised it. I think he was a genuine big man among the Nazis. Not just someone who hangs illegal stuff up in their man cave; someone with some kind of power, someone who's organised. When he got on the plane, he showed everyone, absolutely everyone, where he stands and where he reckons everyone else stands.'

That's what she told me. Saya, the clever one, the one who always sees through things, who knows everything, who is more quick-witted than anyone else. And even so, I thought this sounded like paranoia, and when you read this, you'll have no choice but to assume she's projecting this stuff onto some random stranger. That she's exaggerating. That's not what I'm saying, though; I don't want to sound like you, when you tell us we're overly sensitive and we shouldn't make such a drama out of the things we're confronted with day after day. Instead, I went up to the counter to pay for our drinks.

So, I thought, that must be what it's like when you read too much of what Nazis write, but don't know any personally: you suddenly start seeing them everywhere. I believe I thought something like: God, that poor guy who sat next to Saya.

And so I went over to the waitress, even though I hate being the one who goes up to pay — and not for financial reasons, but because of that uncomfortable moment there always is between you, your purse, and the person on the till. It's one of the many situations in which I miss Lukas, because that was something he always did; even when he had to take my purse, he dealt with the payment and I sat at the table and did nothing. In a way, that was one of the greatest advantages of our relationship: so often, I just sat there, and things still got done. The waitress took her time writing me out a bill, while I watched Saya from the counter as she jotted something in her notebook, and I wondered how she could bear to think like that.

I'd assumed the time when she would spend whole nights reading the comments under various online articles was over; I thought it must be something you'd lose interest in, eventually. But Saya was now carrying out full-blown studies, looking for patterns and inconsistencies in the comments, following and analysing individual profiles. She was like a kid who keeps getting beaten up in the playground, but still somehow wants to invite the bullies to their birthday. You'd like to claim kids like that don't exist, but they do, just as there are people like Saya who hate the enemy, but still can't stop focusing on him and his twisted logic.

The waitress told me what I owed for our two drinks and I gave her a hefty tip that I couldn't afford, just as I couldn't actually afford to treat Saya to coffee, but I thought I kind of owed it to we three women. My purse might have been significantly lighter afterwards, but for some reason I was relieved. Paying for Saya felt like a small good deed, and as unpleasant as the job centre had been, she'd helped me, somehow. It was better to leave there with a ranting Saya than to leave on my own.

As Saya and I walked out of the cafe, because I wanted to go home and sleep, she wrapped her giant shawl around her neck despite the heat and said, 'Oh well, thanks to your job-centre lady I at least have one more story I can tell my students. Great example of the role models you're confronted with every day, and the fact that you don't have to defer to them.' She pointed to her notebook. One more horrible encounter with the world, one more experience of discrimination for her archive, which would now be used for pedagogical purposes.

Saya was a workshop leader for an association that offered one-day workshops to schools, and she really believed in her work. Her specialist subjects were 'Me and My Prejudices' and 'Racism in Schools' — workshops that schools didn't book. Instead, they were always booking 'My Prospects: active career advice', and Saya's boss sent her out to lead these workshops without knowing that Saya placed the emphasis on 'prospects'. She didn't mean looking ahead and making strategic choices based on an analysis of your skills. Saya thought your prospects were more about your individual outlook on life, and the structures you were born into, and the privileges and disadvantages associated with them.

And for that she needed examples, millions of ugly examples from the ugly day-to-day life of a non-white woman.

Saya's notebook is lying here beside my computer, because obviously she didn't take it with her when she got put inside. I've just been flicking through it, though it made me feel like I'd gatecrashed a party, and now I've laid it aside again. For a minute, I thought her entries might be helpful for writing this report, that I could enrich what I'm writing here with a thousand comparable experiences from Saya's own life and the lives of people she knows. But actually I've never understood why people always act like a long list of examples is greater proof than a single one. If you don't believe us after one example, you usually aren't going to believe us after the fiftieth. And because I don't know you, I'm afraid I have to assume that some of you will be those people who act like they're up for being persuaded that certain experiences are part of a larger structure, but then find that our stories somehow aren't enough to persuade them after all.

So I shut Saya's notebook and put it back on her hiking rucksack. It can rest; it doesn't have to yell its anger at me. Now that the notebook isn't on my desk anymore, everything seems very quiet here.

All of a sudden there's a banknote lying beside the computer — the notebook must have been covering it up. In the dim light, it almost looks real, but this is quite clearly fake money that isn't even making an effort to look authentic. It's more like Monopoly money, and it's here because tonight at the wedding we threw it at the happy couple. But we haven't got to happy couples yet — quite the opposite, we're back to Lukas and me again.

∧ ∧ ∧

There's no denying that Lukas was a shit to me, because he fell in love with someone else and left me. A tale as old as time, but shitty all the same. Another shitty thing is that our whole relationship until that point had been extraordinarily beautiful.

The fact that Saya disliked Lukas from the start was firstly because we were always a bit sceptical about each other's partners: no one was ever good enough for us, and they would be out of the picture again soon enough. But the reason Saya found Lukas a shade more unlikeable still was that, clearly, only nice things happened in his life. And obviously that was a hard fact to swallow for a person with a notebook full of negative experiences.

When you first looked at Lukas, for a moment you were reluctant to take him seriously; he not only had a face you thought you'd seen on magazine covers, he was also perfectly proportioned, but in a way that looked natural rather than like he worked out. From the beginning, I myself found that so predictable and boring that I tried to ignore it. But then Lukas opened his mouth and you suddenly wanted to be around him all the time, no matter your age or sex or what kind of relationship you had with him. Because Lukas was kind, kinder than anyone, and he was attentive and fragrant.

It didn't matter how socially awkward you were; you might have said something unnecessary or half-baked, but Lukas would respond to every stammered shard of conversation and talk quite naturally to anyone, however worthless they thought themselves, and everyone involved would come away from it feeling blessed. People fell in love with Lukas sooner or later, whether they wanted to or not. And then he would act like he didn't notice, probably because he was too down-to-earth for that. He accepted it, as he accepted all his successes in life.

Always the class spokesman, always the best at sport, the one who got the coveted scholarship for university, although he was never financially dependent on it. Lukas didn't show off about these successes; he didn't even mention them. Unless you asked him. Then he was honest, without ever bigging himself up. He was more interested in bigging everyone else up.

Lukas would have been the perfect wife for a successful man. Instead, he and I loved each other in a more grown-up and sincere way than either of us had known before. Until, sadly, he had to have a serious talk with me and confess the truth about his new, altered emotional life, which suddenly centred on someone who wasn't me.

Lukas was so sorry he'd fallen in love with someone else that I almost started to worry about him, because he no longer had anyone to tell him it was okay. Saya, meanwhile, could finally feel that her misgivings were justified, because of course it had been hard to dislike someone who was so obviously good for me. Having Lukas by my side *was* good; he made all the negative stuff evaporate, he was enthusiastic about everything, and he infected me with that enthusiasm.

When Lukas and I fell in love, it was summer, and the blond hair on his arms stood out in dazzling contrast to his tan. We kissed for the first and the second time, and arranged to meet for art and ice cream and kissing — all the usual things.

Then I had to move out of the flat with Felix and the riotous New Year's Eve parties, because the rent had gone up. I moved to an area that was still affordable, though I would soon be priced out of rooms in this part of town, too. At that time, of course, none of this mattered to me; all I cared about was how beautiful I suddenly felt beside Lukas, and how beautiful we looked when we walked past shop windows and — as I always do — I checked my appearance in them. Suddenly I wasn't alone; when I looked at my reflection, I wasn't fixating on all the flaws. There were two of us, love's young dream.

When I moved house, I had to organise all the things you need for moving — boxes, a van, removal men — which was all a giant pain in the arse. So much responsibility, so much stress, so little clue. But suddenly there was no more stress. I found a pile of moving boxes in Lukas's cellar; he hadn't known they were there, but of course he let me have them and brought them over on his bike. One stress factor had now evaporated.

We put on some music, packed up my books, clothes, and candle holders, and it all took half as long as I'd feared. Lukas and my friends carried my stuff down to the street while I went to pick up the van. We set everything up in the new flat straightaway, him and me, then ordered pizza and drank prosecco and it was all simple, though only because Lukas had looked askance at me when I went to cook something. At times like these, you get takeaway instead of making even more work for yourself.

Nothing was difficult from then on, because I wasn't doing it alone anymore. Before Lukas, everything had been different, but already I was finding it hard to say how. I couldn't explain it to him, either; I said, 'Until now, I had to do it all on my own.'

'Didn't your parents ever help you with stuff like this, then?' Lukas asked, simple and sincere. And I couldn't even say that my parents hadn't helped, because they might have done if I'd asked them. But I never asked them, because that wasn't how our relationship worked. The way our relationship worked was that I took on as much as I could myself, not wanting to make work for them just because I'd started down this strange path, with university and student flats. Then in the end, none of us would owe the others anything, which had the positive side effect that I didn't need to have anything more to do with them since I moved out.

Lukas didn't understand that, and how could he? His parents were there for all his life events, though sometimes only in spirit. And if they weren't physically present, they would have long conversations about these events afterwards.

It was the first morning in the new flat, we were lying in bed, and I was wondering how to explain it to him. He always wanted to understand everything properly, and his questions were so innocent. We were lying on the mattress, looking up at the light bulb hanging from the ceiling, and I didn't tell him. I could have. I thought of a story, an example, but then I thought what am I going to do if I tell him this story and he doesn't say anything, because he doesn't understand it, and I have to explain? What am I going to do if he still doesn't understand? What do I do if he breaks up with me because what I'm trying to explain to him isn't understandable?

But now I think that if I'd told him my stories, maybe he wouldn't have fallen in love with someone else. Maybe he *would* have understood me. We'd have looked up at the light bulb and I would have said:

I still remember exactly what my nursery teacher looked like, and you used to say nursery school back then and not preschool. She was young and had a stylish short haircut, and was always a bit too serious, but the kids forgave her for that because she was young, and that was a rare thing among nursery teachers and so it gave her power. I still remember very clearly how deep brown her eyes were and how she looked at me, how she sat at the nursery-school table that was meant for children's legs, not looking at the sheet of paper in her hands, but turning her serious eyes on me. Our heads were at the same level, because I was about five, and she sat there and asked: 'How come you can add up? You haven't even started school yet.' The sheet was squared paper, with the squares marked in a pale colour, and it came from one of these pads my father had, with a blue protective cover and a huge number of gossamer-thin sheets inside. Paper on which he wrote letters in a language that I still can't read, to a place where, even now, no one wants to hear his thoughts. When he was out of work and I was starting to do sums, these pads of paper became ours. But I was only allowed to do the exercises from the ancient primary-school maths textbook if I did them neatly, and then he would praise my clear, round numbers and how quickly I was learning. Real praise, from a man who never usually spoke, least of all to me. And so when I was five, nothing was more thrilling than adding up on paper; nothing seemed as satisfying and revelatory to me. I filled whole pages with my sums, and the neater they looked, the prouder he was of me, and so the prouder I was of myself. But for some reason the nursery teacher didn't share our pride. When I showed her the page that I'd brought from home, her tone grew serious and a little severe, and she wanted an answer. 'How come you can add up? You haven't even started school yet,' she said, and I didn't know how to reply. I knew you had to give satisfactory answers, and I didn't know what the satisfactory answer would be in this case. I only knew that we'd made some kind of error in thinking it was great that I could do sums, and I'd made an error in thinking the nursery teacher would be pleased, too. Although I can't be sure that the other two teachers wouldn't in fact have been pleased, patted me on the head, praised my intelligence, admired the page, and shown it to the other children. Maybe it was just this one, this very young and ambitious nursery teacher who thought there must be something wrong at home if I was capable of such things. I knew that my father mustn't be blamed for the whole business. I tried to smile in a way that conveyed sheepishness and pride at once. But she didn't get an answer, and because she had other important things to do, she eventually left me alone and probably forgot all about it. But at five years old, I found myself in a situation that I was already kind of familiar with: my father and I had brought something into this room and now I had to make sure no one thought we were weird because of it. Not long before this, I'd brought into nursery school a little flask that had been given to me as a reward for my sums. A plastic flask in the shape of a robot, a present I'd been given even though it wasn't my birthday. We weren't allowed to bring our own drinks in; you could only drink the cold fruit tea they handed out in metal beakers. I knew that, but I'd brought the flask with me anyway — I just hadn't got it out. And of course, it leaked. The juice started dripping from my pink plastic rucksack as we were having breakfast. The rucksack was hanging from the back of my chair, so the nursery teacher spotted the puddle while I was sitting at the table, oblivious, with no idea I'd been found out. I was so ashamed. Partly because I wasn't honouring my father's gift when I stopped taking it to nursery school. All I told my parents was that the flask had leaked. Not that I'd been told off. The flask disappeared off somewhere, no one learned of my disgrace, and I never again did anything wrong.

I'd spent my whole life trying to avoid any more of these stupid situations. Ever since the day of the robot flask (if not before).

Until I kissed Lukas for the first time, it was clear to me that I, that we, are always on the brink of being called into question. And so, back when Saya's aunts came to visit, I knew at once that Saya was right: people suspected us — and it didn't matter what they suspected us of. It was only when Lukas came and I wasn't alone anymore, when I finally had someone normal, someone unsuspicious at my side, and the two of us became a unit, that this burden fell away.

It was after moving house, after the first night in the new flat, after sex the next morning, when I thought: so this is what it's like to lead a normal life; this is what it feels like. And obviously I didn't want to spoil this normality with pointless stories about nursery school. It was lucky I didn't tell Lukas all that stuff, or I'd have had to watch him struggling to find the right response and failing.

At that time, Saya and Hani were busy with their own lives. For the past two years, Hani had been in a marriage-like relationship with this total dickhead, and we deliberately missed each other's phone calls. Saya was living in another country and surrounding herself with people who'd been actively combating racism for a long time and had stopped getting sidetracked by endless explanations.

And I was alone with a man I was holding things back from, who gave the impression he understood all the same. He must have understood, because he never said anything hurtful, never asked me about my parents in a derogatory way, never presented his life to me as better and more normal. He'd simply understood. We were a unit, like I said.

∧ ∧ ∧

But Lukas isn't here for me anymore. As I left the cafe and started walking home, I tried not to imagine telling Lukas about the job-centre appointment. I also resisted the urge to message Saya and tell her the best train to catch for the market she was going to; she'd lived in this city for a while herself and knew her way around.

So once again nobody needed me, and in an attempt not to feel too down because of that, outside my block I smiled at the woman from across the road who was just unlocking her yoga studio. We'd never met, but I knew her from the many hours I'd spent watching her yoga studio from the kitchen of the flat. She didn't know that, of course. But because she saw a lot of people of my age and sex pass through the doors of her studio, she had to assume the smile was meant for her, and greeted me with a familiar 'Hiii.' I nodded like I was part of her life and tried to sound like her as I responded with my own 'Hiii', and kept walking. Her voice was so welcoming and reassuring that for the first time I seriously considered joining her yoga club. In the stinking stairwell, I abandoned the idea; becoming a part of her beautiful world was bound to be unaffordable.

As I made coffee in the kitchen, feeling incredibly glad that none of my flatmates was home to ask me what I was 'up to today', I could see the woman still standing outside her studio. Eyes closed, she lifted her face to the sun, and now I really wanted to be on her team. I'm not an envious person, but I do long for things. And for a brief second I felt a longing to be like the yoga teacher, though I have no yoga experience at all and don't even know what a sun salutation is. And I always think the words 'yoga' and 'studio' don't sound like they have any business being together.

There were evenings when Lukas and I would watch women doing yoga from the kitchen, the same group every time. Sitting cross-legged on their mats, then getting onto all fours; slowly lifting their arms, not at all synchronised or even graceful. But Lukas and I found it kind of relaxing, and we regarded watching them as our God-given right. The yoga studio was new here, you see, and it was profiting from the evil cloud of displacement that was spreading through the city.

When I moved in, what is now the yoga studio was still a bike workshop. That was a time when people nodded with respect when I told them I'd moved to this part of town. I was baffled by their respect, because I'd ignored the changes in the neighbourhood over the preceding few years, and was just pleased to get the room with its old rental contract. The man who used to run the bike workshop opposite always looked slightly despairing when I came in for a puncture. He would try to explain that I could repair a puncture quite easily myself, or that I could buy a cover for the bike much cheaper on eBay, and then he wouldn't have to take forty euros off me. And I always tried to explain to him that he was completely right, but I didn't want to repair the bike myself, because I'd avoid doing it and would just never ride a bike again.

Then the inevitable happened: scaffolding went up on the surrounding buildings, all except ours. The nice man and his bike workshop vanished. I still think about him sometimes, when I see the guy who sells the homeless magazine outside the supermarket, because they have slightly similar faces, like they could be cousins. Since the scaffolding came down from the building opposite, all its radiant late-nineteenth-century beauty has been revealed, which admittedly looks great, but also projects a warning into our unrenovated flat: your turn soon, it's just a matter of time.

Next to vanish was the woman who sat at the bus stop every day, smoking and waiting, hour after hour, and who I always envied for her consistent style, because she wore a pink coat and pink boots and a pink rucksack and I always grew a little wistful at so much realness. Plus the look in her eyes, day after day, said that, unlike us, she didn't need anyone or anything to help her overcome all the world's adversities. That look convinced me that if it came down to it, this woman would be stronger than all of us put together. But then she vanished.

And not long after that we stopped hearing the man who you would hear but never see as soon as you started opening the windows in spring. The thunderous cry of 'Oo-ahhh!' at irregular intervals sounded like an amazed and scornful comment on the world in which he found himself.

With every building that was renovated, the concentration of children and pregnant women on the street increased. There seemed to be clear guidelines on who could move into freshly renovated flats and who couldn't, and a prolific uterus and healthy sperm — in this exact combination — seemed to be criteria in the application process. That isn't fundamentally a bad thing, of course, and the children with their terrible haircuts and old-man names do at least bring a bit more life to the street.

All the same, the women are questionable, out there with their bellies, strolling down the pavement and being so unpleasantly loud. Why do women's voices only get particularly loud when they're pregnant? As if what they have to say is suddenly so immensely important that absolutely everyone, including people on the other side of the street, really needs to hear it. I feel sorry for them, because what's written on their foreheads is: 'Look, I've done it, I've done my job in this system!' They don't yet understand that yes, this is their job, but they won't be thanked, let alone admired, for it. That, in fact, from now, on they'll be watched, checked up on, and judged by both strangers and friends. That people will disapprove if they try to pay attention to their pram and their phone at the same time, and criticise them if they don't have their children under control, and hate them if they're over-protective. They can't even chat loudly without someone like me coming along and getting annoyed by it.

But I stand by my observation. If you couldn't see the world and could only hear a compilation of all the voices on its streets, you could divide those voices into two categories: men and pregnant women. Though somewhere in among them you might sometimes hear a Saya, shouting and swearing, because she doesn't need proof of fertility to feel important.

Okay, enough of that. Because as I left the kitchen with my coffee, got into bed, and fell asleep before I'd even taken the first sip, my mind was on the yoga teacher again.

The yoga troop that Lukas and I regularly watched wasn't just any old group, you see; it was (of course) a group of pregnant people, who were trying to stick with their cool hobby and do it gracefully despite having doubled their body weight. But we saw straight through their strategies for opting out of the strenuous stuff, and sniggered at the ones who couldn't keep their balance and decided to take another sip from their glass bottles instead. All these women drank tap water out of glass bottles brought from home that must originally have held organic passata or full-fat milk. We sniggered quietly, but for the most part we watched this natural spectacle in silence.

The yoga teacher sometimes got up and moved along the rows of purple foam mats. I imagined her as a younger version of Frau Völker, the woman from the estate who ran the kids' gymnastics club. Frau Völker was clear, fair, and took us seriously. Frau Völker Junior touched the women very lightly on the shoulder or arm and corrected their posture. Even then I thought she must have a gentle voice, because if you want to become a yoga teacher and spend three weeks in Goa while you're training, you must surely get voice coaching as well. She corrected all the women except one, who had the appearance of what yoga people probably think of as a genuine Goan woman. She had long black hair, the complexion to go with it, and wore the same Tchibo gear as the others. Her movements and poses were just as wobbly and misshapen as the others. But Frau Völker Junior still never corrected her.

Every week, Lukas would say he wasn't sure that was true. He'd say there were other women who never got corrected as well, ones who didn't look anything like Princess Jasmine. Sometimes he also said, tentatively, that the woman wasn't actually that wobbly, and maybe she just didn't need correcting. I believed he believed that. But week after week, I still told him he was wrong. And week after week he believed me, too, but said that, even so, it didn't necessarily hold true for every single class.

And maybe that explains why, in the end, we really did stand at the window every week watching the yoga troop. But before I could gather enough hard evidence, Lukas had broken up with me.

In retrospect, I should have started my investigation much earlier. I was already flirting with the idea of signing up for one of the yoga classes, purely for research purposes. Then I'd have found out what would happen when I didn't manage the poses as well as the white other people. Whether or not I'd get a free pass for being the right colour for real, authentic yoga.

Tonight's news is sitting so deep in my bones that I keep imagining I can smell fire. I write, inhale, and think about fire. I stop writing, take another breath, and although I'm thinking about fire again, I definitely can't smell it anymore. But I've written so much about the yoga studio now that I should at least have the decency to get up, go into the kitchen, and check everything is okay over there — just to be on the safe side. See you in a minute.

There are more surprising things in the world, but it surprised me all the same: there's a light burning in the yoga studio right now. Though burning is totally not the right word; I should say a soft light is falling on the Indian wall hanging and on the clean floor, the round cushions, the lonely little bowl of potpourri. The main thing is that nothing is actually on fire, but I'd still like to know who's in this yoga studio after midnight. Maybe someone's broken in, just to upset the idyll. Maybe it's the bike man, come to finally take his revenge after all these years. Or maybe it's just someone who works there and can't get any peace at home tonight. Maybe Frau Völker Junior had a row with her husband and needed to get away. I settle on this option, and at once the light feels reassuring. I'm not alone; even yoga people sometimes have problems and are sharing this sleepless night with me.

But I can see something even more reassuring in the flat above the yoga studio: the TV is on. A really old tube television — not a flat screen, more like a whole globe. Someone is lying in bed watching it, and I would love to just be that person, whoever they are.

∧ ∧ ∧

When I was little, I always used to imagine that Saya and I were characters in a lovely kids' film, and to be honest I was still imagining that once Hani had arrived and the three of us would have been a better fit for one of those atrocious teen dramas. As a kid, I thought that Saya and I, doing chalk drawings on the asphalt, jumping out of trees, burying dead moles and digging them up again weeks later, would be ideal protagonists. Everything we did would have been a perfect prelude. Because at the start, these films always potter along like this, before something unexpected happens and the adventure begins. The adventure in which we are the heroines, with our strengths and weaknesses and most importantly with the power of our friendship. That's what I used to think when other kids wound me up, or that time a couple of older boys beat us up on our way home to the estate: if our adventure starts now, they'll soon be begging for mercy. We just needed to have a little patience, and then we'd show them all. The dream never came true, of course; the adventure didn't happen, and eventually I forgot about waiting for it, because playing, running away, and being a kid was a full-time job as well.

If I wanted to imagine the three of us now, as adults, in some TV format, then for me the only plausible setting would be one of these talk shows from the 1990s. That's what our neighbour, the one above the yoga studio, is watching right now: a talk show where the guests are Saya, Hani, and me.

Remember that talk shows weren't always a vehicle for the political pundits you see now, with a line-up of nasty know-alls. In a land before time, in the neon-yellow nineties, they used to be the television format in which competent people called Arabella, Sabrina, or Vera were given the floor. In which people like you and me, people off the street, were questioned about whether they really behaved in this odd way or held that deviant opinion about the world. Let's gloss over the ones in which lie detectors were supposed to find out if someone had cheated on someone else's half-brother with his cousin, because as we all know, they signalled the demise of this wonderful format.

The early talk shows, the ones from a time when the hosts still had surnames and were sometimes even addressed as Herr or Frau So-and-so, focused on questions that were actually relevant, like: 'Wife-swapping — can it revive a marriage?' or 'Fatherhood later in life — advantage or disadvantage?'

Let's travel back to this time. At the front stands Bärbel Schäfer, short blonde hair, subtle perm, surrounded by her audience, who are sitting there in their Adidas tearaways and Fila hoodies and waiting expectantly for whatever ludicrous thing it is they're going to learn today.

The jazzy music leads into the show, a man's voice tells us what this episode is about, and the camera turns to the three protagonists of today's program, who all hold absurd opinions that really need to be discussed in public. Bärbel has to wait for the thunderous applause to subside before she can start her introduction, semi-shouting in order to be heard.

'I'm the victim, you victim! Who is being oppressed here, and to what extent? We've got a woman on the show today who says "my life is harder than other people's!" and her two best friends, who have to live with it. Let's welcome the three of them: Saya, Hani, and Kasih!'

As she says 'a woman', the camera pans to Saya, and only when she gets to 'friends' does it show Hani and then me, looking at

Hani. The audience cheers like we're rockstars, just because we're sitting at the front and have names. Saya of course gets to speak first; Bärbel asks her if she really means it when she says she's a victim and is being oppressed.

Saya says, 'I'm not a victim! But I am oppressed.'

'How does that work then, woman?' asks a nineties bloke who is suddenly sitting next to us. 'Either you're a victim or you aren't, but you can say one thing without the other.'

'Just a minute,' says Bärbel, much to our relief. 'Tarkan, you'll have your turn later. Saya gets to speak first. Saya, you're a successful, good-looking woman — why do you think you're being oppressed?'

Saya looks at Tarkan and says, 'Well, you can see it, can't you? I haven't even said anything yet and already this guy's been brought in. I can't explain anything without someone interrupting me, claiming to knowing better. Other people's opinions are always considered more relevant than mine.'

Bärbel has really got the wind in her sails now, and she starts to probe further. 'Okay, we saw that, too, and it won't happen again. So tell us a bit about yourself: you're very successful — doesn't that mean you had all the opportunities? You graduated with top marks and went on to do a postgraduate degree, plus now you have a permanent job and you're doing great work with young people.'

'Honestly, Bärbel. Yes, I'm successful. But I also put in ten times more effort than was good for me to get here, and throughout my career I've had to say things ten times while men have got instant applause and recognition for saying those same things once. I had to work my arse off so no one would accuse me of messing something up, and now that I have this success, everyone says: "See, what are you getting so worked up about?" But the point is that it's always been more difficult for me, because I had to start at minus fifty, while people like you started at plus twenty. But you either want to look down on me for my minus fifty or you don't want to hear about it, once I've reached the same level as you. You only ever want to see what currently suits you, and you don't even realise how hypocritical you're being. When I tell you where the three of us grew up, you all wrinkle your noses and say, "ghetto". But decades later, when everyone's opening their cool little bars there and moving into their cheap apartments, they all go crazy over how *gritty* it is. That's the way it is, Bärbel — I'm not being actively oppressed anywhere, but I'm still only supposed to do what's expected of me, and obviously everyone but me gets to decide what that is.'

Tarkan wants to step in and say something at this point, but Bärbel gets there first. A few members of the audience are already standing up, which means they'd like to ask a question and, in most cases, voice their own opinion beforehand. Now it's the turn of a woman whose hair has strands of bleached blonde at the front, while the rest of it gleams in a natural black. She points to Saya and says, 'You said you weren't a victim. So why are you sitting here now whining about it?'

'I'm not whining, I'm raising a valid complaint,' says Saya. 'Pretending you can't tell the difference is a very old ploy, I've heard it before and let me tell you, it doesn't wash with me!'

The woman looks taken aback and sits down again.

Next, her friend gets the microphone. She has a ponytail with a centre parting and two long strands of hair hanging down over her face, curled slightly at the ends. The nineties were definitely the decade of strands. The woman stands up and says to Saya, 'If you're not a victim, then why do you act like everyone else is victimising you?'

Saya thinks for a minute and says, 'Okay. Then I admit it. I am the victim here!' The audience goes wild booing Saya, until she interrupts them, crying out, 'What exactly is so bad about calling yourself a victim?'

The woman with the try-hard strands responds at once, the strands swinging self-importantly back and forth as she speaks: 'That's blackmail! We all disagree with you, but we're not allowed to say so because you have to style yourself as the poor victim! Boohoo!'

Saya roars: 'Okay, fine, then I'm not a victim! But *you* just said I was!'

The woman stands up again and shouts, 'And you said we're all victimisers!'

And Saya shouts back, 'I just told you what my life looks like, and I don't give a rat's arse who's the victim and who's the victimiser! That's not my problem, I have other problems to deal with!'

Bärbel moves away from the woman in the audience; she has served her purpose. Bärbel talks as she snakes her way between the rows. We see her in profile, and we can see that she's keeping one eye on the floor, so she doesn't tread on anyone's feet. She asks, 'Hani, I saw you laughing just now, why was that?'

Hani looks scared and hurriedly says, 'Oh, something funny just popped into my head — sorry, it had nothing to do with what we're talking about …'

Bärbel helps her out: 'Could it be that you don't completely agree with your friend here? Do you think she's exaggerating?'

Hani searches for words, laughs, and looks at me, but is then interrupted by Saya. 'This is all too complicated to describe here. All I know is: if you live like I do, you'll know what I mean.'

There is some applause from the audience at this, but only a smattering, because there aren't too many people here who live like Saya. I join in, because I'm one of them. 'Kasih, you're clapping,' Bärbel says, expertly guiding the discussion, 'but you're not completely happy with the way your friend deals with the world, are you? Can you explain that to us?'

'No,' I say. 'No, and I don't *want* to explain it to you. That's not my job. Saya, it's not actually your job, either.'

'Oh, but it is,' says Saya. 'It's literally my job, you know: I'm doing these workshops with young people alongside my doctorate …'

'Okay, fair enough,' I say, 'but more generally, you're sitting here trying to convince everyone of something that's totally obvious. People aren't arguing with you because you're wrong — everyone knows you're right. They're arguing because acknowledging that you're right would turn their whole world order on its head. If the person you're talking to isn't either a trusted friend or paying you for the privilege, then you shouldn't be giving them an insight into your clever thought processes. You shouldn't be having conversations that get you nowhere, with people who only listen to you so that they can argue back. So give it up: stop explaining, because no one will thank you for it. No one gets applause for telling the truth.'

No one applauds, and for the first time in the history of this program, there's a moment of absolute silence, which I feel confirms what I've just said. But I suspect that really, it's because no one has actually understood what I've just said. Pay her? What for? I see my pale face in the monitor. I'm an attractive person, but suddenly I don't look great. Ordinary and exhausted and boring. I have no business being on this program.

Saya shakes her head and says, 'That isn't the way to make the world a better place. But I don't want to act like the world is fine — that's what white dominant society wants from us. They want us to get so tired that we stop talking about it, and don't keep fighting. But we have every reason to fight! We have to fight against people treating us like second-class citizens!'

'There's a lot going on, though,' I say. 'Just look around you, at the big newspapers, academia, politics. Our voices are represented more and more, people are hearing us and they're letting us speak, there's been so much progress in the last few years.'

'It's not enough,' says Saya. 'These are little crumbs they throw us so we'll keep quiet. And what's that supposed to mean: they're letting us speak? What's that about? Don't you realise what you're saying? We can speak whenever we want, and we should — we shouldn't have to wait for someone who has the power to *let* us. If we stop talking like second-class citizens, then people will stop treating us that way. Then maybe people will stop killing us as well. Killing us! Are you hearing what I'm saying out there? They're killing us, for fuck's sake, what more do you want before you start believing us?'

A few people in the audience get up and leave. The ones who stay brandish their fists and call out, 'Cat fight! Cat fight!' which you will only understand if you've seen American talk shows. Bärbel hasn't, because of course she's from the nineties, when you couldn't just go online and find out what was going on in the USA. So she hurriedly picks on someone from the audience. A man whose name isn't Tarkan, but who says pretty similar stuff.

'Get a grip, princess,' he shouts at Saya. 'I Googled you — you've been to elite universities, and I'll bet you earn more than me. I'm a mechatronics technician and I can't afford those shoes you're wearing. Why don't you listen to your friends and moan a bit less.'

The audience claps enthusiastically. Bärbel is very interested in the precarious existence of a mechatronics technician, and so the man, Michi, is invited down to the front to sit with us and join the discussion.

'Alright, let's work together to convince your friend,' Michi says to me with a wink, and I quickly shake my head.

'No, no, I'm on Saya's side — I just get the feeling she's going to run herself into the ground. I want her to look after herself a bit more, that's all, instead of …'

'Wah wah wah,' goes Michi. 'I haven't heard anything convincing yet today, all you talk about is your *feelings*.' Michi really draws out the word 'feelings'. Then he adds, 'It gets on my tits! You girls need to chill out a bit and come back on the show when the topic is "I'm looking for a handsome man". You'll have more chance of success then.'

Everyone applauds and laughs delightedly.

'Hani, I saw you laugh again at what Michi was saying. Do you secretly agree with him a little bit?' Bärbel asks, and Saya and I look to our left, indignantly.

Hani straightens her top. 'No,' she says hastily, and then, just because she has to say something, 'I mean, everything Saya says is right.' She sounds so benign that the camera can't tear itself away from her. She puts on a little smile.

'So, you agree that women like her don't have the same opportunities as, say, men like Michi?'

Hani looks over at charming Michi, smiles, and says, 'I think Saya's right, but I also think it's a shame she gets so worked up. If no one's going to believe us, there's no point in repeating what's wrong over and over. People either believe us or they don't, but this constant analysing and explaining, and no one taking it seriously, is kind of wearing. It doesn't get us anywhere — all it does is make us sad. We should stop doing things that don't get us anywhere. I saw this book on Amazon recently —'

'You buy books on Amazon?' Saya says, looking aghast.

'Yes,' says Hani, 'and that's the best example. I buy books on Amazon because it's not like I can stand up to Amazon. We can't stop it now, it's too powerful. So I go ahead and buy from there because it's convenient, and I don't waste my time on heroics that no one is going to thank me for, and which would mean I have to pay more and wait longer and in the worst-case scenario actually have to leave the house. Saya, you're a hero as far as I'm concerned, but even you can't actually achieve anything. All you're doing is putting out the little flames, while the whole world's on fire around you — and *that's* why,' Hani proclaims, feeling right at home in front of the camera, 'that's why I buy from Amazon and I'm proud of it!'

The audience goes wild, clapping and stamping and cheering.

Saya starts shouting, because that's the whole point of talk shows: 'It's because of structures like these that …' The audience is still restless, but no longer in high spirits, and Saya starts again: 'In a patriarchal, capitalist society, we get exploited …' The audience boos, and Saya goes on, desperately: 'We're on talk shows, but not in the Bundestag, we never get elected, we're never on the important committees, we're never represented …'

I try to help by saying, 'When we were growing up, on our estate …' but Michi interrupts, 'Exactly: *your* estate! You ghettoise yourselves! You build parallel societies! You want to be with your own people, you don't want to learn the language, but, man, you're still sure you want to be Chancellor!'

The audience applauds.

Saya doesn't say anything more, and nor do I. Hani puts her hand up, because she thinks that's what you have to do on talk shows before they'll let you speak. She actually wants to say something to help Saya, but she can't think of anything, because she's never really understood the whole business about structures and patriarchy. But since the camera is now pointing at her and her justice sensor is going off, she blurts out, 'What about Tarkan, why isn't Tarkan saying anything about all this?'

'My microphone's off, man!' Tarkan shouts, but it comes out very quiet because his microphone really is off. Then he jabs Michi in the ribs and says, 'At least you're a mechatronics technician, you victim, I didn't even get an apprenticeship. I still have to live with my mother and get her to do my washing because no one will give me a job.' And then, with a glance at Saya, 'You're raising a valid complaint? I'm raising one too!' And then his microphone gets switched back on, because Bärbel finds the dispute between Michi and Tarkan interesting.

Saya, Hani, and I don't speak again, and at the end of the program, Bärbel announces, 'Well, we've had some fascinating discussions about victimhood, and we've picked up some new topics for future shows, including "You still live with your mother — are you a mummy's boy?" and "You're successful but still not satisfied — are you obsessed with money?" These are the questions that are really getting us fired up here, so give us a call if you want to be on the show.'

Hani puts her hand up again, because she doesn't think she's given Saya enough support. 'And maybe something about the patriarchy and capitalism as well?'

'No,' says Bärbel, 'that's not something our viewers can really relate to.'

Saya shakes her head.

The jazzy music plays, you see the audience clapping, and the names of the people who work on the program behind the scenes appear on one side of the screen.

The neighbour opposite switches the TV off.

We aren't in the nineties anymore.

We aren't guests on a talk show.

We're three friends who have known each other too long not to understand each other, though in fact, we don't understand each other fully.

We're serious again. This story is serious and sad.

Back to Wednesday, the day that began with the job centre and, for Saya and Hani, ended in the building that burned down tonight.

By the evening, of course, Saya and I had both calmed down. After Saya came back from the market, we spent the day side by side, had something to eat, sat in silence looking at our phones, and waited for Hani to finish work. My job-centre wounds may have been deep, but the healing process was essentially a familiar one. All I needed was distraction. Saya knew that, and once she'd spent enough time tapping away at her phone, eaten an over-sweetened yoghurt, and wrinkled her nose slightly as she looked around the shared kitchen, she turned her attention to planning the evening, and a few hours later we were sitting in an old factory yard, outside a squat and beside a fire barrel, talking, drinking, and laughing, and I had stopped being a job-centre zombie and turned back into the person I really am.

The people around us were rolling cigarettes, budging up so that everyone could sit down, having earnest conversations, and gazing into the fire. It was somewhere between a birthday party and a gig by people we vaguely knew. They kept mentioning a rave we knew nothing about, though that might change soon, if we just looked chill enough and waited patiently.

The people from the squat were of varying ages and beautiful in various ways, as well. If you looked closely, the age range went up to the mid-fifties, though to be honest it was only men who fell into that group. The others were a bit younger, and the women seemed to be doing their best not to look the way women are expected to. That might have been why we felt comfortable in these circles, although in comparison we looked pretty conventional.

I sometimes think we have a kind of special dispensation here; if you're on the left, you either have to look like an outcast, or be one — like us. And that was why, unlike the other women, Hani could turn up in a miniskirt, and Saya didn't have to offset her pretty face with an ugly haircut. But that, as you will have noticed from your inner resistance to this idea, is my interpretation of things. Maybe we were actually entirely unwelcome here and out of place and just didn't notice — or nobody cared about us one way or the other and I was the only one who placed enough importance on this stuff to think about it in these terms. But because I'm the one telling this story, I'm going to stick with my assumption: we were accepted because we seemed different, and we accepted the others because they'd chosen to be different. That was the only reason Saya and I were so relaxed as we sat on the bench, watching the people around us and not saying a word about what had driven such a wedge between us that morning.

I wondered if Saya remembered the time, years ago, when we'd been at a similar party and she'd said it was a mystery to her why the whole world assumed that being anti–right wing was a political position. Being anti–right wing was neither a decision nor an attitude; for Saya, being anti–right wing was nothing other than a survival instinct, and didn't even need a name. She found it odd that people described themselves as anti-fascists and acted like that was something worth mentioning. Being a diabetic — that would be something worth mentioning, in her view, or being a horse whisperer, but not an anti-fascist. If being against fascism was something worth mentioning, then what was the unmentioned norm supposed to be?

Luckily, Saya didn't start on this again now, and I was glad, because I didn't want to hear her puzzling over these things out loud here. We clinked our over-chilled Radlers together and sat in silence, looking around and enjoying a peaceful evening amid — and we were sure of this — kindred spirits. Life was standing a few metres away, tearing up a couple of large cardboard boxes that were needed to light more fires.

Now you're wondering who this Life person is? I thought so, because as we've already established, you never know about the victims. If you'd bothered to find out, you would recognise Life's name, if you'd stopped to look at the photo of him, his wife, and his son. But that evening, Life wasn't a victim; he was just someone we didn't know, someone who at first had no significance for us, and we were just momentarily aware of him in the same way we were aware of everyone else around us. But maybe we glanced at him for a little longer, because he was the only Black person in this white context. Maybe the three of us each made eye contact with him briefly, and maybe someone did something that might pass as a nod. Maybe one of us then looked away in embarrassment. But I don't think so, because I'd remember that.

Saya and I went on looking around, and watching Hani practise her unique art of assimilation. She had popped home after work, put on some thick black kohl, and bought some additive-free cigarettes with filters so that she wouldn't stand out with her usual long, elegant cigarettes. Now she was standing by the fire barrel in

91

her entirely black outfit (unusual for her), talking to Minh, one of many people who had once done an internship at Hani's agency. The agency campaigned for animal rights by producing funky marketing for the species-appropriate treatment of animals before they were killed for their meat and other products. It was hired by companies that slaughtered animals and earned money from their carcasses, yes, but these companies wanted to be fair to the animals beforehand, and were keen to share that fact with the public.

Hani didn't have a huge amount of experience in making the world a better place, or in coming up with advertising strategies, and was employed at the agency as what she called, in a high, sarcastic voice, 'the receptionist'. People like Minh kept finding their way into the agency because they were real activists who were looking for a place where they could earn money without betraying their ideals, and you could see these two hearts beating in the chests of Hani's colleagues, as well. They all looked like they'd once lived in treehouses, but had since got more of a grip on their lives.

Minh was quizzing Hani about whether the working conditions had changed at all. Hani was trying to duck the question — we could tell that even from a distance — because any change would have required her to take the initiative. Minh had left the agency after a six-month internship with glowing references, a slightly longer CV, and the view that commerce and ideals were mutually exclusive, and was now trying to make a career in journalism. Minh had taken a liking to Hani, perhaps because Hani did all the right things to protect the environment — going vegan, buying organic food, avoiding plastic — but seemed somehow helpless, and unlike all the others didn't radiate a rigid morality.

Minh thought this was a nice trait, but I saw through it. I saw through why Hani was asking about the vegan sausages, because veganism was the easiest way for her to eat a socially acceptable diet that was good for her. You can be vegan and still get fat, no question, but being vegan meant you could avoid things in public without having to explain yourself in certain circles, and so Hani avoided things and stuck to vegetables and a bit of tofu. When she shopped at the organic supermarket, she felt safe. She'd spent years desperately trying to buy what other people bought without showing herself up — cf. the Aldi own-brand cola she'd walked around with quite happily, not noticing that the other teenage girls were laughing at her. When she discovered the organic supermarket and realised that, although your purse would come out of there a hell of a lot lighter, you really couldn't go wrong no matter what you bought, she felt so good and so safe that she chose to cut back on other things so she wouldn't have to hide her shopping, and could in fact display it proudly.

Saya and I knew we were thinking the same thing as we watched Hani and Minh, and when our eyes met, we smiled. Two men were standing in front of us, in scruffy black work clothes, with earrings and partially shaved heads, discussing something. We couldn't hear what; we just caught the odd word here and there. It was something about public meetings and demonstrations, well what else would it be, and the organisation of an event that was happening soon, and Saya asked me if I'd been at the last protest against police brutality in my part of town, which had got really out of hand. Since Saya had moved out of this city, she had stayed very well informed about what was going here, and acted like it was only natural that you would go to every protest.

I said no, and felt guilty. When protests were happening, you had to go, of course. But no one does that consistently, I thought, because after a while it starts to feel like you're not taking any real action. In fact, after all the weekly protests against all the things that are going wrong in the world, it always feels kind of like you don't have any possibility of changing anything, because nothing ever does change.

It must have been pretty intense, said Saya; she'd seen videos of it, and it was surprising that something like that could happen here without it being on the news. It was surprising that the police could do whatever they liked again and again, without facing any consequences.

One of the two men, the older one, some kind of craftsman judging by his clothes, heard her words and turned to face us. 'Interestingly, that's also something people on the right claim,' he said to Saya.

'What?' I asked.

'That the press don't report enough on their concerns, on the size of their demonstrations, that they suffer reprisals from the police and the leftists don't.'

'It doesn't matter what people on the right claim,' said Saya. 'In our case it's true, and in the right's case it isn't.'

'That's very short-sighted, though,' said the man, let's call him Markus. 'How do you know that's not true of them? If we make sweeping generalisations about them, they'll keep doing the same to us.'

'What's your deal?' Saya asked, a little louder now, making the people sitting beside us on the benches turn and glance at us. 'I don't care about that — how the right thinks of us isn't my responsibility.'

'And that's the problem,' said Markus, sitting down uninvited next to Saya.

The guy he'd been talking to stayed where he was and gave me an apologetic look. Like he knew Markus, knew he could be a bit difficult, and was trying to tell me that even so, it was bearable, and you just had to bear it. I smiled back and wondered if he'd be a suitable candidate for helping me take my mind off Lukas, but then I remembered that Saya was staying over and so tonight wouldn't be the right time to pick someone up for distraction purposes.

Markus talked for a while, and Saya pointedly didn't listen to him, reminding me of the defiant ten-year-old Saya she'd once been. When Markus paused for a moment in his monologue about the necessity of talking to right-wingers, to ask if we had any filters,

Saya seized her chance and said, 'I don't really care how you deal or don't deal with right-wingers. The fact is, the police, the intelligence service, the system, they have us on their conscience. They have deaths on their conscience. It's their fault we're dying, that we keep on dying — always isolated incidents, never any consequences. I've never heard of right-wingers dying in prison cells, and until I do, I don't care whether they feel disadvantaged or not.'

Markus laughed in the way you laugh at wild, young, rebellious souls when you used to think like them yourself, and I suspected he was doing it to gain some time, because he didn't have a ready answer to that. I thought that if he was smart, he would gain some time and then run away pretty quickly, because Saya was in an unpredictable mood. It occurred to me that there's a gesture among leftists to express agreement without taking up too much space with words — you raise both hands to head height and waggle your fingers, which is sign-language for applause — and so I raised my hands to my head, made the sign while looking at Saya, and earned myself a look of utter horror, which made me stop at once.

Markus said, 'That makes it sound like masses of us are being offed.'

Markus was white. Did I mention that? I could have mentioned it right at the start, but I'm against mentioning these things if there isn't a specific reason for it. Now, however, at this point in the conversation, there was a specific reason.

'You can only say that because you're white,' said Saya, and this time she raised her voice deliberately, because everyone in her immediate vicinity was white, except me, and it seemed like she wanted to say it to everyone. 'Masses of you *aren't* being offed. But we are.'

Markus smiled as if he'd been expecting her to say something like this the whole time. He seemed almost relieved to have teased the word 'white' out of us, though he also seemed unsettled by it. Markus had been at university for quite a while; he had been in classes with young, eloquent people, had read Edward Said, and didn't have all that much to contribute to seminar discussions. But he'd realised that the easiest way to get people to listen and pay attention was to contradict them. Because if everyone was wild and rebellious, you'd be wilder and more rebellious still if you always questioned what the others said.

In reality, despite meticulous reading of all the set texts, Markus hadn't entirely understood what was going on when everyone started talking about white perspectives and white privilege. Maybe that was why he thought it was a great idea to sit with Saya and me; maybe he was vaguely hoping we could explain something that had so far been a mystery to him. But because people like Markus always want to explain things themselves and have never learned to ask questions, and it certainly wouldn't cross their minds to look to us as experts, that was the way he tried to go about it. The way where you join a conversation uninvited, talk a lot, use the words people think they have to use to be taken seriously, and wait to see what happens next.

I don't know why, when people like Markus do this, they always look like they're hoping for some kind of absolution from people like Saya and me. And if they don't get absolution, then they at least want to be the ones who make us think. And so now he said to Saya, 'The whiteness thing — honestly, that's too important to constantly use it as an argument.'

Foolishness of this magnitude left Saya completely lost for words. 'What?' she said. She was perplexed and therefore completely non-judgemental.

'Yeah, well, it's true,' Markus began, taking his time, eyes on the cigarette he was now rolling without a filter, and with such obvious pleasure that I wanted to explode. 'I mean sure, you do have to mention whiteness, everyone knows that now. But the thing is: if we keep on mentioning it, then sometimes we're just taking the lazy option, because we don't have an argument. You didn't have an argument just then, so now you're bringing in my whiteness. If we do that all the time, we rob it of its power.'

Saya laughed, because she now understood that Markus didn't understand anything. 'A person definitely *can* always mention whiteness, because people are always white. You're always white. Remember that. You having a problem with it just tells me that you wish you were a little bit less white now and then. You need to come to terms with the fact you aren't.'

'It's interesting how much you know about me without actually knowing me,' said Markus, and it was interesting that I'd just been thinking the exact same thing. It really is astounding how much you can know about the Markuses of this world without knowing them individually.

'Well, you showed us who you are, without us even asking,' said Saya.

Markus shook his head sadly. 'If you knew all the things I've seen and suffered in the fight against the fascists, honestly. The way we used to throw ourselves into street battles, how many times they beat me to a pulp. And you're acting like I'm the enemy. But you don't even know me.'

As he spoke, he looked so dejectedly at his cigarette that, for a second, Saya felt guilty.

The guy who'd been talking to Markus asked if he could get anyone another drink, and I said, 'Are there any spirits?' and he gave me a brief, knowing nod, and I decided to ask him for his number at some point later. I've never asked any guy for his number, but I liked the idea of it, and luckily for everyone involved, Markus's phone rang just then. Before he got up, he made a gesture that was meant to convey something like: excuse me, I just have to take this, but I'll be back in a minute, and I definitely have more to say.

It was Markus's mother on the phone. She didn't call her son very often these days, since she'd discovered the internet and found a lot of people there who shared her views. It was easier to discuss things with them than with her son; he had a very blinkered world view and refused to see that people from different cultures had different religions and customs and that there were now a lot of customs that, though it was a terrible shame, sadly weren't compatible with our values in this country. But Markus didn't stop trying to talk to his mother, even if it was getting increasingly difficult. He used to be able to provoke her by saying: 'You sound like a Flügel voter!' — but now he had to admit to himself that his mother didn't just sound like one; following the last national elections, she actually was one. A Flügel voter who drank Ayurveda teas and hennaed her hair. He didn't give up on the discussion, though — he now saw it as his mission to convert her. And that was why he answered his phone just then and disappeared behind a construction trailer, and I said, 'Phew.'

'Woah, what a total penis,' said Saya incredulously, and I said, 'You handled him very well.' Saya said, 'Really? You're telling me this now? Why now, when he's gone?' Maybe I should have said that I hadn't found the right moment. That the conversation had been over too quickly. That I hadn't realised she needed my affirmation, and that she'd seemed perfectly up for the argument. 'I did ask someone to bring you a schnapps, though,' I said instead, and Saya said, 'Where's the bloody schnapps then?' and looked around for Markus's friend.

At one time Saya had always carried a hip flask for style reasons, but those days were long gone, and at some point she'd lost it and decided it had found its way to someone who needed it more than she did. For a minute I thought she could really do with the hip flask again now. I could see her hands were trembling as her eyes skimmed nervously over people's heads, the benches, the construction trailer, the beer crates. I could see she was upset, and I remembered her throwing herself against the wall in the night. She only started to look calmer when the guy came back with some little plastic cups, a bottle of ouzo, and a woman who was gently running a hand over his back. He passed the ouzo around, giving me another apologetic look, and I tried to put on an expression that said: it's okay, no worries, thanks for the ouzo.

'I'm Jella,' said the woman, holding out a hand to me and Saya, and we took the hand and the shots and raised our glasses to the strangers, before Jella said, 'You had a run-in with Markus, right? Sorry about that,' which I found odd, because Markus was an adult and responsible for his own sub-par social behaviour. 'He's my flatmate. He's not always easy, but he's basically a nice guy.'

'He's just a bit slow on the uptake and needs to get to grips with the real world,' said Jella's boyfriend.

Jella laughed. 'Yeah, he gets the gender thing now, and he's working on his whiteness.'

Jella and her boyfriend were both white, and the fact that I'm mentioning it now is because I got the impression they were mentioning it themselves. It made me feel a bit awkward, and I could tell Saya was feeling the same as she poured everyone another shot.

'Yup. It's a process that takes some people longer than others,' Jella's boyfriend said seriously, and I nodded.

Because Saya and I were the only ones drinking the second shot, and also the only ones not saying anything, I had the weird sensation that people thought they needed to apologise to the outcasts. It was all very uncomfortable. Do I have to go on? Four people are drinking ouzo together, not really talking properly, and it's all just very uncomfortable. We listened to Hani and Minh laughing, and that was kind of reassuring; it was nice to see the two of them together, just a few metres away and yet somewhere completely different in terms of what they were discussing. Were Jella and her boyfriend apologising for being white? Did people go that far now in leftist circles? Or were they part of a diversity-and-inclusion team tasked with making sure everyone was having a good time at this party? I put an arm around Saya's shoulders, because she'd found herself in uncomfortable situations too many times already today, and I didn't want these two to annoy her further.

'Whose birthday is it, anyway?' I asked, to change the subject and dispel the tension a bit. We'd been invited by Minh and were also here because a mate of mine was in the band that was supposed to be playing. But actually we didn't really know anyone and I'd only realised it was a birthday party when I'd seen the cake and the balloons that were all, quite ironically, printed with various advertising slogans from large companies and had clearly come from factory outlets.

Jella ummed and ahhed a bit, and her boyfriend laughed awkwardly as she said, 'It's Markus's fiftieth,' which of course instantly exposed and thwarted my attempt to change the subject.

'Well then,' said Saya, pouring herself and me another shot, 'here's to Markus!'

'May he grow and mature,' I said, and I could see that Jella and her boyfriend weren't overly impressed with that, but would choose not to say anything, because they kind of wanted to placate us. It worked, thanks be to ouzo, and I can't tell you how relieved I was when Saya and Jella finally got into a conversation, sort of by chance, about Jella's work as a lawyer for leftists and about people who defended fascists. Then they got on to the trial of the far-right murder group, and in a flash Saya's sceptical attitude towards Jella was transformed into absolute fascination. I inwardly made the sign of the cross three times, took a deep breath, erased Jella's boyfriend from my field of vision in an alcohol-assisted move, and looked around.

Hani and Minh had now sat down, and I heard Minh telling Hani she was the only competent person in the company, and I saw Hani categorising that as flirting and being flattered, and without knowing Minh I thought that it wasn't strategic flattery but the simple truth. And I didn't have to know Minh to know this was true; I just had to know Hani, because Hani did what she was paid to do properly, always. She'd learned that from watching her parents: even if people are treating you like dirt and you're the lowliest agency worker, do your work to the very best of your ability. Don't complain, to anyone. And every day you are able to work, be thankful for this fact. Fall into a deep sleep while it's still light outside, and tell yourself it's better than being so worried you can't sleep. It's only when you're ill enough to be in hospital that you're ill enough to be off work. Spend your money as soon as you have it, because you've earned it and that's what it's for.

I turned my attention elsewhere; some distance away, people had started dancing, someone was DJing, and I still didn't know when my mate and his band were going to turn up. I looked at other people's unshaved legs and laughed at them inwardly for thinking it was brave to leave the house hairy, because in comparison to me they didn't have legs you absolutely had to shave, which made it quite easy to be brave. I was wearing jeans because I didn't have any desire to shave my legs, and of course no one thought that was brave. I watched the people who were coolly rolling joints and the people who were watching them and waiting.

There was a good smell in the air, of beer and sweat and weed, and it was only then that I saw he was standing by the fire. Saw that that body, relaxed and at ease with itself, those familiar bent arms, belonged to him. It was kind of unlikely to bump into someone by chance in this gigantic city. Then again, it wasn't all that unlikely when you'd spent years hanging out with the same people, who you'd go somewhere to see.

Lukas was standing by the fire, chatting to some people and looking stunning. My heart raced like it did the first time we met; strange that you have to split up before the feelings you last had years ago reappear. It was also strange that I hadn't spotted him before, and strange that everyone else was able to do anything but look at him. I watched him making small talk with the people around him, and then he glanced up and saw me and hesitated and came over.

'How're you doing?'

'Good. You?'

'Yeah, same, thanks.' A pause. 'Are you here for … ?'

'Yeah, I've been meaning to go and see the band for ages.'

'Me too.' Nervous laughter. 'Have you been here before?'

'No.'

'Neither have I.'

'It's nice.'

'Mm. Yeah, totally.'

'Been inside yet?'

'No.'

'Me neither. But I hear it's good.' An expectant pause. I looked at him, and he looked around. 'No way, is that Saya over there?'

'Certainly is.' Nervous laughter. 'She's visiting for a few days. For the wedding.'

'Oh, of course, the wedding.'

'Yes.' We fell silent then, because we were supposed to be going to this wedding together, as a couple, but then one of us had ruined everything.

'How is Saya?' he asked.

I think she's having a pretty rough time, I could have said. I don't think she's managing to hold it together, I don't think she can wall herself off from all the shit out there and today everyone she's met is weird and she wants to re-educate them all but she can't, and now I don't know if I should be hoping or worrying that she'll get drunk tonight. I want to protect her, but I don't know how and I don't know what from. I could have said that to Lukas, but he wasn't my boyfriend anymore. He wasn't my ally. He was someone else's boyfriend now, and he was white. Why should I tell him about how Saya was hurting and how worried I was for her? 'Yeah, she's fine,' I said.

We looked one another straight in the eye, and I felt hot, and I think he did, too. We had been two people who slept together, and now we were two people who never would again. What a strange realisation. 'Kasih, I wanted, I mean, it's great that we've bumped into each other here, I've been meaning to get in touch, there's something I wanted to sit down and talk to you about.'

'Ah,' I said.

'Yeah, so —' and all of a sudden he sounded very businesslike, and got his phone out, 'so, work's really busy right now, but I can always do Thursdays, even this week, actually, if tomorrow isn't too —'

'I'm always free,' I said, suddenly thinking it was only fair for him to feel slightly uncomfortable at least once in this conversation, and so I said, 'I'm always free: I'm unemployed, you know.'

'Precisely,' he said in a serious tone, to my surprise. 'That's actually what this is about — so would tomorrow be okay for you, then?'

'Sure,' I said, with no idea what this might turn into.

'Well, it was great to see you. I'm going to head off now,' he said.

We hugged, and he left. Because he's a fair person. Because he knew he'd spoil my evening if he stayed. But maybe also because he wanted to get back to his new girlfriend asap, before he suddenly started longing for me. Was his new girlfriend white? I don't know; and in this case, that really doesn't have any bearing on anything. I think.

Hours, chats, and drinks later, I was standing on dusty cobbles dancing to music that I didn't find even remotely dance-worthy, but you take what you can get. Saya, meanwhile, was dancing beside me as if there had never been any music more worth dancing to, which was an indication of how many shots she'd consumed. I found it reassuring. Hani was dancing beside me and looking somehow troubled; she and Minh had finished talking and now Hani had gained a huge sense of self-worth as far as work went, but still hadn't figured out whether there was something between them now.

With every new song, I tried to imagine I'd just put it on myself, so I could really let loose, and I pretended I had never heard anything better in my life, and this illusion helped me to dance pretty well for a few seconds. Hani smoked and danced with one hand in her skirt pocket, which I didn't find exactly inspiring. Saya danced wildly, her hands in the air, and I worried she might injure herself or more likely someone else.

'Do you remember those parties people used to have at the barbecue cabins?' I shouted to the pair of them, and Hani was relieved, Saya slightly annoyed, to have to stop dancing for a minute to listen to me. 'We should have danced a lot more then, the three of us together — things would have been better if we had.'

Hani and Saya nodded, perplexed. They both shifted from one foot to another and then turned away again, back to their own spheres, to dance in the ways they both needed to right then.

There are moments on evenings like these when you think: just stick around a bit longer, it's sure to get more fun in a minute. I had a moment like that just then, and was wondering what had become of the music people listened to before electro existed, and how much longer Saya's condition would keep her going like that, because it's hard work dancing with that degree of abandon if you haven't taken drugs, and Saya had stopped taking drugs years ago; she'd never liked anything that truly called her reality into question. These days, Saya's heart belonged to alcohol.

Eventually, I sat back down on a bench and watched the dancers. Just being an observer has its own appeal, even if, as soon as I'm on the dance floor myself, I suspect all observers of being some kind of pervert. I watched Saya and Hani, dancing side by side for long enough that they evened each other out a bit. Hani started waving her hands in the air as well, while Saya calmed down a little and put one hand in her trouser pocket, and they laughed together over something I couldn't make out, and I heard Hani say something like, 'It's so great you're here,' and Saya say something like, 'It's great to see things are going well for you,' and Hani responding, 'Yeah, things *are* going well, they're going really well,' and then Saya nodded very knowingly and seriously as she kept dancing.

In Saya's world, it might have been incomprehensible that someone could be fine when they knew about Nazi group chats but didn't know the details of them — but at the same time, the most important thing in her world was that everything was okay for Hani and me. She would take care of the Nazi chat thing for us. Maybe she'd find that easier if she did start taking drugs again, I thought, although that isn't a piece of advice you should give your friends. On the other hand, as far as the dancing went, I was seriously impressed with Saya's stamina.

She held out for a while longer, then came over to me, eyes shining and a broad grin on her face, and hugged me and kissed me on the cheek, which she only does when she's drunk. 'Shall we go on somewhere?' she asked Hani and me and the two guys who were standing next to us. Maybe you always gravitate towards the people who are a similar level of drunk, maybe that's why the two guys had joined us; we were pretty drunk, but all still capable of talking and walking and drinking some more. The two guys named a couple of clubs, and Hani and Saya said they didn't fancy clubbing, and they really weren't dressed for it, either, and I said I wanted to go home.

'You can't go home,' said Saya. 'I called Shaghayegh, she's coming to join us.'

'Why?'

'Because I want to know why she's getting married.'

'She's coming out specially at this time of night to explain that to you?'

'Of course not, I'm only going to ask her once she gets here. And she was out already. Hen party with her thin friends, I suspect.' Saya laughed loudly, as if that was the best joke ever.

We'd known Shaghayegh for a hundred years, but didn't really keep in touch anymore, and we weren't at all the kind of people she usually hung out with these days. If I was her, I wouldn't have invited the three of us to my wedding. Markus, today's birthday boy, would probably have agreed that we weren't especially good guests — if he hadn't been asleep on a bench just then. He wasn't snoring, which I found somehow odd.

'Should we draw a penis on his face?' Saya asked, and I said, 'Of course not.' Saya let out a dirty laugh. 'True, why would we, he'd probably only start questioning himself.'

Hani didn't understand any of this; she looked at Markus and asked, 'You're wanting to piss that guy off? But it's his birthday today, isn't it?'

Saya said she didn't think there was anyone alive who had as much respect for birthdays as Hani did. Hani didn't understand, but she took the compliment with thanks, as she takes all compliments in this world. 'I'll tell you all about him when we go for another drink,' said Saya.

'I do have to work tomorrow, you know,' Hani objected.

'But Shaghayegh's coming,' said Saya.

'No club then?' the first guy asked.

'I need to go to bed,' I said, and set off towards the U-Bahn. The fact that the other four blithely followed me told me that I might be a bit more sober than they were.

'I know a club anyone can get into,' said the first guy, at which Saya and I roared with laughter in perfect unison.

'Sure you do, but I don't want to go there,' said Saya.

We kept walking, taking no more notice of the guys. It wasn't far to the station, but in our condition it obviously took a while, and as we walked past a little local bar, the other guy said, 'Hey, this is a proper, earthy, old-fashioned pub, the genuine article!'

I said my goodbyes and watched the others go unquestioningly into the pub. The guy who was very keen to go clubbing stayed with me, not saying anything. For a second, I worried that he might be sad because we'd laughed at him for his suggestion, but then he said, 'I'm Life, by the way.'

'Hello, Life.'

'Hello.'

'And you don't want to go to the pub?' I asked, and Life thought for a moment and then said, 'No. I think I'll go home.' He got out a bunch of keys and opened the front door of the block we were standing in front of. Maybe we hadn't found each other because we were a similar level of drunk after all, but because sometimes at white parties you do end up joining forces. Life nodded to me, looking entirely sober again, and then the door closed behind him.

All at once I felt quite lonely, and headed towards the station. I didn't look back at the building; I didn't turn around. But just so that no fake melodrama creeps in here: it was the rear building of that block that would burn down two days later. We haven't got that far yet, though. And anyone who insists on doing things in the right order can probably cope with waiting. You know the drill: beginning, middle, end.

∧ ∧ ∧

Life went home because he always left when people like Eric (that was the other guy) started going on about earthy German pubs. For one thing, people like Eric were the reason there were scarcely any of these pubs left, and for another, people like Eric never noticed that people like Life didn't have such a good time there as they did. But his desire to avoid this particular pub was also rooted in what had happened on his first and last visit to it, when one of his former schoolfriends had celebrated his birthday there. Life and his girlfriend, Anna, had just opened their cafe on the same street and were gradually getting to know the people who ran other businesses in the neighbourhood. The warmth and the support they found among them was touching; the landlady of the little pub on the corner was the only person they hadn't chatted to yet, and after that evening they knew why.

When Life walked into the pub for the first time, his schoolmates were already tipsy, and there were party hats and plastic horns — people have more childish birthday parties now than they used to when they were actual children. Maybe partly because twenty years ago, party hats and horns weren't produced in China at giveaway prices. The only reason they weren't causing a nuisance was that there was hardly anyone but them in this pub, for which the group were grateful without thinking that it might be down to their presence there. The landlady had a smoky voice and a constant, wheezing cough; a haze hung over the tables and the chairs with their quilted seat covers. Christmassy fairy lights were strung across the walls and the beer was €1.30 for a half litre. At least, that's what people said when they talked about it afterwards. They said they'd drunk in there the whole night, beer after beer, shot after shot, and no one had dropped more than twenty euros.

Life told the story differently. And he only told it to Anna, to whom he didn't have to say too much before she understood. The pair of them had had their reasons, even if they had been unconscious reasons, for never setting foot in the pub before, despite it being on the ground floor of the building they lived in.

So when Life arrived, he realised he would need to drink as much as possible as quickly as possible to catch up with the others, for which reason after saying his hellos and happy-birthdays he escaped being handed a party hat and went straight to the bar. The two bored-looking ladies behind the bar looked at him, but didn't break off their conversation, and it seemed to him that they were making an effort to let him stand there for as long as they could before asking him what it would be. Years of experience had taught Life that the best weapons against this behaviour were his exuberant friendliness and a broad smile.

'I'll have a large beer, please,' he said, seeing himself as the perfect son-in-law.

The women seemed to see things differently, because their faces didn't change. The younger of the two slowly took a beer glass down from the hanging racks and held it under the pump. 'That's two euros,' the older woman, the owner of the place said, putting out her cigarette. The younger one just looked at him as she handed him the beer. She gave him the glass as if she'd prefer he kept his hands off it, a rather peculiar attitude for someone who works in a pub. Life took the beer and thanked her and went back to the others.

Two hours later, when he decided to make a move, the landlady came to the table to settle up before she went off shift. They welcomed her with hoots, praised the choice of radio station and the quality of the schnapps, and marvelled at the small bill. The landlady took their tips, full of jokes and pleasantries, and Life added up just for form's sake, to make completely sure of what he'd already thought at the bar.

'Can I ask you something?' he called out to the landlady, who was in such a fine mood that she gave him a smile and leant over quite cheerfully. 'Why did my beer cost more than the others'?'

The landlady shrank back and the smile left her face. 'What do you mean, more?' she asked, and the friends sitting around him all suddenly seemed busy, with their phones, with their change, with the conversations they'd interrupted.

'What does a beer cost here?' Life asked.

'One thirty,' the landlady replied, already turning to the person who was next in line to pay, as if that was an end to it. 'So why was mine two euros?' Life asked, and she looked at him again with feigned surprise and said, 'Oh no, yours was one thirty as well.' She turned to the next person.

Life smiled and shook his head and avoided looking at anyone. When he'd said goodbye and left the pub, he looked at it again from outside, though of course he had to see it every day. He put the pub on the list of places he would give a wide berth in future. It would pain him when the others talked about their legendary evening there, and made enthusiastic plans to go back. But Life wouldn't reproach them; they hadn't understood what had happened. Just as they didn't understand why he went out of his way to avoid police officers and always factored in additional time for security checks. They didn't even understand why he got annoyed when strangers asked him about drugs. People didn't mean anything by it, they said.

And so in conversations about this pub, Life chose to say things like, 'You would never have shown any interest in dingy old pubs in your own boring towns, but here you call them *earthy* and *the genuine article* and you go mad for them, you bunch of Johnny-come-latelies.' Life was usually the only one who hadn't moved to the city from somewhere else, and so he used this status to browbeat the others, and avoided another terrible evening.

With this information, I'll end my little section on Life. No, let me just add that I thought about going after him and asking him firstly why he didn't go to that pub, and secondly if he would give me his number. But then I realised that he didn't have to explain anything to me; I knew about the problems with these pubs, although I didn't get routinely stopped and searched by the police or have strangers ask me for drugs, and that he had a gorgeous wife waiting at home for him with their newborn. A wife who had really wanted to ask him to stay home with them and not go out to this party, but who knew it was important to let him go, so that one day when she'd stopped breastfeeding, she could do it all again as well. She hated the fact that he was currently running the cafe on his own, too, and was counting down the days until her maternity leave was over. I saw all this from the back of Life's head as he turned away. I felt lonely, went home, and missed out on an evening with Shaghayegh, Saya, and Hani in a genuine earthy local pub.

˄ˆˆ˄

Shaghayegh never stopped to think about things like the permanent no-go areas of a city. She thought it was a great stroke of luck to be pretty. She looked in the mirror and was pleased with what she saw. That was something she did every day, but today she was particularly pleased, because she was slightly on edge, and that evening she would have found it very stressful to feel in any way inferior to Saya and Hani. She thought about me for a second, thought it was shame I wasn't there. Because in her eyes, I always grounded the group, by keeping my opinion to myself if necessary, even if it was written all over my face.

How do I know this? How do I know everything? The backstory about Markus's esoteric mother? The stuff about Life?

I just know, okay.

You always know so much, and you always know better. You know about our habits, you know we put on airs, that we're finicky and have no sense of humour.

So sometimes, I do actually know better than you. And I just know all this. All of it. I know people like Markus and Life, and I know what Shaghayegh thinks of me. I know my reality. That at least is something you can't take from me.

Saya and Hani were sitting in the same corner where Life had joined a childish birthday party and felt uncomfortable a long time ago, though of course none of those present knew that or had any interest in it. And nor were they bothered that Eric, the unknown party guest who was the reason they'd ended up in the pub in the first place, had already left. It was a familiar scenario for Saya: men found her interesting and then, as soon as they'd realised who they were dealing with, they decided to go home. In most cases, Saya was glad of this.

The landlady greeted Shaghayegh with a nod, and the two men at the bar looked at her longer than necessary, but also nodded before turning away again. Shaghayegh interpreted this as a sign of welcome. She went over to the corner, her two friends got up, and they hugged for a long time.

'How long has it been!' cried Hani, patting Shaghayegh's cheeks, first one, then the other, as if she was a hundred years old.

'Much too long,' Shaghayegh said dutifully, and sat down on the wobbly chair. Saya gave her a searching, slightly pensive look. 'Two years, I reckon — you were doing that workshop,' Shaghayegh said, addressing her directly. The other two nodded, though it wasn't entirely clear if they remembered, or if that was actually true. Shaghayegh wasn't a hundred per cent sure, either. 'What were you talking about?' she asked then, because she had the impression that she'd interrupted something, but didn't know exactly why.

'We weren't talking,' said Saya. 'We were arguing.'

'Oh.'

'Doesn't matter. First things first: you need a shot.' Saya turned towards the bar, raised a hand, and snapped her fingers surprisingly loudly to the landlady. 'Three schnapps, and a beer for my friend here,' called Saya, and Shaghayegh was impressed.

The landlady brought three schnapps and a beer over at once. 'Don't swing on the chairs,' she said to Hani, 'they're getting on a bit for that,' and bustled off again.

Hani stopped tipping her chair, raised her shot glass, and said, 'We were arguing about weddings and relationships and stuff. Your good health.'

Shaghayegh laughed and downed the shot, so no one would think she was a lightweight. Saya and Hani talked about things that were only very tangentially related to marriage. Saya's voice grew deeper by the minute, although Hani was the one smoking one cigarette after another. The longer Saya argued, the more she metamorphosed into something like a man, at least with regard to her strange gestures, the way she was sitting, and her voice. Her stance on the issue swung, as it had the previous day on the roof, somewhere between 'getting married is just a means of oppressing women' and the newly added component 'getting married was invented by the National Socialists', and Shaghayegh decided just to choose one thing to agree with and ignore the surrounding guff. She was pretty sure that not everything was a National Socialist invention, but talking to Saya right now felt like a recent call with her mother. Shaghayegh hadn't noticed that she'd muted herself, and kept trying and failing to interrupt, while her mother stoically went on talking. This had made Shaghayegh's mother seem a bit mad. Saya, meanwhile, could hear the objections the other two were making, but she went on talking about Nazis regardless.

Hani countered with the old — and to Shaghayegh's ears, fairly weak — argument that a lot of couples might have split up if they hadn't been married, and were now happy together in their old age. Humans were also unlike most other animals, by the way, in having monogamous relationships. Hani's job, Shaghayegh concluded, was clearly something to do with animals, because animals kept coming up, although so far it wasn't clear why. Actually, she should really have known where Hani worked, and so she was too embarrassed to ask. Hani kept saying that humans exploited animals, but that her employer's aim was to exploit humans for animal welfare, which sounded like a statement that wouldn't make any sense once you started to interrogate it, or have anything to do with the topic of marriage.

Shaghayegh, the only one of the three who was really anywhere near getting married, soon adapted her language and her thinking to that of the other two. It was an automatic process, and also the only sensible thing to do. She yelled, interrupted the others, called for another round of shots — which only appeared when Saya snapped her fingers, legs apart, and ordered again in the world's deepest voice. When the landlady had gone again — not without scrutinising the little gathering and commenting that this was where Rudi usually sat, and he could be coming in any time now — Shaghayegh finally grasped the nettle.

'So, you do know I'm getting married in a few days, right?' she said, and all three laughed, but they also sounded very tired.

'But why?' Saya asked at last, and Hani hissed, 'Well, because he's so cute!' and Saya said, 'But that doesn't mean you have to marry him!' There was a silence, because Shaghayegh was thinking, though that might have been an error, because then Saya went on: 'Listen, if I married every guy who was cute, I'd be constantly getting married forevermore,' and Hani snorted with laughter and Saya snorted with laughter, and because I wasn't there to come in with the words 'Dad joke', the snorting was followed by a brief, awkward silence, in which Shaghayegh ultimately decided to keep the truth to herself.

Instead, she asked, 'What do you have against me getting married?' That was a question directed at Saya. At a wide-legged Saya, who might have been talking constantly but wasn't really responding to anything that was said to her.

'Nothing. Hope the food's good.'

'It will be.'

'How did the two of you decide to do it?' Hani finally asked, in a conciliatory tone. 'I mean, what happened, did he propose to you? Or did you propose? How do you actually get to that point?'

'I think it just happens automatically, because everyone else is getting married,' said Shaghayegh, with what was really only a slight hint of scorn in her voice. 'In my friendship group, at least. Everyone here is married now, and when you're getting all these invitations and drinking toasts to the bride and groom and acting as a witness for them, you start to do some thinking about yourself and your own relationship. And we realised it was what we wanted as well. We're at a point now where we want to tell the whole world. We want to grow old together, we don't want to be with anyone else.'

'And then did he propose?' Saya asked.

'No,' Shaghayegh said seriously, downing the remains of her beer, wiping her lips, and reaching for the second glass that Saya had ordered in advance so they wouldn't have to wait for the landlady again. 'I proposed.'

Shaghayegh was tired. The conversation was getting on her nerves. Everything she said was true. But everything she said was also more or less what her blonde girlfriends were happy to believe, because that's how it was for them, too: they loved their boyfriends, their boyfriends loved them, and they were looking forward to a celebration in which they would be the centre of attention. And their boyfriends, and love, of course. It was what thousands of people did every day. It was what you did when you were an adult. It wasn't the reason Shaghayegh was getting married, but it could have been. Nothing about it was objectionable, and it had nothing to do with chains or oppression or suburban smugness; it was the normality that Shaghayegh wanted. It felt good to act like this was her normality, too.

A small fly was floating in Shaghayegh's beer. She considered whether to return the beer, get the fly out with a fingernail, or just go home.

'Ooooh, romantic,' said Hani, before Saya could make any kind of retort, 'and how did you propose?' She blinked from under her smeared eyeshadow. Hani would never propose to anyone. But she would probably accept any proposal that came her way. Simply because proposals were so terribly romantic. In her world. A world where you put scented candles round the bath and had to differentiate yourself from animals before you made sense.

Shaghayegh had actually proposed to her boyfriend in a romantic way, because she wanted to create a shared memory that would preserve their self-respect, despite it all. She'd waited for Theo on what was to her mind the city's most beautiful bridge, in the spot where they'd kissed for the first time, that night, drunk, back when you could still go out round there without feeling like a tourist. She waited in that spot, surrounded by the smell of piss and the boom of a sound system owned by some wasted punks who were lying on their blankets a few metres away, begging, partying, and resting by turns. She waited for Theo, knowing he'd walk along here — which he never usually did, but a friend had set it up so that he would today.

When Theo approached and walked past first the punks and then Shaghayegh, she threw a pouch at his feet containing the caps from the two bottles of beer they'd bought from the corner shop that first night. First Theo spun round angrily, then he saw his girlfriend coming towards him, and when she went down on one knee in front of him without saying a word, he finally realised what was happening. They'd decided to get married a long time before this, quite unromantically, as they were standing in the queue at a car-hire place. But this made him want to bawl his eyes out: not only had the woman he was so in love with proved over the last few years that she'd stick by him no matter what, but she was also going to make sure they would remain entirely normal people with an entirely normal life. A life that would have no fewer lovely, romantic stories in it than anyone else's.

Saya didn't acknowledge this romantic story for a second. 'A more important and genuinely serious question,' she said, 'is why did you propose? What is it inside you that gives you the urge to ask that question? The urge to get married?'

Shaghayegh hated the arrogance in Saya's voice. As if she was the only person who knew what was right and what wasn't. Like hell was she going to open up to someone like Saya, shared childhood or no. Eventually she said, 'It's about staying together and looking after one another.' She drank her beer, ignoring the little fly in it.

'Time to settle up, girls,' said the landlady, who was suddenly standing beside them. 'Rudi'll be here in a minute, you'll have to move to another table.'

'We can do that,' said Hani, who was still puzzling over Shaghayegh's answer.

Saya said nothing, although she was starting to wonder why the landlady constantly seemed to have some kind of problem. She just looked at Shaghayegh in silence and ignored the landlady when she said, 'Well, you need to settle up anyway, girls. Change of shift.' And then, when no one moved, she added, 'The beers are two euros each.'

∧ ∧ ∧

So, let's be clear about this, Saya. Let's be really clear. None of this is any reason to explode. And you didn't, of course — at least not because of the landlady or Markus or Frau Suter. And actually I'm pretty sure that Saya didn't explode because she happened to encounter a whole series of unpleasant people in the space of a few days. In the end, the only reason she exploded was the news, and one particularly shitty person. But then again, without the series of unpleasant people in the preceding days, maybe that on its own wouldn't have been enough to make her explode.

She came stumbling into my room in the night; I'd given her the key to my flat, and she'd messaged me before staggering out of the pub. Saya switched the light on and said, 'Dude, the kebab shop was closed. What's up with this city? Since when did the kebab shop start closing? At night?' She lay down on me, on top of the duvet; her breath was bad, and she stank of alcohol and the city. 'I bet they're shit-scared at night. Got any bread?' she asked, her face in my pillow.

'Rolls from this morning,' I said, trying to sit up underneath her.

While I was in the kitchen, doing my best not to wake my flatmates, who were now taxpayers with jobs rather than students, she fell asleep. I came back with a roll spread with Nutella and hesitated to lie down beside her, out of fear that she might throw herself against the wall in her sleep again. Ideally, I'd prefer not to be walking around with a black eye, partly because you never lose that hope of being invited to a job interview.

'Saya,' I whispered. 'There's some food here for you.'

'Thanks,' she murmured, but it came too quickly, like a reflex you have in your sleep, without really having heard what the other person said.

'Saya,' I whispered again, 'we don't need to share my bed tonight — don't you want to sleep on your own mattress?'

'I'm not allowed,' Saya replied, again like a reflex.

'Of course you're allowed, you weirdo,' I said.

'I'm not allowed. We're not allowed, Kasih, don't you get it, we're never allowed. That's where Rudi sits.'

Who the hell is Rudi? Rudi is actually completely irrelevant to what happened this evening, but all the same let me just say that at that moment, just like every other Wednesday, Rudi was sitting at his usual table and talking about those bloody people who lived in the rear building, it was an outrage, while the landlady, Chrissi, wisely kept quiet about who had just been sitting at his table. You can forget Rudi again now; but take note of how uncomfortable he just made you feel, or by the end of all this you'll still be thinking the world is a nice place and our biggest problem is that we sometimes have to pay more for beer.

Saya turned away and buried her face in the covers. I put the Nutella roll down on the bedside table and lay down on the mattress on the floor where Hani had slept the previous night. If Saya hurled herself against the wall in the night again, there was a 50 per cent chance she'd choose the wrong side and fall out of bed. Onto me. But at least then she'd explain herself; I'd have to ask. And then I'd be able to calm her down and tell her she wasn't alone and that it just made everything worse when you got so caught up in your own anger. That then you eventually explode. I would have sensible tips at the ready; she'd open up and tell me about it and have a good cry and then everything would be fine. All wounds would be healed. I was sure of it.

'You know when I had to put up with the Nazi sitting next to me on the plane? Well, I saw his boarding card,' Saya said suddenly, stretching her drunk face out from under the duvet and looking at me in the semi-darkness.

'How so? And again: you don't actually know if he was a Nazi.'

'I do now. He dropped the boarding card along with his super German passport, which he had in his hand. Not that there was any need to — everyone knows you don't need one for internal flights. I picked both of them up for him, and that's when I saw his name and it seemed familiar, though I wasn't sure if I was just imagining it because he made me uncomfortable. And then earlier today I searched for him online.' Saya was slurring her words, but she did so with great dignity.

'That's creepy — imagine if he did the same to you,' I interrupted. But of course I still wanted to know what she'd found out.

'I was right. He is a Nazi. Patrick Wagenberg. A certified Nazi. He's been on remand several times, organised protests against mosques and stuff in sad little towns, had official complaints made against him, and he has the balls to write a blog under his real name, spreading some really serious shit. Everything he writes pushes the boundaries of legality. He uses all these foreign words and makes himself sound like he's become a good citizen, left his old ideals behind, and moved on. You need some idea of language to figure out that he's trying to sound educated, but in reality he's just spreading hate and bandying clever words about in the process.'

It was cute to hear Saya saying these things when she herself wasn't quite at her best. She sounded like a detective on *Tatort* who's having trouble with the script but is giving it her best shot anyway. She knew the difficult words she was coming out with, but could only mumble them hesitantly. Still, it was very important to her that I heard all this. I couldn't suppress a little laugh and was glad she was too drunk to notice. The thing that impressed me most was that Saya genuinely did seem to have a Nazi sensor, which I thought was an extremely pleasing development in human evolution. I didn't care about Patrick Wagenberg.

Saya told me in detail about his favourite topics. I won't go into that kind of detail here, because I'm working against him not for him, and if you're interested in his filth, then maybe first ask yourself what's wrong with you, and secondly look it up yourself.

In summary, his specialist subjects are equal opportunity, intersectionality, and urban development. No, I'm kidding. It's race ideology and how you can weave it into everything that's in the papers. He loves to complain that people like to live together in particular corners of a city and open their shops there, where they sell spices and vegetables and speak the language they know best. That infuriates Patrick Wagenberg. 'How am I supposed to explain this to my children?' he wrote under a photo he'd taken, as — so he wrote — he was walking through that part of town.

I interrupted Saya again: 'Saya, if you're going to tell me every single thing he writes, the two of us are never going to get to sleep. Ever again.'

'I wrote to him.'

'You did what?'

'Told him he was a shit.'

'Under your real name?'

Saya lapsed into drunken silence.

'Did you honestly write to him?'

'*I hate you*, I wrote.'

'Did you, though?'

'*Almighty arsehole*, I wrote —' now Saya was laughing '— do you remember, when it rained that time?'

'Saya, are you insane? Don't you know he could be dangerous? You're going to end up on his hit list!'

'Doesn't it make you feel good to imagine that?'

'No, Saya, it frightens me, are you listening, I'm frightened for you.'

'Well it makes *me* feel good. Imagine if I'd pushed him down the steps as we were getting off the plane. He went out ahead of me! I could have just pushed him and I probably would have liked it. Is that really psychotic?' Saya bit into the Nutella roll and grinned as she chewed. There was chocolate spread on her teeth, and although she then shut her mouth again, I could still hear bread pulp and saliva and more than I wanted to hear. 'He must have been absolutely fuming that he not only had to sit beside me on the plane, but I could now identify him.'

'So did you write to him under your real name?'

'I don't have a death wish, Kasih. I used my fake profile.'

'So he doesn't actually know that you're the woman from the plane and can identify him.'

Saya chewed. Then she swallowed and said, 'Okay. Maybe I shouldn't have written to him drunk.'

'You shouldn't have written to him at all! What good could it possibly do?'

'Annoy him a bit.' Saya took another bite of the roll and said with her mouth full, 'Earlier, at the party, it made me so angry to see you talking to Lukas. I was so pissed off with him that I imagined running over and punching him in the face.' She waited for a minute to see how I would react, but I didn't react. 'It feels good to imagine that, doesn't it?' she asked.

'Hmm. Doesn't do anything for me.'

Saya shoved the rest of the roll into her mouth and lay back down. She chewed thoughtfully for a while. 'It does for me,' she said. 'I never liked Lukas, you know. He somehow always reminded me of Leo.'

'In what way?' I was getting angry, in the way you always end up angry with drunk people, because they're annoying, spouting this stuff and wanting attention, though none of what they say is any help to anyone.

'I don't know. Maybe just because the sun shines out of his arse as well.'

'Now you're really being unfair. Those are two entirely different people.'

'Yeah, yeah, true,' said Saya, raising her head and sitting up. She suddenly looked very sober and let out a wide-awake, wicked laugh. 'These white boys all look the same to me. Old racist that I am.'

∧^∧

Leo was Saya's first proper boyfriend, and his mother was her first proper almost-mother-in-law. But the only time she talked about either of them was to make fun of them, which was fairly mean because — apart from having once been extraordinarily important to Saya, but then having ultimately revealed themselves to be kind of indifferent — there was nothing to hold against them. And there was this story about Leo's family (I mentioned it earlier), which Saya never got tired of telling for years afterwards, though it took ages for me to understand what made the story so incendiary.

Saya was twenty when she got her first proper boyfriend. For other girls who were at the same level of cool, that was quite late, but at the same time it gave this relationship a very different kind of seriousness. Because Saya was already something like an adult — and because she was Saya. The advantage was also of course that at twenty, you're not being so closely monitored any longer. Everyone else in our class was eighteen now — younger than Saya, but our heads were already in our university cities; we'd all realised that our school playground and the barbecue cabins weren't actually the centre of the world, but ordinary things that you had to put behind you and leave behind you.

Leo's mum having a round-number birthday and celebrating it in style was an unavoidable routine that came round regularly in the life of someone like Leo. But in the world of young couples, getting a joint invite to a party like this was an incredibly big deal. It was proof of how serious the relationship was. Saya was worked up about it, of course, because she was in love with Leo, and she wanted his family to like and accept her and ideally to think she was great.

She was also worked up because she had no experience of these situations. She wasn't familiar with 'round-number birthdays', which necessarily meant she wasn't familiar with adults' birthdays. When it was her mother or father's birthday, there would be a home-made cake at most, and some birthday wishes at least. Neither of them made any more fuss over it than this, because for them it was just a day that had been picked for the purposes of official documents. No one from their generation and their country of origin actually knew when they'd been born.

Quite apart from that, no one in Saya's family ever went out for dinner. Leo's family went out for dinner. They went out for pizza when there was something minor to celebrate like the last day of the summer holidays or someone's first swimming badge. And they went to fancier restaurants when there was something proper to celebrate, like passing your final exams or getting a raise. They sometimes even went out to a restaurant just because it was a while since they'd been to a restaurant, or when they fancied a treat, or of course when they were on holiday, and that happened at least once a year.

In Saya's life, you only ate out when you had to. When the whole class went for pizza after getting their grades, or the whole gymnastics group went for pizza before the Christmas break. She didn't have any other examples at the time, because Saya, as I've said, was only twenty.

She was sitting — showered, combed, blow-dried, wearing a little make-up and her mother's shoes — at a table in a restaurant, surrounded by adults who were all related to one another. And she was looking much too smart. Going out to eat was dressier than eating at home, that was correct, but going out for Sunday lunch in a rural hotel restaurant by a lake wasn't necessarily something you had to get all dolled up for. Saya's shoes wouldn't have looked out of place at an evening event in a cocktail bar. Here, Leo's aunties went barefoot when they took their children out to the play area behind the restaurant.

But no one seemed perturbed by Saya's shoes, her dress, or her agitation. Everyone loved Saya, because it was so cute how grown-up she and Leo felt, and the aunties and uncles enjoyed seeing little Leo with a girl on his arm for the first time; for the first time, he was almost one of them, but only almost.

Saya didn't yet know that in a sympathetic gathering like this she could get away with pretty much anything. She felt a strange kind of freedom, for which she would never in her life be grateful: if Saya was too dressed up, people forgave her and put it down to her culture. If Saya was too polite, they forgave her for that, too, because everyone was so wonderfully polite in her home country. At first, Saya didn't know what to make of this freedom, which was signalled with an encouraging look and a smile, and so it only increased her general insecurity. Because what if she suddenly did something that couldn't be put down to her supposed culture? How was she to keep up this nice image when she didn't really understand what image of what culture they were projecting onto her?

But luckily the twenty-year-old Saya hadn't started thinking in these dimensions yet, even if she felt it with every fibre of her being.

Twenty-year-old Saya might have started using the word 'racism' in places where that was obviously what was happening, but for the time being she'd stopped again after saying it out loud in front of the lads by the fire pit and quickly regretting it.

But Saya had at least come well-armed for this lunch, having developed strategies for situations like this. When she was invited to lunch at other children's houses, she'd always done the Elbow Check, and she did that now, too, to find out whether it would be a scandal if she rested her elbows on the table. Somewhere, in films or books, she had gathered that parents told their children off for putting their elbows on the table during meals. She wondered whether that was also true of families like Leo's, or if it was something people only did in films and books. So she'd started scanning the table before a meal. If one or two members of the family had their elbows on the table, she relaxed and ate as normal. But if no one did, she started to pay attention. Because that meant this ominous rule applied, and where this rule applied, there might be other rules she didn't know.

So she scanned the table now as well, at this round-number birthday. How were the others sitting, what were they doing with their serviettes, with the slices of white bread and butter that were served before the meal. She watched and did the same. Didn't put the serviette on her knees, although she felt that would be the proper thing to do, but beside the little plate; took a small, dry slice of bread, buttered it, sprinkled some salt on top, and began to nibble. She wondered what the point of this was, and stopped at one slice when she saw that Leo wasn't eating anything.

Leo was talking to an uncle sitting opposite, who had cheerful eyes and a lot of fine laughter lines. The uncle looked like he should be an actor on a children's program, *Sesame Street*, say, or *Löwenzahn*; or a singer-songwriter for nursery schools, a Chris de Burgh for four-year-olds, maybe. 'Quite a few people have got medical exemptions,' Leo was just explaining to him in the serious tone of voice that he, Saya, and everyone else practised in those weeks and months when they were speaking about their much-heralded future. A future that, for the male members of the class, would have to be put on hold for the time being because most had to do military or community service first.

'Oh yes, it was the same for us. We didn't have any desire to march in step back in the day, either. We just moved to West Berlin,' the uncle said, winking at Saya, who, at the same second, snap, smiled back. She liked it when relatives of people her own age told stories from their lives that chimed with what she'd read and learned from documentaries on the Phoenix channel. She wanted him to go on talking about West Berlin. 'But I didn't think you needed a medical exemption for community service,' the uncle said, and Leo nodded very quickly and seriously.

'No, right. If you get an exemption, it's an exemption from everything. But I didn't want to get out of everything, so I didn't ask for certification that I've got some kind of illness. I'm up for doing community service — where's the harm in it? You learn something, and you're helping people, as well.'

Leo's uncle made a pantomime of being impressed, although he did actually approve of his nephew's generosity, and said in Saya's direction, 'What can you say to that!'

Saya might have been in love with Leo, but she wasn't prepared to sit there and look adoringly at him from the side, entering into an alliance with the uncle, just because he'd passed on an exemption. 'Well, it's basically just a gap year of voluntary work,' she explained to the uncle, 'which a lot of people do — girls as well.'

Was Saya still a girl at this point? Are you still a girl at twenty? She still called herself that, in any case; it wouldn't have occurred to her to do otherwise. But what did occur to her was something she'd recently seen on ARTE, which she decided was a super-appropriate topic for this kind of small-talk situation, and so she went on: 'You know, I think everyone should have to do a year of voluntary work.

Like they do in Costa Rica. And there's no army there at all, so there's no military service. Obviously.' She looked from Leo to Leo's uncle and back again, waiting for their reaction, because while she did want to contribute something to the conversation, she also wanted to hand over to the next person asap and pass the attention on to them.

And: 'Costa Rica!' the uncle was already saying. 'Is that where you're from? You know, all this time I've been wondering if Saya might be an Arabic name, but you don't look very Arabian.'

Saya smiled. With that, the subject of voluntary work seemed to be closed, and she shook her head and was grateful that just then, Leo's mother joined the conversation and, despite the uncle's delight, she didn't have to explain that she wasn't from Costa Rica. Delighting the uncle had been far from Saya's original intention; she wanted to be part of this grown-up family world, in which people talked seriously about social issues, decisions about their own future, and things they'd learned on ARTE.

Leo's mother came up behind the uncle, leaned over his shoulder, and kissed him on the cheek. That, at least, was the same as in her family, Saya thought; people kissed each other in front of everyone, because they were a family and they belonged together. Mother and uncle seemed to get on, to genuinely like one another, and Saya imagined the two of them as healthy, tanned children, playing tag on the beach on holiday, making sandcastles, sleeping in tents, and using words like 'dunes'. Leo's mother was still bending down to the uncle's ear, and the fact that they could laugh together so quickly, without a long run-up, reminded her of her aunts' visits again, when Saya's mother and her sisters had roared with laughter.

'Costa Rica? I went there once, it was really lovely. But even so, I wouldn't go back to Latin America,' Saya heard a voice saying on her side of the table. On Leo's left was a girl of about her age, maybe a little older — at least, she spoke as if she was used to making polite conversation with strangers — and Saya assumed that she wasn't a family member, either, or Leo would already have told Saya about her or introduced them. That meant she must be someone's partner, and so Saya felt a great kinship with her from the word go.

'Really? I'd love to go to Latin America, the scenery there must be stunning,' Leo said to the girl, and Saya felt herself start to get impatient, as she always did when people began talking about travel and countries and stunning scenery. She used to think it was just because she couldn't join in. All she knew was Germany and the other country. She didn't know the beaches of this world, or the hidden gems from the very cool guidebooks that only seasoned travellers owned.

Today, she's seen four of the five continents and knows several of the world's metropolises well enough to navigate her way around them confidently, but she still feels bored the second one of these conversations starts up. For her, there is nothing worse than listening to people talk about their trips. About the 'new me' that they managed to acquire for a few days or weeks, when they discovered something fully unknown to them and conquered it. Alright, Saya has never said the conquering bit, but I think it's all connected.

Anyway, in Saya's version of this story, Leo asked the young woman sitting next to him, who wasn't a relative, why she didn't want to go and admire the stunning scenery of Latin America again, and the young woman — let's call her Lena, because she bore some resemblance to Lena from the series *Turkish for Beginners* — began to tell him. The scenery was stunning, she explained, the people were so friendly everywhere you went, the beaches the most beautiful you can imagine, and not yet as touristy as you might think. She'd almost felt like she was the first person to discover these beaches. Alright, to be honest, she probably didn't say that last bit, but it kind of fits with the rest. People do often talk like Columbus when they've seen something new on holiday. Or maybe in reality, I'm the one who doesn't like listening to other people talk about their travels.

'So why didn't you enjoy it there?' Saya finally asked, partly to signal to Lena that she was part of this conversation as well, by the way, and the two of them, as appendages to the family, could maybe stick together.

'Well, for me the main reason was the food,' said Lena. 'I'm a vegetarian, and of course people there just have no understanding for that.'

Leo nodded knowingly.

Saya thought of all the people she knew who would have no understanding for that, either.

'Whenever you asked about something and said you didn't want meat, they always said there was no meat in it, but then it turned out there was.'

'And that's why you don't want to go back? But that might well be the same in other countries,' Saya said, trying to rescue Lena from this basic misunderstanding. No one who could afford to see the world should have to miss out on that because they'd jumped to completely illogical conclusions about it.

'Yes, maybe. But everything was so unhygienic, too. I had real stomach issues for the first few weeks, and a nasty fever. I had to acclimatise.'

Leo nodded understandingly again.

Saya took a sip of the fizzy water that the uncle had unhesitatingly poured for her and everyone else within reach. For a brief moment, she considered whether to say something else, but then she could already hear herself talking. 'That's the fascinating thing, actually,' she said in a friendly voice. 'In countries where services aren't as good and things are less hygienic, people are much cleaner. They wouldn't dream of eating unwashed fruit, for example. And when Western tourists go there, they're just as unhygienic as ever and then they're surprised when they get the runs.'

Lena looked at Saya and blinked in disbelief. She was a nice, well-brought-up girl. Too well-brought-up to say things like 'the runs' at the dinner table, and too nice to attack anyone else. But she didn't like being attacked herself, either. Had this strange girl with the funny name just told her she was dirty? Because she came from a clean country? 'I don't believe that,' was all she said, and Saya took note of these words. So nice and simple and final.

And Saya did actually stop talking for a minute. On the one hand, she wasn't sure whether what she'd just said really was nonsense. It seemed logical to her, and it fitted with what she'd observed. But then, she'd never been to this 'Latin America', and hadn't ever had to acclimatise herself to somewhere.

Just then, another aunt appeared at the table. 'Right on time for the main course!' cried Leo's mother, hugging the new aunt, who, as Leo whispered to Saya, was his mother's twin sister. But twins who, thanks to the relentlessly ticking clock, celebrated their birthdays on different days. Even so, these twins looked similar and had similar-sounding names — Birgit and Brigitte. Like Hanni and Nanni, Saya thought wistfully, imagining the two of them at thirteen, having midnight feasts in their lovely girls' boarding school. They even looked a bit like the illustrations in Saya's *Hanni and Nanni* books. Birgit and Brigitte both had brown hair and alert, hazel eyes.

After popping out onto the terrace to wave and call out 'I'll come and see you in a minute', Brigitte did the rounds of the table, hugging and kissing the other family members, the blood relatives, the relatives by marriage, the partners. When she reached a sunbed-tanned hand across the table to Lena and said, 'I'm Biggi,' and when Lena replied, 'Lena' — or whatever her real name was — with a smile, Biggi beamed at her nephew Leo. 'Your girlfriend!' she cried, with a radiant girls'-boarding-school smile. 'How lovely, I've heard so much about you, *so* much!' And couldn't stop nodding at Lena.

Leo shook his head and said awkwardly, 'No. Saya. Saya's my girlfriend.'

Biggi's smile vanished in an instant, and when Leo put his hand on Saya's shoulder and Saya instantly reached out to shake hands with Biggi like everyone else had, Biggi's confusion was still in evidence. 'Do forgive me,' was all she said, looking from Leo to Saya and back again, until the image of the two seemed to make some kind of sense, and then she quickly added, 'Lovely to meet you, Saya,' and, 'We'll catch up later, alright?' and continued her round.

'And why are you taking that so personally?' I asked, the first time Saya reached this point in the story, which was in fact the end of it. We were sitting on the balcony at Hani's parents' house. They'd just had it built, and the balcony was different in seemingly every way from the one on the estate. But a lot of cigarettes were smoked on this balcony, too, and it was now Hani as well as her parents who filled the ashtray.

'I don't know,' said Saya, 'but it's odd, isn't it, that she assumed Leo's sister's tennis partner, who was there for no apparent reason, was Leo's girlfriend — just assumed it, even though I was sitting beside him as well.'

'It's not odd at all,' I said. 'Maybe she just didn't see you.'

'Of course she saw me,' Saya wanted to say. But she didn't. She was as baffled as we were as to why this had annoyed her, why she'd found this situation so unsettling. She had told us because she wanted to know if she should be annoyed or just surprised.

Hani said nothing, which meant she didn't know what to make of the story, either.

'So from your point of view, would it have been any better,' I asked, when we'd sat in silence for a while, 'if she'd seen you and immediately gone, "Ah, you must be Leo's girlfriend"? Although there was another girl sitting beside Leo who she also didn't know? Wouldn't she then be admitting that she'd been told you were someone unusual, who she'd recognise straight off because there was no one else like you there?'

Saya didn't respond.

Hani said, 'You two. Stop it. There's nothing weird about any of this. Nothing unusual. People mistake people for other people, it happens to us all. Stop moaning about things that aren't actually bad. Stop imagining things you *would* moan about even though they aren't bad either. Just stop it.'

And so we did stop it.

But Saya would still have the last word, because from then on, whenever the conversation turned to relationships with white men, she would start on about this birthday. She never told any other stories about Leo. She never mentioned how loyal her first boyfriend had been, or that she was the one who broke his heart, or that he now led an impeccable, unimaginative middle-class life and earned a packet working for an NGO. Leo had become a joker that Saya would play to remind us (endlessly) that she'd felt uncomfortable in a situation and had every right in the world to be angry about it.

For me, the memory of him is thus also the memory that, as the years have gone by, I've been forced to allow Saya her anger in retrospect, through gritted teeth. Because I've since had my own experience of what happened to Saya then. Of people seeing us and matching us with other people, or not doing that, because it didn't make sense to them that we moved in the circles we were moving in. Of people addressing us in English; of people trying to explain things to us that we knew better than they did; of people asking out of the blue where we *really* came from; or, when we were already three sheets to the wind, asking if we drank alcohol. That was one of our favourite fails.

As she got older, Saya was increasingly able to laugh at this. But she'd encountered her first one of these situations at that round-number birthday, and I'd disagreed with her, instead of saying, 'You're right. Something weird did happen to you. Not bad, but weird. And things that are actually bad happen because people like us are subjected to these weird things every day without anyone questioning them.'

My resistance was the easier reaction, partly because Hani resisted as well. She still does. But her strength lies in not denying the truth of Saya's experience — at least she doesn't do that — and that makes her fundamentally different from the lads by the fire pit.

And you were right about it all, Saya. But that doesn't make someone into a living fire accelerant, does it? That's not why someone starts a war. Not then, and not now.

Maybe we could have listened for longer before we argued with her; Hani in her way, and me in mine.

I've had to hear this story so many times, but it's only now that I'm beginning to suspect Lena — who doesn't come out of it particularly well, and doesn't even have a real name — wouldn't have forgotten it, either. I suspect Lena also talked to people afterwards, to confirm that she had every right to be angry about being taken for Leo's girlfriend, even though she was also sitting next to Alice, Leo's sister. I'd like to tell Saya right now about this penny having dropped far too late, so that we could both be ashamed of ourselves, Saya even more so than me. First we'd be ashamed for not realising, and then we'd feel like insensitive klutzes, and then we'd be ashamed of being the insensitive klutzes we ourselves held in such disdain. Rightly. And yet all these years, when we heard Biggi saying over and over, 'Your girlfriend! I've heard so much about you, *so* much,' we never gave a thought to Lena.

Hani answered the phone instantly, even though it was 6.00 am. She always answered the phone, even when she didn't recognise the number. Saya would never do that; for her, unknown numbers were like the ringing of the flat doorbell years before at her parents' place, when they weren't expecting guests and feared the secret service.

When I rang Saya's doorbell unannounced, I would always hear her voice asking 'Who's there?' before anyone opened the door. The door to Hani's flat, meanwhile, would sometimes be standing open when I came round. Her mother was constantly airing the place out, and anyway they had nothing worth stealing. Or rather: no one in Hani's family wanted to entertain the idea that it might be incautious to live like that. As always, Hani picked up instantly and asked, 'Kasih, why the hell are you awake at this time of the morning?'

'Saya won't let me sleep,' I said. 'She's still drunk, I think — she's tossing and turning and sighing and snuffling, and generally sleeping so loudly that I can't sleep myself.'

'But Saya never sleeps loudly. She's the world's quietest sleeper. What's up with her?'

'That's what I wanted to ask *you*. It's the reason I'm calling,' I said, suddenly feeling immensely relieved that we'd at least almost talked about what Saya was doing to herself in her sleep. Of course, what had woken me was her throwing herself against the wall again. And this time the crash had been so loud it frightened the life out of me, and there was no way I could get back to sleep.

'I'm worried about her,' I said, desperately hoping that Hani would say what she always did: that I didn't need to worry, because everything was fine with Saya; she was just making a mountain out of a molehill again.

But what Hani said was: 'Me, too. She drank so much last night that in the end the bar staff pretty much froze us out, they were probably worried she was going to start wrecking the joint.'

'Really? You think?'

'Yeah. It felt like they were trying to get rid of us.'

'Saya doesn't think it was her fault.'

'When does Saya ever think anything was her fault?' Hani asked, sounding a bit tired, which made me realise it was actually mean of me to call her when she was not only hungover and sleep-deprived but, unlike me, had to go to work soon. Absurd really, that even then I still envied her for having a job and responsibilities she was obliged to go and see to.

'Look, sorry for calling, Hani, but I wanted to ask what we're going to do with Saya?'

Hani laughed. 'The same as usual. Just don't argue back too often, or it's only going to get worse. Tell her she's right about everything.'

'And is she right?'

Hani considered this. That wasn't like her; Hani never considers anything. She has internalised her strategy towards the world to such an extent that she just de-escalates situations whenever necessary, always and everywhere. Even when she contradicts Saya, she does it so that later she can toast an amicable end to their discussion. If she missed this part out, she would never again contradict Saya; she'd just stop listening. That's why I'd called her: I wanted peace, I wanted her to tell me I was exaggerating and we didn't need to worry about Saya.

'She's got this Nazi chat thing on her phone and she's reading it all the time,' said Hani. 'It's not doing her any good.'

'Was she reading it yesterday as well?'

'Yes. Drunk on the U-Bahn. She read bits out loud. All the other drunk people heard. It was really embarrassing.'

I was too tired to tell her that Saya had also written to the Nazi from the plane and told him he was an almighty arsehole and she hated him, and, oh yes, that's right, that the story about her flight was pretty much entirely made up as well. Just thinking about where to start with a plausible explanation of these facts was too much for me, and so I kept quiet.

Instead, I asked the only relevant question: 'What are we going to do with her?'

'Distract her,' said Hani. 'That might be all you *can* do. She needs to stop reading that stuff, it's not going to get anyone anywhere.'

'Distract her. Okay.' That sounded like a good plan.

'Exactly. Distract her, cheer her up. But there was something I wanted to ask you, as well.'

'Please, please, talk about something else.'

'It's about yesterday. So, do you think Minh is interested in me or not? Just going on body language and that?'

I called up the image of Hani and Minh standing by the fire. I saw Hani's posture: definitely interested. I saw Minh's posture. 'Hard to say. Anyway, you were talking about work, right? Not so much about personal stuff?'

'Yeah. Unfortunately. It's so ridiculous that people always talk about work.'

'Well at least you all *have* work.'

'Yes. Sorry. So what now?'

'Minh kept on saying you're too good for that job, right?'

'Yeah, whatever, but is that what you say when you're interested in someone?'

'I think it's what you say when someone's too good for their job, Hani. Look, I've been wanting to tell you this for ages, anyway: I genuinely think you're too good for that job. Everyone offloads their shit onto you, and no one thanks you for it.'

'Yeah, whatever — look, I just want to know if I should call Minh or not. How are we interpreting the general body language?'

'Okay, being real about it: I'd say not.'

Hani was silent and I felt sorry for her. I wanted to say something different, but there would have been no point. And to be honest, it felt kind of good, even though I was sorry for her. When you're going through relationship woes yourself, you begrudge everyone else their cute flirtations.

'I'm sorry,' I said.

'Okay, thank you.'

'But maybe you could take to heart what Minh said, all the same? About your job?'

'Meh — right, I need to go. What are we doing this evening?'

'I don't know. Drinking, maybe? Distracting Saya?'

'Why don't you take her out somewhere today. Go and lie in the sun or something, I'm sure that would do you good.'

'Okay.'

'One other thing.'

'Yes?'

'Saya kept going on about some trial starting today. I think it's the Nazis again. Maybe you could make her just forget about that.'

'Ha. Sure. Like Saya would ever forget anything. But okay, I'll try.'

'See you later.'

'See you later.'

We hung up, and I went back to bed, while Hani started her day in the way people in a capitalist society do, when they aren't unemployed or drunk. She showered, had breakfast, got on her bike, and thought about what Minh had said to her the day before. 'You were the only one in that office who I always knew would be there, and when you'd be there, and that you'd be getting on with things. Everyone else always tried to make themselves invisible and be as opaque as possible, which has a certain style, but when you're doing an internship it's just annoying.' Hani retrospectively relished the praise, not yet guessing that it wasn't her interest in Minh but these golden words that would keep gnawing at her.

She pushed the pedals hard, looking forward to the buffer-cigarette she would earn by riding as fast as she could. That was the real reason she cycled rather than taking the bus. All three of us live in mortal terror of being late for things, and so we always get to places a good ten minutes early. Even places we have to go to every day, when we can estimate to the minute how long it will take to get there on public transport. On her bike, Hani could choose to extend this unnecessary time buffer and use it to smoke outside the office.

Besides which, buses were the least reliable form of transport in the city, and anyway Hani had lost her faith in them since the day our bus stopped going to the estate. That was also the day we adopted 'almighty arsehole' as our number-one favourite swear. Not because it sounded cool, but because it brought together all our rage and energy in exactly the right proportions. So there was something good, something illuminating about that day; it was an important day in our transportation biography.

∧^∧

The day our bus stopped going to the estate was the first time I had an inkling the estate was going downhill. Though downhill is a misleading word in this context, because on the day the bus stopped going, Saya, Hani, and I walked up quite a long hill in the pouring rain. It's also hard to imagine that an area where the scum of society has been housed for generations can actually go downhill. But it can, and it does, when the people in charge really put their backs into it.

Saya, Hani, and I were still hanging around outside our blocks in the afternoons, which put us in a bad mood because there was absolutely nothing going on there. We tried going to each other's flats, but since we and our problems had got bigger, the flats seemed ever smaller to us, and the smell of the carpets ever more musty. We sometimes went off to the little woodland play area to sit ironically on the swings and watch Hani smoke where no one else could see her. And then someone killed themselves on the playground and it was dismantled. We weren't even sad about it, because the playground had never really belonged to us.

Maybe it was lack of alternatives that made us start going to the children's centre, which of course wasn't in our neighbourhood, but on the opposite side of town. Even back then, Saya was volunteering there, doing activities with kids' groups, which she regularly raved about to us. Eventually, of course, Hani and I went to join her, and together we organised outings for disadvantaged kids and supervised their craft sessions. The social-services staff loved us for taking work off their hands, and although they never cared about us being there on time, it was the first context in which I realised how obsessed Saya, Hani, and I were with punctuality.

No one ever monitored or evaluated us, and of course no one was paying us either, but for whatever reason, we behaved as if they were. The only real benefit it brought was that after two years of volunteering, we were given a certificate, which at the time I thought would be useful. At the time, I didn't know that one day I'd have a whole pile of certificates and still no future. But for Saya, working with these kids was the thing that prompted her to do a degree in education, and Hani, who usually would have lost interest in the place and the work after a few weeks, realised that once she'd moved to the new-build estate, this was an opportunity to keep seeing Saya and me every day. She also secretly thought that the social workers had a very cushy time, sitting there with their computers and their coffee cups, making phone calls and planning things.

Anyway, on the day the bus stopped going, we'd taken the girls' group on an outing, which was no fun because it had rained the whole time. We'd been to a museum that looked imposing and steeped in history, but wasn't of any interest to anyone. We were really only there because there was a play area with a summer toboggan run in the museum grounds. But it was raining, and the fifteen grumpy little girls hated the three grumpy group leaders for not simply taking them to the cinema.

When we'd handed the children back to their parents, we were in a hurry to get home, back to the estate. It was only when we were standing at the bus stop outside the children's centre waiting for the bus and stuffing our faces with the leftover apples and muesli bars that we saw that our bus had been cut. It wasn't just that one bus had been cancelled; they'd discontinued the whole route, cut the connection that had existed between the estate and the rest of the world, without even giving us any warning. That morning, Saya's dad had driven us in. And now there we were with no way back. Saya's dad was at work, my dad had to sleep because he was working nights, and Hani's dad didn't have a car. Our mums played no part in these calculations. While we were coming to this realisation, the rain kept falling on us, as if a merciless authority was trying to punish us for something.

'Right then,' said Saya, and stalked off.

I looked at Hani, whose lower lip was thrust forward, like Saya had just told her off. She was probably still thinking the rain would stop any minute. 'You can have my umbrella,' I told her. 'Come on, or we're going to lose her.'

Hani took my umbrella, held it above my head and hers, and we trudged off after Saya. The walk would take at least fifty minutes of our lives, and the hill on which the estate stood was a steep one. It didn't take very long for Hani and me to abandon the idea that two people could use one umbrella, and Hani realised that this was a type of rain against which an umbrella wasn't going to protect even just one person. Saya was still walking ahead of us, though we'd caught up to her by this point. It seemed to lessen her anger that she was at least faster than Hani and me.

The rain had swept all life from the streets of our small town, and when from time to time a car passed by, it sprayed water everywhere and sounded like a noisy, roaring crowd of people. Who were laughing at us. Everyone is laughing at us, I thought, as the three of us battled against the wind in the middle of the road; there are probably people sitting in the cosy flats around us right now, looking out of their windows and wondering what's wrong with us. As a teenager, you always think everyone you see has nothing better to do than wonder what's wrong with you.

I looked at the wet ground and screwed up my eyes against the angry, pounding drops, and when I moved my eyes slowly upwards, they fixed on Saya's backside. That couldn't be helped — not because of the rain, but because I always look at the backsides of people who are walking ahead of me, though it's a mystery to me what you're supposed to think is great or not great about backsides; for me, at least, they've never been a factor in people's attractiveness. Certainly not Saya's backside, which I knew as well as my own.

We knew each other's backsides better than we wanted to, which is to say, we had a code that we'd whisper in public to let each other know if our trousers had slipped so far down that everyone could see our bum cracks. The code was: 'You smell nice today.' Sounds like a compliment, but in reality it was an emergency service. I don't know how long it is since you were at school, but let me just say that in a room full of teenagers who are at the mercy of constant growth, a hell of a lot of bum cracks are unintentionally displayed. Which is all the more dramatic when you know this is a room where everyone is constantly watching everyone else and at the same time is terrified of doing something embarrassing.

When we inducted Hani into our code, however, it lost its effect, because if you tried to alert her to a wardrobe malfunction by saying, 'You smell nice today,' she just felt pleased, and only a few minutes later would it occur to her what the supposed compliment signified, and she would turn red and cry out 'Oh, I *see*!' as she pulled her trousers up.

Anyway, I was looking at the wet asphalt, the rain, and Saya's pugnacious backside striding ahead of me, when I had my first realisation of the day, which was to do with the rain and not the estate. By this point, I was completely soaked. My socks and shoes were wet through; my jeans had become a second, unpleasantly slimy skin; my thighs, the back of my neck, and my collarbone were freezing; my clothes were sticking to me and wrapping me in a spiteful layer of cold. But my realisation was that, now we'd been walking for long enough, all this had stopped bothering me. I'd become indifferent to the cold, the slimy skin, the water in my shoes; I was one with the wet world. The only thing that still annoyed me was the fucking rain, the drops needling me in the face, the endlessly falling drops that seemed far too energetic. They were hyperactive nuisances who couldn't see that no one wanted to play with them.

The longer I thought about it, the worse every single drop became: sheer provocation, sheer harassment. And when a raindrop — one of the really fast and vicious ones — flew right into my eye (for the tenth time today, but this was once too many), I lost my shit. I stopped walking, turned my face to the sky, and shouted, 'Was that really necessary, you goddamn motherfucking bastard rain?'

Saya stopped ahead of me, Hani beside me, and they both started laughing, and then Saya turned around and yelled into the next gust of wind, louder than I had done, 'Was that necessary, you bastard rain?'

'You dickhead rain!' I shouted.

'You wanker rain!' shouted Hani, who can yell at quite an impressive volume when she wants to.

'Fuck you!' Saya yelled at the sky. 'Fuck you, clouds!'

'Fuck you, clouds!' the three of us yelled together, and it seemed like the rain answered, by hammering down on us even harder.

'I hate you!' Saya shouted up at it, even making the effort to cup her hands around her mouth. 'You almighty arsehole!'

'Almighty arsehole!' Hani and I shouted.

We couldn't stop saying these two words, they came out with such beautiful anger. We walked slowly on, trudging along the road in triangle formation and yelling whatever came into our heads, though always coming back to 'Almighty arsehole!'

When we reached the estate, the rain eased off and the sky looked almost friendly, and Saya kicked the chewing-gum vending machine that stood like a welcome sign at the bottom of our road. She kicked the side of the machine with all the force there is in an Adidas Superstar. Saya had saved every last cent she could to buy these shoes, and she's the only person in the world who looks after the things she's saved for so well that she can wear them again when they come back into fashion years later. And the Adidas Superstar was clearly tougher than you might think; it isn't just that Saya is wearing these same shoes today — the wet shoe even survived a hefty kick to a chewing-gum machine without a scratch.

'Fuck you, you almighty arsehole!' she shouted.

The machine was a relic from the seventies; it was blue and had that eternal Wrigley's logo all over it, which can't have changed since the baroque period. No one in the estate still went to the chewing-gum machine to buy chewing gum, even though it was right next to the cigarette machine. The old machine had heard worse words from worse children in its lifetime, and although Saya's kick made it wobble for a moment, it seemed otherwise unimpressed. Saya took that as an insult. She'd sworn at raindrops, clouds, cars, fences, and stones, and now it was the chewing-gum machine's turn, and her wet hair whipped across her face as she kicked the machine again, and kept kicking it until it finally keeled over, slowly, almost casually. First it listed to one side, silent and defenceless, then it crashed forwards onto the wet pavement. If it had had arms and hands, it would have clutched at its heart.

Saya, Hani, and I looked at the machine, which until that point had been part of our childhood, part of our everyday lives, and suddenly felt a deep humility. As if we'd chopped down or at least injured a wise old tree. Saya bent down and picked something up off the ground. In her hand were two packs of Wrigley's. Between us, we three could have picked the machine up and raided it. What a giant haul of chewing gum we'd have got. But no one wants ancient chewing gum — even if the machine had preserved it remarkably well all those years. The gleaming white gum should have ended up between the gleaming white teeth of healthy, well-nourished seventies teenagers. Instead, it was now lying on the wet ground, at the feet of such sad figures as Saya, Hani, and me. Saya lobbed the chewing gum into the bushes, and we kept walking.

By the time we reached the buildings of the estate, the sky had lightened to a pale grey, and the rain had stopped. Its hammering had been replaced by the subdued twitter of birds. We'd exhausted ourselves, not so much with the walk and the rain, but with yelling and cursing. We said goodbye without saying much more. When it had rained, the buildings looked even worse than usual, though every time you'd hope the water would wash away the dirt. Instead, it just smeared it across the render.

The fate of the chewing gum machine became a kind of accidental prophecy for what was going to happen to the whole estate. That dawned on us a few days later as we walked past the machine, which no one had dealt with in the meantime, not the local authority or a public-order office or a vending-machine company — no one. In fact, people had clearly made things worse and thrown it around the street. But it hadn't disappeared; the chewing gum was scattered across the asphalt, and a lot of people seemed to have made it their mission to get at the money inside the machine, though no one had managed it. After a while, people began to ignore the dead machine, and it just lay in the bushes, quietly rusting away. Until to cap it all, a pile of poo appeared on it, which judging by the size and composition must have been human. The prophecy was not an auspicious one.

If we hadn't been sixteen and preoccupied with our own stuff, the cutting of the bus route might have rung alarm bells for us. But a few months later, what was happening to the estate had become too obvious to imagine that it might just fix itself: it was emptying, bleeding out; it was sick and had started to stink. I don't know if the rent elsewhere had been radically reduced, or the interest rates on mortgages had fallen, but suddenly a large number of flats were unoccupied and fell into disrepair, which is sad when you think how lively the estate had once been.

Sometimes new people would move into one of the flats, but they weren't families with children who brought the laughter back;

strangely, they were young, feral people, of the type who wore vests in public, lit barbecues on the grass in summer, and forced every last tenant who wanted to hang their laundry out in the sun back to the washing lines in the cellar, with drunken caterwauling and faecal language. One of them kept setting light to some big wheelie bins, dangerously close to the buildings. These things never used to happen. No one ever peed in the corridors, and no one threw rotten fruit at the windows.

There must have been some strategic, political reason for so many flats remaining empty and everything suddenly starting to smell of fish and vomit; that doesn't just happen by itself. The estate had persisted for generations, because everyone who got sent there simply stayed forever and felt at home. New benefits claimants and foreigners were probably being sent elsewhere, while their predecessors now seemed to be living a better life in a better area, as if by magic. That was why Hani's parents would soon be talking about the prefab house and the new-build estate on the edge of town; it was why Saya's parents had long since signed a building-loan contract with which they would be investing in the purchase of a nice, solidly built flat for two as soon as Saya moved out; and it was why my parents would eventually move to another run-down residential district, just like their friends and their friends' friends.

Of course, we didn't know that at the time. To begin with, we just felt betrayed by all the buses of this world, and got ourselves bikes. By the time they were nicked from us, one by one, we'd already lost faith in the world anyway.

∧ ∧ ∧

I had another bike nicked a while ago — one that I'd bought specially for guests, because at that time none of them had the money to take public transport, and they liked having to find their own way around the city. I wasn't actually bothered that someone had nicked the bike. I'd forgotten where I'd put the key in any case, and by then my guests could afford public transport and didn't want to arrive drenched in sweat for the meetings that were the real reason they were in the city. The bike was nicked and forgotten. Someone in greater need will have been glad of it, I thought, because it could hardly have been nicked to sell on. I should just have put it in the cellar when it stopped being used; it was sheer laziness to leave the bike parked in the back courtyard, sheer laziness to let fate decide whether it would still be there in a few weeks' time or not.

If I could have offered Saya a bike today, she wouldn't have been on the U-Bahn, watching people. She wouldn't have got so angry she had a meltdown. All it would have taken to stop her seeing what she saw was a bike. I really don't want to put any of the blame for the whole thing on myself; I wasn't put on this earth to get bikes out for other people so that in the end, no one dies. But quite honestly, I wish testicular cancer and haemorrhoids on the guy who stole my bike. Now, all this time later, may both be visited upon him.

'How do you know it was a man?' I can hear Hani saying as if she was sitting behind me, and I feel like getting up and giving her a good shake. Because I just *want* to know, without having to feel bad about that. I know it from the very fact that I've been on the U-Bahn, and it's men on the U-Bahn that are the most annoying thing about taking the U-Bahn. If Hani wasn't always defending every possible group of people, she would see that, too. Men on U-Bahns are the real reason I seek out job ads for places I won't have to travel too far to reach.

When I get on, I never know what the lesser evil will be: sitting beside men and letting them invade my space, or sitting opposite them and exposing myself to their eyes. And there is nothing worse than overcrowded carriages. Not because someone's going to grab your arse or anything; that doesn't happen very often in the daytime, and if it does, then thanks to Saya, I know what to do. No: I hate overcrowded carriages because there's nothing to hold onto in them. The loops attached to the top bars are at the perfect height for men's arms, but not for mine, presumably because men built the carriages and tested them on men. The bars that people of any height can hold onto are usually occupied. Not by other people who need to hold on, but by people leaning against them, and it's really, really only men who do that, firstly because they don't know that people like me have nothing else to hold onto, and secondly because they don't realise that if you do somehow timidly hold on there, you're doing it timidly because you don't want to get too close to them. And any person who isn't a man will react to that with some sensitivity and move straightaway to make room. Men don't do that. Men sit on the train with their legs apart and don't realise that no one can sit next to them. A manspreading man is not a rucksack you only have to point at for it to be removed. A manspreading man on the U-Bahn is like two occupied seats on the U-Bahn.

For that reason and that reason alone, it had to be a man who nicked my bike. And if that man hadn't nicked my bike, Saya wouldn't have had a meltdown today because of people on public transport. I *hate* manspreading men, and I'm going down to the corner shop now to buy some cigarettes and a beer, because I've just lost the thread of the story.

But now I realise it's yet another man who is stopping me from going down there — the corner-shop guy with the pseudo-charming one-liners, I mean — and that makes me furious, and even so, I'm going to do it, really, I'm going down there now in my pyjama trousers, and if he says I'm getting prettier every day and phrases it like a question, I'm not going to answer, because I won't hear him, because I'm going to put my headphones in and pretend he doesn't exist. See you in a minute.

The young gigolo wasn't there. It was a woman. I've never seen her there before. She seemed pretty competent, though, and I felt a bit ashamed, first for going in there in my pyjama trousers, and second because I had my headphones in, but the wire fell out of my pocket and she could see straightaway that it wasn't plugged into anything and I wasn't listening to anything and I'm so poor that my headphones are still attached to a wire.

'Marlboros, please,' I said, being as cool as possible, and she placed a packet on the counter with a tremendously laid-back air and said, 'I'll come out for one with you.' So we smoked together, she and I, on the plastic chairs outside the shop, I to the left and she to the right of the door, and she told me about her son, who used to be such a smart kid. Sometimes you meet lost souls this way, who suddenly lay their whole lives out at your feet, but she wasn't one of those. It seemed like she was very on the ball, and like there was a good reason she'd selected me to talk to.

Her son was away, she said, at the airport; her husband couldn't drive, weak heart, too dangerous on his own, and his brother, her son's uncle, was passing through and was in the transit area of the airport. Did I think they'd be able to see him, even though he didn't have a visa for Germany and the pair of them didn't have plane tickets that would let them through to the transit area? She asked that quite sincerely in her smoky voice, and her black eyes glinted beneath her painted eyebrows.

'Which airport?' I asked, thinking: some airports are so small they might be able to wave at one another through the glass.

'Frankfurt am Main,' the woman said, and when she said Frankfurt she sounded like Saya's parents. They used to say it a lot, because in the nineties, I think, everyone who came to visit Germany flew into Frankfurt am Main.

'Then I don't think they'll be able to see each other,' I said, and she nodded solemnly. She'd clearly known beforehand that it was pointless to let the husband with a heart condition and the clever son drive right across the country to the airport in Frankfurt.

'My son said the same. He didn't want to go, but my husband

hasn't seen his brother for thirty years,' she said, her round head turned towards me, underlining every word with her hands. 'Thirty years.'

I nodded. That's the way things are; there are people out there who don't see each other for thirty years. You can't shock me with things like that.

'That's my son,' the woman said, showing me her purse, in which there was a faded photo of the son, who of course I knew, because he was the guy who usually sat here. In the photo, his hair was full of gel and he was looking past the camera. She looked at the photo for a while, without any emotion in her face; she was much too cool for sentimentality. But her son was her son and so he was everything to her, and that's why he was allowed to live in her purse in her bum bag.

I wondered what she'd say if I told her that her son was the reason I'd spent quite a while not wanting to come down here. But my problem wasn't just her son; it was the other men as well. I couldn't have told her that, though, because she didn't seem like someone men could do any harm to. If I'd tried to explain, she would have answered quite drily, 'Oh, come on, no one else is awake now anyway,' and she would have been right. In other parts of town, it didn't matter how late it was, every street was lined with convenience stores and kebab houses, groups of people swarmed around the crossings, and someone was always sidling along the dirty pavements. Not here, though — or rather: not here, these days. It was silent here; everyone was asleep, and only the woman and I were quietly making the tobacco crackle.

I don't know what I was hoping for from the cigarette — that it would distract me, maybe — but all it did was make me jittery, because at some point quite soon it would be finished. I opened the beer, because after the cigarette I wanted to have another reason to sit with this woman outside her shop. She made me feel safe. Even if someone was still awake and got too close to us, she'd destroy him instantly. Her face, her wrinkles, her strong hands — everything about her spoke of a woman who fought back. Maybe that was why the son thought he needed to show women it was okay to simply be pretty and not a warrior. Or maybe the son was just a pain in the arse.

'What do you do for work?' the woman asked, lighting a second cigarette from my pack, and I had to think for a minute before recalling that I'd told her I had to get back to work soon. That was before I'd figured out whether she was okay or a nutter.

'I write,' I said, thinking: we've just got to Thursday morning, and Hani, cycling to work, and that's why I was writing about buses and the rain, and then bikes and men on public transport, and I went way off topic because my mind keeps coming back to Saya, even when I'm writing about Hani, and maybe that's just poor Hani's lot in life: someone is always slightly more important than her.

'You write,' the woman said, nodding. It felt really good talking to this woman, because she seemed to take everything seriously, even things that were semi-invented. 'Then you're a writer,' she added, and I thought, if I nod now, that will actually be the closest thing to the truth. I'm more a writer than I am an unemployed person, because you can't *be* an unemployed person. What is that apart from a state that says something about your bank account and your troubles, but nothing about your interests or what you actually do. 'I'm a writer, too,' the woman said, and I nodded.

'What do you write about?' I asked, but that appeared to be something writers didn't ask one another. At any rate, she didn't answer me; she just looked along the street to see if anyone else was coming.

'I don't write anymore,' she said then, and her mind seemed to be elsewhere, or at least no longer with me and our conversation. Maybe she's just a phony who calls herself a writer so she can then say in a voice pregnant with meaning that she has stopped writing, now. That's possible. But it's also possible that I was sitting there beside someone who's capable of making up the coolest, coolest shit ever. Someone who sits down, moves a biro across the page, and answers all the questions we have in life, in five or six sentences that are striking, clever, witty, and poetic as well. Maybe she has drawers full of these sentences, or maybe they've been printed, in a language that is spoken as soon as the shop door closes and there's no one else there. Maybe she's the greatest author of all time, this person who just called me a writer.

I thanked her, picked the cigs up off the table, and considered leaving some of them for her. Then I remembered that she ran a whole shop full of cigarettes, and I raised my beer to her briefly and said, 'Have a good evening.'

She nodded and gave me a little wave, with the hand holding the cigarette. How different people look when they're smoking, I thought. Hani would never do that; cigarettes were noble and beautiful things for her, and you didn't wave them around like that.

I felt sick then, and I still do, because I really don't like the taste of cigarettes. I'm a tiny bit tipsy, and it's good to be back at the desk, to keep writing. The woman is sitting outside, taking care of us. And from now on, I'm a writer. Because if that's what she calls me, then it must be the correct term.

So, Thursday morning, and back to Hani, who is cycling to work, and whose general air of serenity we may envy.

∧ ∧ ∧

Hani got into the office on time. It smelled of plum tea. She spent her days with cups of plum tea, because it stopped her drinking one coffee after another and getting yellow teeth.

The people in her office weren't the type to drink one coffee after another just because that was what you did in offices. They were people who would never have thought they'd be working in offices one day, and for that reason found it all the more acceptable to have ended up there. Their deep-seated scepticism proved, you see, that they hadn't just stumbled into the hamster-wheel of capitalism. They'd retained their ability to make independent decisions and were simply here to fight for animal rights.

Hani's desk was in reception, and so hers was the first face people saw when they came into the agency. Another reason to always arrive freshly showered and to look good, she thought, and the fact that her office always exuded a faint scent of plum tea was no bad thing, either. If anyone had asked her how she was, Hani would have told them that she'd been out late last night. But no one asked. On her way in, she'd ridden past a man who was on the phone, telling someone he'd been 'out with the boys', and she'd felt a real connection to him. Not that Hani would ever say she'd been 'out with the girls', but sometimes she got the feeling that talking like that would suit her.

If her boss, Carolin, a woman with a sidecut and a handful of dreadlocks, who had reared cattle on a communal farm in the mountains before becoming a businesswoman, told her with a vague smile that she was wearing particularly nice earrings today, Hani instantly knew that her boss meant particularly nice *for someone like her*. The boss, Carolin with no e, as it seemed important to her to point out, would never wear earrings that weren't handmade, imported from another country, and sold somewhere outdoors. But when it came to Hani, Carolin didn't seem bothered by fake-silver earrings in striking colours from C&A.

When Hani thought about it a bit harder, then actually everything Carolin said to her in her friendly, worldly-wise way made her question whether they'd accidentally misinterpreted her personality here. 'I *love* your earrings, wow, great colour!' was something you said to people who told you they'd been 'out with the girls' last night. Hani switched on her computer, dusted the keyboard with the sleeve of her pale-pink cardigan, looked at the shadows under her eyes in her reflection in the monitor, and wondered if she was one of those people. She wouldn't mind if she was, but somehow she did mind that Carolin thought she was.

'Morning!' her colleagues sang out as they walked past her office door, beaming as if their breakfast smoothies had been spiked with happiness hormones. Hani beamed and greeted them back, calling each of her colleagues by name. People were never this cheerful in other companies, not even just before the Christmas break — Hani knew this all too well, and so the morning greeting-and-beaming ritual was Hani's daily affirmation that she belonged here.

There were emails waiting in Hani's inbox with requests from various colleagues. 'Just checked the homepage, the pictures from the last project really need changing, see server, professionals can tell the difference!!!' they said, or 'Next Christmas party: found a great venue, check it out, think it might be a goer? Give them a call and get a quote!' or 'Didn't manage to contact the press office for Project C before the weekend, afraid you'll have to do it, thank you and have a good rest of the week!'

At the bottom of her colleagues' emails, a footer said: 'Paper eats up resources and trees — please only print me out if you really have to! Thank you!' Hani had come up with the wording of the footer. To this day, she was extremely dissatisfied with the result, but the fact that her colleagues appeared to take no notice of this part of the company signature reassured her. Otherwise someone would long since have asked her to rewrite it. Probably no one read it; probably when people got to the signature, their brains started playing lift music, which always kicked in whenever it was time for the obligatory do-gooding moment.

Hani wondered why a colleague was emailing to say that she hadn't managed to fit something in 'before the weekend', when she'd sent that email yesterday, on a Wednesday afternoon. Sometimes Hani wished she worked for a company that kept set hours, where no one disappeared into an impenetrable part-time existence because of childcare, or to take life more slowly, or both — an existence that seemed to consist primarily of writing emails like this on the two days they were actually in the office.

'Morning, Hani!' trilled Carolin, appearing in the doorway and staying there. She only did that when there was something to discuss, which Hani dreaded. Carolin took a sip from her bamboo coffee cup and didn't bother to wait for Hani's response. She got straight to the point: 'I've been asked to pass on best regards to you,' she said, her voice sounding bored but wide awake.

'Thanks!' Hani said with a smile, waiting for what would happen next and hoping that after such a strange opening, the substance of the conversation wasn't going to be about some error or other. When Carolin wanted something, it was usually either to talk about herself or to rectify mistakes — she never knew precisely who'd been responsible for them originally, and so Hani had to turn investigator or fix the problem herself. But today it was hard to tell what Carolin had in mind. 'By who?' Hani finally asked, and Carolin smiled, bobbing her coffee cup up and down a little.

Hani knew a thousand people who owned these cups, herself included, but they never looked the way they did on Carolin: like the coolest object on the planet, like you had to hold it and move it that way and purse your lips at the same time. Sometimes it felt as though Carolin had spent time on the farm in the mountains standing in front of the mirror, practising ways to draw people's attention and keep it with the least effort.

'Someone who's really delighted with your work here,' said Carolin, and Hani didn't register the slight smirk; Hani thought of the overtime she didn't claim for because she was afraid they would think her too slow; she thought of all the times she'd stayed in the office until the middle of the night to finish the annoying fine-tuning on her colleagues' projects before a deadline; she saw herself cleaning the sticky oat milk off the milk frother again and again, though it was clearly everyone's job. She was the only one who ever did it, and she didn't even drink oat milk. She didn't even drink coffee here. Who *did* drink coffee here? Why all the oat milk?

Carolin, who was standing in the doorway and seemed to have finally realised Hani's worth, was one of the reasons to take on tasks like the milk frother and to always arrive at the office on time and well groomed. Good work was always rewarded in the end, Hani's father had said, when he got home from the building site and fell asleep on the sofa in his work clothes. He'd never complained, and instead made sure there was never any reason to complain about him. In his eyes, that was the whole deal. And even if he was just a builder's labourer among fifteen other labourers: at least he was a labourer. Unlike other people from the estate who didn't get a proper contract on a building site where they took safety seriously. And so he made an effort to be a particularly good labourer, so that nothing about this status would change.

Hani looked at Carolin, waiting for her to finally come out with it.

'Thorsten, the photographer from the last expo! I ran into him yesterday, and I think he'd like to have you in front of his lens again.' She winked at Hani — a gesture she used sparingly — and performed the necessary spin in her imitation-leather boots to detach herself elegantly from the doorframe, call out 'Morning, Stefan', and saunter off.

Carolin never wanted to be called Boss. 'We have a flat hierarchy here!' was one of the things that had been repeated most often in the job interview. It was something you could then tell other people with pride, because of course that's how everyone wants to work. But Hani had no problem with hierarchies, and never had done; in hierarchies, she was firmly convinced, everyone at least knew where they stood and what they had to do. If there had been a proper hierarchy here, Carolin and Hani's conversations would be more frequent and more substantial. Hani would be given tasks directly by Carolin, and Carolin would then have an overview of which of these tasks made sense and which didn't, which of them were accomplished with devoted care, and which should have been done by the colleague who was actually responsible for them.

Hani stared at her screen again, started marking important emails in her inbox with the 'important' symbol, and wished as she was doing it that Carolin was a normal boss with a severe, analytical eye that noticed when someone had done something good. Not something ordinary like treating Thorsten the photographer with respect. Hani's mood darkened with every email that she marked 'important'. There were a lot of emails, and that meant a lot of work and a long day. And she didn't actually think what she was doing was important at all. She thought her email program should have an icon that meant 'important in the context of this job, but completely irrelevant in the wider world'.

The same could be said of what she had to do outside the email program. If, at the end of any given workday, Hani had been asked to summarise what the focus of her work had been, she would probably have said, 'Tidying up.' Or, if she was being honest, 'Tidying up after the others.' She might never have phrased it in such concrete terms before, but after her talk with Minh it was hard to escape the realisation. It must be nice to be like Carolin, Stefan, and all the others, to wake up every morning in the knowledge that you have the best job in the world, because you're making the world a better place and that's more important than anything else.

If you believed their stories, Hani's colleagues had dedicated themselves to making the world a better place all their lives. The animal part of the world, at least. When it came to the rest of it, there didn't seem to be much that bothered them. They'd always been concerned about the meat issue — obsessed with it, in fact. They'd become vegetarian while they were still in kindergarten, gone on animal-liberation missions when they were students and later worked in editorial for vegan lifestyle magazines. Finally got really serious, came to work here with a good conscience, and created advertising campaigns so that everyone would consume more again — but in the right way.

Hani liked this last part. No one here ranted about an obscure enemy called capitalism; they wanted to improve capitalism, and that was nice, thought Hani, because no one had to flagellate themselves over it. It seemed logical to her that people would eventually show some insight, grow up, and start eating whatever they fancied. Though it didn't seem logical that they were now putting all their energy into making sure animals had a 'good life' before they ate them. What is the point of that, she secretly wondered as she checked photos of green landscapes and friendly-looking pigs for resolution and format. What on earth is the point of someone having a good life until they get eaten?

Hani was capable of anything when it came to food. She could look into a pig's eyes and admit to herself that she could tuck into this animal. She'd been able to even as a child; she'd been present when pigs were slaughtered and looked forward to the food while it was happening. Including the crackling and bone broth and black pudding — uses for leftovers that Hani's colleagues didn't even know existed before one particular contract. Hani liked to eat. She liked vegetables, meat, everything. The whole to-do about it she found a bit tedious. But there were people to whom that did matter, and who — instead of giving up meat — still ate it, but wanted to ensure vague improvements beforehand. And that was so …

Hani faltered. While she was marking as read the emails that came at the end of a chain and so didn't require an answer, she imagined that Saya would end that sentence with 'German'. That was so German. A concept formulated with such thorough logic that it lost its actual sense. So concerned about doing everything right that it missed its own joke.

How would it be, thought Hani, if I gave someone a really nice life, cherished and cared for them, and petted and stroked them, and then, in the end, ate them? Better than if I were to hit and kick them and then eat them. There is that. But hitting and kicking are things you shouldn't do to anyone, under any circumstances. You don't have to throw yourself a giant party every day for not doing that.

Anyway, 'German' isn't a characteristic. Especially not when you're Saya and you call the word 'German' an identity construct and reject it for that reason, but then always use it when you want to say something's shit.

Good job Saya didn't work for this agency, Hani thought; she'd probably have been sacked by now, if she hadn't quit immediately. Not because of the animals — Saya could be won over to any cause that made the world a better place, and even if there was something paradoxical about it, she'd accept it with a shrug. No, the thing that Saya wouldn't have been able to stand were the conversations that happened over lunch, either at the Vietnamese cafe or the vegan galette place. Hani could only stand them because she liked her colleagues, was now familiar with their quirks, and could laugh with them. And yet: these conversations often took place on another planet. That was something she realised in her very first week at the company, when the lunch conversation was about Tiny Houses, which really are tiny and might just save the planet.

At first Hani was impressed by what she heard, until the subject turned to houses in general, and two colleagues started talking expertly about prefab houses and laughing at them. How did they know so much about prefab houses? They probably knew nothing at all about them, except that you didn't really have to take them seriously as houses and that this fact was entirely incontrovertible. Prefabs were evidently the high-school dropouts of the housing world, the intensively farmed pigs of the housing world, the cut flowers from the Netherlands, the winter tomatoes from Morocco, the PET bottles of the housing world. Prefabs represented everything they'd cut out of their lives. Anyway, they all lived in beautiful pre-war apartment buildings or in old cottages outside the city, which they renovated themselves, never complaining about the ice-cold water and the tiled stoves. It was all cool. Prefabs weren't cool.

Hani realised in her first week that she would listen, learn, and keep quiet when it came to these subjects. Her parents had built their own house after their years on the estate, and this of course had a symbolic value for them: not only had they escaped hell, they'd put down new roots in Germany. They hadn't bought an existing house, because it was more difficult to get a mortgage for that at the time; they'd just built one to suit them. They'd studied catalogues of floor plans and layouts of facades with great enthusiasm, and finally chosen a house, their dream house, a prefab house.

A few weeks after the conversation about houses, they celebrated Carolin's birthday in the agency's office with a catering package that consisted of various soups. By this point, Hani had realised she'd need to find a way to deal with the lunch conversations. The soup-fest involved a lot of little bowls and one soup after another, and Hani kept stealing glances at the clock because work was piling up on her desk and she knew she was still going to be hungry even after ten bowls of soup. Her colleagues, meanwhile, were talking animatedly about a public debate that had arisen around a football match.

Some fans had insulted a player after an apparent foul by making monkey noises, and the referee simply let the game continue, which triggered weeks of discussion about racism in sport and zero consequences. Hani's colleagues were outraged, both at the incident and at the way the subsequent debate had played out in the media. They were genuinely annoyed that animals were still being used as insults, and that a society could conduct a heated debate about such an incident without even being vaguely aware that they were disregarding the dignity of animals. It made them angry that humans had no sensitivity to this form of discrimination: people outside your own 'bubble' were so ignorant in this regard you didn't even know where to start. There was no further mention of the football player.

Hani longed for her bubble, which seemed to be a different one, and started to mull over out loud to herself what spices might be in the soup, impressing everyone with her knowledge of herbs. That went down well; herbs were almost as important as animals. Hani's grandmother had taught her about herbs and spices, and reviving this niche knowledge and putting it to use was something she now enjoyed. She wanted to be able to go on laughing and beaming with the others, and stop imagining what Saya would do in her place: bang her fist on the table, quit her job, slam the door behind her, and disappear forever.

Hani took a deep breath and realised that there was no more mindless sorting of emails to do and she would have to start her actual work. Thorsten crossed her mind: what did Thorsten look like, again? She decided to find out later — and not on her work computer. She would do it in her lunchbreak, or en route to the loo, on her phone. Though actually, why not now?

Hani took the device out of her handbag and saw that Saya had sent her a message. *Worst hangover of my life, but man, thanks for a great evening, I really needed that.* Hani was pleased and responded with a heart, though she could see that Saya was already writing something else.

She was putting Thorsten's name into the search engine when Saya's next message arrived. *It felt good to talk to someone about all that shit. Thank you for listening and for your support.* Hani stared at the message and at the Thorstens she'd found, who of course were all the wrong Thorstens, because when you put the name of a photographer into a search engine, what comes up are pages of his photos and not all that many photos of the photographer himself.

What could Saya mean by that? Thank you for listening. But all three of them had listened to each other, beer after shot after beer, laughed, talked, tried to drown out the cheesy radio station. What shit was Saya talking about, exactly? What support? This time,

Hani responded with three hearts and put the phone down, her work ethic preventing her from devoting any more time to Saya or Thorsten.

If Hani had given all this some more thought, she might have realised that Saya didn't mean what had gone on in the pub. That Saya meant what had happened after the pub. On the way home, which Hani couldn't properly remember and didn't consider now, either. In the state they were in, it had taken forever, and Saya had got all the shit off her chest and found Hani to be a scarily good listener who didn't argue with a single thing she said. Hani just nodded and nodded and finally wrapped her arms around Saya in a long, fierce hug. Her mind had already been in bed. She hadn't listened to Saya, and had now forgotten that she hadn't listened. Even so, it cheered her right up to know that she'd made Saya feel good.

Hani could hear Carolin talking to Stefan in the corridor. They were having a conversation about a contract, a conversation that in Hani's opinion they should have been having in one of the offices, not in the corridor. Nothing had a proper place here. When Hani had decided to pursue office management, it was still called administration, and one way or another she'd chosen it because the work seemed to have good boundaries. You would seldom have to do overtime, and you'd primarily be communicating, sitting on the radiator and becoming the boss's closest confidante. How pleasant, how safe, she'd thought at the time.

Carolin and Stefan were talking about an agricultural business that was planning to make every single step for every single head of beef cattle accessible online, over years, so that you'd become part of that animal's life and could be certain that everything in it had been done right. Stefan was telling Carolin about an idea that had come to him in the night, and which he'd discussed at length with the other three members of the team the day before — an idea that would mean completely changing the current concept once again, but also fundamentally improving it. Carolin's voice sounded tired, as if she wasn't convinced by the substance of what he was saying, but wasn't about to argue with him and thereby with the other three as well.

Hani's own name came up too often for her liking in this conversation that she wasn't involved in; she kept pricking up her ears because, of course, it felt like they were addressing her, but they were probably just talking about various tasks they'd give her, not larger areas of responsibility to which she'd have to contribute ideas. In conversations between two colleagues, you should only hear your name mentioned that often if you're the boss of the whole company, Hani thought. It was tempting to imagine herself as the secret boss, but her salary wasn't high enough for that.

Hani suspected that the conversation in the corridor was gradually nearing its end. Carolin agreed with Stefan, though it was clear that she thought what he had in mind was nothing like what the farmer wanted. What good does having a flat hierarchy do, Hani thought; who benefits from everyone eventually agreeing on something just so they don't have to keep talking about it?

Yesterday, she'd tried to defend her colleagues to Minh. 'But they're all so incredibly nice,' she'd said. 'You don't get that kind of working environment everywhere.' Minh hadn't said anything, which probably meant they had different definitions of 'nice'. The memory of their conversation was starting to get on Hani's nerves, to the extent that she flirted with the idea of deleting Minh's number on principle.

'I'll just pass that on to Hani,' she heard Stefan saying. Oh, great. Whatever had just been decided out there clearly meant more work for her; that was always the way when a concept had been changed again at short notice. She sighed, but only briefly, because a second later Stefan was standing in the doorway. Hani smiled.

We watched TV. While Hani was updating her to-do list with all the tasks that Stefan's revolutionary idea had generated, and the rest of the city's inhabitants were distributing themselves around the streets and their workplaces, Saya and I lay on the sofa staring at the television with the sound off.

'TV? Don't you have streaming services?' Saya asked, pressing the button on the remote for a popular streaming platform, which only produced a blue screen.

'The wi-fi isn't good enough,' I said. A long, boring story that you could spend hours on in the kitchen of a shared flat. Routers that stopped working, old routers that had to be exhumed, a poor signal, and no one ever calling someone from the phone company out, because somehow you just learnt to live with the slow, old wi-fi. Unless you wanted to stream anything.

So you might say that our internet situation is to blame for everything. That instead of having a meltdown today, Saya would have been relaxed and even-tempered if she'd known she could just come back to my place and distract herself with the positive feelings that the end of every episode and the start of the next released in her. And right now, I'd much rather be distracting myself with box sets instead of writing — or did you think I was enjoying this?

We were sitting in front of the TV, then, and I had to explain to Saya that there was no streaming, and she looked incredulous.

'So you watch actual TV? Like people used to?'

'Yes, like people did in the war,' I said, shaking out my sofa cushions in the hope it would make things more comfortable. Muted light shone through the closed red living room curtains, and although all the windows were open, it was warm and sticky. It was a hot summer day that we were deliberately ignoring, despite Hani's advice that I should distract Saya with sunbathing.

Sometimes, when it was really hot outside and I was sitting in the flat and everyone else had gone to the lake, I would have liked to message Saya. Something like, 'I'm missing you right now,' or, 'Today would be a perfect day for watching TV with you,' or something. But we didn't write kitschy stuff like that to each other; we'd never started, and to start now would be to break our unspoken pact that we knew what we meant to one another without all that.

We drank tepid tap water, and Saya channel-surfed. First she said, 'Cool, remote control,' and then she started to get impatient. At first I thought it was because the only things on TV were boring documentaries and the tenth repeat of sexist sitcoms. 'So white, TV is so white,' she said, and just then, unfortunately, she was right. 'That's why I only watch stuff online now — at least there are people like us there. What must the Nazis be watching? Do they put the TV on all day and end up hollow?'

'Maybe they watch things online, too, and end up hollow. They're probably watching different things to you. Things with white people in them, because that makes them feel all warm and cosy.'

'Hmm. Look, this is still on,' said Saya. She'd stumbled across a German telenovela that had been going since our childhood: white aristocrats in the countryside with horses and scandals. We used to love it, and rediscovered our enthusiasm at once; ten minutes in, we were idolising the new female lead with our whole hearts, and we watched one episode after another. We immediately grasped the relationships between the characters, empathised with them, were able to laugh at them when we felt like it, and were eager to know what would happen next.

At some point, we started speaking when the actors spoke, overlaying the bad dialogue with our own, and then we turned the sound off altogether to put our own words in their mouths. Saya's voice was very earnest; what she'd come up with for the people on TV was too important to her, and I was the one who couldn't make the actors give her a proper answer because I was lying on the sofa laughing. Saya laughed too, but not so much that she missed her next line, and sometimes, when it was clear that I really was laughing too much to advance the dialogue, she would start laughing, too, and eventually we were both laughing and couldn't stop, and then the door opened.

Robin was standing there in his boxer shorts, with no top on, which never usually happened here — he must have stumbled in straight from bed, his hair more tousled than I'd ever seen it. He actually looked pretty funny, like a dreaming schoolboy, but he clearly wasn't in a funny kind of mood. 'Are the two of you always this shitty, or are you making a special effort today?' he asked, shielding his eyes with one hand as if even our curtain-darkened room was too bright for him. He spoke so quietly that the words sounded even more threatening than they already were.

We stopped laughing at once, and because the TV was muted there was a minute of silence between the three of us in which Saya and I looked at Robin and he looked at us. 'Are we being too loud?' I asked eventually. I felt sorry for him, sorry about everything, but I had no idea what was up with nice Robin.

A long thread dangled from his boxer shorts. I wondered for a second if he'd noticed I was looking at the thread, and thought how I hated it when men looked at my breasts and genuinely assumed I wouldn't notice. Looking at the thread, I wondered whether men also noticed when you accidentally and without any meaningful reason at all looked at such ridiculous places as a thread on their leg. Why shouldn't they notice? They do have eyes. And yet: they wouldn't, because you don't have to notice things you don't care about. I do care about people looking at my breasts, because people who look at your breasts indiscreetly might also touch you indiscreetly, and people who think that's okay are found in so many innocuous places that you can never stop being on high alert, and the memories of it are always on your mind. I don't know what it did to Robin, when I stared at the thread that was hanging down his hairy thigh. A white thread, emerging from a pair of light-blue boxer shorts. Why do men wear so much fabric on their arses, when it's much more comfortable to keep pants as minimal as possible?

'I can't believe you're even asking me that, Kasih, it's super ignorant,' Robin said then, seeming not to have found the business with the thread all that important for the time being, if he'd noticed it at all. 'You're well aware I've got my exam today, I don't really need to tell you again for you to show me a bit more consideration, do I?'

I would love to write that Robin was shouting and banging his fist against the doorframe, that he yelled at me with his face so close to mine that I was staring into his bloodshot eyes and fearing for my life. But obviously I wouldn't live with someone like that. Robin is nice, and he sounded angry and firm when he said what he said, but still like a normal person.

'You were ridiculously loud when you came home last night, and then you've had the fucking TV on since first thing this morning and didn't even put the volume down. And now you're laughing really loudly, thinking of no one but yourselves.'

Saya and I were still staring at him. We really hadn't thought about him for a single second. 'You're completely right. Sorry,' I said.

Robin took a few deep breaths. He seemed not to have any more experience of dealing with a situation like this than we did, because he didn't even know what to do with my apology. 'Not cool,' he said, pulling the door closed behind him. He looked sad.

'Not cool,' Saya said quietly, giving me exaggerated puppy-dog eyes, which still had a sheen on them from her tears of laughter. 'Not cool, Kasih, for you not to spend day and night thinking that the white man has an important exam, and arranging your life accordingly.'

'Tss,' I went, staring at the TV.

Robin wasn't a white man. No, actually, Robin was the epitome of a white man. So white that he didn't even know he was white until recently. But he was still in the right. Because sometimes, Saya, it really doesn't matter if someone is a white man or a blue cockatoo. Mostly it does. But sometimes it doesn't.

'Yeah, but you always want everyone to show *you* some consideration, I think,' I said to Saya.

'Do I?'

'Yes, constantly, everywhere — on the plane, on the U-Bahn, you're always angry and going on about no one being considerate towards you, and when someone says that to you for once, you make fun of them?'

'Yes,' said Saya, 'because it was funny. Your flatmate is funny. Does he always walk around half-naked? You know, some people really don't appreciate you doing that without first asking them if it's something they want to see. You might talk to him about that. And then he can start on about consideration.'

I had no idea what else there was to say about the whole business. I wanted us to be able to barricade ourselves into my secure cave without Saya having to get annoyed about something, but apparently that wasn't possible. More than anything, I wanted to protect Saya from the things that made her angry, but quite honestly, Robin was right, and I couldn't pretend he was the one with a screw loose just because Saya was going through a bad patch.

'Robin lives here, and he can do what he wants,' I said, thinking that this was the most democratic thing to say, and yet it still felt like I was stabbing Saya in the back.

'Why should I have to enable that? *I* can't do what I want. Not here, not at home, not outside, not anywhere in the world. When I say for the thousandth time that I'd like to be shown some consideration, too, pretty please, then for the thousandth time no one is going to hear it. But good for your housemate, it must be nice to go through life with people doing that for him, with people adapting themselves to his needs. Good for him. But it's also unfair.'

Something about the situation actually did feel unfair. All at once I had a vision of myself lying in bed at night, desperate to be asleep, only someone was making a noise. Someone bellowing in the stairwell, the sound echoing through the flat; someone smoking underneath my window with his mates, singing and laughing. Someone putting the stereo on at four in the morning. It might be Robin and his girlfriend coming back from a night out and slamming the front door behind them rather than closing it quietly as you learn to do when you grow up in a rented flat. Or one of my other flatmates vacuuming at 7.00 am when everyone else was still in bed.

I thought about all these situations and how, instead of going and launching into some angry tirade like Robin just had, I lay in bed feeling annoyed and merely imagined telling them what I thought of them. I began to envy Robin and to curse Saya for the fact that I did kind of understand where she was coming from. But remonstrating with people like Robin just because they do manage to complain also seemed ridiculous.

'Shall we just keep playing?' I asked, meaning our dubbing game.

Saya put the sound back on, seeming to ignore the fact that I'd just used words I hadn't said to her for years. 'Keep playing' had once been such a vitally necessary thing. You were really deep into something, with Barbies, with cuddly toys, with something, with various professions, and then you were interrupted. Afterwards, someone would use the magic words, 'keep playing', and the interruption was forgotten. It took a moment to collect yourself and pick up again where you'd left off. You had to find your way back into the role of the Barbie or the lawyer, and for a minute the game felt alien and new, or sometimes just boring. But you kept playing anyway, because eventually, the game would gather pace again. Everyone knows that.

Saya changed the channel. 'I don't want to now. I'm going to look for special bulletins on the trial. Okay?'

'You're looking for what now?'

'You know: the trial starts today. There might be images of it already, they're allowed to film in court at the start of the day.'

I had no idea when and where this trial was taking place, which one of this Nazi group was in the dock, or exactly what for — and I was glad, to some extent, that Hani had mentioned it, so I didn't look completely clueless. I could guess the enormous significance this first day of an apparently 'watertight' legal case had, and that a lot of people, including Saya, had been waiting for this beginning for days and months.

That day, yesterday, Saya's status update was the now-legendary post by a lawyer for the victims' families, who had been subjected to racism herself and whose words seemed to resonate with a lot of people: *Germany, up until today you have failed. Germany, from today you can try to come to terms with your failure. From today, we will try to trust you.*

These lines went viral at the opening of the trial and were shared and reposted endlessly, and I knew so little about it all, not even the name of the lawyer. The only thing I knew was that these Nazi chats had been leaked a few days earlier, and that journalists, and the lawyers for the joint plaintiffs, meaning the parents, husbands, wives, and children of the dead, had something to do with making the messages accessible to everyone. Saya knew all this. She knew the names of the people who'd been killed and the relatives who'd spoken out in public; she knew what the murderers had done and which charges had been brought against them.

'There they are!' she cried delightedly. You could see the defendants entering the courtroom, their eyes on the floor. One was hiding his face behind a folder, one had his hood up, the other two turned their faces away. There was an indistinct hum of voices; camera bulbs flashed all around the room. You couldn't really see people, only bodies. Bodies of murderers.

I didn't want to see them and turned to Saya, whose eyes were shining. As if we hadn't just almost argued, as if she wasn't seeing horror personified in this courtroom. The images were already starting to come round again, but then hardly anything had happened today apart from the trial opening. The program, which really was a kind of special bulletin on the trial, now turned to the lives of the murderers, their childhood in neglected, run-down places, the waystations of their bleak biographies. Saya looked spellbound. And for a minute I was grateful to the Nazis for getting Saya and me out of that weird discussion about Robin and his bare chest, but of course that gratitude was all kinds of wrong. Much like the fact that Saya's fascination with the Nazis unsettled me more than the Nazis themselves.

'He was, like, the intellectual of the group,' she explained in passing. 'He only joined recently.' He looked very young — juvenile, almost, and like someone who would play the word juvenile for all it was worth. 'Her, that one there! She lured the women into the traps, gained their trust and stuff. On the outside, by doing a lot of chatting on the stairs, she made them look like normal tenants, and the neighbours believed it.'

I pretended to be listening, because that was the only favour I could do Saya right now. The Nazis looked like people you wouldn't care about. One even looked quite nice, and one was kind of attractive — I couldn't associate anything worth knowing with them and was worrying that Saya might work out I hadn't even learned the names of these murderers. They looked so random.

The male voice guiding us through the program was outlining who the members of this group were. Everything about their biographies was boring. When it finally moved on to the murders, I considered leaving the room. It hurt to look at the photos of the victims. They looked so painfully normal. Normal and real.

'This girl here was murdered after her school leavers' ball,' said Saya when the photo of a young woman appeared. 'They did serious research into which of the leavers was some bloody foreigner, so they could murder her after their certificates had been given out, after the party.'

'Really?' I asked. I had been prepared for anything after our own leavers' ball, except for someone taking any interest in it. Even then, the idea that it might motivate someone to kill would have been unthinkable.

'Right outside the school hall, can you imagine that?' said Saya, and all I wanted to do was get away.

My phone was in my room, I realised, and I had a sudden urge to check whether Lukas had messaged me. He might have cancelled our meeting later, and if not, I wanted to have a shower and get ready, sort my eyebrows out. I needed to look good to meet Lukas, or I'd feel uncomfortable. I wanted to get out of this room right away. Saya seemed to be somewhere else already in any case.

'Saya,' I said, 'I need to go and get ready, I've got plans for today.'

Saya didn't even take her eyes off the TV. 'Oh yeah,' she said, 'you're seeing Lukas.'

How could she speak with such disdain about my meeting Lukas and with such fascination about Nazis?

'Just imagine, though, if after our leavers' ball, someone had …'

'Saya, I just really need to find my phone,' I said.

'Go on, then,' said Saya. 'I wanted to have a little nap anyway. All they're doing is showing pictures I've seen a thousand times before.'

Maybe, I thought, you'd be better off if you'd never seen them at all. But I didn't say anything, just walked out of the room and left Saya alone with the Nazis. It felt weirdly like I was doing her a favour.

∧^∧

I've just taken a break from writing, for a few minutes. You didn't notice, because without me generously doling out information you'd be screwed now; without me, you wouldn't be getting any of this. You need me, but I can also fool you without you noticing. The keyboard can hold its tongue while I scream and yell and freak out without you ever knowing. But I'm making an effort at transparency here, so of course you'll get to hear every detail of what I'm doing — otherwise I might as well give up right now.

I took a little break from writing and tried to focus on the people who were killed, and failed once again. I looked for and found videos in which the relatives tell their humiliating stories about police investigations that yielded nothing and were also suffused with racism. I wasn't strong enough to listen to them; I forwarded straight to the end, to the moment they take up the words of the lawyer and say that they hope they'll be able to trust the justice system again after this trial. They sound convinced.

I looked at photos of the people who were murdered: twenty-two photos of twenty-two different people; a row of young women and a row of older men. The Nazis never explained why they chose these people. Or at least they never explained to anyone who wasn't a Nazi themselves. When you find the photos on the internet, you get the feeling your own family album is suddenly online. I don't know why. I don't know these people. They have black hair, dark eyes, and they come from somewhere. All things I could be entirely indifferent to, but which, as soon as they were killed, and not me and my friends and our fathers, suddenly make me look at these strangers like people I know. That's why I can't look at them and that's probably also why Saya couldn't stop looking at them. Especially the young woman in her prom dress, who, if you like, does actually look like Saya in her prom dress. Except they're not similar at all: different hair, different build, completely different faces. And Saya never wore a dress like that.

Our leavers' ball was lovely. Which is to say, Saya's, Shaghayegh's, and my leavers' ball. I'd almost forgotten it was Shaghayegh's ball, too, because we didn't see much of her that evening. We no longer saw much of her in our breaks and free periods, either. She spent them with two girls who liked to wear white, the three of them mostly doing homework, higher-level biology and things. Or they'd sit outside, roll up their sleeves and their jumpers, and sunbathe, talking about which gym offered which aerobics classes, and thinking they were so grown-up that until just now I'd somehow assumed they were already adults back then. That's why I have no idea where Shaghayegh was sitting during the ball.

I was sitting with Saya and her parents. Both were wearing black, her father in a suit and her mother in something with shoulder pads and gold chains. They sat there, sincerely proud of their clever daughter, but also not really knowing what to do with themselves. They hardly got up all evening, and our little group were the last ones at the buffet, because there was such a stampede at first that they just remained seated, and drank mineral water all evening. When the waiter who'd been hired for the event came round to fill the glasses, he first had to put down the wine bottle and then refill the water glasses, even if only a few sips had been taken. Who drinks mineral water by the litre, I thought. But then they did have to drink something.

Saya and I each had a glass of sparkling wine, which we nursed for as long as her parents were there, partly as a slight provocation, because we knew that Saya's parents were refusing to acknowledge the new order that would prevail from today for everyone involved. To acknowledge that, from this moment on, we could make our own decisions about what we drank. Which was ridiculous, because if Saya's parents hadn't been there, we would have been at least three beers down by this point and wouldn't have bothered with the sparkling wine.

After the exam certificates had been officially given out and the speeches made, the four of us sat and ate the oily, salty remains of the buffet, while the other families had long since started moving towards the bar. We pushed overcooked peas onto our forks in silence. The reservations that Saya's parents had about German cuisine were once again proved correct, and the pair of them were wondering how much longer they'd have to stay.

Saya sat beside me, making no effort to start a conversation, although she was the link between her parents and me — but then what did we have to say to each other? I saw other parents recognising one another and saying hello; I heard them laughing indulgently at how grown-up their children were now, and talking about the speeches that the students, teachers, and principal had made. I saw the boys from our class, in their suits, standing together in groups of five or six, suddenly looking slightly threatening. I saw the few couples in our year having their photographs taken — worst-case scenario: with a teacher — and looking like they were standing on a red carpet in a storm of paparazzi flashes. Everyone, in fact, was constantly having their photos taken with each other, because everyone had bought evening wear specially for this occasion and had their hair done, and of course that had to be captured for posterity.

And when I write that Saya and I hadn't known you needed to get all glammed up like that, it sounds ludicrous even to me: we weren't outsiders, recent arrivals, novices. We'd just dismissed the talk of dresses and hairdos as superficial crap, from which we would naturally distance ourselves. We thought it would be like always: the show-offs overdo it, the majority of people are normal, and Saya and I make an effort to be a little bit cooler than normal. Which meant that I was at least wearing my black flares and leather boots rather than trainers, and Saya's neckline was lower than usual, which in Saya's case, meaning in the case of a well-defined collarbone, also fulfilled the function of jewellery.

I don't remember how much thought we gave to this stuff at the time, but these were situations in which we felt very acutely the lack of knowledge from parents, older siblings, older cousins that we might have fallen back on when it came to something as basic as:

how formal is a formal party for teenagers actually going to be? We weren't alone in this, at least: the outfits of at least five other people bore witness to a similarly leaky spot in their biographies, to their own failure to clue themselves up about the fashion at leavers' balls.

But as different as we were, we all spent the whole evening collectively waiting for the parents to leave so that we could celebrate normally, like we usually did, with the rest of our year.

Saya and I were also waiting for Hani, who would give the whole thing some down-to-earth normality. We didn't yet know, of course, that Hani would turn up in an evening gown that would put the dresses of all the other girls there to shame, but that's another boring story. Just as boring as the fact that, later, everyone was so drunk that no one still looked red-carpety, but more as if they'd been to a riotous fancy-dress party and ended up in a downmarket hotel.

In this company, Saya and I finally came up trumps with our un-ruinable outfits. We danced with the outsiders, we danced with the smart kids, with the ones we'd always envied, and the ones who had never been nice to us. We talked to people we'd never talked to before, and laughed with them about the people who usually laughed at everyone else.

And in the end, we took photos as well, with big digital cameras and small analogue cameras, because obviously no one had a smartphone yet, and we were in that transition phase when people still thought the digital revolution might just be a short-lived fad. All our photos were of the three of us — Saya, Hani, and me — taken with the camera of a person whose name I can no longer remember and who drunkenly assured us that yeah, yeah, deffo, he'd send them all to us, which of course he never did.

At the end of the night, when everyone was saying there was nothing left to drink, we found another crate of white wine and went off at regular intervals to hide with a few select others and help ourselves from it. As we got drunker and drunker, the hall started to empty out, because who stays around when they're sobering up and alcohol is calling to you from elsewhere.

At the very end, someone gave Saya the key to the hall, because the next day the clean-up team was supposed to come in and clean up. That was what students did back then. Ridiculous. Saya and I were on the clean-up team, because everyone had to join a team. Cleaning up was the least popular job in the whole affair, only a few volunteered to do it, so in the end we'd taken pity on them.

It was a bit sad to see the hall so decorated and colourful and empty. Saya, Hani, and I sat in a corner, feeling a little disappointed after all, when everyone had gone.

'Is anyone else coming?' Hani asked us, and we let out a wine-drunk laugh and repeated her words several times, and Hani of course didn't get it. 'Was that it, then, or what?' she asked, looking at her watch, a delicate special-occasion wristwatch decorated with glittering gemstones, and then said, 'But it's only half-past four. Is that how short these Gymnasium balls are? You spend so much time studying for those exams, and so little time celebrating afterwards?'

We laughed for a while longer, until it became clear that there was no point going home, because the clean-up team had to start work soon. So we sobered up by starting to collect the glasses, rinse them, and pick up the broken ones. When the other people from the clean-up team arrived, there was still a lot to do, they didn't see how much we'd done already, and so we just carried on with them. Hani in her ballgown, although it wasn't even her ball.

At my brother's ball, I did things differently. I told my parents you had to go. It wasn't something that some people went to and others didn't. I told my brother he needed to buy a suit and get a haircut.

I sat with my parents in the family rows, and my brother sat right at the front with the other leavers. When they called people up to collect their exam certificates, his name, our name, was mispronounced, as expected. I don't know if that was the same for me, but now, with my tired parents beside me, it was suddenly embarrassing, although there was really nothing I could do about it. I was also embarrassed when the prizes for the highest grades, then the second- and third-highest, were given out. When three teenagers we'd never heard of before went up to the front, because we had no idea what the people in my brother's class were called. It was strange, too, to watch the other proud parents clapping their children, while my own brother probably only went down the university-entrance route by chance.

But the strangest thing was seeing the girl accepting the prize for the second-best grades and then going back to her seat, with her flowers and her trophy, to join her fellow students. She looked lovely, uncomplicated and warm, and she congratulated the other two prize winners, which was a huge thing for someone her age to do — or any age, I thought. Her dress suited her, and her hair looked like she'd done it herself, but because she had lovely curls, it didn't matter what she did with them anyway. She sat happily in her chair, following the rest of the action on stage. Live orchestral music and speeches of thanks and more the-future-begins tomorrow nonsense. Then she turned halfway round, as if she knew what was about to happen, and a boy appeared behind her, maybe a little older than her, who laid a hand on her shoulder, kissed her, and handed her a glass of sparkling wine. She took the glass in the way adults take glasses from people, smiled at him, raised the glass towards her parents, and then turned back to the stage. And I wondered how many worlds lay between that gesture, that girl, and Hani, Saya, and me.

As we were lining up for the buffet later on, I asked my brother if he was on the clean-up team, too, or what other part of the event he was involved in, and he said, 'Clean-up team? We're paying some Polish people to do that,' at which I felt like puking, and not just because there were overcooked peas in a lake of oily brine again.

I will admit, I just made that bit up. My brother didn't go down the university route, but I think if he had, that's exactly how his leavers' ball would have gone. Though I doubt my parents would actually have come with us. That pea-buffet came at a steep price, and cooking was something my mum could do herself to mark the occasion, thank you very much.

But I want to take the made-up story a bit further, to say that my brother's geography teacher, who was also my geography teacher, was standing behind my dad in the buffet queue and thought this would be a great opportunity to get to know him a little, while my dad thought the opportunity here was to eat at least as much as he'd paid for.

'I've been wanting to meet you for a long time!' said the teacher, and my dad was sure the teacher must have mistaken him for someone else.

'Why?' he asked, looking at the gleaming red meat in the hotplate trays. Because of course he had no idea who this unknown young man with the large glasses was.

'Well, let me tell you,' the teacher said — let's call him Mr Geo. 'In class, when we were looking at climate change, we compared water use per head per household, and your son gave us figures that not even my wife and I could get below. Then we wrote the number on the board, and you must know, I told the students, look at this, it's possible to reduce your water use, we don't have to live like lords the whole time. The other numbers were horrendous, of course, as you can imagine.'

'What?' my father asked, fishing a lemon out of the meat because he couldn't bring himself not to take anything from these trays.

'So — great stuff!' Mr Geo said now, a little louder and slower, suddenly worried that my father might be having trouble understanding him. 'It's great that you consciously managed to reduce water use in your family!'

My father looked at Mr Geo, nodded, nodded, and nodded, and then, when he finally reached the schnitzel, picked up the tongs, put one on his plate, and said, 'It's expensive, water, it's so expensive, if you don't take care.'

Mr Geo also nodded, hastily, to disguise how fully unexpected this reply had been, and then the two men had no more to say to one another and never spoke again as long as they lived.

I know, I've already revealed that they never spoke in the first place. But if the opportunity had arisen, the conversation would have gone exactly like that, I swear. My dad definitely had the potential to become best friends with various ecowarriors I've met, because he did all the things they approved of out of sheer lack of money. My dad even liked dogs, which you could tell from the way he always smiled at them and tried to befriend them on the U-Bahn. Mostly without even clocking who these dogs belonged to, so he didn't notice when the Nazis who were with the dogs weren't wild about him flirting with their four-legged friends.

I could go on telling funny stories about my dad now, and eventually someone would say, 'Look, this is where your strengths lie, in describing your dog-loving, accidental-ecowarrior father — just cut the rest and keep writing about him!'

'That's a wonderful idea,' I'd reply, 'why didn't I think of that myself? The scene with the father is actually the best thing I've written so far, and the funniest, too — my dad's a total comedian. Forget the rest, I'll write a novel about my dad and we'll turn it into a film with Christian Ulmen in the title role.'

'But Ulmen is a proper, homegrown, socks-and-sandals German, no one will buy that,' they'll say then.

And I'll say, 'True. Then let's just use Moritz Bleibtreu, like always, he's a real chameleon, looks like he could come from anywhere, and he's funny, too. Deal?'

'Deal.'

And I'll get rich and famous and thank my father.

But now back to what happened in reality.

In reality, the television was still showing the images of the murder victims. In reality, I was, however, far more interested in the fact that Lukas had messaged me, maybe sounding a bit distant, but confirming our meeting and suggesting a particular cafe, and I was so full of adrenaline my heartrate wouldn't calm down.

I was sitting by my bedroom window, as I am now, plucking my eyebrows. Next door were Saya (asleep) and the TV (on). Next door were Robin and his tablet. All somehow a long way off. Maybe right now, Saya was dreaming of a reconciliation with Robin.

But Saya wasn't asleep. She was lying on the sofa, her cheek pressed into the fat cushion, feeling the springs inside this ancient piece of furniture sticking into her ribs. Her eyes were closed. The alcohol from the previous night pulsed against her forehead from the inside, and she kept her eyes closed because she thought the most sensible thing to do was fall asleep. She knew that when she woke up and saw me again in a few hours, we'd just carry on as if nothing had happened. Saya's facial muscles relaxed.

What *had* happened, anyway? She'd made it clear to me that there was nothing in this world I had to just accept, and one day I'd understand that and admit she was right. Saya concentrated on the words coming from the television, because that murmur was the best sleeping pill there was. After a while, the theme music for the news came on, which she hated. It was kind of synonymous with her mother's stern voice, which was deployed in various situations, but especially at the start of the news. Because you had to be quiet during the news, and to little Saya that always felt like you had to stop existing.

The newsreader greeted Saya, and Saya opened her eyes for a second to see what she looked like. White. That's what she'd thought. She closed her eyes and tried to keep following the words, to help her fall asleep. The best way to vanquish a hangover like this one was to sleep. Maybe she should have done that straight after breakfast — then the blond flatmate wouldn't have got so hysterical.

Hysterical. A word, Saya thought, that should be used more often in relation to men, to show how outrageously exaggerated it was. People are never really hysterical.

Saya opened her eyes and realised she'd missed the top story about the trial; the report couldn't have been that in-depth, then. The newsreader was now speaking live to an expert in Washington. Saya's right eye opened tentatively and closed again a second later. The expert was white. Things were happening in Washington, and Saya imagined the expert saying that the US president had been hysterical. Saya tried to imagine the hysterical US president. In her fantasy, he'd just flipped the table over and was crouching Rumpelstiltskin-fashion on his executive chair, flailing his arms around. His face bright red and twisted in a yell. But even that couldn't be called hysterical, thought Saya. That was aggressive — which was what you said about men. So what would a hysterical US president look like?

The newsreader now turned to the stock markets. It was the part of the news that Saya really never understood, and it would probably send her straight to sleep. One last glance and off to no-man's-land, she thought, and there was her third tick: white. Check. Three women in five minutes, all from one group: privileged. Saya turned her back to the TV. Why did she have to keep checking over and over that what she already knew was still true?

Meanwhile, in the flat above ours, a woman was sitting in front of her own TV, doing her tax return, and following the program with half an ear. It was also a long time since she'd last watched the news on a big screen rather than on her phone, and her sole reason for doing so now was a desire to distract herself from this mind-numbing data entry with something smart. She smiled when the stock-market item came on. What a great quota, she thought. Three people in the space of five minutes in such prominent positions, all from one group: the disadvantaged. On the news programs of her childhood, women had done the weather report, at most. Today, they were much more present.

In the flat downstairs, it didn't even cross Saya's mind to be pleased about that; she'd already turned her back to the television. That was an end to it for her. Her thoughts mingled with the words she was hearing, were displaced by them, and dissolved into the remaining alcohol in her system. She fell asleep, and the thick fog of news language descended over the images of hysterical politicians: Syria, Federal Chancellor, budget, anniversary, refugees, right to a family life, upper limit, borders.

Saya heard the recordings from the Bundestag — and she didn't hear them, as well. Anyway, they would only confirm what she already knew: they draw a distinction there. There are Germans and there are refugees. We don't exist in this world. Here we're neither Germans nor refugees; we aren't newsreaders or experts. We're some kind of joker in the pack, and they don't know if they can use us for anything.

The last words that Saya caught were 'Minister of the Interior'. Then she fell into her sleep paralysis, and I would really love to know whether all the words left her head again a few minutes later, when she flung her sleeping body into the back of the sofa and felt its springs poking her in the ribs. Whether injuring her own body helped, and whether the words 'Minister of the Interior' at least had the decency to be the first to leave Saya's body.

Saya didn't hear that the program ended with some breaking news on the trial. Saya slept and got the update like most other people, as a push notification on her phone. One of the Nazi women had been the first to take the stand; she was the only one of the terrorist group who wanted to make a statement. She'd spoken about the murders and stressed that they hadn't been racially motivated. That right-wing people were capable of committing crimes for reasons that weren't specifically right-wing. That the media had jumped to conclusions and was judging them purely on their political persuasion. The media totally freaked out after that, saying the case now had to be looked at from a completely new angle.

Saya saw this on her phone when she woke up, while I was with Lukas and Hani was still at work. She was alone and didn't talk to anyone about it. She had the impression it wouldn't particularly interest me, and she didn't want to message Hani at the office again. When Saya read the update, she was as powerless as she'd been when she first heard about the murders. This woman could just make those claims, even though the whole world knew she was lying. She trumpeted a lie out into the world, and it would be described as a defence strategy and not a lie, although any idiot could see through it. Even if the judge wasn't going to believe this woman in the end, the lie was out in the world, and as a rule — Saya had observed this often enough before — people did give the far right's lies a tiny bit of credence, no matter if they came from politicians or from murderers on trial.

Saya made the photos of the murder victims into her phone wallpaper and wrote me a message: *When are you back? Hope it goes well with Lukas. Even if he is a wanker. At least don't be a wanker yourself, and get drunk with me today.* I replied with three hearts, because I'd got the same push notification and was wishing that, just this once, the world's push notifications could be about what was happening to us, and nothing else. 'After the split: Lukas and Kasih are meeting up!' they would say. And underneath: 'Saya's thoughts are with Kasih.'

Lukas was sitting at one of the outdoor tables, looking at his phone. Because you have to look at something while you're waiting for someone, I thought. Or because he urgently had to message someone, his new girlfriend, maybe. She might have just asked if she should make dinner for him this evening, I thought a second later, angrily, suddenly convinced that his new girlfriend always cooked amazing meals for him, and he could just enjoy her food without having to lift a finger, and both of them were happy with this arrangement. I was so sure about this that it made me hate her, the new girlfriend, even more than I did already.

I pulled the folding chair — a light one made of wood — back from the table quite forcefully so that I could sit down. I'd hoped jerking it like that would make some noise, but unfortunately it didn't, and then I hoped that my disappointment over this wasn't too obvious.

Lukas broke into a sudden smile. 'Hello,' he said a little too quickly, putting his phone down at once, as if he'd just been looking at some dodgy website. He hugged me across the little table, which as expected was not a particularly elegant manoeuvre.

I sat down, got my phone out, and placed it on the table beside his. I have no idea why — I mean, he already knew I had a phone — but maybe I wanted to put us on an equal footing from the start. Maybe that had secretly been my problem in this relationship. But there was no sense in going over old ground now, because by this point Lukas's hormones were partying elsewhere.

We made a handsome pair, the two of us at that table, I was sure of it. The cafe dog, who was loitering outside the building with a mournful look on his face, immediately came and lay down in the shade of our table, like we were his family. A small, taciturn family.

'Kasih, I'm so glad this worked out, us seeing one another — I mean, I really value it,' said Lukas, and as he said the last half of the sentence, his face changed, like he'd suddenly remembered all the guilt he'd piled on himself by talking, laughing, messaging, and making eyes at the wonderful woman next door. Like he'd forgotten all that until a minute ago and only just recalled how much he should hate himself for it. For bumping into her in the university canteen and having lunch together, for going for a walk with her and — oh, how should I know exactly how it all started? Maybe his expression also changed because just then the putrid smell of the idyllic canal wafted over to us.

Lukas fell silent, and I looked calmly into his small, bright eyes, envying him once again for his naturally curling eyelashes, and making an effort not to look afflicted, but like a person enduring laryngeal cancer with dignity. There are these women in films who fall terminally ill at an advanced age and then, bald-headed, find their true strength, and everyone admires them for it. That's the energy I was projecting, on this small wooden chair.

'It's good to see you, too,' I said with a very noble smile. 'How are you?'

Lukas considered this, snorted, looked at his phone, as if the answer was written there, and then looked away again instantly, as if the answer he'd just seen wasn't meant for public (i.e. my) consumption. 'I think I've had too much coffee today, but otherwise pretty good.'

'Too much coffee, is that possible?' I asked, though in reality I was thinking, what a neat answer.

'Well, for a person who takes their coffee like you do, probably not, but if you drink proper coffee, then yes,' he said, and I laughed, because at a stroke I'd gone back to being someone he knew well enough to take the piss out of. I liked that role much better than the bald-headed sick woman.

'Then maybe my coffee strategy is actually superior to yours?' I said, and was pleased when he laughed as well. Coffee was one of these subjects about which we'd kept having petty arguments. The kind of arguments you don't actually care about, but which you are also weirdly determined to win. When Lukas made coffee, it was always too strong for me, and when I made it, it was too weak for him. Each of us got seriously annoyed about this on a regular basis, and at the same time we liked ourselves in these roles, winding the other one up.

When the waiter came, a guy who was taking care not to hurry, as if that was proper gastronomic etiquette in this city, we both ordered a cup of coffee and smiled at one another. We probably both felt like our meeting was going pretty well, and breathed a little sigh of relief.

Lukas didn't ask me how I was the whole time we were there, incidentally, which I chalked up to sensitivity, though you might tell me it was ignorance. But I know him better than you do; Lukas was sensitive, like he always was. He was sensitive and a bastard, but those things aren't mutually exclusive, you know.

The people in the leaked murder group chats were terribly sensitive, too, when it came to the strange things they were frightened of, but that's a subject that doesn't belong here now — it doesn't belong anywhere, really, but just then I was thinking: if Lukas and I run out of conversation, maybe I can tell him that I just had to watch this special bulletin and that Saya is constantly reading this stuff, because if I know Lukas, who is forever and ever a well-informed newspaper reader, he will definitely have something to say about it that I can repeat word for word to Saya later on. Something legal-sounding. That was the anchor I was clutching from this point on, poised to drop it into any silence: Nazis and Saya. I'd even be able to pass it off as something that had just occurred to me, because a man at the next table was reading a news magazine that had the Nazi gang's symbol displayed in threatening red on its cover.

Apropos of which, news magazine: seriously? That's what you put on your cover for the first day of the trial? I hope there were at least some interviews with the relatives inside. With the victims' relatives, I mean, not the perpetrators'.

'It's great you had time today,' Lukas said. 'I thought it would be better to meet up than call you. I mean, I know you don't like talking on the phone and stuff.'

For a moment I imagined we'd spoken by phone and his new girlfriend had overheard. That was more likely to be his real reason. Meeting up with your ex-girlfriend looked grown-up, but phoning her looked like you had something to hide. 'Yeah, this is much better,' I said. 'So what was it you wanted to say?'

The waiter brought our coffees, made a great performance of putting them down, and spilled half of them into the saucer with the little almond biscuit on it. Thanks for that, wanker, I thought. If I'm going to sit in an overpriced hipster place like this, I'd like to enjoy every last sip I've paid for.

When I was ill as a kid, my mother always used to pour my tea into the saucer, blow evenly all over it, and then hold it to my lips so I could slurp it without scalding myself. I could do the same with my coffee now, and let's see the looks on their faces then, the chilled-out people sitting around me with their MacBooks. You'd be better off in the shisha bar next door, they'd say. Shisha bars were the emblem of this city; but shishas were only considered cool when they were in front of certain people. Otherwise, they were a synonym for gangster clans, drug cartels, and other terms you could pick up from German TV dramas and regional papers.

We thanked the waiter very nicely, and he took the rollie out from behind his ear, moved a few paces away, and started smoking as if he'd just completed some very arduous task. Maybe I should become a waitress, I thought; it seems to be better for the ego than what I'm currently doing.

'Well, I know you're still looking for a job,' Lukas said.

I lifted my cup, took a sip, and knew Lukas would need sugar. There was no sugar on the neighbouring tables — I'd already clocked that — and he would have to ask the smoking waiter or go inside. He would either have to interrupt what he'd been about to say or put off drinking his coffee. Lukas picked up his cup and put it down again; he seemed to be wrestling with something.

'And, like, I know all the stuff you can do, Kasih — I mean, you helped me with my dissertation. And I also know you're super smart and reliable and you do things well and think for yourself.' He turned his head discreetly to the side and scanned the next table and the one beside it for sugar. 'I remember us printing that essay out again in the middle of the night because you wanted to make everything perfect and you'd found an error in the footnotes. I remember you reading it through over and over, even though it was my essay, not yours, but you're very proper about everything.' He turned his head discreetly to the other side and finally reached the conclusion that there was no sugar.

'That was an awful night, when we took the printout into university and obviously the building where the pigeonholes were was locked,' I said, wanting to chip in to cover my embarrassment.

But Lukas just nodded and turned his head towards the cafe, only to realise that the waiter was taking a cigarette break. Lukas looked at his cup and sighed. 'You're right, it was,' he said. 'I'd forgotten that bit. What stayed in my mind was how much work you put into that essay and how impressed my mum was when I told her. That you would take so much care over it and be so willing to help.'

That was right: his mother wasn't exactly easy to impress, but the way I'd kept reading and correcting that essay somehow seemed to live up to her standards of how hard you had to work and how much you had to support one another. I'd never quite understood these standards, which she herself mainly lived up to in her work as a gynaecologist in a fertility clinic, and I was surprised to find I'd met them once in all those years by accident.

'She still talks about it, you know,' Lukas said, smiling at me. I had not one single regret that his mother was out of my life, but the apologetic smile he was giving me suggested he was trying to comfort me for the fact that I no longer got to see her every Sunday. 'Kasih, I'm sorry,' he said abruptly, getting to his feet. 'I need to pop inside and get some sugar.'

I could have told you that this whole time, I thought. Just as I could tell you now that it's your mum's birthday in three weeks and you should start thinking about what to get her. I could tell you

Neil Young happens to be in town a week after her birthday, and if you thought about these things a bit further in advance, you'd have an amazing present for her. But sadly, at the time the tickets went on sale, you were busy splitting up with me, and I, the person who could have pointed this out, was fucked if I was going to help you.

Lukas came back with the sugar shaker and all at once looked much more relaxed than before. He would probably start thinking about a present two days before her birthday, and honestly I was pleased that he was going to be royally screwed. For years I'd given him great ideas for things to buy his family members, and he'd always got the thanks, without ever stopping to consider that someone in my own family might occasionally have a birthday — though okay, none of them actually celebrated their birthdays.

The sugar was pattering into Lukas's coffee as I was taking my last sip. Then I started on my softened biscuit and watched the sugar as it just kept on pattering into the little cup. Lukas took a huge amount of sugar in his coffee, I realised. Really, it was a lot. I suddenly thought that, of course, it was easy to insist on strong coffee if you were then going to sweeten it like you were making cocoa.

'So, what I really wanted to say is that I think I can get you a job, but I don't know if that's an appropriate thing to do,' said Lukas, finally putting the bloody sugar back on the table.

'What?'

'Yeah, and now obviously it does sound kind of inappropriate, but I think you deserve the chance to get out of this quagmire at long last, and I have a chance to help you, and I'd like to. But maybe this is completely out of line, after everything that happened. I'm still not sure. I guess that's something only you can decide.' He stirred his coffee, looking kind of helpless.

My heart was pounding as if a spotlight had just picked me out of the crowd, to come on down and take the jackpot home with me. All at once, everything made complete logical sense: our relationship, the split, this surprising turn of events here. It would all be so fair and right and good.

'So, I genuinely think I can help you: it's a friend of my mum's who is looking for someone with your qualifications. She wants sociologists to apply, and if you do, we can casually mention that you're not just one applicant among many but, like, first prize.'

I thought that sounded totally fair; I'd never in my life had anything like a leg up, because for that you had to make the effort to develop your own network, or dive into a pool of family and social contacts dug by previous generations. Lukas was telling me in very vague terms about his mother's friend and the institution, but I couldn't listen properly because in my mind I was stepping onto the gameshow stage and being handed the banknotes, smelling them, throwing them in the air.

'I just really don't know if I'm the person who should be helping you, when I'm also the one responsible for the quagmire,' Lukas went on.

For a second, I considered cutting the whole thing short by saying something like, 'Hey, don't stress about it, I'd actually be glad if you turned out to be some use in the end,' but I suspect that would have made him cry.

The waiter rolled a second cigarette, looked over at us, and seemed to be considering whether to stick it behind his ear or light it. The dog under our table had fallen asleep, and I couldn't blame him. There were two men at the next table; the waiter shot them a resentful glance and then looked elsewhere for a moment and defiantly lit his cigarette. Maybe because the two men had got their vapes out. Since it had become socially acceptable for grown men to smell of gummy bears and Spice Girls body spray in public, I had the impression we'd taken a step closer to gender equality. But the waiter looked as if instead a new front had opened up in the battle over real masculinity.

'Okay, well, I need to get going,' said Lukas. 'I'm sorry I don't have more time, but I thought it was important to meet up as soon as possible — these application deadlines come round pretty fast, and you should hurry. If you do want me to get involved, I mean.'

I nodded and said I'd pay for his coffee, just so that we didn't both have to sit and wait for the waiter. He looked relieved and guilty at once, because you can do that if you're Lukas, and I was suddenly in a really good mood — though it was only after we'd hugged and he had left that I could breathe freely and smile at everyone and everything.

The waiter looked back, unmoved.

∧ ∧ ∧

The thing I really hold against Lukas isn't even the business with the other woman. Of course I hold that against him, but my feelings about that, its effect on me and my sense of self-worth, are things you could find in a thousand soap operas, Hollywood films, and pulp-fiction books. And let me tell you: the way they portray it is exactly how it is, not a single difference. Come on, you've been unlucky in love, you know what I'm going through. But for that I have my diary and you have your TV; the subject has no place here, and it's none of your business.

But because Lukas has suddenly become a character here, even though I didn't want him to — he just barged his way in, like male characters always do — I will have to mention one more time that he abandoned me, and I can't just say *he ended it, now you imagine the rest*. Because the word 'abandoned' is meant very literally here. I feel abandoned since he's been gone. Not because my heart is broken, and not because I hate the new woman so much, and not because I've become a puddle of tears in a tracksuit. It's because I have a colour again since he's been gone, and I'd come to really rely on never having one again in this life.

I mean, yes, maybe there would still be the looks on the street, or the confusion when I say my name, or having to answer unpleasant questions and talk about where I supposedly come from, though I have no desire to engage with any of this — fine, you can never escape from these things, I know that. But I did think that from the moment we started calling ourselves a couple, my biography had become a proper, unremarkable, ordinary biography.

Lukas and I had talked about children, in some unknown future; that's the kind of thing people do. It clearly wasn't going to happen any time soon, because then as now I had no idea what I'd be doing this time next month, but eventually we would be in a taxi, me having contractions, him with a handsomely anxious expression; we'd fill the labour ward with my screams and warm it with his calmness; and then we'd be holding a peaceful little human bundle in our arms, surrounded by the purity of the hospital bed.

The way I used to picture the scene, he then kisses the top of my head and I sigh and am radiantly beautiful despite the marathon of the birth. From that moment on, our lives go the way everyone else's have always done. Looking for a flat? No problem. We send out enquiries from his email address, and his name sounds like steady income and fitted kitchens, like regular rent payments and a strict adherence to the cleaning rota for the staircase and landings.

I ignore the fact that we have been accepted for a flat because all the other applicants were refugees and people on benefits — maybe I even forget it. The fact that we get a nursery place in a city where no one gets a nursery place, because 'mixed-race couples' are so cute: it's a gift. The fact that my joining the parents' association gives it a bit of diversity without anyone having to expose themselves to the risk of foreign cultures or the horror of a language barrier: well, so what. Sometimes you should be able to benefit from the thing that usually makes your life more difficult. We just magic the obstacles away, Lukas and I, the handsome couple, who smell of round-the-world trips, a wide circle of friends, and unusual furnishings.

We dress our child in the organic wool of thirty years ago; his wooden toys are free of toxins; the cot is where his grandma once slept, and his father built his high-chair for him. The baby equipment my parents had for me, meanwhile, was all plastic and chipboard crap even then. No one knows which skip or cellar it ended up in, but that doesn't matter, because we're protected by an ancestral gallery of totally normal people, which he brings with him to our high-ceilings-and-stucco life.

When we enter rooms, it's the sound of our voices and the joyful greetings that count; when we want to go to pubs, we do; when we want to eat somewhere, we check the menu and just go. When we're in the supermarket, we put our shopping in the rucksack and no one follows us round until we've paid for it; and no one rolls their eyes if we decide to leave something at the checkout, because the papayas aren't as cheap as we thought. If people annoy us on the train, we give them a piece of our minds, and someone films us and posts it online as an example of how to be a good citizen. We're popular and don't stand out; we're normal people among normal people, maybe even slightly better and more special, wrapped in his protective cloak of invisibility. Everyone brings something to a relationship.

Oh, the world out there and your day-to-day lives aren't as rosy as all that, you say? And sooner or later I'd have found out that people are sometimes spiteful and mean even to someone like Lukas? But you *can't* know what would have happened, you know-alls, sitting there saying if wishes were horses etc. I, on the other hand, know very well. Now I sometimes walk out of the front door and see how white my neighbourhood is and how male the next neighbourhood along. I'm like a crumb that's fallen off the table but is still claiming to be a biscuit. That's a funny image. But it's wrong. I'm not a crumb at all; I'm a member of the scum of the earth.

A man did such-and-such to a woman, because he comes from such-and-such a place and believes in the wrong god, says the digital news screen on the train. I'm sitting under that screen, and people read it and then give me a long look. Since Lukas broke up with me,

I have gone back to being what I've been since birth. An eternally open question: am I really as bad as you suspect I am, or only a little bit bad? Am I a problem case that you can ignore because I've assimilated and am keeping my trap shut, or will the evil swirling in my bloodstream eventually come to the surface?

Since there has been no more Lukas, I'm an eye-catching visual for anyone looking for something tangible to hang their 'party policy' on, which comes straight out of the swamp of race ideology. *That's* what I hold against Lukas. He could have taken a moment to consider that before he left. But how were we to know that the post-Lukas world would be a more sordid one than the world we got together in. That in the meantime, the looks and the race ideology would have begun a steamy affair that now colours the streetscape, even though we live in a cosmopolitan metropolis.

But the cosmopolitan metropolis has become a place where you speak your language quietly, change into your drag outfit once you're in the taxi, leave your kippah at home. The cosmopolitan metropolis said, 'Fuck you, you losers, this isn't what we signed up for,' set fire to a few cars in one of the south-eastern districts, and left. She didn't say where she was going, or I would have followed her. For her, I would have shown my vulnerable side, but not for Lukas. Never. Lukas remains the man who broke my heart and is now offering to donate a kidney to me. He's not someone you run after.

∧ ^ ∧

When I opened the flat door, I could hear voices from the kitchen and Saya's laughter. An oddly tranquil scene greeted me there: Saya, sitting at the table with Robin and his girlfriend, Iris, eating pasta. 'There's some left if you want it,' she said.

On the hob stood a dented pan of tomato sauce that I instantly recognised as Saya's. Strips of green capsicum and cubes of eggplant in a red mush with large pools of oil. The atmosphere of hostility I'd left her in this morning had gone, and in its place a scent was hanging in the air, a mixture of domesticity and Saya's perfume. Here were the sauce and her laughter; I could breathe easily.

'Robin passed his exam!' Saya said, and her eyes said that this announcement was meant to inform me there had been a broader development. The development was peace, love, and harmony. And that's how the three of them looked, with their half-empty plates and prosecco glasses.

'Hey! That's great news, Robin, congratulations!' I exclaimed, more out of politeness than joy, because actually the fact that something like harmony now reigned here was far more important to me than Robin's career heading in the right direction.

'With top marks,' said Iris, putting a hand on his knee, for which reason I quickly turned back to the pan and muttered something like, 'That doesn't surprise me.'

I put pasta on my plate without knowing if I was hungry or not. I wanted the sauce, that was the only important thing. There was a laptop sitting on the small kitchen table, and the three of them had squeezed themselves around it, angling it so that they could all see the screen. 'What are you watching?' I asked, and stayed standing at the cooker with my food, showing wise foresight.

'Far-right trolls,' said Iris, with a laugh, and Robin leaned forward to scroll down the page of the social network, and said, 'We'll read you the highlights, okay?'

Saya gave me a guilty look; her eyes and Iris's expression hinted that they had spent quite a while in front of the laptop and had laughed a lot.

'They're genuinely completely nuts, the stuff they write is so far removed from reality it's hard to imagine they're actual people.' Robin showed me a man's profile page that must have particularly amused them — which I understood at once, because the profile looked so cliched that the three of them could easily just have created it themselves. The photo was of a man in a 'Deutschland' bucket hat. He described himself as 'patriotic', seemed very concerned about the microwave radiation with which the government and his Syrian neighbours were conspiring to attack him and his wife, and was seeking other victims of state-sponsored torture so they could form an alliance.

Then they showed me the profile of a woman who liked crocheting, was worried about the future for her grandchildren, and had commented on one of the Deutschland-hat man's posts, advising him to stick strong magnets behind his ears. She herself had been assaulted by the state's microwave radiation recently, in the middle of the autobahn. It had been so severe she'd had to pull over.

I laughed for the sake of the others, not wanting to be rude, but these two people seemed more worthy of pity than amusement to me. I'd rather have shaken my head sadly. Hadn't anyone explained to the man and the woman that the whole world could see what they were writing? Didn't they have anyone?

I also laughed because I had such a nice image of what it would be like if I could *really* laugh with Saya and Robin and Iris; what a nice time we'd be having. We knew each other in the way that flatmates and friends of flatmates do, meaning actually hardly at all, but sharing a kitchen is usually all it takes for people to swiftly gravitate towards the topics that interest everyone. I've sat in these kitchens on these evenings so often and thought about how weird it is that people always have things to tell one another and get along when external circumstances, like the kitchen of a shared flat, happen to bring them together. As if a common denominator as miniscule as this was all it took for them to let each other in.

'At the bottom here, we have to show you this, there are two people having this bitter row over the fact that there are non-white people on some new advertising posters, but they don't include any Asians,' said Iris, scrolling down, scrolling past pictures of German cities destroyed in the war with sad captions, and Saya added, 'It's mad: they're so far right that they're arguing about why Black men are being depicted with white women and not the other way round — they've ended up having the ultimate diversity debate and they don't even realise.'

'And at the end there's always an argument about grammar and spelling,' said Robin, giving me a sympathetic look.

I chewed, nodded, still over by the cooker, waiting for their presentation of horror to end.

'Oh, I've lost it now,' said Iris, still searching. 'Saya, while I'm looking, why don't you tell her about your Nazi friend.'

A sudden, massively unsubtle exchange of looks between Saya and me.

'The guy from the plane replied,' she said. 'Remember, I messaged him yesterday when I was drunk.'

'Did you really do that? I was hoping you'd made it up.'

Saya bit her lip to stop herself from smiling. 'No, I'm afraid I did. I couldn't remember if I'd written to him, or exactly what I wrote, but it's actually really funny, and the funniest thing is that he replied. Here, see for yourself.' Saya handed me her phone with her DMs open on it.

Maybe the messages between the two of them will be published anyway. So it doesn't really matter if I put them here or not.

Saya wrote to the man using her fake account, which, as I've said, she always used when she couldn't hack reading any more excessive Nazi opinions and felt she needed to get involved in the discussions of these far-right losers. True, so far it hadn't changed any of their minds, but at least Saya was distracted from her own powerlessness for a bit before she had to go back to just anonymously reporting hate speech as violations of the social network's community guidelines and getting one-twentieth of these comments deleted.

Saya's fake profile transformed her into Monika Stein, a middle-aged white Christian woman. I don't know why she had to be a Christian specifically, but maybe Saya had realised that people don't like morality that only comes from someone's own humanity or powers of reason; they're much better at coping with it when it's backed by a religious institution. Left-wing people always get called 'idealists' and 'do-gooders', but religious people seldom do, and Saya was trying to exploit that, which suggests that her hope for this whole campaign was that her comments were, in fact, going to change someone's mind.

So she'd written to Patrick Wagenberg from her fake Christian profile at four in the morning. The time was the only thing that hinted at her drunkenness, because linguistically Saya was always on top form no matter how drunk she was. What she wrote was more or less this:

Dear Patrick Wagenberg.

I saw you on the plane. You are an unkind man who acts like he was sent by God. Why? And why, then, don't you also believe that all people are equal before God and before you?

Best wishes, Moni Stein.

'Seriously, Saya, that's what you wrote to him?'

Saya laughed and looked at Iris and Robin rather than me; she shook her head like she couldn't quite believe it herself and said, 'Yes, I don't know, either. I think I just wanted to see what would happen. And I'm almost glad I didn't really call him an almighty arsehole, because he'd have found my IP address and be lying in wait outside my front door.'

'At least that would have been a political statement and not utter bullshit,' I said, but then placated her at once by putting on a very stern voice to make the next bit sound like a joke: 'Anyway, he would have been lying in wait outside Robin's and my front door, if you were using our wi-fi.' This idea did actually frighten me.

Around me, the others giggled softly, as I turned my attention back to Saya's phone. The man whose face I was now seeing for the first time had replied:

Dear Frau Stein,

I thank you for your message and your interest in myself. It's unfortunate that I can't see from your profile which city you come from, but since you recognised me on the plane, I assume you are familiar with my blog, which does have a certain reach. I would be glad to answer your questions.

I don't believe that I do act as though I was sent by God. It's possible I may have been a little unkind to one person or another on the plane — that happens to us all from time to time. I was on edge and annoyed by things that may also be familiar to you. We live in interesting times. The establishment politicians are all about maximising their own profits through the asylum industry, rather than looking after the wellbeing of ordinary people like you and me. For that reason they also have no regard for the fact that you and I have no security for our old age and that you, I may assume, can't walk down the street alone at night.

You seem to be a woman of faith, which makes me sympathetic towards you. It is not least the traditions of our Judeo-Christian culture that will be lost if the German state sticks to its immigration policy, which is making people like you a minority in their own homeland.

I must also take issue with you on another point: all people are equal in my eyes, too. If you actually engaged with my views instead of relying on prejudices informed by the mainstream media, you would know that. What I stand for has nothing to do with hatred of other nations. I endorse ethnic plurality and fight for it to be upheld. And that necessarily means defending myself against the current flood of migration and the great population replacement taking place in Europe, right outside our own front doors.

When I look out of my window, I see the rear building in our apartment block, which my grandparents also looked out on. But that building is not the same building my grandparents saw. What I see are windows from which you can hear yelling in various languages, quarrelling people who have a different mentality to us. This is also why they stick together and entrench themselves in a parallel world, because they like to be with their own kind as much as we do. I have some understanding for these people and therefore support a policy of improving the conditions in their countries of origin, instead of making conditions in ours worse by them coming here.

I would ask you to honour the trouble I have taken over this reply, by fundamentally rethinking the fairy tale of multiculturalism, which you have got used to, perhaps without wanting to.

With patriotic greetings, Patrick Wagenberg.

I gave Saya her phone back and sat down on the chair beside her. Robin spooned the last of the sauce from his plate and said, 'Unreal, right?'

I nodded.

'Especially,' he said, 'because I can imagine that in the end, a Frau Stein would decide there's some truth to what he's saying.' We sat in awkward silence. 'I find that a lot,' he went on. 'Reading their rubbish, I can see where they get the logic for their illogical arguments, and I have to keep reminding myself what they're leaving out.'

I didn't say anything, because that had never happened to me. Saya didn't say anything, because that had happened to her quite a lot, but she'd decided you didn't have to just admit it like that.

'Do people really read his blog, then?' Iris asked.

Saya said, 'I don't think so. It's pure megalomania, thinking he gets recognised in public.'

'Yes, but he *was* recognised,' I said. This was starting to make me angry. I'd spent the last two days racking my brains over how to protect Saya from bad people's bad thoughts, how to distract her, and meanwhile she was becoming pen pals with these people for laughs — albeit slightly panicky laughs. I was also angry at being forced to read Wagenberg's gibberish. I'm sorry you all just had to read it, too. But you've been on the internet before, so it probably wasn't the first time you've read stuff like that. And if it was, then I'm afraid I've got another shock for you, because that was just my diluted version; the real message was worse.

It's like the newspaper article right at the start — remember? It said Saya shouted 'Allahu Akbar' before the fire and all that; the real article was much worse, too, so just be glad you've only got my version.

'Bullshit,' said Saya. 'I just saw the name on his boarding card and happened to be able to place him. The guy's a nobody — the only people who share his blog posts write equally racist blogs themselves. They copy off each other, refer to one another, and where it all ends up is that woman advising someone to stick magnets behind his ears.'

'They're the ones living in the parallel society he's so scornful of,' Robin nods. 'That's what I mean by how illogical their logic is.'

'Let's not start unpicking exactly what he's wrong about,' I said. 'I mean, it's impossible to know where to start, or if you can ever stop.'

Robin didn't interrupt me, but he came very close to it when he said immediately, 'Yes, that's true — but maybe that's the work we should be doing, even if it is a lot of work. We need to crash their parallel society, make our comments even louder than theirs, stop what they're doing.' This was Robin, who'd never been to a protest, never so much as signed an online petition, and the full extent of the action his anger had spurred him into may well have been telling Saya and me how loud we were being that morning.

Just to avoid any misunderstanding, he then added, 'We need to talk to these right-wingers. Anything else is gross negligence.' I had some misgivings about Robin's euphoric activism; I put it down to the good mood he was in after passing today's exam, which allowed him to be infected by Saya's charisma. Tomorrow, he would have forgotten he'd just worked out a precise strategy for combatting the far right.

Robin suddenly reminded me of Markus, the left-wing birthday boy with the above-average need to talk. Why had all men suddenly become so obsessed with Saya and me talking to right-wingers?

'The whole foundation his philosophy is built on is false, and unless he ditches that, our arguments aren't going to change his mind,' I said. 'His philosophy is founded on the idea that he, as a white man, gets to decide what's good for a non-white person, what they should be allowed to do and what they're worth, and as long as he thinks that, however well he hides it, he's disqualified himself as someone you can talk to.'

Saya was just about to say something, but she didn't get a chance.

'Got it!' Iris cried suddenly, and showed me the screen with the next funny Nazi on it, and I laughed with the other three, though it was clear now that laughing with me was a different thing from what had been providing such harmonious unity not long before.

'Isn't it a bit difficult to laugh at them like this, though?' I asked. 'I mean, actually, these people might be dangerous?'

Robin was about to say something, maybe to argue that these people are only dangerous if we start taking them too seriously, or something along those lines, but Iris changed the subject. She did it in such a natural way that we didn't even notice; what she said was interesting and funny and immediately got us all on side. She told us about this incident with her flatmates that was funny and also not entirely undangerous, but mainly just very funny, and thanks to Iris we were suddenly talking about shared flats and that automatically led on to flatmate auditions, and we never stopped to wonder what had happened to our previous topic of conversation. Secretly, we all breathed a sigh of relief and were grateful to Iris.

Finally, we were laughing with an equal distribution of enjoyment. We laughed about flat shares where new flatmates were put on a six-month probationary period to make sure they knew the value of toilet brushes and cleaning rotas, and then got thrown out for personal reasons at the end of it.

Saya joined in, being the charming and interesting conversationalist that she could be, and was generally — in a way she hadn't been for the past few days, though she'd perfected the art — polite. She listened to the others, didn't interrupt anyone, nodded her agreement, asked follow-up questions, summed things up, and topped up our prosecco glasses when they were empty. If I were Robin or Iris, I'd have thought that someone like Saya should actually come to stay more often.

When Iris told us that she was off to an event very soon, on a topic that was important to her, Saya grew quieter. Iris was as normal as a normal person could be, neither ghetto girl nor horsey girl, neither public housing estate nor Steiner school. She was the child of divorced parents, had one brother, had done a degree in something or other because that was just what you did, and had now got a job somewhere through the church, without ever having given any real thought to the church as an institution. Iris's life was okay; she had problems the same as everyone else, spent hours watching box sets with her boyfriend, knew a bit about art-house films, and was bang up to date with books and the debates in newspaper supplements.

She hadn't really noticed the term 'feminism' starting to take root in the conversations she had with her friends, and appearing on her cotton tote bags, and becoming the subject of the events she went to; the term was just there, in the same way other contemporary terms were, and of course she'd describe herself as a feminist if you asked her, because what sensible person was going to say they weren't a feminist. But no one in Iris's social circle did ask these questions, because there was a consensus on them.

The event that seemed to be important to her, the one she was going to that evening, was pure consensus — and so she didn't ask us if we'd be interested in it, just whether we were planning to go, too, like it was safe to assume that we'd already put the question to ourselves and answered it. I mean, what else would we be doing that evening when faced with this unbeatable offer?

Saya looked weary and shook her head. Robin said he didn't really feel like it, either; he wasn't after any additional input after such a big day. Though having said that, he was definitely feeling the need to go out and be among people — and the two of them went to get ready and left Saya and me alone in the dirty kitchen. If they had stayed, we'd have had a nice evening. Talking about Robin's exam would clearly have been as personal as the conversation got, but then who's to say that personal stuff is automatically better than pleasant and superficial stuff?

I think that for Saya things were actually much too personal with me and Hani; when we were there, there was no filter to stop her anger at the world erupting, even if she did keep trying to pull herself together. I mean, all she did was make fun of Robin when she and I were alone together — but the minute I left the flat, she was cooking pasta with him. What good do our safe spaces do us, really, if they're where we give in to our uglier side? We should eat pasta with Robin and Iris much more often.

Before she left, Iris popped her head round the kitchen door one more time, waved, and asked, 'That wedding you're going to, is that tomorrow?' And Saya and I nodded, at which she beamed and said, 'Well, then, in case we don't see each other, have a great time!' Her expression suggested that weddings were the epitome of fun and joy, and as she said it I thought, actually, that's exactly what they are. Justified political objections aside, it's a party at which a nice thing happens; that's the whole point of it. Everyone you love and who loves you comes to eat and drink and celebrate the fact that you love someone else. And that is no reason to look like Saya and I looked as Iris said these words on her way out.

'Regarding the wedding,' Saya said hurriedly, to fill any potential silence, 'I was wondering: does Theo have money?'

'Who the hell is Theo?'

'Shaghayegh's fiancé.' In Saya's mouth, 'fiancé' sounded like a creature from a fantasy world — something that intrigued her, but which she assumed didn't exist in real life.

'Oh, him. I have no idea, I don't know him that well.'

'She said she was marrying for the security, and in plain German that means because he has money.'

'Or because she has money. And if he doesn't, then together they save on taxes. You terrible sexist.'

'Okay, but he isn't a crown prince, then, otherwise you'd know.'

'To be quite honest, I don't think I would. He could have won the lottery and I wouldn't have heard about it. Shaghayegh and I basically never see each other. I'm not entirely sure why she invited us.'

'Because she knows where she came from, dude. "I'm still Jenny from the block," remember?'

'All too well. Unfortunately. Saya, look, can't you stop wondering about it and just, I don't know, be happy for Shaghayegh?'

That, friends, was the extent of the critical questioning to which I subjected Saya this week. I will reveal that here and now, and I probably don't even need to mention that Saya acted as if my objection had never been made.

'Well, I think it's very touching that Shaghayegh invited us. Because in the pub yesterday she seemed like she couldn't remember exactly why we know each other. So — how was your meeting with Lukas?'

I told her, and she swore.

'Do not do that under any circumstances,' she said, wiping the sauce from her plate with little pieces of bread until it looked like there had never been anything on it. Look, that doesn't need washing up now, the child version of her would have proclaimed, with a proud, gap-toothed grin. 'There's no way you should be accepting his help. It's weird. He's only doing it to try and clear his conscience. You don't need that.'

This sounded good but completely out of touch with reality — and it suddenly hit me: 'Maybe I do need it. Maybe I'll just never get a job without people like him.'

'I don't believe that,' said Saya, as her phone vibrated. 'You're too good for that.'

Hani had sent her a voice note, at which Saya and I both let out a little groan. Voice notes are an abomination, particularly when they're sent by people like Hani. This one went on for six minutes and was a live broadcast from Hani's meandering stream of consciousness, as she justified why she was too tired to leave the house again today and meet up with us. Information that could have fitted into two sentences.

In a second voice note, recorded immediately after the first, Hani apologised once again for being too exhausted to leave the house.

With a dark look on her face, Saya sent a voice note back: 'No worries, we're only hanging out in the kitchen anyway.' She put her phone down again.

'Saya, I do know I'm good, you don't need to tell me that,' I said, picking up the conversation as if it hadn't been interrupted, 'but I'm sure we both also know that in the end, that isn't what counts.' This of course chimed with two strange convictions of Saya's: the belief that people like her and me can't rely on getting what you would call a fair chance in life, and the belief that we can do anything we want to.

'Even so,' was all Saya said, despite this, 'no white saviours. Tell Lukas no, whatever wheels he's set in motion.'

'He hasn't set any wheels in motion. The way we left it was that I was going to have a think about whether to accept his help or not, and let him know if I was, so he could send me the job spec and sing my praises to this woman he knows.'

'What kind of job is it?'

'No idea.'

Saya laughed.

'No idea,' I went on, 'he told me something vague, but I wasn't really listening. And I actually don't care. The main thing is that it's a job someone would give me. I'll take anything.'

Saya cleared the plates. She'd wiped mine with bread, too, but obviously they still had to be washed. I watched Saya get up and it suddenly hit me how old we were. How grown-up. We were the people who washed up the plates, not the ones whose plates were filled for them.

'Being completely honest now,' said Saya, 'I'm worried about you and I'm worried about Hani.'

I almost laughed out loud. The madwoman who read transcripts from Nazi group chats the way other people injected heroin, who threw herself against the wall at night and looked for arguments everywhere she went, who seemed more unbalanced than I'd ever seen her, was worried? About everyone else? 'Well, you don't need to worry about me.'

'Pff,' went Saya, as if she was the very embodiment of an orderly, ordinary life. 'You turn into such a bundle of nerves after a job-centre appointment that you cry your eyes out in public, you toe the line, you leave parties early, you subordinate yourself to a man who was a shit to you — I'm worried! You never would have done this before. You'd have found some clever way to let the job-centre lady know she was letting you down, you'd have made *her* cry, not the other way round, and you'd never have given someone like Lukas the time of day again after he turned out to be a dead loss, let alone gone for coffee with him — you'd have done it all differently.'

When Saya said these things, I was tempted just to believe her. But in fact, I thought she was talking about a version of me that had never existed. It had been a puzzle to me ever since childhood that she thought I was the strong one, when really nothing qualified me for that position.

'And Hani is a whole other matter. The stuff she puts up with in that shit job — and she can't even see there's anything wrong with it. Sometimes I think I need to move back here. You two aren't looking after each other at all.'

How good it would be if Saya moved back here, I thought. As long as she didn't bring with her this beef she seemed to have with the world in general. I'm worried about *you* — that would have been an appropriate response. Move back here and we'll make you okay again, we'll all make each other okay again, I should have said. 'So, what did you think of Iris?' I asked instead, subtly trying to change the subject.

'Well, nice, obviously. We could do with having more nice people around. I looked at Iris and thought: if you had more friends like her, I'd feel a bit more reassured.'

'I wouldn't call Iris a friend, though.'

'Why not?'

Why not indeed. I don't know. Because I didn't choose her. Because we only hung out from necessity, seeing as her boyfriend was my flatmate. We had good chats, we got on well, but that wasn't enough for a friendship. You need to share more than those things. At least one childhood, at least half a lifetime, at least two categories of discrimination.

I could talk to Iris happily for ages, until eventually something would start to feel a bit weird and I'd want to wriggle out of the conversation. I remembered, after one of these events we'd been to, the two of us talking about terminology that was new to us, like 'body positivity' and 'sex positivity'; us, two thin women who, okay, weren't super hot, but were more or less in the same ballpark as current ideas of what constitutes beauty. The two of us sat in the kitchen with these astonished faces because we'd just learned terms that turned a vague feeling we'd never paid attention to into a describable reality.

We got ourselves worked up over our memories; Iris said that all these years she'd slept with men and then, when she stopped sleeping with them, felt ashamed that she'd expressed her needs to them. As if that was something embarrassing, when it was actually incredibly important — and I listened and nodded and said that I, in turn, wanted to sleep with men and felt ashamed when I realised that they knew this, but weren't interested in me. And that the shame came from my interest, not their disinterest. Iris nodded, because she recognised that as well, and we confirmed to one another that it was okay to want sex, that in fact it was our right, and once again it was sad that the world didn't allow us that.

And just as we were nodding with such agreement and confirming what the other had realised, Iris said that if she knew anyone who was totally sex positive, it was Hani, and I thought wow, you can be so utterly wrong about people you don't know. Hani had always had a lot of sex and she'd always enjoyed it, but she never talked about it. She was too honest to keep it secret, but she was too ashamed afterwards to express any kind of opinion on it. That is what the parties of the past, the years, and the rumours had done to her: she'd become a bright-red, stuttering face that turned away as soon as the talk turned to previous dalliances.

In Iris's world, just having regular sex was enough to make you the doyenne of sex positivity. And she would spend seconds — seconds, I know it — struggling to compose herself if you then said that, of course, Hani's sex life didn't only involve men. Or if you told her that Hani's first time had been in the middle of a civil war, just before she and her parents managed to escape, and that she'd been twelve. Or that we three were surrounded by sex positivity on our estate: another kid's parents shagged on the balcony, and nine months later we giggled when the balcony-baby was pushed past us in a pram. Iris would probably see that as an indication of how shit our neighbourhood was rather than as a feminist statement by a mother of two.

Anyway, Iris would have to take a minute to collect her thoughts after receiving all this information, and that was why I wouldn't become friends with her, or only a little bit, but not properly. That's why I haven't found any new friends since the estate. Always just flatmates and their friends, and then Lukas. Actually, Lukas in particular.

Saya was now washing up Robin and Iris's plates and whatever else was lying around, chopping boards and muesli bowls and coffee cups; she was broad-shouldered and had to bend down slightly over the sink because of the sloping ceiling. She had rolled up her sleeves — I mean of course she had, she was washing up, but no one could roll up their sleeves like Saya. From behind, with a view of her broad back and her sleeves, she looked like she was about to build a whole house, a whole castle, stone by stone with her bare hands, then dust those hands off on her thighs, roll her sleeves back down, and have a contented cup of coffee in the turret. This was the woman I knew: the one who was washing up the things no one wanted to wash up, and thereby dispensing with the arguments no one wanted to have.

In the exact same way, just when she was a lot younger, she'd stood at her mother's ironing board ironing leaves, which stank to high heaven and crackled worryingly — and yet she had to keep going, because Hani hadn't done her homework.

Hani was supposed to have created a portfolio of leaves — rowan, sycamore, birch, the whole lot. She'd had six weeks to find, collect, and press them, and hand them in to her teacher in a folder. But Hani had no clue whatsoever about rowan, sycamore, and birch and didn't know how and where to start, how to connect things that grew in nature — which were completely random and impossible to categorise — to these words and this mammoth task, and so she'd just let the six weeks slip by. Six weeks in which she had diligently done her maths and general-studies homework in front of the TV, but hoped that the 'leaf folder' project would just vanish from her homework diary if only she waited long enough.

Saya, Hani, and I were sitting on the steps outside one of the blocks, reading magazines, when eventually Hani asked: 'Do you guys have to make leaf folders at your school?' We laughed at her and said hell no, that's baby stuff, leaf folders, we're drawing cells and joints, look, and we got our clever Gymnasium biology books out of our school bags, which we would carry around until the late afternoon when we finally went indoors, and showed her the sketches we'd copied off the board. Hani looked at our paramecia and started to cry.

Do you people out there know stuff about trees? Do you walk through the woods recognising what's growing around you? Do you know what grows out of the ground, what ferns and brushwood are, what resin is and what it smells like? Do you hear birds and know more than just that those are birds? Then you have some idea about nature, congratulations, but no idea how lost Hani felt in her cluelessness.

She hadn't repressed the folder business because she was lazy — Hani, as I've said, had never been lazy. She hadn't made a start because for six weeks she hadn't known how, or who to ask about it. And now, when it was due in, she'd asked us and we'd laughed at her.

'Alright — then we'll just get on and do the folder now,' Saya said, jamming her copy of *Bravo* — which she now bought herself — into her rucksack along with the biology book. She was a little ashamed at not having understood what a big deal this was straightaway, which made her all the more determined to act.

'We can't,' said Hani. 'That's the whole problem, you have to press the leaves for weeks, we can't just do it today.'

Saya looked at Hani like a disappointed teacher might.

'And I don't know anything about leaves, either,' I put in quickly.

Hani gave me a look of relief; this was the thing she hadn't dared to say out loud. But then she was straight back into panic mode, because what were the chances that Saya would nail this thing if I was clueless as well?

'That doesn't matter. The main thing is that tomorrow, Hani has some kind of leaves and not nothing. We'll just figure something out. If we get a move on, we'll have it done before *GZSZ* comes on TV,' said Saya, and spat on the ground. We always used to spit on the ground like that, it was a kind of exclamation mark you could actually see. You just had to make sure you didn't step in it afterwards.

So we walked through the woods, which was boring as hell, collecting everything we saw — if it was green and grew on a tree, we were having it. We went back to Saya's place with bags full of leaves — in our minds, full of garbage — where the first thing that happened was that Saya got an earful from her parents. In the language that is so familiar to me that, whenever I happen to hear it somewhere, it gives me a greater feeling of home than the language my parents and I actually speak with each other. Of course, I couldn't understand Saya's language then, or now. There was a heated exchange of words; in Saya's house, that was what passed for a row, though in ours it might have been classed as a pleasant conversation.

In the end, the three of us sat down with Saya's parents in front of four books, turning the pages, while outside darkness had long since started to fall. The two adults searched through dusty encyclopaedias for illustrations of leaves, which we then compared with our garbage, before looking up the corresponding word in the dictionary to find the German name for the tree: so much work for a result as mundane as 'birch'. Finally, Saya's mother got out the iron, ironing board, and blotting paper, proving just how clever she was. If you have an iron, you don't need six weeks to press leaves; you can do it in about thirty seconds.

In the midst of all this, Hani sat in silence. The rest of us were having a great time, brimming over with enthusiasm, and Saya's parents talked in their language and laughed. They'd initially told Saya off because you don't leave your homework until the night before it's due in, but they'd soon stopped because they were smart people and had begun to grasp the situation. This clearly wasn't Saya's homework at all; she was just looking for a way to get her parents on board.

Hani ended up with a leaf folder containing four of the ten specified leaves, plus a few others the teacher hadn't named. Saya kept ironing long after Hani had disappeared back to her own flat with the glue stick and the loose-leaf binder. I had a view of her back as I said goodbye, when I finally went home after an eventful day and a job well done. She was standing at the ironing board like an adult, saying nothing, ironing stinking leaves without reason, without purpose, lost in thought, that whole evening, as if it would save not only Hani's biology grade but the whole bloody world. She missed that night's episode of *GZSZ*.

Now Saya was humming to herself as she constructed a professional draining tower out of the stuff she'd washed up. Maybe everything was fine again, I thought. Perhaps that was all she needed, half a day alone in my flat, a nice conversation with pasta-eating people who weren't affected by racism and who brought a levity to the situation that rubbed off on her.

'There's a brand-new documentary about the Nazi group on tonight,' she said then, starting to dry up with the grubby tea towel, because the sloping ceiling didn't allow for a very tall tower. 'They've interviewed the parents and some people they grew up with.' She turned to look at me and, quite honestly, her face was warm and affectionate. 'Do you want to watch it together, in a bit?'

Of course not. Nazis and Nazi parents? Horrific. In the end, they'd be nice people, and what do you do then? I nodded all the same, slowly.

Saya's phone was vibrating again. Hani saved me from my obligation. 'I'm feeling bad, people,' her guilty-sounding voice-note voice said. 'I really don't want to stand you up — Saya's flying back the day after tomorrow. So here's another suggestion: let's meet round the corner from my place, then I don't have so far to go, and we can be out in the fresh air. I know a good bench where we can sit.'

Saya hung the tea towel over the back of the chair. 'Well hallelujah,' she said, 'on to the next challenge.'

∧ ^ ∧

In summary: Saya was frustrated with Hani and me because I was *too* weepy and Hani wasn't weepy *enough*. And when Saya flew here, she'd thought she was coming to visit two ninja turtles who were going to help her save the world. Where she got that idea from is something she didn't reveal to us. And it's kind of flattering that she thought we were ninja turtles, but I quite often wondered if

Saya had ever actually taken a close look at her two friends. When it came to us, Saya was deluded, and there was no way in hell I was going to set her straight. At least there was one person who was a massive cheerleader for me. The accusations re: weepiness that Saya made against us a few days into her visit therefore carried no weight, and so we made no further comment on them.

And we didn't have to, because Saya made some very specific demands of us: firstly that Hani either hand in her notice or slam her fist down on her boss's desk and tell her what she was doing wrong, and secondly that I decline Lukas's help and from now on submit job applications in which I presented myself as the jackpot I was. Like I wasn't already doing that.

Hani and I were so confused by the fact that Saya was affectionately frustrated with us that we just assumed the roles she'd assigned us without any objection. We had done everything wrong, and were therefore in no position to worry about her. She, meanwhile, seemed so content and relaxed after telling us these things that we would have allowed her to accuse us of anything.

We were sitting on a park bench; it smelled of dog shit, and the people walking past didn't look at us, and paused their conversations until they'd passed our bench. As if they sensed that we would make fun of any scraps of conversation that might reach our ears. We cracked sunflower seeds and added to the existing collection of light-coloured husks under the bench, evidence of many other good conversations between other friends.

I looked at Saya's legs and then mine, and realised first that this was the constellation of legs on a bench that was most familiar to me, and second that Saya always did everything absolutely right in life. What was so wrong about her reading these Nazi group chats? I mean, they were Nazis, and you had to know your enemy, right? That's why the messages had ended up in the public domain in the first place: a lot of people, not just Saya, had an interest in knowing what danger surrounded them; every bit of information was illuminating. She also seemed able to laugh at these people. Maybe Saya had thrown herself against the wall in the night — or maybe I'd just dreamed it. I'd never heard of a phenomenon like that; surely I must have imagined it. And if not: who was to say it was something she did regularly? She might have stopped again now. After all, the strange business of her resenting my flatmate for no reason at all was over, too.

'Wow, I'm so glad we're out again after all,' said Hani. 'Sorry for all the back and forth.'

'Will you stop apologising for everything,' said Saya, and Hani nodded quickly; there was something she wanted to add, and she started with, 'You're right, sorry.'

Saya rolled her eyes and I felt good. I was sitting between the two of them like a baby between two people who are there to take care of her.

'I genuinely didn't want to go out, but then you said you were just sitting in the kitchen not doing anything, and that sounded so tempting, but kitchens are always too far apart in this city.'

Saya and I didn't say anything to that because it was such a trite statement.

In Hani's life, it was anything but trite. One time, years ago, we'd talked about our earliest childhood memories, and Hani's might have been less spectacular than Saya's with her escape over the mountains, but it was still a powerful testament to how one person's life can develop.

Hani's first memories included sitting on the cold tiles of the kitchen floor while her mother and her mother's sisters sat smoking round the little table and talking about their lives in a fast-paced language with rolling Rs and throaty laughter. Hani didn't understand; her mother always spoke to Hani in her father's language. In Hani's ears, her aunts' conversation was one big concert, in which she could hear the notes and melodies, but hadn't been given a program with the titles and lyrics in it. The conversations began cheerfully, with everyone talking over one another, sometimes with all of them laughing, and sometimes just the person who was talking; the women gesticulated wildly, and when one of them turned her eyes towards Hani, she was filled with a wild delight; they rubbed Hani with an ointment made of joy and an abundance of sweet phrases.

But then, as Hani also remembered, there would be a moment where the mood changed, the women grew more serious, and eventually all you could hear was the soft crackle of cigarettes and one of the women crying. It was always a different woman in tears. It was always the rest of the women who would then start to speak calmly, each taking their turn. At some point, one of them would get up to fetch more cigarettes. And by the time they'd finished, no one would be crying and the conversation would have returned to normal. No noise, no chaos, no weeping or comforting. Then the aunts would leave, before the men got home.

Sometimes, on special occasions, the aunts would come over with their husbands, and then Hani was always glad when they left again and the only man who remained was her moustachioed father. He always looked like he was glad the other men had gone, too. The men didn't seem to fit with the loud aunts at all; they never bothered with Hani, just sat on the sofas and barked incessantly at one another in their deep voices. The way Hani remembered it, they had never spoken a human language. When the aunts and the men had left, her father would sometimes get quite silly, lying down on the kitchen floor with her as they watched her mother tidy up.

When the war came, the women met more sporadically, depending on curfews and bombardments, but they still met, even if their numbers were slowly depleted as one by one they left the country or went into hiding for a while.

Later, in Germany — where they were allowed to remain because, once concern had passed about the war, which had given them that right originally, they'd been able to prove that Hani and her brother were doing well at school — Hani still did her homework on the kitchen floor, while the sounds of the lonely television could be heard from the lounge. Her mother might have stopped smoking in the kitchen, but she still had a stream of visitors. Not her sisters — they were scattered across the planet and now wept either alone or in the kitchens of people she didn't know. Hani's mother had visits from the neighbour with the hijab, her and her great aunt, and the young single mother who lived downstairs from us. They went out to smoke on the balcony, and because they had to get by in German and Hani was now old enough to understand their problems, it was only there that they unpacked the real, important details.

Once again, all that reached Hani through the glass pane was a confusion of speech melodies, the content of which remained unimportant to her. The melodies were the same as she used to hear from that other kitchen floor, and these women's tears might have flowed more quietly and less naturally than the aunts' had, but they flowed all the same. Hani's mother usually listened, sometimes spoke, ended up laughing with the women — and now, too, popped out to buy more cigarettes when necessary.

When Hani was old enough to smoke in front of her mother — though in most families, she wouldn't have been regarded as old enough to smoke full stop — her perspective changed; she went from being the child sitting on the floor to one of the women sitting at the table. Even when no one was visiting, she and her mother sat there and talked, and it was a mystery to Hani how her mother managed to say helpful things even though Hani never even hinted that she had a problem. When the girls at school laughed at her, when the boys gave her the cold shoulder because of the stories they'd heard, but at the same time made secret passes at her, there was no way in hell Hani was going to tell her mother. But her mother would tell her about this situation and that, one person and another, affairs, machinations, bold decisions, and everything turning out well in the end, because the people involved were good and good people always find one another in the end. It was that simple, and the next day Hani went to school with her head held high.

Eventually Hani's mother swapped the cigarettes for eucalyptus lozenges. In the new-build area where they had built their beloved house, the other women may have been open-minded enough to drop round for tea with Hani's mother occasionally, but they never seemed to bring problems with them that you could talk about in the light of day and in other people's houses. So now the radio was always on in Hani's mother's kitchen, with talk of operas and social issues, though Hani's mother had never been to the opera or read a newspaper, and it wasn't even switched off when the voices and faces of Hani's aunts appeared on her phone, briefly creating the illusion that the room was once more filled with living human bodies.

Hani missed her mother's kitchen. Partly, of course, because she missed her childhood, but also because she had this sense that the world would collapse if we didn't maintain its kitchens, and the idea that Saya and I were sitting in my kitchen without her made her feel she was passively contributing to the kitchen's demise.

So Hani was thinking about kitchens and her mother, and I was thinking about cars, because some massively expensive set of wheels had just shot past us as the lights turned green. It must be insanely stressful to drive like that; how stressful, if that was part of your everyday life, using your car and your driving style to feel like the person you wanted people to see you as.

I always used to wish one of the three of us would finally get a car; in summer, we'd drive out into the countryside with good music on, looking at the view with earnest, dreamy expressions. Well okay, my real dream was to be in a car with a sensitive boy, just the two of us, but because that seemed so unachievable, I imagined the more realistic version, in which Saya earned enough with her side-job as a personal tutor that she could buy a stylish car and drive us around, now that we felt too grown-up to sit on the steps outside our buildings. We'd laugh and chat and spend the night sleeping in a cornfield somewhere. We've never done that, and none of us enjoys driving, not even Saya, who is otherwise so obsessed with control and forward motion. But driving a car was too boring for her, and too daring for Hani.

'Right, I'm going to get us something to drink,' Saya said, getting up from the bench. No idea what she'd been thinking about for the last silent minute and a half. 'Requests?' Hani and I shook our heads.

It was only when Saya left that we realised we'd gone very quiet. 'I think I should probably give my mum a call,' Hani said, almost by way of explanation. That was enough to tell me what had gone on in her head in the minute and a half since her statement about the distance between our kitchens. We've known each other a long time. You people know tree species off by heart; we know each other off by heart. Everyone has different priorities in life.

I want to say something else about Hani's mother quickly, and then I'll tell you about Saya coming back from the corner shop. You're probably pleased about that, because while I'm telling you about Hani's mother, I might happen to reveal which 'ethnic group' she belongs to, and why this was the reason her family had to flee and exactly where from, in which year, so you can compare that against the news stories you found so terribly moving at the time, and open the right Wikipedia articles, to be sure you're not misremembering any of it. But obviously I'm not going to tell you that stuff; all you'll find out is what you need to know about Hani's mother for her to be recognised as a heroine and get her name in the closing credits.

When we used to get ready and put our make-up on in Hani's

flat so that people could then leave us standing on our own by the fire pit, having gone off to the toilet and not come back, Hani's mum never told us not to do things. She never said stuff like: 'No alcohol! No drugs! No sex!' She didn't even give well-meaning instructions on how to improve rather than worsen our appearance with a kohl pencil, though in retrospect I don't know if I do rate her quite so highly for that. She spared us the drug talk, probably because she already had some idea of what we were consuming and in what quantities. She nodded at us from the small kitchen table, waited until we were standing in front of her, and then she would say, 'Stick together.'

And fundamentally, that was the only important thing. A drunk daughter sleeping with the biggest tosser of all time was not the problem. The problem was if she was alone. If she stayed alone, tried to get her head straight alone or get home alone. The life advice I got from Hani's mother was that I could drink and smoke weed and didn't need to be scared of what would happen. I could let myself go, let myself fall, and I always knew I wouldn't lose myself completely because, in the end, Hani and Saya would be there and they'd stick with me.

'Say hello to her from me,' I said, moving her mother's name further up the end credits.

'Nice people, the guys in the shop over there,' said Saya, when she finally sat back down on the bench an eternity later, sounding very cheerful. It really felt like the day had soothed her a bit, and her extended visit to the corner shop had been the icing on the cake. She was wearing a broad smile, and the brief glance that Hani and I exchanged told me that neither of us knew whether we could lay our worries to rest now or not.

'What kind of people?'

'Brothers!'

'Real brothers? Or is brothers a combat term?' asked Hani.

Saya laughed. 'Both,' she said, and finally told us: 'Two boys, both around our age, pretty hench, you wouldn't want to get on the wrong side of them. They look like twins, but they're just brothers. Only, one of them has just had twins, and the other one had a baby in the same week, and all three are boys.'

'Oh come on, they were lying to you.'

'No! Honestly, I've seen photos of the three babies, and it gets better. The bakery opposite, which is one of those little newsagents as well with magazines and tobacco, is owned by their other brother, but he doesn't look anything like them.'

'Hmmm.'

'And wait till you hear this: they took over the shop from their father and his brother. The two of them opened it twenty years ago, and *they* are actual twins.'

'I'm out — too many twins,' said Hani.

'It's an inherited thing, you know,' I said. 'It always skips a generation.'

'That's not important,' said Saya. 'What I really wanted to tell you is something else. The father and the uncle opened the shop when everyone who lived round here was scum, people like them. No fucker wanted to live in the area around the park over there, and the shop just stagnated. But now that all these blocks have been renovated and the yuppies and the rich nuclear families and the children's shops and startups are arriving, now when the rents are going up and the flea market in the park is in the tourist guidebooks, now that everyone comes here to chill and shop, not just the scum, they've still got the only corner shop that's open late, close to the park, close to the station, and all three brothers are raking it in, because no one else has this location.'

We drank a toast to the three brothers and the generations of brothers before and after them.

'One day we're going to build an empire like that, too,' said Saya.

'Except we're not sisters,' I said.

'Pfff. People have never been able to tell the difference between us, so it doesn't matter, does it?' Saya laughed, and then we started talking about what it would be like if we had a corner-shop empire, a whole street of them: we'd tell various different stories about which of us was related or possibly married to which; we'd keep throwing out the words 'twins' and 'triplets', and for special customers we'd whip out our phones and show them photos of babies off the internet. We thought up names for our babies and imagined how we'd keep correcting our customers, how we'd make them repeat the names of our made-up babies, which their gammon tongues weren't capable of pronouncing, and how we would attach great worth to people being able to pronounce the three to five names of our babies correctly. And as we were imagining this, the people in the flats around us pulled their blinds down, so they wouldn't have to hear us laughing.

'But be honest for a minute: has anyone actually mistaken you for sisters before?' Hani asked.

'Yes, all the time.'

'You've never told me that.'

Of course not, Hani. That would have meant telling you that no one ever mistook you and us for sisters, and we couldn't bring ourselves to do it. Then you might also have understood a few other, more painful things, and we wanted to shield you from that. Besides which, we have in fact mentioned it in passing loads of times.

'Oh!' Hani cried then, slapping Saya on the thigh. 'I've finally figured out which shop you're talking about! Of course! I thought those two lads were a couple!' And we carried on talking about corner shops and brothers and sisters and babies and couples, and banished our serious voices again.

'Laughing about it is good,' said Saya. 'I want to start laughing about it more. Earlier, with your flatmate and his girlfriend, I could finally laugh honestly about all that crap. I want to do that more often — I don't want to be angry all the time, and I don't want to have to constantly explain to everyone what they're doing wrong. I want to be like a Robin or an Iris, who can choose what to focus on and then laugh about it.'

Hani and I exchanged a quick glance, the last one before the fire, and then leaned back. So, everything was okay.

'You just have to decide to do it, right? I mean, it's just a question of your own attitude.'

For the second time that evening, I imagined Saya moving in with us. Making pasta with Robin, taking good care of Hani as she did the washing up, giving me advice, and always humming softly to herself, when she wasn't blessing objects and living things as she passed. Everything about this picture was wrong. Everything. Because I'd seen the Nazis on TV just that afternoon and still had the photos of the murder victims in my mind — and if Saya was humming and laughing, who would remind me that a section of humanity was out there killing people like us?

'We should probably make a move, if you still want to watch that documentary about the Nazi terrorists,' I said.

Saya looked taken aback. She'd forgotten about the program. I know, I know — sometimes I just do everything wrong.

We're getting closer to the horrific, decisive day, attentive readers. Are you still there? I'm still here, and I don't know why. Why *am* I still here? I've been sitting here breathing and writing, and have stopped thinking. The last few hours have passed, and I find it incomprehensible that hours can just keep passing like that, when people who were here so recently aren't here any longer. It just goes on; nothing stops, that's the strange thing, and it makes no sense at all. The clock has no respect — the clock is the only traitor here, not me, not you. It could be on our side, but it doesn't care what's driving us to despair, or what's important to us. It just carries on regardless and laughs at us for all of it. But I refuse to acknowledge that it's stronger than me, and so I type, I type faster than the second hand can move. I can do what it can do; it doesn't get to rule over me, though it rules over you out there, setting your alarms and switching them off and going out to get the paper and looking at your phones and searching the internet for news — you're the junkies, but I'm free of that; I'm the one writing, and as long as I'm writing, I am the clock. I am time. And so I'm going to stop looking at the clock. At some point it will get light, at some point the morning will arrive, and at some point Saya will be released, and until then, I dictate the tempo — and everything else, by the way.

I woke up in the morning surprised I didn't have a hangover. You have the most mundane thoughts in the morning. Even on days when terrible things happen, everyone just wakes up and thinks really normal stuff. You're glad you haven't woken up with a headache because you gave someone the last of the headache pills yesterday and if you had a headache now, you'd have to march down to the pharmacy before doing anything else. But you can spare yourself that walk because after three evenings with your best friends, your alcohol tolerance has finally gone back to what it was in your first year of university. That's what you think. That's what I thought, at any rate, when I woke up.

By this time, Saya was already on her way to her workshop. She was going to help a class of school students with their future careers, and afterwards get her travel expenses paid by a school that was hoping Saya would tell their students what apprenticeship or degree course would suit them. But Saya, as I've said, approached these workshops in the same way as her racism-prevention workshops: every student first had to take time to reflect on where they came from and what skills they had that were of no value in school or in a capitalist society, although they did have real value.

It was only at the end that she handed out the directories from the careers information centre. The young people regularly asked if these weren't available online. 'Sure,' said Saya, 'but I'm giving you hard copies anyway, or you won't look at them.' Students don't usually laugh at something like that, because it's the kind of pronouncement made by annoying teachers who think they're better than you. But with Saya they did laugh, because they realised she was right, and they were surprised at this themselves. When the students laughed, Saya knew it had gone well.

So, when I woke up feeling glad I didn't have a headache, Saya was on her way to the school, and Hani had gathered all her courage and was intercepting Carolin outside her office. 'Do you have time for a chat today?' she asked, feeling grubby even as she said it — pushy. Like she was being self-important, faking an illness, or hiding poor work behind a show of activity. She was doing it for Saya, she thought, so that Saya would be pleased when she told her about it later.

'Yeah, sure,' said Carolin, principally out of curiosity over what might lie behind this shy but determined request, and suggested a time. I hope Hani isn't pregnant, she thought; no one could replace her, even for a short period, and having one more employee go part-time would be a bridge too far.

Hani went back into her office grinning mechanically, and felt like throwing up there, even though she wasn't pregnant.

A few hours later, I was sitting in the kitchen among the yogi teas and writing Lukas a message. I'd enjoyed seeing him, I wrote; it was super nice of him to want to help me with the job and I'd like to apply. Could he forward me the job description. Afterwards, I felt just as good and just as empty as after writing an ingratiating application. On the one hand, I'd done something that would get me somewhere and make me an adult. On the other, I had sold myself — for less than I was worth, that was clear.

At the same time, Hani saved the document she'd just opened, put her computer into hibernation, got up from her seat, and smoothed her skirt, before walking into her boss's office for a conversation she never would have requested off her own bat.

At the same time, Saya was heading back to my flat, having finished her workshop. The sun was shining and Saya was exhausted. The way you are when you've been concentrating hard with a group of ambitious young people, giving your all to do a good job.

One girl had said she wanted to work with refugees one day; her mother did voluntary work with them, and it had made her realise how good her own life was, how much she had, and how much she could give. Once the girl was done with school, university, and looking for a job, Saya thought, today's refugees would long since have settled down and ceased to be people in need, for whom you had to sort and distribute clothes. But there'd be others; this line of work wasn't about to die out. She had told the girl she should start to think strategically and learn a foreign language that would be needed then.

Arabic, Kurdish, and Persian were currently in high demand. If only someone had told us that when we were kids, Saya thought on her way home, instead of acting like our languages weren't proper languages, just another deviant habit that we cultivated to annoy our fellow man.

The sun was shining and Saya walked to the tram that would take her to the U-Bahn. The sun was shining just as wearily as Saya, exhausted by knowing it was doing the right thing.

Another girl had said she'd rather go into politics if they were talking about helping refugees. People were giving their lives to save other people from drowning in the Mediterranean. They shouldn't have to do that; it should be the job of the politicians. Saya's jaw dropped. She hadn't expected words like these, and it was probably Saya's enthusiastic nodding that meant the kids with sceptical looks on their faces didn't start a discussion about it. Objections had hung in the air, but Saya was the one pulling the strings here. This discussion wasn't going to happen. Though it was sometimes fascinating when it did.

In another workshop, she hadn't been so quick and so dominant, and a boy had launched into a monologue about how Muslim cultures didn't fit in with the culture here blah blah blah, and refugees didn't want to integrate and committed crimes blublublub, to which another boy retorted drily, 'Well so what. That doesn't mean they should drown.'

Sometimes, it was that simple. Saya loved her work. Today, too.

She got on the tram with a cluster of other people who had all just finished work or school, feeling very content. She snaked her way through the crush like the seasoned city-dweller she was, found the gaps between people who were talking to one another as they boarded and thus wasting precious time, and spotted a free seat from some distance off, somewhere to sit down and take some deep breaths. Now everything really was good; even though she was only going two stops, in the daily battle of the big city, seats were the currency in which success and experience were measured.

The people in front of Saya were packed in tightly, and in a nearby corner a man was standing with his two daughters. He was looking straight ahead with his arms around his daughters' shoulders, holding them close so that the three of them looked like a little family island. The daughters were primary-school age and looked like they didn't know that pushing and shoving could get you the seats that had eluded them. The three of them weren't looking at one another, just standing there as if this was their proper allotted place. As if they were already pushing their luck by being allowed to stand here, in this country, in this city, on this tram.

Saya looked at their feet, at their cheap, well-cared-for shoes, and wondered what paths they might have trod.

When the man — who was still very young, just a few years older than Saya — noticed her looking, she got up from her seat, made an inviting gesture, and pointed to the children. He flashed her a very brief smile before declining, as if they were already standing in the right spot for them. Possibly because a single seat wasn't actually much help for two children. But much more likely because they would then have had to push their way through the people in between, and that would have meant inconveniencing the other standing passengers, which he didn't want to do. He looked away and pressed his daughters a little closer to him, as if that offered some kind of protection.

Two young women then inserted themselves between the three of them and Saya, blocking her view, enveloping her in a cloud of perfume and swinging a rucksack into her face. It smelled of fake leather and Primark. 'If she messages me today, I'm going to make her wait,' the rucksack woman was telling her friend, 'she can fuck off, I'm not her servant,' and both women laughed.

Saya dodged the rucksack and saw it moving towards one of the little girls, ending up right in her face. The girl, at that moment a million miles away from her father, whose eyes were fixed on the street, didn't dodge, because there was nowhere to dodge to; she didn't say anything, and she didn't move.

'Careful,' said Saya in her friendly-but-firm workshop-leader voice, which she would only manage to drop several hours after a workshop. She caught the eye of the young woman who was looking down at her. Saya flashed a smile, gestured at the rucksack, and said again, by way of explanation, 'Careful with your rucksack.'

The young woman, who was in the middle of saying something else about not being someone's servant, turned around briefly to the girl and her father, and then gave Saya a look of incomprehension.

'Your rucksack is in that little girl's face,' said Saya, wondering as she always did in these situations just how polite she needed to be.

The tram stopped and a few people got off, and the crush in front of Saya and the others thinned out a little; the young woman automatically moved away from the little group of three and only then took another look at the girl, and then at Saya. In her eyes lay a stressful day in a school that didn't interest her, with people who didn't appreciate her, in a world she didn't understand. The young woman looked at Saya, saw her watchful gaze, her flawless features, her shiny hair. She saw that Saya's hair was black, and so were her eyes and her eyebrows, that her complexion was darker than her own and still would be when winter came. She saw a woman she couldn't pigeonhole — the only thing she knew about Saya was that here, in this tram, this woman shouldn't be telling her what to do. The tram was one of the few places in the world where no one automatically had any say.

She looked at her Primark companion and shook her head. 'The rucksack, yeah?' She laughed, and they both raised their eyebrows, because that's what you do when shaking your head like that.

Saya's ability to read a room, unlike her voice, was not still in workshop-mode. She didn't notice that the two of them had practised this form of expressing their incomprehension, whatever they were faced with, and could call on it at any time. She didn't notice that this wasn't about the rucksack or the little girl; it was about not letting people tell you what to do. The two young women were friends because together they were better able to stand up to people. To teachers, fellow students, parents. To all the people who gave them nothing but a sense that they were useless. But what Saya did notice was that the woman didn't have any regard for the people around her, and that made her furious.

'You know, *I* take my rucksack off when the tram's full,' said Saya loudly and firmly and with all the aggression she had been carrying around inside her for days, which had suddenly returned as if it had never left.

The two women laughed. 'Good for you,' said one. '*I* leave my rucksack on when the tram's full.'

This cheap retort disqualified her from being someone you could argue with, and so Saya chose to fume in silence instead.

The two women now looked over at the man and the two girls, who had remained oblivious to this war of words. Luckily. They looked at the two girls, with their long, braided hair and their different faces. The young woman turned back to Saya, clueless and full of righteous indignation: 'Why don't you just let your daughters sit down if that's so important to you?'

— and with that, Saya's self-control was gone. 'She's not my daughter,' she shouted. 'For fuck's sake, is it too much to ask for you to just be aware of other people?'

The father looked a little sheepishly in Saya's direction. The two women exchanged a glance, which said that, okay, it might have been a touch embarrassing to assume erroneous family relationships, but that it wasn't completely unreasonable, either, given how Saya looked and how high and mighty she was being.

'That's not my daughter,' Saya shouted again. 'Those are three people who should be allowed to take public transport without getting your rucksack in their faces!'

The tram had reached the U-Bahn stop and people were getting off, without giving any sign of what they thought of the whole thing. The two women looked at one another, laughed, and shook their heads, which Saya realised was something like the last word. She got off the tram and avoided checking whether the man and the girls had caught any of what had just happened. The last thing she wanted was people who didn't even feel worthy of a seat discovering that they had been the cause of this escalation. Saya wanted to grasp both women by the scruff of the neck and bang their heads together. Though obviously not hard enough to kill either of them — and without the man and the children seeing. That goes without saying.

Instead, Saya got on the right U-Bahn, but going in the wrong direction.

∧ ∧ ∧

Meanwhile, in another place, a man was laughing loudly to himself as he pushed a stroller with a toddler in it, and talking, although not to anyone who was actually there. The child didn't look neglected, but the man did. People watched them go by, wondered if they should intervene, and then decided that even unkempt old men sometimes babysat their grandchildren. They made a mental note of his face in case there was a police hunt later. That's the kind of neighbourhood it was.

Life saw the man from inside the cafe and nodded to him. He'd known him for years and knew no one needed to refer him to social services. Since Life and Anna had become parents, they'd had regular conversations with the man about nursery places; he was surprisingly knowledgeable about the childcare situation in their little neighbourhood. Life was waiting for someone to come and take over from him. It had been an okay morning; no one had wound him up by saying the cappuccino wasn't hot enough, ignoring the fact that this was the proper temperature for cappuccino. He'd even found the time to keep checking his phone for updates about the trial.

Two people had been sitting at one of the tables for hours, arguing loudly in English about not being allowed to kill wasps. They'd been noisy even before they started arguing; they sounded like the people from American TV dramas that you watched in the original English because of the social circles you moved in. Life was sure that the pair were only talking in such a loud, affected, passionately artificial way because they'd learned it from these streaming shows. He wondered how many other people hurled their arguments at one another with such passion and said 'you know' and 'wait' and 'like, really often' in that faux-emotional tone because they'd seen it elsewhere, and how dreadful this English must sound to native speakers. He imagined a world in which everyone spoke German like they'd learned it from soap actors on *GZSZ*, and made a great display of that, too.

Until just now, Life hadn't known you weren't allowed to kill wasps, and that it could actually incur a fine. But it made sense; people who sat outside had every reason to want to kill a lot of wasps, and yet he never saw them do it.

The girl who was supposed to be taking over from Life was late, as usual. If Life wasn't Life, he would have fired her a long time ago. But he couldn't bring himself to do it; she was always cheerful, the customers liked her, and so he just accepted that he was often late home because of her. If Anna hadn't been on maternity leave, the waitress might have had less luck, but right now he was the boss here and he compensated for his own faint-heartedness through self-exploitation. But the waitress's continued non-appearance was starting to make him nervous; he was more impatient than usual and wanted to get home to Anna and the baby.

Little Nikolai could in good conscience be described as a crybaby, and so they stayed at home most of the time. They didn't dare venture into the noisy outside world, fearing that the baby would cry even more if he was overstimulated, and they'd be doing it all wrong yet again. In his mind's eye, Life saw Anna waiting for him at home, and he felt sorry for her.

'Have you got anything that isn't Ramazzotti or Jägermeister? This is all faggot stuff,' said the old man who was sitting outside amid the wasps, and Life was aware that this was one of those situations where you were supposed to speak up, and he didn't. 'Sherry?' said the man. 'Cognac? Some kind of schnapps?'

'All I've got is what's on the menu,' said Life, and although that was the end of it, he knew the old man saw him as the one responsible for this, the one to blame. Life liked to pretend he wasn't the owner of the cafe, just one of the employees, which in any case was what his customers already thought.

The old man ordered a cappuccino with a shot in it. Life wondered if he was some famous old dude, one of these white West Germans who'd been important in the nineties and retained the attitude from that time, though they had nothing left to say. Life hoped the waitress would get here soon and deliver him from this guy. He brought the man his cappuccino, and the man didn't even glance at him.

Life went back inside, looked out of the window, looked at the clock, and messaged Anna to say he was going to be a bit late.

Shame, she replied, *but the important thing is that you sort the rug out today, I finally flogged it.* This was followed by a thumbs-up emoji. Since Anna had been on maternity leave, she'd started 'flogging' things on eBay — it had become something like a second job, because it was easy to do from your phone.

We can do that, he wrote. And then he added another message: *Yes We Can.* He didn't know if it was funny.

Outside, a young woman walked past and smiled at the cappuccino-drinking old man, a slightly pitying smile, but mostly wistful, as if she was thinking about her own beloved grandpa and was wishing all the old grandpas of this world well. The man looked gravely at his newspaper and didn't respond.

Life's phone vibrated. *Second day of the trial: application for a private hearing granted.* Life's heart raced, but his face showed no emotion. Well of course. From now on, they would all be finding things out later, via more convoluted channels. That was always going to happen. He clicked on the notification. One of the defendants was so young, he shouldn't have to have any false allegations against him aired in public, the story said. The media had prejudged him, according to the defence lawyers, and it was the job of the court to regard political views as a defendant's right and not as a starting position from which to form their judgements. They had to 'make very sure that these views are not what is being punished'. Even the state prosecutor had likened the press's attempts to investigate and the public statement by the relatives' lawyer to an 'incessant swarm of flies'. It was a victory for the defendants. The internet was going ballistic.

Life took a deep breath and stuck the phone in his back pocket. That was enough for today. That was enough full stop. He recalled the lawyer's post, just the previous day, in which she'd announced that 'we' would try to trust Germany again in this trial. So much for that.

Then Life heard the clattering and yelling from outside. The old man shouting at her to kindly stop doing that, and the young woman shouting back that he needed to shut up, as she kicked the cafe's pavement sign.

'Hey, what the hell? Have you lost your mind?' Life cried as he came rushing out of the door and saw her kicking and yelling until the sign clanged onto the ground. Then there was silence. It was only when she inhaled loudly and tucked her hair behind her ears with a weary hand that he recognised Saya.

'Goodness me,' the old man exclaimed, 'is that the kind of thing people do these days?'

'Yes, it is! They do what they like! Why don't you go back to your paper, dickface?' Saya shouted, though she seemed to calm down a little when she saw Life. It was unclear, however, whether that was down to her surprise or because he looked at her not with panic or condemnation, but with interest. 'Oh, it's you,' she said as he bent down and righted the sign — with an air of calm that rankled because it seemed to neutralise the ball of rage inside her.

'Why would you do that?' he asked.

Saya just held up her phone.

'Oh, I see,' said Life — and then, after a pause: 'That was always going to happen though, right?'

Saya shook her head. But she was slightly soothed by the fact that he knew what she'd just read, and had probably just received the same notification. She considered telling him what had happened on the tram, but that would take too long; it wasn't an easy story to tell. That was always the way, she thought, thinking of the old story about Leo as well: you can't just tell everyone about things like that, they aren't really stories at all, they don't have any real punchline, and people who aren't close friends always want a payoff at the end, they want clear stories, a clear build-up, a voice from offstage summarising the rights and wrongs of the whole thing.

Life was horribly tired. They hadn't been getting much sleep since the baby arrived. 'Listen,' he said, 'if you want to work off your aggression, fine, but don't take it out on my cafe.' He checked the sign, ran his hand along its edges. These things were expensive; he and Anna might not have had a lot of start-up capital, but they did have an unconditional love of detail. 'Why don't you go down to the pub on the corner, at least they're genuine bastards.' He jerked his head down the street.

And only then did Saya realise where she was, and that she'd been there before, the night before last, and that this pub was 'earthy' and 'authentic', though that wasn't what people like Life would call it. 'Oh, yeah!' she said. 'Nazis, right?'

Life nodded. Not necessarily Nazis, he thought, just your standard racists; they probably even voted for the left-wing parties. But he didn't say that, because Saya didn't seem in the mood for this kind of nuance.

'I'd like to pay, if you don't mind,' said the old man, putting his cup down slowly, with a dignified rattle.

Where on earth do these people learn these moves, Life and Saya both wondered, as they saw each other for the last time in their lives.

'Of course, right away,' said Life.

Saya took a few steps towards the old man and sent his cup flying off the table with a well-aimed swipe. Then she set off towards the pub on the corner, yelling something that sounded to Life's ears like 'Almighty arsehole! Almighty arsehole!' at which he couldn't suppress a laugh — but then he hurried back inside, because he could see who was standing at the end of the street, about to encounter Saya. The neighbour with the sticker on his letterbox. Life had no desire to even witness this encounter. That may have been another piece of cowardice, but he really didn't have the energy for any more conflict, besides which he had a job to do. He went back inside to get the man some serviettes.

∧ ∧ ∧

There is always something ceremonial about getting ready. I remember my mother getting ready before we went to parties. She would dress me and my sister — back then, we each used to get a smart dress once a year, and these would finally be brought out of the wardrobe, out of their plastic covers, and put on. White lace tights underneath — imitation lace, obviously — and patent-leather shoes. A white lace collar over the top of the dress (because this is the early nineties we're talking about here). On those days, my mother smelled of make-up, which she never wore otherwise, and her nails would shimmer pale pink. She painted them after the housework was done, when the real preparations started.

I always wanted a handbag to carry around on these occasions, but I never got one. Saya had a handbag that I was always envious of. An oblong black bag embroidered with little black glass beads and a few in different colours. Very stylish, little Saya.

So yesterday, when Saya and I were getting ready for Shaghayegh's wedding, I was in a very festive mood — though nothing was any different to the days before. We were still in my grubby shared flat, standing barefoot on the sticky wooden floor. Most of the clothes that Saya had brought for this trip were by now distributed all over my room, and every place she had sat since Tuesday was marked with empty glasses and bottles. As if she was trying to balance out the tidiness she'd brought to our kitchen and living room with a suitable level of chaos in my room.

Everything was like it had been before, apart from Saya's bizarrely good mood, which didn't align with the jumble of stuff she started telling me the second she walked through the door. She took her sandals off, looked at me through the tangle of hair that was hanging over her face, and launched into incoherent descriptions of women on the tram and coffee-drinking old penis-owners. And because she looked so relieved and happy, I laughed a bit and wrote it off as more of the usual, which she'd decided that from this moment on she was going to process by seeing the funny side. I didn't sense any danger, and that might have been due to her eyes, which spoke of such total normality that she might just as well have been out doing some stressful Christmas shopping and had a few whacky thoughts along the way. That kept me from saying anything.

I know that sounds ridiculous. But I've known Saya for more than just a few hundred pages, unlike you. I've known her my entire life, and the things she then told me about in more detail once we were in my room — rude women on the tram, a small meltdown outside Life's cafe — were nothing that she hadn't been through before, so what was I supposed to do?

I could have asked why she was laughing so madly. She looked like the Joker from Batman. You're right, I could have asked her that. But I clung to the thought that a madly grinning Saya was better than a madly angry one, and to be honest, I just wanted to look forward to the wedding.

And I swear: she didn't tell me what had followed the incident outside the cafe, so I concluded that after that, she'd just come home.

'What are you going to wear?' Saya asked, disappearing into her hiking rucksack and pulling out more stuff that she scattered across the floor. Saya travelled with a lot of clothes and even more books. When did she find time to read them?

'A black dress,' I said, looking sadly into my wardrobe. I never really missed my mother, but the annual new-dress service had been a pretty good thing. Saya gave me a quizzical look, one arm in the rucksack. 'I've only got one smart dress,' I said apologetically, 'and it's black. It suits every occasion. What are you wearing?'

'A black dress.' Saya threw something that looked like quality fabric and special laundry cycles onto my bed. Her black dress would definitely look better than mine, but that wasn't going to surprise anyone.

'Is it kind of disrespectful to Shaghayegh that we haven't bought new outfits for tonight?' I wondered aloud.

'Don't be ridiculous,' said Saya. 'A white dress is the only thing that would actually be disrespectful towards her.'

'Is she going to wear white?'

'Of course. If you're getting married, you wear white, don't you? If you're going to be silly, might as well do it properly.'

'Why are you even going to this wedding if the whole thing annoys you so much?'

Saya considered this and said, 'To find out why she's getting married. Do you want to swap dresses?'

'Absolutely.' I was clearly the one benefiting from this, but I didn't say that. My dress would look better on Saya than it did on me anyway, so it didn't matter. The main thing was that we were both wearing something new.

Saya picked up the invitation card between finger and thumb, scanned it, and asked, without looking up, 'Did you get back to Lukas?'

I nodded.

Saya rolled her eyes and put the card down. 'I hope this job working for his grandma is the best thing since sliced bread, at least.'

'It's not working for his grandma.'

'How do you know? You never even asked him what kind of job it was.'

I had no wish for Saya to go on talking and take away the sense of pleasant anticipation I could quite happily live with. Since making the decision to accept Lukas's help, I'd been feeling wonderful, and could already see the signed contract sitting in front of me.

I looked at the wedding invitation. It was classy: expensive card, elegant font, delicate illustrations of ivy and wedding rings. I read Theo's name for the first time, and only now realised that Theo was short for something else, and that his real name probably caused as little delight in public offices as Saya's or mine, or indeed Shaghayegh's. They'd had a quote from a clever love poem printed on the card, which I hadn't previously done more than glance at. I turned the invitation over and only now did I see that something was printed on the other side.

> *We have gone through tough times and we have overcome them. On this day, help us celebrate leaving the worries of the past behind us once and for all. Help us celebrate the fact that we have each other.*

'Er, Saya? When you were out doing shots with Shaghayegh, did either of you ask her what this thing was all about?' I held the card out to Saya, who was rummaging in her rucksack again.

She skimmed the text without interrupting the rummage, and said, 'Nope. I didn't even see that. But there's an easy explanation. Theo was ill! I reckon Theo was really ill and now he's well again and they were so happy they decided to get married — *now* I get it. It's like in hospital dramas: a near-death experience, followed by love. It doesn't make it any better, but at least it's understandable.'

Saya finally pulled her arm out of her rucksack and held it aloft. She'd found the small glittery handbag that I'd envied her for as a child, and which she'd clearly held onto. Still chic, no question.

'Now we do rock paper scissors for who gets to carry it.'

We played, I won, and for a brief moment I loved everyone and everything in the whole world.

∧^∧

Carolin was on edge ahead of her conversation with Hani. She was often on edge, and wondered why she'd ended up in this leadership position in the first place, and at what point everyone around her was going to realise that she was completely the wrong person for it. That she'd made it this far through sheer luck, and people favouring her: shaky foundations on which you shouldn't really build, even if they did seem helpful at first. But sooner or later she would make some bad decisions, and the company would go to the wall, declare bankruptcy, and she'd lose face in front of the whole sector. It was inevitably going to happen one day; it was just a matter of time before everyone saw through her facade of competence.

Since taking this job, she'd started talking encouragingly to her own reflection again. She'd last done that as a teenager. Of course, she wasn't a boss like other bosses; she was aware of that. She'd never been interested in power and exploitation. Her sole focus was the animals she loved, and being able to pay her colleagues. Though sometimes she had a strange, nagging suspicion that maybe she didn't love animals as much as she should, or as much as the others did. But this doubt, at least, was easy to shake off when she thought of her days on the cattle farm, and her three horses, and of how many clients she'd won in the past few years and how many animals' lives she had thereby upgraded.

Carolin was a boss who maintained a flat hierarchy with her colleagues — not only because of the idea from which her agency had originally been born and grown, but also because there was no way Carolin wanted to bear the sole responsibility for anything. Yet after years of living in cooperative housing projects and farms, she also knew that things took forever when you let groups decide them, and so there had to be someone in charge, and that someone was her. It was her, goddammit!

She stretched her spine and slid her backside to the front of her chair so she could sit up straight. She swallowed and blinked twice, knowingly. Hani was sitting opposite her. Hani who, Carolin suspected, would be the last person to ever cast doubt on Carolin's competence. Carolin had liked that about Hani from the start: her quite open admiration for people like Carolin. Hani actually seemed to enjoy admiring other people. Carolin was touched by this, but that on its own wouldn't have been enough for her to argue as vehemently as she had done that Hani should get the job, particularly since the others had been more sceptical. They didn't say it out loud, but it was obvious that Hani's whole persona was very different from theirs, and she didn't seem to come from the usual background.

Carolin was interested in someone like Hani because for Carolin in particular, this position came with a level of intimacy that she feared. The secretary's office was next door to hers, and the secretary would be the first to notice Carolin's mistakes and bad decisions. The secretary would also be able to hear most of her phone conversations, including the private ones (and Carolin's private life was a complete fiasco, though that doesn't concern us here), no matter whether Carolin tried to prevent it or not. Hani's position was only that of a secretary — but it was a bloody powerful position if the boss had something to hide. And so the job really needed to go to someone like Hani.

Carolin looked at Hani. To Carolin, she still looked like the young thing who had started work for them all that time ago; she was looking observantly around Carolin's office, which she appeared to like. It seemed like she was trying to work out what actually made an office into an office. She was so sweet, thought Carolin. And she was definitely pregnant. She'd been looking tired for days now, had a slight gleam in her eyes, seemed unfocused. That wasn't like her.

Recently, Carolin had had quite a few conversations like the one she was probably about to have. All at once, her insides clenched and her heartbeat told her what she kind of already knew: she was panicking. If Hani left — maternity leave, maybe a few extra months, then she'd be sure to go part-time, or even worse: hand in her notice! — then Carolin was screwed. She had no idea exactly what work Hani was doing at this point. She had merely observed that the others were passing more and more work on to Hani, mainly for selfish reasons.

A secretary who was that busy would hardly be able to find the time to expose their selfishness. The theory worked brilliantly, and soon everyone had abandoned their initial scepticism towards Hani, and Carolin could rely on her to keep her business running smoothly. Hani kept smiling, and so everything was great.

If Hani left, Carolin would have to employ someone else. Whether temporarily or for longer: she'd have to contend with the old uncertainties again, and she'd end up with someone who shut the office door behind them after eight hours, performed only those tasks that, on their insistence, were agreed with Carolin in advance, and came running to her over every little thing. And okay, the new person might be more devoted to animal rights, but that didn't matter to Carolin.

She watched Hani, who was fully occupied in squeezing out her teabag with the aid of a spoon and placing it on the plate beside her cup. 'So then, Hani,' said Carolin, and found that her voice sounded appropriate, appropriately serious and appropriately sensitive, even if she was on the point of exploding with panic, 'what's up?' Hani looked at her, and Carolin filled her eyes with bonhomie, blinked again knowingly, and sent a little prayer up to heaven.

'Yes, so,' said Hani in her childlike voice, raising the teacup to her lips with both hands. She wasn't looking at Carolin anymore.

Was Hani even in a relationship? Was she not just pregnant but soon to be a single mother? That wasn't Carolin's problem, of course, and yet it would explain why Hani wasn't beaming with joy. On the other hand, the most recent colleagues who'd come to announce their upcoming hiatus to her hadn't beamed, either; they looked like they'd accidentally eaten the bin for breakfast. They'd only beamed as they were leaving Carolin's office again.

It astonished Carolin that, one after the other, they seemed to have forgotten how to behave. Not one said anything about having actually planned to get pregnant; they always seemed to have stumbled into it by accident and were now just accepting their fate. But Carolin didn't notice that, when they felt no one was watching them at their desks, they would stroke their bellies and laugh with one another, or that their voices had a note of self-satisfied excitement. In Carolin's eyes, it was incredibly self-centred to bring children into a world that could really do without additional CO_2-emitters, but of course you couldn't talk like that as a boss and so Carolin now made an effort to look slightly less affectionate and a little more severe, because bloody hell, Hani really needed to get on with this.

'I wanted to talk to you about my work.'

Carolin laughed. 'Oh, Hani — I thought that's what this would be about,' she said.

'I've been working here a long time,' Hani went on, as if she hadn't heard Carolin and had learned what she wanted to say off by heart. 'I've been working here a long time and, I don't know, I think I do a good job — at least, I really put a lot of effort into it.' You could see she was embarrassed to be saying this.

Carolin relaxed a little. Hani was being a bit odd, but as yet this didn't sound like pregnancy. 'I've been thinking about that today as well,' said Carolin. 'You don't just put the effort in, you're doing brilliantly!' Carolin took a deep breath, lowered her tense shoulders slightly, and felt what she had just said spreading through her. 'You're always there for everyone, you're considerate, you're quick and organised in everything you do, and anyone who comes into contact with you likes you.' All of this was true, and she wasn't saying any of it because she thought she needed to charm Hani. She went on: 'You know, when I passed on that feedback from our photographer yesterday, I felt it was important to tell you that — to let you know that I'm pleased with you. You're representing our agency to the outside world and making a good impression. That professionalism is really important to us. I do also see, Hani, that you're taking on some responsibilities that no one has explicitly given you. That's why you're such an asset.'

Hani looked like she couldn't believe what she was hearing. She looked at Carolin as if Carolin had just told her that God did actually exist, and was inviting her to a massive god party. After a while, it occurred to her to respond with a whispered, 'Thank you.'

Carolin nodded, saying nothing, letting her words take effect. If Hani had been considering not coming back after her maternity leave, these words might prompt a change of heart. Time to get real now, though. 'But you probably didn't come into my office so I'd say nice things to you,' Carolin laughed, not noticing that Hani didn't laugh with her and was now collecting herself. 'So, how can I help you?'

Hani took a sip of her tea and burned her tongue. Carolin was wrong. There were two reasons Hani had come to her office. One was that she'd promised Saya she would, thinking that if Saya was struggling as much as she believed, then it might soothe her to have her advice taken on board and followed. She also definitely *had* come to be told nice things. That was actually all she needed.

No, if Hani thought about it a bit longer — and in order to do that she had to pretend to take another sip of her much-too-hot tea — she didn't actually need to hear these things. She knew them already; Carolin didn't have to give her absolution. It was nice to hear, but that was all. Anyway, every time Hani left the office at the end of the day, every time she tidied her desk and threw away all the to-do lists she'd worked through, she already told herself that she'd done her absolute best and had earned every cent of her salary. She wanted to just put her cup down, thank Carolin for the chat and for giving her this insight, and get straight back to work. But Hani had asked for Carolin's time — so how could she allow herself to do that, when Carolin's diary was so full and she was now expecting a clear answer to the question, 'How can I help you?'

'I think we agreed to a salary increase, but I haven't had it yet, can that be right?' Hani now said abruptly. What? Money? Agreement? Hani instantly regretted what she'd said. There had, in fact, been an agreement that Hani's salary would follow a fixed scale, and according to this table she should have had several increases by now, starting some time ago. But when you were merely 'following' something, the crucial question was who was doing the following, and it didn't matter that Hani had an eye on this agreement if she was the only one who did.

'Yes, of course,' said Carolin, beaming. 'Of course, you're right! I've been meaning to talk to you about that for a while, so I'm glad you've brought it up!'

Carolin naturally hadn't ever considered this and wasn't glad Hani had mentioned it at all. Now she would have to deal with it, although she'd forgotten what their original agreement had been and didn't know if she could afford a raise or whether that would mean everyone else wanting more money, too, and it would then be bloody difficult to carry on being a fair employer and liked by everyone. No matter. The main thing was that Hani stayed. The main thing was that no one took Hani away from her. Hani, who was the only one who always seemed to be really awake.

'Thank you for coming to me with this,' said Carolin, getting up to find a copy of the employment contract, because that looked competent and business-like and masked not only her consternation but her delight. She could have hugged Hani.

∧ ∧ ∧

We clinked glasses.

'Salary increase!' Saya kept calling out, as if that were the reason 200 people had gathered on the lawn outside the lavishly decorated hall. Hair done, dressed up, with smiling faces and red, swollen eyes.

We didn't say 'cheers' or (as we had been doing for years, to make fun of old-school pub-goers) 'your good health'. We cried out, 'Salary increase!' and clinked our glasses together, doing both so loudly that the other wedding guests turned to look at us.

The ones who were having fun themselves, standing with their people and laughing and talking and smoking and being noisy either didn't notice us or wished us well, some of them raising their own glasses and crying, 'Salary increase!' with long, drawn-out vowels and the wrong emphasis.

The ones who were sitting around uncertainly, as if afraid the Mafia was going to turn up to the party any minute, merely gave us sideways glances and were probably going to leave the wedding early anyway. Or so I thought at the beginning.

I didn't yet know that later everyone would be dancing arm in arm and roaring with laughter and having the time of their lives. But then I also didn't yet know about the horrific conclusion to the evening, or that it would eventually wash me up here, on this desk.

At the start of the wedding, then, we were standing at fancy round tables — which you probably have to set up for a champagne reception by law, although everyone always just keeps their champagne glasses in their hands — eating salted nuts from little woven baskets and celebrating with Hani, who had banged her fist down on the table and told her boss, 'This will not stand. Either you give me more money, or I'm off.'

Saya couldn't get over it. 'You're such a badass,' she kept saying. 'You really asked for more money, genuinely, wow!' Then she would raise her glass again.

We didn't actually drink that much; we just kept making toasts. Hani would have liked to buy everyone a drink, but of course she couldn't, because we were drinking on the happy couple's tab. Instead, she kept offering us cigarettes, and Saya and I smoked with her, as if rewarding Hani for her heroic deed. The three of us smoked and looked like three women who always smoke together, and that was a lovely thing; it suited this wedding party, where a lot of little groups seemed to be having a good time together while they waited for the bride and groom.

Hani drank a little faster and a little more than us and hoped that Saya wouldn't ask about exactly how the conversation had gone and exactly how Carolin had responded to Hani saying her working conditions were problematic. Because this part of the conversation ultimately hadn't happened, though it was the main reason Saya had urged her to go and see her boss. But on this point, luckily, Saya is as straightforward as everyone else in the world: as soon as more money is offered, everything's good. She didn't ask — and I only asked later, when Saya had left.

I assured Hani that it was okay if personal recognition wasn't important to you and money actually was. It felt grubby to say that, but from where I was standing, it was the simple truth. Just ask the people at the job centre.

Anyway, when we'd been standing at the champagne-reception tables for quite a while, the car drove up, a fancy vintage one, gleaming black and decorated in white. The driver honked the horn, and the wedding guests started clapping and cheering and making a loud, rapid trilling sound with their tongues to create a howl of joy in which Saya instantly joined, and which made Hani and me fall silent, because we couldn't even begin to figure out how you made those noises with your tongue.

The bride and groom sat laughing in the car, and when they got out, they were met with a hail of tiny white sugar pearls, which fell on them as if in slow motion, and at first it looked like the guests were throwing piles of banknotes around as well, but it was only Monopoly money, made to imitate some kind of foreign currency. The children in their suits and puff-sleeved dresses fell shrieking on the notes, with no idea of the realisation that was to come.

Shaghayegh laughed and beamed, and Theo took her hand, raised it above their heads and couldn't stop laughing either. Theo's and Shaghayegh's parents came and kissed their new and old children, wept, and cupped their hands around the couple's faces. Then the next lot of relatives came to kiss and throw their arms around the bride and groom, and I looked at Saya just as she was wiping a tear from her cheek.

'Aha!' I said, raising a forefinger, and Saya cried, 'Salary increase!' and raised her glass, and the people around us all cried, 'Salary increase!' and raised their glasses too, and then everyone raised their glasses and roared, and I believe no one has ever had a wedding where there was so much bellowing and laughter, although most of the guests didn't know each other beforehand, and would never have met otherwise.

Shaghayegh looked like a bride from a bridalwear catalogue — no, she looked like she was on TV because she was marrying the heir to the British throne; she looked like princesses looked when I was a kid, sitting on the carpet in front of the TV eating crisps, eager for an adventure that as far as I was concerned could end with a wedding.

Even Saya seemed so moved by the whole thing that she refrained from commenting. She didn't so much as say that Theo definitely had a swimming pool full of gold that he regularly dived into, because this wedding surely cost more than what I lived on for three years, and Shaghayegh wasn't rich enough to afford that by any stretch of the imagination. Saya didn't comment that Theo's wealth could indeed be the reason all this was happening and so she could consider her detective work successfully concluded.

Nor did Saya comment on the fact that Theo was Black. Of course not, because there's nothing to say about that; I mean, we're not you. But Saya, who had been referring to 'the groom' in such scornful tones for the last few days, like he was privilege personified, might have felt caught out. Because in her mind, a bridegroom called Theo who was marrying a woman was going to be a white man. A rich man or a sick man as well, maybe, or a man who'd got Shaghayegh pregnant, and probably a boring man, or he wouldn't be getting married — this had all been very clear in Saya's mind. She could now have done a contemplative little tour of her own prejudices, but that didn't occur to her. Sometimes, you see, we *are* like you. Instead, she wiped away another tear and laughed when Hani offered her a tissue.

The remaining guests were gradually approaching the bridal pair, but keeping strictly to an unspoken order based on how close you were to the couple, in both family and friendship terms. I looked around and realised I didn't know anyone except Shaghayegh's parents, who of course had once been my neighbours. They'd always been nice, and today they'd greeted Saya, Hani, and me like we still lived next door, like we were still children. But all the same, after that, we sadly had nothing to say to one another.

For some reason, I'd hoped that Shaghayegh would invite other people from the estate. People from our childhood who I vaguely remembered and would now be reunited with. We would hug and be pleased to see each other; we'd marvel at what had become of us all, and then talk in distant but affectionate terms about the place no one ever wanted to be, though it had given us a happy childhood. We'd go over what had happened when it started to decay, and how weird it was to think that a few people had stayed and were still living there.

We don't know those people, or we could have asked them if they'd installed smoke alarms in their flats now, just for safety's sake. The fact that we don't know them might also be proof that the strategy of letting the estate bleed out had been successful. We didn't band together; they had no need to be afraid of us. And so no one from the estate was at Shaghayegh's wedding. But we three were.

When we went to congratulate the happy couple, the bride hugged us long and hard, one after another. She didn't necessarily like us. She'd always feared that one day we would show her up, and she sometimes looked down on us for not being able to behave like everyone else. Always wearing the wrong clothes, always laughing loudly, always arguing someone into a corner with an illogical theory. That was okay when it was just us, she thought, but when anyone else was there it made her uncomfortable. Right now, though, Shaghayegh hugged us and was relieved that we'd come, because we represented a part of her that no one else here did, though it was still very much a part of her. Shaghayegh seemed to hug Saya a little tighter than Hani and me, and Saya kissed her on the cheek, which as I've said is a total rarity for her, at least when sober.

We went back to the other guests, and stood around until one of the bridesmaids initiated a cute game in which the bride and groom had to cut a heart-shaped hole in a length of fabric, through which Theo then carried Shaghayegh — you can imagine the rest. It was a textbook wedding, a picture-book textbook wedding, only slightly better.

By the time we all finally put down our champagne glasses to move into the decorated hall, the guests already seemed a bit tired out from sheer euphoria. No one spoke as they gradually joined the long queue that had formed outside the entrance, until only the last of the smokers remained on the lawn, taking a few hurried drags and finishing their conversations so that they could join the queue as well. Saya, Hani, and I still had no real idea of what role we were playing at this wedding, and where we came in the hierarchy of guests, and so we let everyone go ahead of us just to be on the safe side, and lined up with the straggling smokers.

Behind us were two men who weren't an obvious fit for either Theo's or Shaghayegh's side, in terms of their age and their demeanour, which was friendly but a bit distant. Hani watched the two of them stubbing out their cigarettes and bringing their murmured conversation to a close, and seeing them confirmed what she had already suspected when she first received the invitation. *On this day, help us celebrate leaving the worries of the past behind us once and for all.* For someone with Hani's history, that was easy to decode, and she had seen at once that the happy couple's joy was genuine and that at the same time, the relief in their faces was an existential thing.

This wasn't a case of two people getting married because that's just what you did; the marriage was allowing them to stay together, and above all, to stay here. Hani smiled at the two men as she pretended to need the ashtray again, recognising them as the people who supported and backed celebrations like this, the ones who had taken care of the necessary information and legal safeguards beforehand. People who could actually be living a completely different, untroubled life, and instead chose to help others.

Hani smiled at the two men, but they didn't smile back, firstly because they couldn't know that Hani understood what no one else did, and secondly because they didn't see her.

We entered the stairwell of the hall in silence. Hani imagined telling Saya that she, unlike Saya herself, had actually discovered why the couple were getting married. She imagined the bafflement in Saya's eyes, which we usually only see in white people who are only just hearing that they're white and therefore enjoy privileges. Not at the moment they hear it, but at the moment they understand it. When they have to place their own viewpoint and their own experiences second, which they aren't used to doing. When they recognise that, although they're good people, there are people who have a much better idea of how shitty things are, because they experience it every day, firsthand, without ever getting to stop for a breather. Saya's face would be that of a person who knew she'd had it good in life, but had forgotten that fact. Because so far, her German passport had made it easy for her to travel, to learn, to look down on and make fun of 'Germanness' — while forgetting how things would have been if she hadn't had that passport and that safety. Hani placed a hand on Saya's shoulder, but Saya didn't notice, and nor did Hani tell her about her realisation.

Just then, my phone vibrated and the name on the screen made my heart race like it used to. Lukas had forwarded me an email; he'd been in touch with his mother's friend, and she was looking forward to receiving my application. He said that he hadn't considered the fact that the job wasn't based close by, and he didn't know if that would be an issue for me. But if it was, he was sorry, etc. 'Anyway, good luck!' he wrote.

When I opened the attached document, I heard myself laugh. It was a loud laugh. But not a long one. The next thing I wanted to do was cry. I'd seen this job ad before. Thanks, Lukas, that's sweet of you. It was the job at the Migrant Services office. In northern Bavaria.

I put my phone back in the glittery children's handbag, glad that Saya and Hani hadn't noticed.

There was a soft rumble of thunder, and we turned round again. We could see dark clouds gathering in the distance, but they were still too far off for us to need to take any real interest in them.

'About time we had a bit of rain,' one of the two smokers said, and I nodded. Then we walked up the stairs together in silence. We would spend the rest of the evening in the hall.

What comes next is ugly and happened just a few hours later. It's ugly and it hurts, because Life, Anna, and Nikolai were happy — though not even especially happy, they were just in the world and they were fine with it.

The storm was a short one, and it had passed over already. There was a series on TV Anna wanted to watch, and Life put up with it because he was mending the rug at the same time, just as she was feeding Nikolai at the same time. He'd wanted to suggest going for another walk, now that the storm was over, but the rug had to be mended by the following day; Anna was gloating over the fifteen euros she was going to earn from it. So he dealt with the rug at once and made his peace with the idea of spending another evening at home.

He'd come to understand that sitting on the sofa with a warm baby pressed to your warm body absolutely counted as work, though he still didn't *really* understand it. But he had now accepted the fact, at least — even if he found it hard to recognise as work something that you could do while sitting down and watching TV and selling things online.

When he started glancing around, trying to place the strange smell, she didn't even look up. Smells, sounds, lights: the city is always full of mysteries, even when you're sitting in your own flat. But when he got up and said, 'You know, it smells like fire in here,' Anna did take notice for a minute.

The baby had stopped feeding, and his strange, vacant baby eyes were looking around. Everything about this creature seemed so confident and yet helpless to Anna — the way he waved his little arms, as if they had marionette strings attached; the noises he made, the gurgling, the white drops clinging to his cheek. She lifted the baby's warm, round body over her shoulder, patted him on the back, and said, 'I can't smell anything.'

It was only when the baby had burped quietly and she'd covered her breast again that she started helping him to track down the scent, which she still couldn't smell, just so that she'd be able to sit back down as soon as possible. They walked through the rooms. Everything was quiet, the TV on pause. Just to rule out every eventuality, she opened the flat door, with the baby held in one arm.

What confronted her was the force that knocks you to the ground, that takes away your right to exist, that punches you in the stomach and rams its steel toecap into your crotch. Imagine all the fears you could have, all the panic, in all its unmitigated power, and transform it into a black, innocuous-looking cloud of smoke, and you will know what confronted Anna and Nikolai here.

'Fire,' Anna said, and then she shouted, 'Fire!' and ran past Life, who didn't understand; she grabbed her phone as she passed through and rushed out onto the balcony. Into the dark, into the cold air that had followed the storm. There was a brief moment when she could breathe more easily, when Life finally came onto the balcony and pulled the door shut behind him; when he'd understood. Then the fear returned.

Anna leaned over the railings, the baby on her shoulder. Life wanted to take him from her, but she turned to him and said, 'No.' Through the window behind him, she could see their living room already vanishing in the lazily advancing cloud of smoke. It would be so simple. So simple. The sofa they'd just been sitting on, the rug he'd just been mending, the water glasses, the peach stones, they were simply engulfed by the cloud that had come to bring silent death.

Life took Anna's phone and called the fire brigade, yelling into it, arguing with someone. He needed to calm down, he was being told, the fire brigade was already on its way, 'No need to stress, my friend.' And of course there was no stress for the man on the other end of the line. The stress of knowing that this cloud of smoke was coming for you. The stress of seeing the fear on your brave wife's face, the baby over her shoulder as she stood beside you. The stress of knowing you couldn't protect that tiny body from death, that tiny body that needed you to rock it to sleep. The stress of having to rely on white people in uniforms again, at a time like this.

By the time they heard the first cries from down below, the living room was hardly recognisable. The flat was nothing but smoke. On her dash for the balcony, Anna had forgotten to close the front door.

They conferred frantically, above the baby's alarming screams, above the screams that were coming from the three lower floors. They communicated without knowing how; Anna turned her back to the window and yelled down to neighbours they didn't know, because no one said hello on the stairs. The people from the lower floors were standing on their balconies, too, though in groups of eight or nine rather than three, and seemed to be asking Anna something; they called out, but Anna couldn't understand their language, and they couldn't understand what Anna was shouting down to them, either.

Life, meanwhile, couldn't stop looking into the smoke-filled living room. Their things would be unusable, if they survived this. If he could only close the flat door, they could save at least a few possessions. Nikolai was crying, his little face twisted into one of the three expressions in his range. Among the things that were currently being smoked out, his were the most valuable: the solid-wood crib, the organic mattress — they'd bought everything new.

Life looked at Anna's phone. It was an eternity since he'd called the fire brigade. They weren't here. They wouldn't be coming that quickly, either. 'No need to stress, my friend,' the man on the phone had kept saying, which told him first and foremost that *they* weren't about to start stressing. Life wondered what language the downstairs neighbours might have been speaking when they called the fire brigade. It occurred to him that he'd dutifully given his surname on the phone, though his gut instinct had told him not to.

He looked at Anna, who was staring straight ahead, her knees trembling slightly, singing Nikolai the song that her father used to sing to her at bedtime. The language she sang in was an imitation of her father's, because Anna had grown up speaking German, and this song didn't exist in German. Nikolai quietened down, and Anna looked like a baby-rocking robot.

The fire brigade didn't arrive. The room behind them had disappeared.

'I'm going to go in, shut the front door, and open the window,' Life said to Anna — he yelled it, in fact, but she just kept staring, until finally she said, 'Stay here, you can't go back in there.'

'Our things,' he said.

'Our things have had it,' she said. 'The fire brigade will be here any minute, they have to be.'

Life was convinced that Anna was wrong. That the fire brigade was taking its sweet time. That the people who thought panicking when your building was on fire was just 'stressing out' were the same ones who wondered whether people fleeing to Europe should be saved from drowning or not. If they let us drown out there, they'll let us burn to death here, Life thought with a sudden clarity.

Anna, though, was still sure that every noise, every clatter, every cry echoing through the courtyard came from the fire brigade, who must now be arriving. She thought the things they had in their flat weren't all that valuable. That they'd always been in danger, wherever they'd lived, but that danger had never been life-threatening, and nor was this. Anna realised that the screams around them were getting louder, that heavy things kept falling from the balconies above and landing with a dull thud, and that she could stop herself from thinking about that. That everyone around her was doing the wrong thing, that Life was doing the wrong thing by worrying about their possessions in the flat, and only she knew what had to be done; she realised that she was slowly calming down, that the longer this endless waiting went on, the closer the fire brigade was getting.

'The longer the better, the longer the sooner,' she said to herself. Nikolai had fallen asleep to her rocking and her mantra.

In the end, she thought, still murmuring to herself, she would jump if she had to. It would be very simple; she'd shield Nikolai with her arms and land on her back, and Nikolai would survive, one way or another, and that was the only thing that mattered.

'The fire brigade is coming, I think,' said Anna, as she heard the latest clattering sound coming through the courtyard and the front part of the block, but Life had made his decision already. He'd taken one final look through the living-room window, totted up roughly what their possessions were worth, and remembered the things his mother had left him and the box that held Anna's childhood diaries.

'I'll be back in a minute. I'll hurry,' he said. He pulled his shirt over his nose, opened the balcony door, and disappeared.

Anna stayed on the balcony with the sleeping child and her clarity and started the song from the beginning again. Until she understood that the dull thuds did not herald the fire brigade. They came from the bodies hitting the ground below.

∧ ^ ∧

'Huge numbers of domestic accidents. It must have been a frying pan. If the fat in the pan catches fire, you must never put it under the tap. Never. That only fans the flames — fire and water aren't the opposites you got told they were as a child. What it comes down to, in reality, is oxygen, plain and simple,' said a nice, distantly related uncle of Theo's when the news of the fire was no longer just a line on our phones, but — underscored by gentle music — a topic of conversation at the white-clothed wedding tables. He was one of these teacherly uncles, but because he seemed friendly and was attentive to what other people were saying despite his teacherliness, we forgave him for his manner.

We listened and kept peering discreetly at the dancefloor to see if anything was happening again yet, after the collective group dance and the break when cake was served. The guests were either old and had thus already gone home, or they were drunk and looking for some reason to stay awake. Hani, Saya, and I hadn't required cake and were almost annoyed at the interruption. That is to say, Hani and I were almost annoyed. Saya was silent and inscrutable.

'The pan lid will save your face, your skin, and your body. Put it on the pan as if you're making steamed dumplings, and that's how you smother the flames, which is kind of ironic, when their plan was to smother *you*.' The uncle laughed. He'd been a fireman — not in Germany, and not this century, but fire is a subject you can never get away from once you've had dealings with it. You smell it everywhere; you scent danger and feel responsible whenever you realise someone still hasn't fully understood this element.

The uncle's digression was keeping us from thinking any more about the actual fire. We were too preoccupied with the chemical processes of fire to be able to consider what our phone screens had just told us: *Most devastating fire since the Second World War — several dead and injured.* It sounded like an accident, initially, and with accidents you didn't have the usual reflex of hoping that some non-white person hadn't been to blame, providing the next piece of so-called legitimation for an increase in the Nazis' vote share. We could choose to be shocked or to get another round of schnapps in, to regard this news as a potential topic of conversation or not.

'When there's a fire in the stairwell and you open the door to your flat, you're giving the fire what it needs. You're giving it oxygen,' said the uncle with a sigh. The look he gave us three polite listeners said he hoped we would never open doors in that situation.

'It's called the chimney effect.'

The tenants of Bornemannstraße had little interest in details of this kind. They were sitting in an old bus, where they were being given medical attention; they were in ambulances on their way to hospital; their bodies were being detached from the wet paving slabs of the courtyard; they were being found on the stairs, in their rooms, outside the doors of their flats, and identified. Most hadn't succumbed to the flames; they had died jumping from windows or fleeing down the stairs.

A statement from the fire brigade in the hours immediately after the fire said that the magnitude of the disaster was due to 'issues of culture and mentality'. Instructions had been given, they said, for residents to stay in their flats with the doors shut. Even with a quickly spreading fire, this would keep you comparatively safe. The tenants hadn't understood these warnings, hadn't heeded them. Many had tried to escape down the stairs, and had suffocated on the way. In future, fire-prevention leaflets would be translated into other languages.

The source of the blaze was very quickly identified as a stroller in the stairwell, which, the fire brigade suspected, had been deliberately set on fire. There was currently no indication of a xenophobic motive. This may have been mooted at first, since the victims were of various different origins and the area was inhabited largely by people with foreign roots. But in fact, there were several potential causes and motives for the arson attack: statistically speaking, it was more likely to be jealousy, revenge, or insurance fraud. It could also have been children playing with matches. The area was a hotspot of deprivation.

'Where did you say the building was?' Saya asked. She wasn't breathing, and her face was white — whiter than I'd ever seen it. Saya went red when she was angry, and blood-red when people didn't take her anger seriously, but she never turned pale. She looked like she'd eaten something you should never, ever eat, shouldn't even touch.

'Bornemannstraße,' I read out. 'I don't know it. Must be in one of those north-western districts.'

Saya coughed, knocked her hand into her glass, didn't notice that she'd spilled wine over the table, got up, and left.

'Oh, wait,' said Hani. 'We were there this week. The pub after the party.'

Saya didn't hear that. But of course, she'd already known it.

What did Hani and I think? Nothing earth-shattering. We thought it was a shame Saya was leaving so early, when the last few days were supposed to have been the overture for this evening, when we could really let our hair down. And we had let our hair down, too, with loud, blaring, sinuous music, exuberant dances, human chains moving rhythmically around the room, laughing faces. We wiped the beads of sweat from our foreheads and waved shyly at the past.

But that had only been one part of this party, and it suddenly felt slightly pitiful to be sitting here now with the informative fireman-uncle. While Hani and I were wondering if we should have done anything differently over the last few days in relation to Saya, the uncle was providing us with what he considered to be relevant details, because his phone had just given him more news about the fire. The man must lead a very stressful life. Whenever someone gave us a new piece of information, he felt it was his duty to add some explanatory comment.

Everyone else in the group, which at this point consisted of Hani, me, and two nameless relatives of Shaghayegh's, looked at him in silence as he did this, because anything else would have been rude, and yet there was no ignoring the fact that we were all a bit embarrassed. This was like something from another age. He might have been one of the last of his kind, a kind who sat at tables giving lectures. But the benevolent look he gave us all after the fifteenth piece of information about the chimney effect was an indication that he didn't yet know this. He didn't even know that what he was doing prevented all other conversation, or that we weren't anywhere near as grateful as our nodding suggested. That, on the contrary, we pitied him; that we scorned what he was doing for emancipatory reasons and at the same time tolerated it for social conformity and politeness reasons.

To be honest, though, his monologue did also bring a bit of normality to the situation. Saya leaving couldn't be all that momentous, I thought, otherwise things wouldn't just have carried on without her. Nothing about her departure was any more dramatic than all the other stuff she said and did.

The music changed, people started clearing away the cake plates, and the wedding guests moved back to the bar. The uncle finally stopped talking and looked over at the people around the bar, before abruptly saying goodnight and going off to bed. As if we were no longer providing sufficient entertainment for him, I thought. I imagined that he'd been bored this whole time as well and was wondering why no one but him was keeping the conversation going.

'I'll try giving Saya a call,' said Hani, picking up her phone and then, after failing to get through several times, putting it back on the table. I didn't even react; we looked at one another and then wordlessly watched the people who were starting to dance again.

'She must have gone to bed,' I said, and although I remembered the last few nights all too well, I pretended that was a reason to be relieved. 'Or she just needed to be alone for a while, and she'll be back any minute.'

So Hani and I stayed sitting there, unable to think of anything better to do than wait for Saya's return. The alternative would have been just to leave Shaghayegh's wedding, and we couldn't bring ourselves to do that. But drinking without Saya was no fun, and nor was dancing, and because Hani and I weren't interested in meeting new people and we feared further uncles, we both kept our eyes glued to our phones.

Until, hours later, when the happy couple were saying their goodbyes, mine rang.

It was Jella, Saya's lawyer.

∧ ∧ ∧

Hello, my name is Kasih R. You'll confuse me with refugees you've seen on TV and you'll pronounce my name wrong or be too ashamed to try saying it at all. You will doubt everything I say a little bit and tell yourselves you know better. You might be right, just as I am. I'm right, and as I've been writing I have sometimes lied, okay, but I'm still right; lying and being right aren't mutually exclusive, and that's true for me, too.

My friend, my closest and oldest friend, has been locked up, as I've said already. The papers are reporting on her, the internet is in an uproar, everyone hates her, and reading through it all, it seems like a miracle to me that this is the first time my friend and the internet have come to blows, because when you look at everything that happens on the internet, it's like it was made for taking people like Saya apart. A digital courtroom where even the most miserable loser is allowed to pass judgement, an arena in which the audience is the opponent.

But Saya won't be finding that out; I have no idea what prisons look like in the real world, outside of American dramas, but I'm pretty sure that alongside the right to legal representation, you don't get a right to check what's happening on the internet.

I checked what was happening on the internet and stopped again immediately. I'm not Saya, not addicted to seeing with my own eyes how much the people sitting in front of their cheap computers with their hands down their trousers hate us.

Instead, I searched for our public housing estate online. No idea why. Maybe because I never had before.

And not searching until now was the right thing to do, as well, because something has happened: the estate has been sold, renovated, and reanimated, and if you do a little more research, you'll find current property ads. I look at the details and the numbers and imagine moving back there; I open the photo galleries and feel like I've broken into my own past. Empty rooms — I can smell them, the sweet mildew, the cheap plaster on the walls even though the place has been renovated, the smell of rancid vinegar in the stairwell; I can feel my bare feet on the carpet, and the spring breeze blowing through the open windows.

People will soon be living there again like they used to, in safety. Children will wear their door key on a length of wool around their neck. Teenagers will snog outside the blocks, standing close to the wall of the building so their parents won't see them from the floors above. Adults will look at the neighbourhood and assure themselves over and over, despite all the changes, that their families are still safe here. Not completely safe, but safe enough.

In one of these flats, some friends might be having a sleepover right now, and laughing themselves hoarse under their My Little Pony duvet covers. Telling each other jokes and being surprised at how good they are when you say them out loud, making fun of other people and repeating words and phrases they've invented for them. Laughing as quietly as it's possible to laugh, into the covers, certain that they've never heard anything this funny, until the dark chipboard door opens and a weary mother, a weary father talks to them in a language that all children understand, no matter where they come from, and the friends hold their breath to stop themselves bursting out laughing at the worst possible moment. Until the door shuts again and they find they can't laugh like that any longer. It's a shame.

That's all happening right now in the flats that I have found empty and deserted on the same hate-filled internet where Saya is currently being eviscerated. I want to think about these flats and not about the flats I've had to see thanks to Saya and her interest in the lives of Nazis. Flats inhabited by stinking, lazy Nazis with stinking, lazy Nazi parents, who neglected their ugly children and raised them without love and, would you believe, are now talking about it on TV. But they too hung white plastic curtains at their uncleaned windows, and their Christmas decorations were a single string of multicoloured fairy lights, which constantly changed colour and flashed and lent the room a kind of cosiness for a few weeks every year, if you pulled the blinds down and switched the main light off and sat on the radiators. Because the Nazi kids didn't have flat radiators neatly mounted on the walls, either; they had proper, boxy metal radiators wide enough for two children to sit on, watching TV and drinking cola.

I don't like thinking about these Nazi flats, but when I do think of them, I can't help thinking they're kind of comfy, and maybe that was something else that fascinated Saya. In their brokenness, these childhoods resembled ours more than those of our classmates, flatmates, and partners. But Saya would never put it like that, and I would never bring it up with her, and I'm only writing it down now because I'm getting to the end of this story, which I am somehow trying to put off.

I'd rather carry on reflecting on Nazi flats for a while longer than think about the flats where the flames turned to smoke and the smoke to death, where people suffocated before they could burn, flats from which people jumped because they were living on the fifth floor with no papers or their husband didn't come back from the smoke-filled living room. From which people jumped, thinking they could protect the child in their arms with their own body, even if they themselves wouldn't survive the fall. Because jumping is the last thing you can choose to do. You've understood the language being yelled at you through the megaphone perfectly. You've just never trusted it.

When I got home from the wedding, I looked for Saya's notebook, which was only lying on top of her hiking rucksack because it didn't fit in her smart handbag. I just needed one last piece of the puzzle to understand what had happened after Saya had her meltdown outside Life's cafe. After she'd learned that the trial of the Nazi group was going to be held behind closed doors, and that the disaster of state failure would therefore continue out of sight. After Saya called a man an 'almighty arsehole' and swept his cup off the table, and before she came home to me to play rock paper scissors for custody of her childhood handbag.

∧ ∧ ∧

Saya was standing outside the pub with a stone in her hand. It was a beautiful cube of red brick, rough and heavy, and a pleasant shudder ran through her as she raised the stone and tried to recall the sequence of movements involved in shot-putting.

The pub window was as ugly as the pub itself; it was featureless, old, the kind of window you'd walk past and think the place was either already dead or soon would be. Really not somewhere you wanted to go for a beer, Saya thought, wondering how she could have been drunk enough to walk in there. No wonder Life and I had gone home early that evening — what the hell had been wrong with her own sensor?

She swung the brick back.

'Well, well,' he said, 'Chrissi's beer not to your liking, or what?'

Saya didn't want to turn around. In her mind's eye, she'd already hurled all her rage away, transformed the window into a lot of little shards on the pavement — though that triggered disquieting associations rather than heightening the anticipation. When she did eventually turn round, it was because of the strange smugness in his voice. 'Are you Chrissi's bouncer, then, or what?' Saya asked, before recognising him at the exact same moment he recognised her.

His expression changed, transforming from charming fellow citizen to disgusted paterfamilias. 'No need to get hysterical — just explain what you're doing here, or if I should call the police.'

'And what are you going to tell the police?'

'That you're out of control. Committing vandalism. That you're threatening good honest people in good honest establishments and disturbing the peace.'

Saya laughed out loud. It was absurd enough to suddenly find a person whose words you'd only seen written down standing there in front of you — but being confronted with this mindless ideological guff was the final straw.

'Patrick Wagenberg, what a lot of big words you know,' she said. 'Have you always known them or do you learn them at home, on the internet, from the other arscholes?'

'And how do you know my name, Miss?' Wagenberg said, pulling himself up to his full height. Being recognised could be risky, but it was also a mark of distinction. When that happened, you'd made a name for yourself in the movement, you'd become a dangerous figure to the enemy. Dangerous because you were speaking the truth, because you were standing up for the protection of your own people and against the collapse of this country's values. It didn't occur to him, of course, that Saya had caught sight of his boarding card on the plane and then looked him up. And naturally it would never have occurred to him that she was the Christian Moni Stein from the internet — how would it?

Saya had to laugh at him suddenly addressing her as 'Miss'.

'The internet, my friend,' she said, 'is a place that does have some relation to the real world, you know? When you write things online under your real name with your cock hanging out, then people are going to recognise you and your cock in the real world, too.'

Wagenberg's lips quivered; he was still thinking up a snappy response.

The conversation could have remained on the level Saya had chosen, and they could have had a wonderful argument: an exchange of blows between two people who openly hated one another. Saya's voice was already so loud that the curtains were twitching in the window behind her. But then she saw the brightly coloured little badge on his ugly jacket, and was amazed that it amazed her. Far-right attitudes were common and ever-present, and yet the idea of displaying them in public, almost naively, took her breath away.

It was the symbol of the Nazi group that was currently on trial. They were sitting in the dock, Saya was sitting and looking at photos of the dead, and someone somewhere was earning money selling merchandise to losers. So this was a genuine, textbook Nazi standing in front of her, and she still had the brick in her hand and the afternoon's rage in her belly, the rage from the day before and the day before that, from a million days. An obvious impulse would have been to raise the brick again and smash it into Wagenberg's head. Saya would spend the rest of her life wondering why she didn't have that impulse at that moment. Why she didn't just shatter that hate-filled skull.

'You stink of shit!' she screamed instead, taking a step towards him and ripping the badge off his dignified chest. She hurled it to the ground, where it tinkled innocently, and as she stamped on it, in the crazy belief that she could destroy a tiny metal pin badge that way, she went on shouting: 'You stink of not getting enough love and not having any money or any future! You stink of your mum being wasted when you were conceived and leaving it too late to get an abortion.'

The textbook Nazi looked at Saya; he was standing there as if frozen to the spot, trying to remember that he and his people were stronger than the enemy, since they didn't come from primitive stock; in his head, an audio tape of affirmations and wise sayings was providing a soundtrack to the image of the hysterical Muslim woman. It would have been easy to just cave her head in, but it was broad daylight and the days when you could afford to make headlines like that were over.

Saya misinterpreted his silence. How could she have guessed that she was dealing with someone who'd been ordered to stand out in public only for his good manners and open, friendly smile, when he used to be a man who chased people down the street just for daring to exist? Saya concluded from his silence that her words were too feeble, that she couldn't damage her opponent's ego with them because he didn't seem to have one. And so she took a step closer and swapped the yelling for a whisper, a hiss:

'Patrick Wagenberg, you're a lot quieter in real life than you are on the internet. Is it because you're still wondering how come I can speak German? Weird that I went to university and you didn't, isn't it? When my genes are flooding the country and making it stupider, because they're geared towards herding goats, while your genes — sorry, what is it they specialise in again? Oh, that's right, losing wars!' Saya laughed and was pleased to see the emotion in Patrick's face. 'Funny, isn't it, that I could take your job from you if I wanted, but you don't actually have a job. It isn't a terrible thing to be unemployed, Paddy, really — I bet your father and my father used to sit next to one another at the job centre, feeling all sad. Is that what makes you so jealous, yeah? That I'm smart and rich, and you're just as much of a loser as your father and his father before him? Has it ever occurred to you that you and your friends always start exploiting the latest murder or rape for your own ends when one of us has just scored a goal for Germany? That you're always just responding to our successes? That you torch houses owned by hardworking people when you can't afford a home of your own, because no one wants to do business with you? That you shoot shopkeepers dead in their shops because you yourselves would never get off your backsides and build up your own business? That you shoot up synagogues and mosques and shisha bars because we're comfortable in there, while the only community space you have is some horrible, ugly pub with resident alcoholics? That you shoot people right after their university entrance exams in case they end up teaching your kids? Why do you live here, Patrick Wagenberg, why do you burden the people here with your existence? This neighbourhood isn't for people like you, don't you get that? This neighbourhood is one of our successes that you're so afraid of. This is where people like us live, and only people like us — we own the corner shops, the shisha bars, the breakfast cafes and the greengrocers, and people like you end up here by accident and then can't sleep at night because you've suddenly realised you've got no one, no community behind you, no kindness of strangers — you've got nothing because you've just kept passing on your Nazi genes while we've got really comfortable here in the parks and on the benches. And you end up setting off your stupid nail bombs because you can't accept how lonely you are, or you start another discussion about how we're creating parallel communities and never come out of our ghettoes, because you're afraid of our communities and our ghettoes, because we might just band together against your shit, we might form gangs to fend off the spread of your ideology, or just have a better life than you, plain and simple. Then you start blubbering again and shooting us dead. The stronger we become, the more stuff you set fire to, but you know what, you little arsehole, this is the end of you. We're so strong, so much stronger than you — in the end, our ghettoes always grow back somewhere, and we're working for newspapers and writing about it, and we're becoming members of parliament and argu-ing about it, and we're organising protests and shouting about it, while you're on the internet cheering on a few pathetic murderers.

You've lost, all of you, you've lost — you can't burn down enough houses with your little lighter to stop it, it's too late for that. But you don't even know how the whole arson thing works, you can't even bring yourself to punch me in the face now, can you? You almighty arsehole!'

Then she walked away. She walked fast, and then faster; what she had just done was gradually dawning on her. She had tickled an angry bull, without knowing what she was hoping for. That he'd explode, the way she wanted to explode herself? Saya started running and laughing, a feeling of exhilaration in her belly, the ground carrying her like a conveyer belt that wanted to help her get away as fast as possible. A long, long way from Patrick Wagenberg, the pub, and the apartment building. She ran without turning round, hoping he didn't have a gun to shoot her with as she went. He didn't have a gun, and he didn't follow her. He'd followed her words, though, which from then on would play in his head on an endless loop, for hours, right into the evening.

It's Saturday morning, 5.58 am. Outside, the sky is bright and clear. The day wants people to fall in love with it; it's acting harmless and like it's bringing with it something new, unforeseen, unprecedented. Something new, unforeseen, unprecedented would have happened yesterday if Saya had killed Patrick Wagenberg or at least injured him, or if she'd actually set fire to the building on Bornemannstraße where Patrick lived. But most days, nothing unforeseen happens, as I've been saying from the start.

For an hour now, two photos have been circulating on the internet: one of Saya at twenty, drunk, at her leavers' ball, which the right-wingers have unquestioningly taken to be a current photo, and one of Patrick W., looking serious and smarmy and middle-class. He vanished without a trace yesterday evening, and so the right-wingers are mourning him as another victim of the fire.

Neighbours and residents observed the two of them arguing in the afternoon, and alerted the police early on — which was the only reason that, when Saya left the wedding and ran up Bornemann-straße, they were able to identify and arrest her immediately.

Over the last few hours, then, Saya has gone from being a member of the Islamic State group to a left-wing Nazi-hater, radicalised by feminism and acting alone. If I didn't know better, I'd believe it, given how much you can find on the subject. Because I do know better, I just laughed out loud. Nothing has changed.

And what about you? A person can never be entirely sure what absurdities you people will take as true and what you won't, whether and what you'll believe from us, and exactly what you think people like Saya are capable of. Did you think she set that block on fire? Are you horrified that I'm implying you did? I'm sorry about that. But a person can only ever half trust you; we want to, and we usually do. But then we still never know if you've actually heard about the murders of non-white people that kept us awake at night and made us shut our shops. If you actually know about the houses that were burned down, because of which we bought walkie-talkies back then, and now install smoke alarms in every new flat. Or if you were away on holiday when all these things happened. On the Mediterranean coast, perhaps: it's so lovely to put one foot and then the other into the cool water, to leave your cares behind — wonderful.

But if, in turn, you happen to know about things we've never heard of, if you've ever heard of Nazis winding foreigners up and the foreigners then killing the Nazis and setting their houses on fire, do let me know.

Saya, at least, is neither a member of the Islamic State group nor an avenger of the oppressed; Saya doesn't strike back, and nor is she planning to. Saya screams while everyone is somewhere else. Her body has never been physically injured, not by prison guards, not by foreign intelligence services, not by other kids, not by men, not by strangers, not by Nazis. Right now, this very second, she suddenly hurls it without any warning against my bedroom wall. With an impact that must surely shatter her bones, but nothing shatters, nothing is broken — I let the keyboard fall silent and turn to look at her. She is lying in bed asleep. Beside her, Hani lifts her head briefly, her hair sticking up in all directions, then shifts herself closer to Saya, burrows one arm under the pillow, puts the other around Saya, and pulls her close.

A push notification about the trial appears on my phone. I feel nauseous: it's going to be the biggest trial since the Federal Republic of Germany was founded, and a huge crowd of both national and international media is expected. Plus for two days, we have officially known that the far-right terrorist group that had been underground for years and had killed Muslims in particular, Muslim women in particular, had a group chat going with other Nazis, which has now been leaked to the public. Bastards chatting to other bastards. Murderers chatting to their accessories. The far-right terrorist group can expect many years on remand and a long, anxious wait for the verdict. But hang on, we all knew that already, we've all heard this before — are you still there? Are you still listening?

An hour ago, a quote was published that people are already saying will go down in history. A lawyer for the victims' families, who herself has been subjected to racism, posted: *Germany, up until today you have failed. Germany, from today you can try to come to terms with your failure. From today, we will try to trust you.* She probably knows herself that the response to this will be death threats, like it always is, just like the last time and the time before. And why do you even believe me when I say that quote was just published an hour ago? You read it earlier; I already told you that Saya had it as a status update a few days ago, and that Life thought events had already proved it wrong just before he died, but I swear, I've got the page in front of me now, and that quote was only published an hour ago, even though I already wrote about it — how can that be? I knew that I knew a lot, but how could I know that?

Someone (not me) commented under the post: *Every great challenge begins with the first step. Every trial with the first day.* The trial is only starting today, even if everything does always feel like a repetition. I pick up the Monopoly money from the wedding and try to figure out what foreign currency it's meant to be, and then I think that today must actually be Thursday morning, not Saturday morning. The banknote evaporates.

Why did you believe me, if you've been sceptical all this time? And why were you sceptical about me, anyway, when I was the one who was continually unmasking *you*? Did you really believe Saya had been locked up?

Today is not only the first day of the trial, it's also the day of my meeting with Lukas, who will see that I've been out boozing all night. My meeting with Lukas, which we arranged yesterday by the fire barrel in the old factory yard, outside the squat. Which definitely won't be about some dubious job offer. We will instead talk about our relationship, and he'll say once more, calmly, 'I'm sorry.' He'll say it should all have been different, but that he can't undo any of it — 'much as I might want to.'

I will listen and understand and I'll say, 'I'd like to undo it, too.' Because the world out there scares me, and it was nice to have a boyfriend who didn't feel such panic at the world since, although he's affected by it all, none of it is there specifically to affect him, and Lukas will tell me that my fear is justified, and that on those evenings when we watched the women doing yoga, he'd known I was right, and had disagreed with me anyway.

'Because I wished you were mistaken,' Lukas will say.

And I will reply, 'But I can't be mistaken, that's my life, I'm the woman who never gets corrected in yoga even though she's doing it all wrong, I know about these things, I'm the expert here.'

And Lukas will say, 'I know. And there's something else I wanted to tell you,' and I will be afraid that this is when he's going to start on about his dissertation and his mother and the job, but instead he'll say, 'The yoga teacher thought she wasn't *allowed* to touch that woman. She thought that women like her must belong to some impenetrable religion that prohibits all touching.'

'Yuck. That isn't any better,' I will say, and give myself a little shake before asking, 'If not even I know that, then where did you get it from?'

'From myself? From my life?'

'From your life as a woman who teaches yoga?' I will ask.

And Lukas will laugh and say, 'Yes.' And after laughing, Lukas will say that he's there for me, even if we're not together anymore, he's still there and so are other people; I'm not alone, and nor is Saya.

That's how our meeting will go, and it will be years before I realise that Lukas and I have stayed friends, though we avoided using those words.

I turn to Saya, who is alone in bed, because of course it's Thursday morning and Hani, as you know, didn't stay over the night of the party in the factory yard, because she had work in the morning. Hani slept in her own bed, if you remember, so she could have a shower and cycle to the office as normal.

Only, I didn't tell you that Hani's bed isn't in a flat in the next district over, but in another country. So are her bike and her office and her plum tea and her boss and the colleagues who take advantage of her diligence and kindness. When an end was declared to the bloodthirsty, merciless war in Hani's former homeland, people like her and her family were sent back, no matter how well they were doing at school.

Did you honestly think anyone would have been interested in Hani's good grades? Hani, her parents, and her brother said their goodbyes, left their few sticks of furniture outside the block, gave away their books and toys, and emigrated to the USA, where they would have more opportunities and security than in their old country. In their old country, former traitors were still traitors, even if they were no longer killing each other in such large numbers.

Hani became a memory, to which I add her current reality when I type her name into the search bar and discover her new life displayed in a huge number of photos. The face of a teenager who has become a young woman, hazed over by a nostalgia filter, in the midst of her family. Her face beside the faces of her children — they look into the camera, and Hani seems to have forgotten Germany and us.

My phone vibrates and with half an eye I read a message from Robin: *Internet is back up, no need to waste any more time reading! Stream to your heart's content!*

We will stream in the coming days, of course, because the coming days will otherwise grind us down, numbing us with images and news from the trial that we don't have the strength to deal with, and from which we have to distract ourselves with drama box sets that seem decades more progressive than our reality. They will also distract us when we hear about the fire, the largest since the war, the latest caesura in our timeline. We'll cycle through the city to burn off some energy, until the red lights stop us, and eventually we will stand, sweating, outside the apartment building and weep for people we don't know. We won't be able to forget the picture of Life, Anna, and Nikolai.

But the coming days are the coming days, and we don't know any of this yet. We haven't yet seen the picture of Life, Anna, and Nikolai, or the faces of the others who died.

Maybe it really is too much to expect for you to trust me and believe me; I mean, I've lied at least as much as you have in your lives. But the pictures — look at the pictures when they start circulating a few days from now, look at the faces. They're real.

I switch off my phone and the computer and lie down beside Saya, shift closer to her, burrow one arm under her pillow, lay the other arm on her arm, stretch a little further, and hold her as tightly as I can.